'A super-fast-paced, high-oc[...]
throat and carries you t[...]
I absolu[...]
Sarah Bonner, aut[...]

'Very topical and desperately urgent. I absolutely loved it'
Daniel Cole, author of *Ragdoll*

'As dark and gritty as it is pacy and original. So vivid, real and
now I had to keep telling myself it's fiction. *A Clockwork Orange*
for the twenty-first century'
Janice Hallett, author of *The Twyford Code*

'An intelligent, breathless read – has you questioning everything.
Hard-hitting and thrilling'
Deborah Masson, author of the DI Eve Hunter series

'

A brilliant, pacy thriller that hits the ground running and never
lets up! I raced through it in a day ... Highly recommended'
Guy Morpuss, author of *Five Minds*

'Superb. My favourite book of the year so far'
Keri Beevis, author of *The People Next Door*

'A wrong-man thriller so nightmarish and intense that it should
come with a health warning'
Matt Thorne, author of *Eight Minutes Idle*

Dan Malakin has twice been shortlisted for the Bridport Prize, and his debut novel, *The Regret*, was a Kindle bestseller. *The Box* is his second novel and his third will be published in 2024. When not writing thrillers, Dan works as a data security consultant, teaching corporations how to protect themselves from hackers. He lives in North London with his wife and daughter.

THE BOX

DAN MALAKIN

This paperback edition published 2023

First published in Great Britain in 2022 by
VIPER, part of Serpent's Tail,
an imprint of Profile Books Ltd
29 Cloth Fair
London
ECIA 7JQ
www.serpentstail.com

Text design by Crow Books

1 3 5 7 9 10 8 6 4 2

Printed and bound in Great Britain by
CPI Group (UK) Ltd, Croydon, CRO 4YY

A CIP catalogue record for this book is available from the British Library.

ISBN 978 1 78816 843 4
eISBN 978 1 78283 871 5

For Amelie

PROLOGUE

At first, she liked it in the box.

There were toys to play with, paper and coloured pens. Sometimes cartoons came on the screen, and when she was thirsty, she bent the straw into her mouth to drink sweet apple juice. She felt warm in there. Safe.

Outside the box was the silent maze of unwelcoming rooms, full of things she wasn't allowed to touch. Outside the box was the large cold man, who pointed at the chalkboard and made her repeat the same things, over and over, staring her down when she made a mistake.

Then one day, it changed.

It changed with her waking up to see the large cold man standing over her bed. He lifted a strange and bulky set of clothes, a tail of cables streaming from the back.

'You're ready,' he said, his face in shadow. 'Put these on.'

The clothes were stiff around the elbows and knees. Metal sewn into the fabric pressed cold to her skin. As she dressed, her heart beat harder and she wished more than anything to stay in her soft pyjamas.

When they got to the box the toys and coloured pens were gone. Climbing inside, she no longer felt safe.

Images appeared on the screen. She'd played this game before and knew how it worked. When a car appeared, she said 'car'. When a ball appeared, she said 'ball'. But this time was different.

Sometimes when she said the word her clothes grew pleasantly warm, other times they seemed to spark for a moment, making her whole body jolt.

She couldn't understand this new game – the rules made no sense. Soon the jolts became stronger, lasted longer, leaving her shaking and desperate for breath. She wanted it to stop, wanted the man to let her out, but no matter how much she pleaded he didn't respond.

The images came faster. Hot desperate tears ran down her cheeks. Sobbing and heaving, she put the straw between her lips but instead of sweet apple juice what came out was liquid fire.

Once she started screaming, it seemed as though she would scream for ever.

1

6.20 P.M., FRIDAY

I peeked around the dining-room curtain to look at the men at the top of our driveway. There were four of them, the same ones that had been outside my office all day. One holding leaflets, another shouldering a camera big enough to make him look as though he was from the nightly news, two more waving placards with my face in a red circle, a diagonal line through it, like I was some kind of menace. A danger to society.

Behind me, Gabrielle said, 'Please, Ed. Just call the police.'

'And say what?'

'They're filming us. It's harassment.'

'Borderline. It's a public road.'

'They've got signs with your face on them!'

'I'm perfectly aware of what's on their signs.'

They'd been following me around all day, ever since the courts granted the injunction to take down the Men's Learning Centre website – first outside my legal practice, picketing clients as they came through the door, and now here, at home. I'd tried reasoning with them, threatening them with the police, but they'd laughed and filmed my frustration. It would be hard to prove they were breaking any law, and they knew it. The last thing I wanted was to take them to court to explain why I *wasn't* a danger to society.

I dropped the curtain and faced my wife. She was standing

behind a dining chair in her long puffy coat, not even attempting to hide the fact that she'd been out back for a cigarette. Neither of us had slept well since Ally went up against that website, and we were both slipping into bad habits, doing things we shouldn't.

'I told you not to carry on with this,' Gabrielle said. Her grey eyes were murky from exhaustion, and a tight pink line had replaced the smile that usually came so readily to her lips.

'Protecting our daughter is not *carrying on*.'

'Ahhh, right. So protecting her means making it ten times worse. I get it now.'

'This *isn't* my fault. Try calling her again.'

'Her phone's still off. I've already left her three messages.' Gabrielle sighed. 'Oh, I don't know. She's probably fine.'

'No call. No text.'

'She's sixteen!'

'It's *Friday night*!'

We weren't religious – bacon sandwich Jews, that's what I called us – but both Gabrielle and I were brought up in Orthodox houses that stayed in on *Shabbat*. We hadn't raised Ally and Mitchell that way, and we didn't partake in all the holy stuff, like lighting the candles and saying the prayers, but we still set the table nicely, placemats and everything, and ate a family meal. It was the one time of the week everyone came together. As the children grew older, the further I felt them slipping away from me, and the more important those couple of hours had become.

Ally was out most of the time these days – she was a teenager with an active social life – but on Fridays she always came straight home from school. *Always*.

I pointed to Gabrielle's phone. 'Anything from her friends?'

'Jasmine said they had lunch together.'

'That's it?'

'That's it.'

4

'You called all her friends?'

'The ones I know.'

I grabbed a couple of wine glasses from the sideboard, poured myself a drink from an open bottle of red, and nodded to Gabrielle.

She shook her head. 'Go easy. It's still early.'

I sipped the wine and peered round the curtain again. My chest seized as I saw a man handing a leaflet to one of our neighbours, who accepted it with a bemused expression. They were trying to intimidate me into withdrawing the injunction, that much was clear, but I'd told Ally I wouldn't.

Promise me, Dad, she'd said. *No matter what they try.*

She didn't come to me for help much these days – it's our kids who outgrow us, never the other way round – so I'd promised. I didn't want to break that. But what if those men were the reason she wasn't home? What if they had her in the back of a van, and their next move was to start sending us pieces of our daughter in the post?

Gabrielle moved round the table and took my hands. Her fingers were cold, so I lifted them to my mouth and warmed them with my breath.

'Alison's got her own life,' she said. 'We don't know half the things she gets up to.'

I stopped warming and looked my wife in the eye. 'Something's wrong. I know it is.'

Fear is infectious, especially when it's paired with conviction. Gabrielle's reassuring air slipped, and I saw that her bravado had been an act, to convince herself as much as me that our daughter was safe.

Her chin trembled. 'So go out there. Speak to them.'

'I've tried speaking to them.'

She fixed me with a stare that could break rocks. 'If you think those *men* have anything to do with Alison not being here then you go out there right now and … and *demand* they tell you where she is.'

Cold sweat ran down my neck. What if that was their plan? To force a confrontation? To say I wasn't much of a fighter would be putting it mildly. Even if those blokes were blind and turned the wrong way, they'd mash me into the pavement before I worked out what to do with my fists. The court was my boxing ring. Tomes of law reviews were my gloves.

Gabrielle started for the front door. 'If you won't—'

'I'll go,' I said, pulling her back. I took a reckless swig of wine, which turned into the whole glass, and was about to say something brave and funny so she wouldn't see the frayed nerves holding my smile in place, but instead I spluttered Merlot over the dining table.

'You can do it,' she said, nodding harder than necessary, as though trying to convince us both that this was true.

I headed to the door. As I pulled it open, a muffled ping came from the kitchen, the oven telling us the chicken was done. Any other week that was my cue to put the roast potatoes back in to crisp, while Gabrielle did some magic to make her always perfect gravy. I can't explain it, but as I stepped out of the house, I knew our carefree Friday nights were gone. Maybe for ever.

2

The sun was low as I approached the four men, the light grainy. An autumn chill to the air. When I got to the top of the driveway, they booed like I was a pantomime villain. The closest one to me, a ridiculously handsome guy, leaned his placard of my face against the front wall and lifted his arms, as if we were old pals readying to hug.

'Edgar!' he cried. 'So pleased you could join us.'

I bristled at my full name. I hated it, I'd always hated it, and to this day wondered what was going through my parents' heads when they named me. Did they think I was going to grow up to be a Victorian gentleman? No one called me Edgar now, not since my mum passed away – except for Gabrielle, on very rare occasions, usually in shock at some catastrophic act of stupidity. To everyone else, I was Ed.

One of my stock-in-trade tricks was to go hard on the first question, try to catch someone out. That initial reaction often said everything.

I stopped in front of Handsome. 'Have you hurt my daughter?'

We were about the same age and height, but that was where the similarities ended. He had more hair, enough to blow-dry into a silky brown side-parting, hollows where a normal person's cheeks would be, and the air of someone who got everything he wanted

7

in life simply by flashing a charming smile. Definitely not the case for me. I hated him on the spot.

He dropped his arms, snorted and glanced to the side. *Who, me?*

Inconclusive.

'Murph,' he said, leaning round to look at the shaven-headed slab behind him, the sort of thug you wouldn't just cross the road to avoid, but leave town, change your identity, and spend the rest of your life in hiding to avoid. 'His daughter … didn't you bang her last night?'

'Fucked her inside out,' Murph intoned. The other two idiots snickered.

Handsome smiled back at me. 'Answer your question?'

As expected, I had nowhere to go with this. I wasn't Liam Neeson, able to whip a Glock from my waistband, jam it under his chin, and demand to know where he'd taken her. I wasn't Liam anything. I was nothing to them. They could say whatever they wanted to me, and I couldn't do a thing.

'All this is meaningless,' I said, waving at the leaflets, the camera. 'If you've kidnapped my daughter, you're facing *twenty years* in prison. Is it worth it for a bloody website?'

'Listen, Edgar,' said the suave shitbag intent on ruining my reputation. 'We're just members of the community informing other members of the community about an *unsavoury* character in our midst.'

'What community? You don't live here!'

He gestured for his mates to look at me, as though by losing my temper I'd proved his point.

I glanced down the street. We'd been on Oakfield Road for fifteen years, moving here from our poky Clerkenwell flat soon after Ally was born. It was pleasant enough, quiet and tree-lined, only five minutes' walk to Finchley Central Tube, the kind of street where hedgerows were trimmed into geometric shapes and almost every car was German.

Thankfully, it was quiet now, the kids and commuters home. Even so I could sense the twitching curtains, the peering eyes. Without a doubt we'd be the main discussion over dinner. I'd never given much thought to my 'good name' before, but you don't, do you? Not until someone takes a dump on it, then passes the photos round your neighbours. What was on those leaflets? What were they saying about me? I wasn't perfect. I'd done things that made me ashamed. Things not even Gabrielle knew about, let alone the whole neighbourhood.

'Look,' I said, forcing my voice to be calm, 'imagine if it was your daughter being harassed by a website. I couldn't just do nothing. Wouldn't you want to protect your family?'

'But you're a dangerous person, Edgar.' Handsome's smile went sly. 'You want to shut down free speech. Just like the Nazis, eh? Kind of ironic, don't you think.'

He made a sound through his teeth like escaping gas.

He was trying to trigger me – and it was working. The throb in my temple had intensified so much it felt like my whole face was pulsing. I was clenching my jaw so tight an ache had spread down my neck. I glanced at the house and saw Gabrielle by the window.

'Not bad,' he said, giving her a little wave. 'May be worth a ride, after all.'

'If you touch her—'

'Then again, there's four of us here. We'll probably just wait for your daughter to get home and have a party.'

I stepped towards Handsome, finger out, ready to say he'd gone too far, but the giant fucker behind him shot out an arm and gave me a sharp slap to the face with a hand that I'm pretty sure was hewn from granite. I staggered sideways, disorientated, clutching my eye, pain vibrating down my spine. Someone stuck out a leg, tripping me. I dropped to my knees on the pavement.

'That's a warning,' he said. 'Next time, I'll cave your fucking head in.'

My vision swung to the dining-room window, Gabrielle standing there, her hand over her mouth. I forced myself to stand.

The big bloke's face soured. 'Did I tell you to get up?'

I shook my head quickly and dropped back down.

'Good boy,' he said.

They started chatting about the Arsenal game, like they were down the pub instead of outside my house. I stayed on the ground for a few minutes, staring at the moss growing between the paving slabs, too scared to move, too ashamed to lift my head. Too weak to fight for my family.

Soon the shame became too much and I darted for the house. They laughed as I ran, but didn't come after me. I stormed back into the dining room, straight to my whisky decanter, poured myself a triple, maybe more, and drank it with a shaking hand.

Gabrielle put a hand on my back. 'Oh my God, Ed. Are you okay? Do you want some frozen peas?'

The pain from the blow had faded after the initial shock. I tried to count myself lucky not to be speeding to A&E with a broken nose, but it failed to calm me down.

'Did they say anything about Alison?' she asked.

I finished my drink, wincing at the burn. 'Yes … no … I don't know.'

'That's *it* now, Ed. This is too much. I've tried to be supportive, but it's stupid what you've done. You don't know these people—'

'I promised Ally—'

'She's a child!'

I spun, suddenly giddy, wanting to lash out. 'I thought she was old enough to *disappear* on Friday night without telling her parents.'

'For someone so smart,' Gabrielle said, 'you can be a real idiot.'

'I don't know what to do.' I slumped against the sideboard.

'You *know* what to do.'

'Ally made me promise not—'

'One of them just punched you!'

'Actually, it was a slap.'

'I can't *do* this, Ed.'

By 'this', she meant our little dance, our particular pattern of bickering, Gabrielle getting increasingly irritated with my nippy lawyer comments until she stormed off. Every couple has their routine for having a row, and this was ours. Most of the time we were great together – we laughed a lot, we supported each other, and even after twenty years we remained affectionate – but ever since Ally got on the wrong side of that website, practically every conversation ended up in the same death spiral.

'Come on, Gab,' I said. 'It was meant to be a joke.'

'Oh yes. Violent men outside our house. How *very* droll.'

Her phone buzzed on the table as a text came through. She grabbed it and unlocked the screen. 'Alison!'

And just like that, the tension keeping me rigid dissolved, leaving my legs so weak I had to grip the sideboard to stay standing. I'd been picturing her bound and gagged in some grimy basement, or being found dead in a park by someone out walking their dog.

'She's gone to Brighton with friends,' Gabrielle said. 'Back Sunday.'

'She's gone *where*?' It was one thing to stay out late without texting, another to disappear for the weekend, only telling your frantic parents while hurtling down the motorway in a campervan.

Gabrielle sighed. 'At least she's safe.'

'Does it even say who she's with?' I was furious with Ally – I couldn't believe she'd do something so selfish.

'It doesn't say much.'

I took the phone and read the message. Gabrielle saw my look of horror.

'*What?*' she asked. 'What's wrong?'

'This text,' I said. 'Ally didn't write it.'

3

Hampstead Heath, near the bottom of Parliament Hill, on the edge of the tree line. Forensic officers in crinkling paper suits snapping on purple latex gloves. The tech team setting up sodium lights to capture decent stills in the dawn gloom. Constables barricading the area with blue tape, or looking for evidence in the nearby bushes, or speaking to curious members of the public taking an early walk through the park.

DCI Jackie Rose crouched by the murdered girl – mid- to late teens, pale and supine in the centre of all this industry – and felt that sickening crunch inside her stomach, the same one she always got when she thought about the parents, how they'd react to the news of their child's death. She knew only too well the prayers they'd say to turn back time, to hold their baby once more. But there was no going back. Only the chance to stop it happening again.

'Ma'am?'

Jackie straightened and took in the woman who'd addressed her. Five-ten, mid-twenties, brown hair, brown eyes. Nervous air, like someone who wasn't sure if they were in the right room. White blouse open at the top button to reveal a small silver crucifix.

'And you are?' asked Jackie.

'Detective Sergeant Charlotte Keyes.'

Clearly this was another of Superintendent Drum's new recruits to the Rapid and Serious Unit: a twenty-four/seven operation, set up to investigate rapes and homicides in the capital within minutes of them being reported. Shame this detective sergeant looked barely experienced enough to run a bath, let alone a crime scene. Since when did RAS become a fucking training ground for newbies? Their 'crime solved' stats were ten points higher than the Met Police average for a reason.

Jackie shook her hand. 'DS Haggerty around?'

'Sorry, ma'am. I've not met—'

'Doesn't matter. Looks like we're working together. So, what we got, Sergeant?'

'I just want to say what a privilege it is to work with you. I'd asked three times for a transfer into Rapid and Serious, and—'

'Let's do the pleasantries later, eh? For now, just fill me in on what's going on.'

'Sorry, ma'am.' The sergeant went to the start of her notepad. 'Just after six o'clock this morning we received a call—'

'Keep it simple. We got a name?'

'No ID.'

'Who reported it?'

Keyes nodded to where a dapper old man with a couple of poodles on a double lead was chatting to a constable. 'Says he does this same route every morning.'

Jackie crouched by the girl again. Her face was on its side, her brown curls loose in the dirt, her eyes staring into the grey sky. If it weren't for the way her neck kinked – you didn't need a post-mortem to know it was broken – she could have been mistaken for daydreaming at the clouds. Such a waste. *All those lives now ruined for ever.*

The girl was dressed in navy Tommy Hilfiger tracksuit bottoms and a loose pink sports vest, but something about the style said loungewear rather than jogging. Straightening, Jackie said, 'Time of death?'

'No rigor mortis yet, but it was cold last night. Anywhere between midnight and three. Pathologist should get a better idea.'

'She's not dressed to be out.'

'Could've had a coat.'

'What if she was dumped here?'

Keyes looked confused. 'You mean killed somewhere else, and brought to the park afterwards? But why...?'

'Exactly. Why *here* as well?' They were near the Parliament Hill entrance, close to the path. The body was bound to be seen within minutes of sunrise. 'If you're going to the trouble of hiding a body in the park, why not stick it in the trees? Even better, bury it.'

'They got disturbed?'

Jackie looked into the murdered girl's unblinking eyes, and saw Verity again. That last look from the front step. Seven years ago almost to the day, but never more than a few seconds from her mind. 'Or maybe they wanted the body to be found.'

*

Jackie hurried back to HQ to give the briefing. When they first started RAS, her and DCI Aleksy and Superintendent Drum, they'd worked out of a basement in Croydon Police Station, a fusty, mouse-shit-scented hole with Thatcher-era office furniture and carpet squares that shifted when you walked over them. Due to their success they'd been upgraded to a set of swanky rooms on the sixth floor of the new CID building in Victoria.

The open-plan office was busy with detectives, over thirty now in the unit, scanning CCTV footage at their desks, or poring over burgeoning case folders. Jackie passed through, nodding and saying hi, heading to Incident Room 1. On the way, she grabbed

DS Milou Ramya, and DS Weston 'Trav' Travis, who headed up the tech team. Some senior investigating officers filled their incident room with every constable and their dog for the briefing, but Jackie preferred to have just the detective sergeants, whom she trusted to control the flow of information.

DS Haggerty was already there, on his knees by the A/V suite, a disconnected cable in each hand, staring at the ends as though he were holding them back from a fight. Thirty-two, smart and serious, he was keen to rise up the ranks. They'd been running cases for three years, and she liked how he worked.

'Missed you this morning, Nick,' Jackie said.

'I take it the super didn't tell you about my promotion,' Haggerty replied. 'Inside sergeant.'

Jackie pulled a corkboard from the corner and placed it in front of the blank screen. 'Bit young for a desk job, aren't you?'

Haggerty smiled. 'Bit old to be chasing down criminals, aren't you?'

'Your humour is duly noted, Sergeant.' She gestured to the chairs, where Ramya and Travis were already sitting.

Jackie pinned three stills of the girl to the board. One close-up and two from wide angles, to show the surrounds. 'Found this morning.'

'No attempts to hide her,' Ramya said, his mouth set in the usual amused smirk that most people took for belligerence. They were right, too. Without a doubt, his attitude had contributed to him being 'stuck' at the rank of detective sergeant for much of his career, although the higher ranks' loss was her gain. He was tough and to the point; no one messed with Ramya. Perfect for the uncompromising atmosphere at Rapid and Serious.

'Clean clothes,' Haggerty said. 'It was raining yesterday afternoon. Any kind of struggle, there'd be grass stains on her knees, her elbows.'

'I'm certain she was taken to the park *after* being killed,' Jackie said. 'And left there to be found.'

'SOCO get any forensics?' asked Haggerty.

'She was clutching some strands of hair.'

'Winner, winner,' said Ramya.

'We'll see,' Jackie replied. It wasn't like on TV – a strand of hair meant nothing if none of the follicle was attached. Even if they got the follicle, if they didn't have the killer's DNA on file it was as much use as a boot print in the mud. 'It's all gone to Grace Street for analysis, so we should have the results soon.'

She nodded at Travis. 'There's CCTV on every entrance at the Heath, so get busy.'

'On it, boss,' he replied, giving her a little salute.

'Let's get her onto the mispers list,' she said, addressing all of them. 'She's young enough to be a runaway. I want to know who she is, what she was doing last night, and who she was doing it with.' She tapped the close-up of the girl's face. 'This is someone's daughter. There's a family who loved this girl more than anything in the world, and she's been taken from them. Understood?'

The sergeants left the room, and Jackie studied the pictures again. It sickened her that the life had been stolen from someone so young all because some pervert in the park took a shine to her. Or maybe she chose the wrong psycho boyfriend and he dumped her body there after a row. Either way, they wouldn't rest until they found out.

Superintendent Drum's PA stuck her head round the door. 'There you are,' she said. 'Andrew would like a word.'

'Tell him I'll be in soon.'

'He said it was important…'

In other words, get your arse over here *now*.

4

Jackie had worked with Superintendent Andrew Drum for eight years in the Met's Major Crime Unit before Rapid and Serious, following him up the ladder, always one rung behind. Always wondering whether she'd beat her way into the old boys' clubs of the senior ranks – less than thirty per cent of superintendents were women. But looking at how Drum spent his time now, on the phone all day, stressed to bursting trying to placate some irate chief, she was fine to stay on the front line.

'Have a seat, Jack,' he said.

'You know we've got a live—'

'Just five minutes, please?'

She sat down. 'What's up, boss?'

Drum leaned back in his chair, shirt buttons straining against his chest, and steepled his fingers under his chin. He was still a big man, with a rugby prop forward build – quite the player, apparently, before a busted knee ended all that – although his muscles were less defined now. At least, that was the polite way of saying it.

He took a long slow breath and regarded her. She knew from his sombre expression, his tentative air, what this was about. 'How you doing today, Jack?'

'Busy.'

'You know Aleksy can take this one if—'

18

'I'm taking it, boss.'

'I know what day it is tomorrow.'

'I *said*, I'm taking it.'

Drum's eyes drifted to the framed photo on his desk. His family on a skiing trip, the white peak of Mont Blanc rising in this background. He had three girls; the youngest was eleven. *The same age Verity should—*

Jackie leaned forward, clearing her throat. 'Listen, Andy, stop worrying. I'm fine. It's *okay*. Whoever killed that girl last night, I'm going to hunt them down.'

He sighed, like he had more to say but understood it would be pointless saying it. 'I know you will.'

'I need to get back.' She started to rise.

'Just another minute,' Drum said, motioning her to sit. 'RAS is expanding, so you might have noticed a few new faces round here.'

'I noticed I was babysitting the newbie.'

'DS Keyes comes highly recommended. She was a rising star at MCU.'

'Seemed a bit slow off the ground to me.'

'There's additional scrutiny on us now,' Drum said, giving her a hard stare. 'You know what I'm saying. Keep the investigation … conventional, okay? The higher echelons are watching. They love our stats, and they want to know how they can replicate them.'

Jackie prickled. Rapid and Serious was a success because it was built around a focused, hard-working, *selected* group of detectives, not because there was some secret recipe that could be passed around to other units. This wasn't a fucking KFC franchise.

'Noted, boss,' she said, and made to stand again. 'Anything else?'

'Carry on.' As she got to the door he called after her, 'And be nice!'

In the main office, Keyes was at her desk, leaning in close to her screen.

And be nice!

Jackie girded herself and went over. 'The Super tells me you were hot stuff in MCU.'

'Well, I wouldn't like to say,' Keyes replied, cheeks flushing. Her hand went to her crucifix. A nervous tic. 'But I did receive a commendation for bravery at the Commissioner's ceremony last year.'

'You must have been very proud.'

'Just doing my job, ma'am.'

'I may come across as a bit tough, but if you work hard we'll get on fine.'

'Thank you, ma'am. I intend to.'

Keyes seemed keen now, but Jackie had her doubts about whether the sergeant had the stomach for RAS. The scum they chased down, the sadists and rapists and child abductors, you needed a certain way about you, and Keyes simply didn't have that air about her. It was nothing personal.

Still, she was here now, and they had to work together.

'How was the post-mortem?' asked Jackie. 'Anything interesting?'

Keyes pulled the report from the case file, and handed it up. 'Cause of death was an upper cervical spinal injury—'

'Broken neck,' Jackie said, scanning the document. 'Any evidence of sexual assault?'

'None.'

'Heard back from Grace Street about those hairs?'

'Not yet.'

The way the girl had held onto them, the three strands curled in her fist even as she died, Jackie had no doubt she'd pulled them from the attacker's head so he could be identified later. Smart kid. Hopefully, it wouldn't be in vain.

*

Jackie took the case file to her office and shut the door, pleased to mute the chatter of the main bullpen. She read through the scene log and incident report and witness statements. Studied the stills again. Was the killer a commuter, coming from far away to commit the crime, or a marauder, someone local to the girl? Was he a stranger or someone she knew? It had the feel of a botched sexual assault – she's accosted in the park, starts screaming, he tries to shut her up. That was how it *felt*. But like Haggerty said, no grass stains. Could the assault have happened indoors? So why take her to the park? And after taking the risk to get her there, why just dump her where she was going to be found? Was it a cry for help? Was the killer taunting them?

Next time Jackie checked the time, it was after midday. News of the murder was already on the internet, so they had the press lined up at half past. She stopped by the tech team on her way to the media room, but DS Travis had nothing to report from the park's CCTV. Haggerty had the opposite problem; the Crimestoppers hotline had taken over two hundred calls already.

As Jackie was getting to the lifts, Keyes ran up behind her. 'Ma'am! Ma'am! The lab results.'

Grinning, she handed over her phone. Jackie took it and, reading the email, her smile quickly matched the sergeant's.

From: SusanJiangCSI@met.police.uk
To: DCCharlotteKeyes@met.police.uk
Subject: Hair strands

Hi Charlotte, wanted to get this to you asap. Full details to follow but just to tell you we got a DNA match for the hair strands recovered from the scene this morning. Name is Edgar Truman.

5

'Edgar Truman,' said Gabrielle, 'that is the biggest load of bollocks I have ever heard in my life.'

I stabbed my finger at the message, supposedly from our daughter. *Gone away 4 the weekend to Brighton.*

'Ally *hates* text speak,' I said. 'She thinks it's really lazy.'

'Where's the text speak?'

'Look.' I jabbed the *4*.

I rang Ally back, but the phone was off again. I forced myself to hang up before the answerphone beep. This situation was not going to be improved by me venting onto her voicemail.

'Maybe she was in a rush,' Gabrielle said. 'Maybe one of her friends wrote it for her.'

'I thought you'd contacted them all.'

Her mouth twitched, like she wanted to tell me something, but then her chin hardened. 'For God's sake, she's a teenage girl. You think we know everything about her life?'

'But—'

'Maybe she's got a boyfriend, or something. Have you thought of that?'

'What boyfriend?'

'Could be more than one.'

'Don't wind me up.'

'So it's okay to wind *me* up with your stupid comments?'

And so it began. One more ride on the quarrel carousel. Gabrielle saying how if I took more of an interest in the kids when they were growing up then I might know them a little better, me replying that I may not have done the picks-up and drop-offs and playdates but I worked incredibly hard to pay for it all, so I wasn't *completely* useless, both of us furious with Ally but taking it out on each other because our daughter wasn't there. I couldn't believe she'd disappear for the weekend without checking if it was okay with us first! Especially with friends we didn't know. Double that if it was a *boyfriend* we didn't know.

Or maybe more exactly, that *I* didn't know.

Gabrielle ended the row with a sweep of her hand.

'Just, *enough*. I'm teaching all weekend, and I need to get my head in the right place, and all of *this*' – she made a show of passing her hands around the room, but mostly keeping them near me – 'is not helping.'

I stepped back in surrender. 'Fine. *Okay.*'

Going back to teaching was a big step for Gabrielle in re-establishing her career. She held a PhD in Curating Fine Art from Goldsmiths, and before getting pregnant with Ally was working as an intern at the National Portrait Gallery. I was earning close to six figures at a city law firm, so it made sense for her to stay home with the baby. At the time she talked about getting back into work quickly, but when Mitchell came along a couple of years later, that was that: from budding artist to bored housewife.

She started drawing again a few years ago, when Mitchell went to secondary school, and I couldn't be prouder of what she'd achieved since then, setting up a website to sell her pieces, even securing an exhibition at Hackney Arts Centre, and now running the weekend introductory courses at the London Art Academy.

It was amazing. *She* was amazing. Although I wasn't quite so on board with all the changes of late. I didn't like the fillers. She'd first had it done about six months ago. I couldn't believe it when I came home and there she was, her cheeks shiny and slightly bulging, like someone had gone at the front of her face with a foot pump.

'I just got sick of seeing a middle-aged frump in the mirror,' she'd said.

I'm not saying she needed to run it by me first. I just thought she looked beautiful before. Those curls, those stunning grey eyes, that sexy little smile she still gave me on special occasions – I found her as attractive as the first day I saw her on campus, over twenty years ago. I guess what hurt the most is that she didn't care about my opinion. At best it felt like I was an afterthought. At worst, an obstacle.

I mean, I tried my best. I exfoliated, I moisturised, I went to the gym at lunchtimes, although no amount of treadmill miles made a dent in the bulges over the back of my jeans when I buckled my belt. But like strip poker or skinny dipping, vanity is a young man's game. Extra pounds invariably appeared on the scales, even when I'd been living on kale smoothies and chicken salads all week. My hair, tragically, continued to collect in the plughole.

'I'm going upstairs,' Gabrielle sighed. 'Don't drink too much.'

'But you've not had dinner!'

'Eat with Mitchell.'

'I'd rather eat on my own,' I muttered, but not quietly enough, judging from my wife's withering expression.

Mitchell, our son. Now there was a whole thing. I just didn't really *understand* the person he was becoming. When I was fourteen, I took my bike out in the evening, or kicked a ball around with friends. I mean, the amount of time he spent in that pit of a room, his curtains drawn, a smell somewhere between mush-rooms and mucus coming from under his door, Gollum probably got more fresh air than him. He was so disconnected from the world, so disinterested.

'How about *I* go upstairs?' I suggested. 'And *you* eat with Mitchell.'

Gabrielle spoke in a sharp whisper. 'Would it kill you to spend time with your son?'

'Oh, come on. It's not just me. No one likes him. When was the last time he had a friend come round?'

'Oh, *God*,' she moaned. I thought it was in reaction to what I'd said, but she was looking over my shoulder. I glanced round and felt myself deflate.

These days, I struggled to see much nuance of emotion in Mitchell's face. It was at that awful in-between stage particular to early teenage boys, where different parts mature independently, in his case giving him a grown man's nose and forehead, but the mouth and jaw of a young child. Usually it was fixed into an expression that might best be described as apathetic petulance, but right now he didn't seem anything less than very, very upset.

He looked from me to his mother, then back to me – complet-ing more eye contact in those few seconds than in the previous year – then said in a voice cold enough to shatter my heart, 'I hate you so much.'

I covered my face and groaned as he stormed out the room. 'That's so bad. Like therapy bad.'

'Not your finest moment as a father.'

'I feel awful.'

'Because you said it? Or because he heard you?'

'That's helpful.'

She eyeballed the door. 'Well, go on…'

Things felt unresolved between Gabrielle and me – further

evidenced by the way she followed me up the stairs and went into our bedroom without another word.

I stopped outside Mitchell's door, and my eyes drifted to the tableau of peeling Optimus Prime stickers still gamely clinging to the paint. Was it only five years since he was obsessed with *Transformers*? That version of my son seemed as far away as the creased little bundle of limbs handed to me by the nurse minutes after he was born. I had such hopes for him back then. *Mitch*, people would call him. He'd be popular and sporty and fawned over by all the girls in class. Not because I wanted to live vicariously through him, but because I didn't want him to struggle like I had. Instead he'd turned out even more nerdy and unpopular than I'd been.

As expected, Mitchell ignored my knock. I called his name, loud enough for Gabrielle to hear, my voice echoing on the empty landing. Still nothing. Long gone were the days when I'd shout to him from the bottom of the stairs and he'd hare out of his room to see what I wanted. Now when it came to communication between my son and me, if he could get away without responding, then that was what he did.

Nevertheless, I stumbled through an apology, saying how I was sorry, really sorry, it was just a stupid comment, and tried not to think about him on the other side, wishing I was dead. It hurt to hear him say he hated me, even though I knew he didn't mean it. Probably. As a kid, I remember thinking that about my own dad enough times. To say I had a fractious relationship with my father would be underselling it – in those final years, once Mum was gone and he was in a home, I peddled every lame excuse to get out of visiting him. And yet here I was, driving my own son away. Maybe we're all just fated to turn into our dads. I rested my head against the wall, dejected. *Good luck, Mitch. You're going to need it.*

I traipsed back downstairs, finished my whisky, poured another.

Was it any surprise that many parents drank so much? It was dark outside, the streetlights on. The men had disappeared from the top of the drive, but it didn't matter, the damage had been done. No one would forget seeing my face on a placard.

Did Gabrielle know who Ally was with? Or at least, did she have a good idea? I pictured my daughter on the beach, taking a slug on the bottle of vodka going round a campfire, and giving her phone to a friend because she was too drunk to text us herself. When did my little girl grow up? Why did I feel like I'd missed it all?

I was too twitchy to watch television, too annoyed with Gabrielle to attempt to make up, so I set about dismantling dinner, saddened by the sight of the dried-out chicken. That filled twenty minutes. I eyed my bag by the front door – my usual rule was never to work on Friday night, if only because I worked pretty much the rest of the time. Work was my saviour. It kept me sane. It quietened the undertow of existential dread forever dragging on my mind (*Is this it? Is this everything? Shouldn't I be happy by now?*), allowing me to switch off, lose some hours, and when I finished, unlike so many other things in life, I invariably felt contented instead of disappointed.

Steve and I did good things at our practice. As legal aid solicitors, we made an important contribution to the community, focusing on family law and often working *pro bono*. We tried to make a difference in people's lives. After seeing what happened to my mum, it was a calling for me.

I took my bag to the dining table and got out the file for a tricky case. The client had reported her husband's psychological abuse against both her and the kids, and I'd applied for an occupation order to get him out of the house. The trouble was, he controlled the money. He'd hired a top city firm and was trying to use her antidepressant prescription as evidence that she was delusional, despite our letter from her doctor saying that she neither exhibited delusion nor could develop it as a side effect of her medication. I started to read the supporting statements, but just couldn't concentrate.

Ally. That text.

Was that handsome bastard and his cronies involved in her absence? But if they were, all they had to do was show me a picture of her tied up in the boot of a car and I'd have capitulated on the spot. Even so, a lifetime of simmering in the British legal system, of listening to people lie and prevaricate on a daily basis and very occasionally tell the truth, had given me a gut instinct I trusted like my right hand. And something just didn't *feel* right.

I got out my laptop. First, I checked Ally's social media. Fortunately, she wasn't as embarrassed by her father as some of her peers, so unlike many parents I was friends with my daughter on TikTok, Instagram, something called Snapchat, which I knew little about, except that it was to be feared, and a few other things I'd created accounts for, but which now seemed to be used by no one.

Between sips of whisky, I made longhand notes on a legal pad. The last photos of Ally I found were on her friend Jasmine's Instagram feed, taken the previous night at 6.22pm. They were going to a 'social' (we weren't stupid, we knew what that meant), then having a sleepover at Jasmine's. Photos of the party weren't hard to find, but most were either blurred or filled with indistinct forms flinging their arms in the dark. I didn't see my daughter in any of them.

For many hours, I worked through Ally's friend list in Instagram, cross-referencing it with anyone tagged in the party photos, searching for something – or someone – suspicious. Most were kids from her secondary school. It was a decent place, it cost enough, and no one whose profile I delved into seemed like a total reprobate. They all seemed like good kids. No evidence of a boyfriend, either.

Still scrolling, I went to pour another whisky, but when I tipped the decanter nothing came out. I slumped back in my chair, breaking the screen spell, only then realising how impressively drunk I'd managed to become. Back in the real world I was due at Westminster Magistrates' Court in the morning for a paid case.

I was looking at my phone, doing the morning maths for how long I could reasonably sleep in and still be on time, when deep in my subconscious something clicked into place.

Her phone.

We had a family contract. I had access to everyone's itemised bill.

I logged into Vodafone, raced to Ally's bill, and scanned the list of phone numbers. Right at the bottom was Gabrielle's – the text sent to her tonight. Above that was a call to a mobile number, at 9.38 p.m. yesterday.

The last call Ally made.

I copied that number and pasted it in the search bar of the bill. She'd never rung that number before. I typed it into my phone. It was late, but fuck it.

I pressed dial.

6

10.53 P.M., FRIDAY

Phoenix shoved her laptop away and sighed. She'd been digging through router vulnerabilities, hunting for ways to hack into the Wi-Fi of the office building next door, but her eyes were too tired to carry on reading the screen. She'd try again in the morning when her mind was less frantic, her nerves not quite so electrified. *Yeah, right.* Not much chance of that happening.

She kept looping through last night, what went wrong, the *exact moment* it all got messed up. *Oh, God.* What had she done? She got up off the mattress, darted to the grimy window looking onto the busy London night, and searched for the people she knew were hunting her. The post-theatre crowd had cleared, but it was Friday night, the pubs and bars were packed. Girls and guys her age busied the street below, shouting and laughing, fearlessly enjoying themselves, and for a moment she wondered what it would be like to be one of them. To be trussed up in hot pants and heading to a night club, where she'd dance and smile and meet cool people, then at the end of it stumble home to a safe warm bed. Wasn't that what normal girls her age did? But she'd never been normal – at least not by other people's standards.

Was she safe to come here? Should she have gone straight to the hideout? She was in a small room, on the second floor of an abandoned office block near Pall Mall, now run as a squat by the Autonomous Nation of Anarchist Libertarians; she'd found out about it on a No Shock Doctrine march against austerity cuts. She'd been homeless at the time, having run away from her boarding school days after her fifteenth birthday. Usually a spiky-haired club promoter called Vanna stayed in this room, cluttering it with old flyers and incense sticks burnt to the stub, but she'd gone back home to Leeds because her mum was sick. Unlike some of the places where Phoenix crashed, this squat was the right side of grubby, with running water and electricity, at least in certain parts of the building. No one knew she used this place, not even Ally. They'd planned it that way.

Ally should be here.

They should be here together.

Phoenix lay down, pulling the worn blanket over herself, hoping the exhaustion in her bones would spread to her brain. She'd been awake for coming up to two days now. How was that even possible? Through the rolled hoodie she was using as a pillow she heard the faint *whub-whub-whub* of a bassline. A party on the fourth floor – she'd overheard people talking about it. She tried to focus on the sound, thankful to have something to distract her from the panic frothing in her chest, the monologue of blame going through her mind.

What was that?

She jerked up, heart pounding. It sounded like a voice. The pale glow coming from her laptop was enough to show that no one else was in the room. She heard it again – someone was on the phone in the corridor – and slumped back down, hand to her chest, quivering from the adrenaline.

Calm. The fuck. Down.

No way was she getting sleep any time soon. She might as well do something useful and try again to find a way onto the office next door's Wi-Fi. The sooner she could get the videos uploaded, the sooner she could bring those bastards down, the sooner she could get Ally free. It was their only chance.

Phoenix activated the security token on her watch and entered the six-digit number into the laptop, unlocking the screen. *Okay, come on. Concentrate.* The Wi-Fi was using a Cisco 800 router. Decent, but not impenetrable, depending on the firmware. She scanned her documentation repo for bug lists, patch histories, trying out things that sounded feasible, an HTTP subscribe attack, a WSD protocol exploit, but nothing was working. She found a software release note luckily saved to her hard drive for a similar model, which contained what sounded like a ridiculous suggestion – connect to the admin and type a password longer than the maximum allowed characters – and barely suppressed her howl of delight when it worked. *Yes!* Thank heavens for poorly written software.

She connected to her secure server and set the videos to upload. After encryption they were so big it would take the best part of a day to complete, but that was at least three times faster than at the hideout, which had only a satellite connection.

And then what?

Don't think about that now. One step at a time. These videos gave her options. They gave her power. If she was smart, she could still bring them down *and* get Ally back.

Phoenix lay on her side. The music from the party was still going. She focused on it again, taking meditation breaths, wanting to sleep with a desperation that she knew would only keep her awake for longer. What if they were tracking her? They were developing some sophisticated AI facial recognition software at the centre. She'd tried to be careful, but there were cameras everywhere in London. What if they'd found her already? What if they were already on their way? What if they burst in the room and dragged her back there? Her hand flew to the scar on her neck. She'd rather *die* than go back to that—

A quiet buzz from inside her bag, her phone vibrating with a call. She sat up in alarm. That wasn't possible.

Only one person had that number.

7

I all but shouted into the phone – 'Hello? *Hello?*' – but they hung up. I rang again and this time the phone was off. '*The person you are—*' I tried again. Same thing.

I pressed the phone to my forehead. *What am I doing?* I'd probably just woken, I don't know, the Uber driver who took them to the party. Sleep. That was what I needed. And not to have gotten so wasted. Then again, I said that most nights.

Gabrielle had to be right. Ally was with her mates, no doubt not even giving her parents a second thought. And yet . . . and yet. I didn't believe in God, had always found the idea of an angry old man in the sky demanding we say nice things about him faintly ridiculous, but even so I shut my eyes and prayed that she was safe. Then I grabbed the spare bedding – so well used of late that describing it as 'spare' seemed gratuitous – and set up on the sofa.

After an hour I was still awake, so put the news on low on the television and lay there miserably listening to all the death and destruction happening in the world, hoping that hearing about the plight of others would make my own more manageable. It must have worked because next time I cranked open my eyes the clock in the corner of the screen said 7.32, the morning present-ers were swapping cheery banter, and my head was pounding like someone was trying to break it down.

I showered and dressed and forced down a coffee thick enough to tarmac a road, all the while engaging in a silent war with Gabrielle that I neither wanted nor knew how to stop, then flew out of the house for the Tube. I was meeting Steve at Westminster Magistrates' Court at nine, but because the God I didn't believe in hated me there were problems on the Northern Line. Cue a frantic dash back to the house to get my car and offer my second prayer in twenty-four hours, this time to not get pulled over by the police. No doubt I was still a unit or two over the limit.

Gabrielle was right, though. This couldn't go on. When I got to the office that afternoon, I was going to write to the court and file a notice of discontinuance to pull the injunction. Let them keep their shitty website. As long as they left me and my family alone.

Ally's voice – *Promise me, Dad. Whatever they try.* I didn't want to let her down!

I turned on the radio, hoping to drown out the row in my head. When I heard who was being interviewed, I wished I hadn't bothered.

William Carmichael.

The man responsible for ruining my daughter's life.

Until last year, I saw William Carmichael as a minor internet nut job. A psychology professor who dressed like he bought his clothes from a catalogue called Drab, and uploaded his webcam musings on the problems with modern progressive culture to – I thought – a small but appreciative audience of despondent misogynists. Turned out, I was wrong. Carmichael was *huge*. Like a hundred thousand YouTube views *a day* huge. And that mattered when his main line of argument was some incoherent conspiracy theory about how the liberal agenda was being forced on the population by sinister corporate forces, driven by the super-rich elite, for profit and control.

I remembered seeing him on a *Newsnight* panel about the rise of national pride as a response to multiculturalism. 'The liberal agenda demands change,' he'd said. 'With change comes new opportunity. Take the transgender "movement".' He actually did the finger quotes. 'Who benefits from that? Is it the person, who must deal with the trauma of the situation? Is it the family, whose conflicting beliefs may cause it to break apart? Or is it the pharmaceutical company, who now has new customers, popping hormone replacement pills for *the rest of their lives*, to cure a disease they don't really have?'

Right now on the radio, Carmichael was arguing that the rise of feminism, far from making women happier, was the biggest contributor to female depression, especially post-natal. 'Women have had their place in the world stolen from them,' he said. 'They've been conned into thinking that being natural at nurturing is a bad thing.'

It was his voice, the measured way he delivered his views, that gave him credibility. He wasn't loud or angry or red in the face. Unlike most cranks, he sounded intelligent. That made his *views* sound intelligent. And that made them the most dangerous kind of nonsense.

'Think of the impact this nurture gap has on the children,' he was saying. 'The mother is at work. The father is at work. So who is nurturing these children? Some bored young girl on minimum wage? In every report, rates of serious mental illness, anxiety, depression, body dysmorphia – they all rise exponentially the more a country pursues progressive policies. The more liberal a country, the greater the amount of mental illness. That's a fact.'

Maybe it was our fault that Ally became obsessed with William Carmichael. Her mum was an artist, passionately liberal, and she'd been subjected to my rants about how justice should not be the reserve of those who can afford it since birth, so perhaps it wasn't surprising that she turned into our little social justice warrior. Although considering Mitchell's complete indifference to suffering in the world, I guess the jury must stay out on the nature/nurture debate.

When Ally was eight, she went on her first march with Gabrielle, against the sale of arms to Saudi Arabia. Aged twelve, she became editor of the school paper, writing an article on empowerment through inclusivity that had everyone talking in the staff room, at least according to her form teacher. Only this year on her sixteenth birthday, I drove her out to a field in Hampshire so she could picket a new fracking site. I couldn't have been prouder than if she'd come home with straight As, which, to be fair, she usually did.

Then, six weeks ago, she milkshaked Carmichael as he came out of his Men's Learning Centre campus. *Definitely* not something I condone. Although the video of him that went viral – dripping with glutinous strawberry slop and shaking with rage as he intoned that she would be a happier human being if she spent her time bearing children instead of harassing innocent people – was pretty hilarious.

Carmichael's devotees rose up to take revenge. One forum in particular, on the Men's Learning Centre website, took the lead, digging into Ally's life, publishing her email address, her phone number, details of all her social media accounts. I wrote to Carmichael repeatedly, asking him to remove all information about my daughter from the website, but instead users in the forum kept posting new stuff – her medical records, her school reports, even, somehow, her bank statements.

Eventually, I filed a claim for harassment, and at the hearing on Friday morning the judge granted an interim injunction forcing Carmichael to take down his website until the trial.

Hence last night, his men outside my home.

And now Ally was gone.

8

Phoenix stared at the phone, now off. *Who the fuck was that?* Some guy, sounded middle-aged. Was it one of *them*? She fought the urge to jump up from the mattress, grab her rucksack and run from the squat. Skulk through the Friday night party crowd until she cleared London, then head straight for the hideout.

It *had* to be them. Ally was the only person with that number. They must have tortured it out of her – and right then, Phoenix saw it, Ally beaten, sobbing, tied to a chair, that *psychopath* approaching her with a slick grin and a glistening scalpel.

A number had come on the screen when the phone rang. She turned it back on. It was her burner phone, a Nokia 3301, no internet, no GPS, impervious to even the best spyware, so she didn't need to worry about it pinging a nearby tower. She checked the call log. The call came from a mobile. On her laptop, she put the number through a reverse-number look-up site. The results came back with his name and phone carrier: Ed Truman.

No way. Ally's dad.

How did he get this number? Did Ally give it to him? What if she made it back home, but lost her phone and was using his? But why wouldn't she call? Unless she was hurt. Phoenix weighed the burner in her palm. Could she call back and ask about Ally quick enough not to get traced if he was working with the Men's

Learning Centre? She went cold. Was that possible? Surely not Ally's dad. The plan would never have got this far if he was one of them!

Still, it was possible. If she got caught as well, last night would have been for nothing. As much as she was terrified for Ally, she couldn't let that happen. *Ally* wouldn't want that to happen. This was so much bigger than both of them. Nothing could jeopardise what they were doing.

But what if Ally was safe? How amazing would it be if she was here with her? She was so smart with the strategy stuff – it was what made them such a great team.

Phoenix opened a new web page and searched for Ed Truman in an identity information site. She had to find out, but she'd do it her own way. His whole life appeared on her screen. Address, phone numbers – mobile, home, and work – his social media accounts, all with minimal privacy settings. She despaired of people sometimes. Every day they were told about scammers and identity thieves, and what did ninety-nine per cent of them do about it? A big fat nothing.

She clicked into his LinkedIn profile. A lawyer. She'd have to be careful. But even the smartest mark only saw what they wanted to see. Normals craved the normal, the everyday. Most of them couldn't handle anything else.

He ran a private legal practice called Smith Truman Solicitors, and she found the email address on their website. That was good, they used their own domain. She fired a blank message to blah-blah@smithtruman.co.uk, and got a reply in less than a minute.

Delivery to the following recipient failed permanently: blahblah@ smithtruman.co.uk

Technical details of permanent failure:

The recipient server did not accept our requests to connect. [mail.
smithtruman.co.uk. 212.188.249.149: socket error]

So 212.188.249.149 was the webserver address. Phoenix fed
it into an IP lookup, tapping impatiently by the trackpad as it
searched. *Please let it be local, not some Russian email farm.* The
results came back: the server was located at 18 St Peter Street,
Finchley. Same as their offices. She smiled. Almost too easy.

Getting onto the webserver was simple, as it had clearly been set
up by someone who knew as much about internet security as an
empty crisp packet. Windows 2003? *Come on!* That was rubbish
fifteen years ago. She could've hacked into that still in nappies. A
quick scan of the ports showed the SMB service was open on 445.
She tunnelled through that to start a remote shell.

She found the firm's email archive, scanned some conversations,
quickly figured out an angle. Ed's business partner was called Steve
Smith, so she sent Ally's dad a message spoofed to appear as if it
came from Steve's address, steve@smithtruman.co.uk.

Hey Ed, can you PLEASE look through this in time for court tomorrow.
I want to get your take on it before we're called in. Cheers! S

If Ally's dad tried to download the attachment from his phone,
it would silently install a piece of software, allowing her to turn on
and view his GPS location.

Then she was going to meet him in person and find out for herself if Ally was safe.

9

9.29 A.M., SATURDAY

I was supposed to meet Steve at nine, but that was long gone by the time I found a parking space near Baker Street, paid the GDP of a small country into it for the privilege of parking there, and stayed in the car a further ten minutes doing battle with myself, eventually losing and taking two quick pulls from the flask under the driver's seat. Using the sudden burst of energy, I ran the rest of the way to Westminster Magistrates' Court, arriving in the kind of ragged, gulping state that always gives clients confidence that they chose the right representation.

Until recently, courts only opened on weekends for overnight remand cases, but the ever-increasing backlog of prosecutions, along with the accelerated rollout of the flexible criminal justice system model – which basically amounted to everyone working harder and longer for the same money – meant that all too often I spent my Saturdays here. Although smart on the outside, with its glass front and modern square design, inside was as much of a zoo as any other magistrate's court: a hotbed of busted dealers, ASBO kids, joy riders, drunk drivers and battered spouses, festooned with stressed solicitors forever looking for a private room to go over their statements, while petulant ushers ordered everyone around with the compassion of trainee fascist dictators. All of this was against the backdrop of an incoherent Tannoy system, whose constant, crackling announcements seemed to be directed at both everybody and nobody at all.

Steve was waiting for me in the lobby, all smiles, although our client's face told an entirely different story. One that perhaps involved parading through Regent's Park with my head on a spike.

I'd known Steve since school, and we'd always been close. Our wives became friends too, and we'd made a frequent foursome, to dinner or the theatre. But when Faith walked out on Steve, Gabrielle sided with her because he'd cheated, despite the fact their marriage had been in a perilous state way before his fraught, doomed-from-the-start affair with crazy Rowena from our squash league. I argued that Steve and I went way back, we had a business together, whereas all she and Faith did on their own was meet for lunch every few months and bitch about the mothers who smoked by the school gate. Gabrielle wouldn't be persuaded. She started to hate it when I grabbed a post-work beer with Steve, as if he was some kind of human herpes, and 'having an affair' was a contagious disease.

As always in these situations, the children got dragged into the middle and booted around, especially when the split was so acrimonious. They had two boys, Vince and Nicholas, and Faith was always trying to get Steve's access curtailed. I didn't know everything that went on between them – I only heard one side of the story – but it *was* very difficult to get a court to file much in the father's favour. And I'd been friends with Steve long enough to know he wasn't the monster she liked to paint him as. These days, he did a lot of free work for men in the same situation as him, but who didn't have the money or expertise to take the mother to court to fight for shared custody; without public legal funding, many who'd done no worse than their spouse in the break-up weren't able to see their children at all.

This client, however, wasn't a freebie. Otherwise I wouldn't be there. I was an extra bum on the bench, to show the client was 'lawyering up'. His Swedish-born wife had returned to Stockholm with his three sons and refused to come back. We wanted the judge to agree to the motion of international child abduction, which would allow us to file an extradition order.

'Good job they're always running late,' I quipped as I shook the client's hand, a tall pinstripe type, who scowled at me like I'd brought him the wrong coffee. Again.

'I'm going to the lav,' he fired at Steve.

'You, my friend,' Steve said, once we were alone, 'look bloody awful.'

'Sorry … Ally didn't come home last night.'

'I thought she was going to a party.'

'That was Thursday. We got a text last night saying she'd gone away with friends, but she didn't ask us first. And we don't know who she's with.'

Steve rubbed his forehead, pained. It'd been over ten years since he worked for a city firm, but he still presented himself in that corporate style: side-parted crew, tailored three-piece suit, something on his cuffs glittering in the shadow of his jacket sleeves. 'Nicholas is the same,' he said. 'A couple of weeks ago he disappeared for the weekend with his mates and made me cover for him. Faith was fuming when she found out.'

'I bet.'

'Let's grab a coffee after the hearing. We can commiserate about being surplus to our children's requirements together. In the meantime, what's your take on the consent question? Could his wife use the mail from the fifteenth as proof that he acquiesced to the move?'

'Was that in the email you sent me this morning? I tried to download the file but it wouldn't—'

'What email? Jesus, Ed. Are you …' He leaned in, somehow

looking more pained than before, and took a sniff. 'Have you been—'

'I didn't sleep very well. That's *all*.'

'Okay. Okay.' Steve threw his hands up in surrender. 'Listen, am I still okay to pick Mitchell up tomorrow? I'm taking him over to see Vince.'

'Sure, of course.' Mitchell went over to Steve's place once or twice a month – it was nice that he still had at least one friend in the real world.

The client was coming back. Steve smoothly slid his hand into the small of his back and guided him towards the chairs. 'Why don't we get comfy until we're called.'

As they turned away, he caught my eye and grimaced pleadingly. *Please go clean yourself up.*

I needed to sort my head out. Much as I saw my work as a mission, we still needed to pay the bills, and clients like this were crucial. In the heat of the lobby I felt woozy, breathless, bloody drunk again – I knew those gulps from my car stash were a bad idea – so I stepped outside, into the chilly morning.

Come on, Ed. Get it together.

I turned without looking and slammed into someone, a young girl about Ally's age, sending, for some reason, a pile of vegetables cascading into the air.

10

For Phoenix, what she did was a kind of method acting. Becoming the part. Today she was a sweet-young-girl-in-the-city, doing some grocery shopping on the way to class. Hence the vegetables. And her hair, the fringe from her platinum bob spilling from beneath her feminist-style bandanna. And the black ink stains on her fingertips – she was studying at the Slade School of Fine Art, if he were to ask. These little details made the lie so authentic he wouldn't even realise being lied to was an option.

People believed anything as long as you presented it right, and most of the time she knew exactly what to say. She'd spent her whole life trying to convince everyone she was one thing when really she was something else. This was just what she did. The art of it came easily to her.

Ally's dad gasped, reaching to help her. 'Are you all right?'

Phoenix winced as he pulled her up. In person, he was even more of a dad than on his social media. He just had that air about him, like you could ask him for a lift and he'd say yes. Ally hadn't said much about him, but Phoenix figured they had a good relationship. It was people who had a bad relationship with their parents who talked about them all the time. Well, usually.

Adrenalin had beaten out the exhaustion from before. When she looked forlornly at her broccoli – which had tumbled off the

45

curb and lay an inch deep in grimy road water – she infused her expression with genuine regret at her lost lunch.

'I don't think I'll be eating *that* now,' she said. Together they gathered the rest – carrots, cabbage, a leek that had luckily rolled a centimetre shy of a patch of fresh pigeon poo. 'I should have got a plastic bag, but I've got a bag of them already at home. A bag full of bags, right?'

When she laughed, he returned it, already more relaxed. She felt the shiver of anticipation across her back. She loved this part. The switch.

'*Hey!* Mr Truman, right?'

'Sorry, I—'

'You're Ally's dad. It's me, *Katie*. Katie Carlson. I'm at school with Ally, or I was. I actually left last summer. Got into art *college!*' She sang the last word, swinging her body so he could see her port-folio case, containing, if he were to ask, intricate Hindu *samsara* paintings, which she'd borrowed from a gothy earth mother at the squat called Niama. She touched his arm just above the wrist. 'You don't remember me, do you? I was more Jasmine's friend, but I've been to your house before. Probably not since I was thirteen. I had the worst mullet *ever*! I've not seen Ally in *ages*. How is she?'

'She's, *errr* … She's …'

Keep smiling, keep sunny. 'You know, I might give her a call tonight. Have a proper catch-up. Do you know if she's around?'

'Actually … she's away with friends.'

'Ooh, how lovely. Gone anywhere nice?'

'Brighton, I think. I don't know. She texted last night.'

Phoenix felt her face freeze. Last night? Did that mean Ally got away? How was that possible?

'Ooh, how lovely,' Phoenix said. *You already said that!* 'I mean, it's lovely down there.' *Stop saying lovely!*

Ally's dad frowned. He cocked his chin to the side. 'You

wouldn't happen to know, ummm ... I mean, we're not sure who she's with.'

'*Me?* No ... I've not spoken to Ally for like ... I don't know – a while!' She'd blown it. Curtain, dropped. Phoenix backed away, hugging her veg. 'I'd better ...'

'Sure, sure. Sorry. Just out of interest, were you in Ally's class at Hargraves?'

Abort! Abort!

'Sorry, I'm already a bit late. Good to see you, Mr Truman, and say hi to—'

'Wait – hold on.'

'Sorry! Got to dash! Bye!'

Phoenix hurried away, taking the first corner in a trot, ripping off the stupid bandanna and dumping that along with the vegetables into the nearest bin.

How could Ally have sent that text?

*

I watched the girl go, bewildered. Something about that whole exchange didn't feel right. I mean, sure, I was unlikely to pick too many of Ally's friends out from a line-up, especially if I hadn't seen her since she was thirteen. At that age they were an indistinguishable mass of spots, hair and braces to me, and no doubt to them we dads were little more than paunches, sad eyes and hairlines in various stages of receding. She probably looked very different now, with the nose ring and the trendy T-shirt and the silvery hair. It was just the way her eyes went sharp when I mentioned Brighton. For a millisecond, but I saw it. She knew *something*. About what, I couldn't say. But I was determined to find out.

I started after her. The back streets here were a maze, so I tore

47

round the corner, hoping she hadn't turned again. I saw her up ahead, by a bin. As she hurried on I checked what she'd dumped. There they were, the vegetables, discarded on a coffee-stained copy of the *Metro*. The truth hit me like a slap. She never went to school with Ally. Everything she'd told me had been a lie.

I knew it. I knew it when she froze.

I carried on following, wondering whether to confront her, but deciding to keep my distance. It was Saturday, the streets were busy with tourists. What was I going to do if she started screaming? At least I was able to stay hidden while keeping her in sight. We came out near Marble Arch. The 94 bus was coming. She quickened her pace to get it. She sneaked onto the back, keeping low, heading for the stairs. Only a couple of people had got on. It was readying to leave. Screw it. I'd apologise to Steve later, say Gabrielle called me home urgently. I jumped on the front, pressed my debit card to the reader, and stayed near the driver among the throng of other standers.

We passed Bond Street, turned at Oxford Circus. The stop after Piccadilly, there she was, a flash of silver hair, darting down the stairs. She slipped out the back of the bus. I shoved my way off the front. She took a right onto Pall Mall, and hurried to a grand old building, the kind with columns along the front. She looked left and right as she pushed open a side door.

On second glance, the building was in a bad state. Windows were cracked, a few smashed, and inside was dark. An official-looking notice was pasted to the main entrance.

I hesitated. Should I go in and speak to her? What if it was a crack den? The last thing I needed today was to get filleted by some druggie looking for Saturday night fun money. But what else was I going to do? Wait here until she came out? What if there was a different exit? What if—

My phone vibrated in my pocket. Gabrielle. I answered, 'Hey, honey, you al—'

'Ed? *Ed?*'

I felt my scalp flush 'What is it? Is it Ally?'

'It's not Alison. It's *you.*'

'What about me?'

'You're in the *news*, Ed!'

'What ... what—'

'Look at the link I sent you. Call me back!'

'But—'

She hung up. A moment later a WhatsApp from her arrived, containing a link to the *MailOnline*. I clicked on it and staggered backwards, hand to my head, feeling like reality had switched to something new, weird, and altogether worse. And the old one wasn't coming back any time soon.

DOMESTIC ABUSE LAWYER ACCUSED
OF SEXUAL HARASSMENT.

11

They were waiting for her in the car. The handsome man flipped down the sun visor and checked his reflection, smoothing a misplaced hair, biting his lips to get some colour into them. He practised a smile. Such an easy thing to do, to shape your mouth that way, to crinkle your eyes along with it, and yet people were fooled almost every time.

'That her?' asked Murph, shifting forward in the driver's seat, the belt straining against his bulk.

Helen McAllister. Dumpy and drawn, lank black hair, the sort of sallow complexion that spoke of too many sad nights alone in front of the television. She'd come out of the corner shop with a shopping bag in each hand. Good. The last one almost managed to claw his face. Murph had made sure she wouldn't be doing anything with that hand for a while.

'Let's go,' the handsome man said, opening his car door. He knew he should probably delegate this kind of thing, that his time was no doubt needed on a million other pressing matters, but nothing else gave him a thrill like being on the front line. Besides, this bullshit with the website had been going on long enough. Time to finish it off before Truman found out the good news.

They started after McAllister, staying on the other side of the road, their pace leisurely, pretending to chat. She glanced at them a couple of times, but didn't speed up. Clearly, she didn't think they were a threat.

More fool her.

As they came to the right point – an alleyway that ran behind a couple of disused offices, most of the windows boarded up – the handsome man called across the street in his most helpful voice.

'Excuse me! Miss! You've dropped something.'

She paused and looked at him. He knew how attractive he was to women. He knew he had brooding eyes, and that his jaw slanted into a strong chin. Match that with confidence and it became a killer combination, as irresistible as a cold beer on a summer's day. It was those looks that gave him time to get close.

'I think it was a fiver,' he said, crossing the road, but focusing on the ground behind her.

Her attention was on him now. She'd turned and joined him in searching, distracted enough for Murph to move into place, light on his feet for someone so big.

'But I . . .' she said. 'I don't think . . .'

The handsome man ducked to the pavement, so it seemed as if he was snatching something from the ground, although he already had the five-pound note palmed.

'Here we go,' he said, holding it out to her.

She took it from him, a smile appearing on her sour face. 'Thanks, I didn't even know I had—'

Murph stepped in behind her. One hand around her mouth, so huge it covered her nose and chin, the other around her waist. Lift and carry into the alleyway. She kicked and bucked, uselessly flailing her shopping bags. They took her behind the offices to a scratch of cracked asphalt, the weeds coming through it grown to knee height. Except for the insistent bark of a distant dog, the morning was quiet, enough to hear a scream from a block away. And this one looked like a screamer.

'My friend is going to put you down,' the handsome man said. 'And we're going to have a chat. If you listen and agree, I'll let you go. Understand?' Eyes wide, head nodding. Moaning behind the massive hand. He flashed her a grin that in other situations would have her falling in love with him. 'Now, are you going to scream?'

Her nods became a frantic shake of the head.

'I'm so pleased you're willing to co-operate,' he said.

He liked working with a big man, that old pairing of brains and brawn. So much easier to get things done. He'd found this one, Murph, about four months ago at an AA meeting. Always a good place to recruit, as you got a lot of security workers. Must be the night shifts, the long hours with no one to talk to and nothing to do but wonder what you could have done differently to avoid this being your life. His was a typical sad-sack story. Drank away the wife, the house. Kids grown up and gone away. Cut adrift by society, and heading only one way: down.

Perfect, really.

They'd struck up a conversation at the end of the meeting, and carried on talking on the phone that night, the two of them trading *waa-waa* tales about the woman that had ruined their lives. Soon the handsome man was taking Murph to Men's Learning Centre meetings, the support group he'd created to recruit new members, introducing him to the guys. *See what happened when you yoked yourself to a woman?* they told him. *I bet you were a feminist too. Ha! Like the turkey who voted for Christmas!*

Now Murph followed him around like a Rottweiler rescued from a dog-fighting ring. There was no warrior more loyal than one who'd been saved.

The handsome man smiled at the woman. Would it kill her to put on some make-up? If you didn't play the game, how could you expect to be anywhere but at the bottom?

Even before he finished explaining what he wanted her to do, she was shaking her head, murmuring, 'No, no, please, I can't.'

'We can be *very* persuasive,' he said, gesturing to Murph, who tightened his grip on her shoulder.

She began to cry. 'Please. If . . . if anyone found out, they'll take my kids. I can't . . . I can't . . .'

'Such beautiful children too. How old's Finn? Six, isn't he? A lovely age. So inquisitive, and yet so innocent. And the baby, Bea. Or I guess not so much of a baby now she's three. Hard to keep an eye on them *all* the time.'

'If you touch them, I'll go to the police!'

He leaned into her. 'If you go to the police, I will dismember your children and feed them to you piece by piece. And when I've finished, I'll *still* make you do this for me.'

She stared at him, too stunned to speak. He knew how his face would look to her now, the smile gone, his eyes cold.

'Do you understand?'

Her lips trembled. '*Yes.*'

He reached for her face, her eyes following his hand, her breaths going fast as he pushed the tips of her greasy fringe out of her eyes.

'There,' he said. 'That's so much better.' He paused with his fingers in her hair, then drifted them down her cheek. 'You know, you really would be more attractive if you made a bit more effort.'

He leaned in and kissed her neck, tasting sweat and cheap soap, feeling the pounding of her pulse against his tongue. He reached under her coat, found the crotch of her jeans, flicked open the top buttons. She squirmed, but Murph held her again, covering her mouth, wrapping his arm around her chest. The handsome man pushed his hand inside her underwear. Tears slid down her cheeks as she sobbed and shook her head and tried to squirm away.

'You've got until the end of the day,' he whispered in her ear. 'No second chance.'

12

In the black cab on the way back to my car, I sent a grovelling text to Steve to apologise for disappearing, then frantically read about what I was supposed to have done. The story had spread from the *Daily Mail* to *Buzzfeed* to *HuffPost*, and on to an endless number of internet news sites I'd never heard of before. It was a great piece of clickbait, the abuse of power giving it a deliciously salacious angle. Just a shame it was about me.

Three of my clients had reported me to the police. *Three!* I put my heart into those cases, spending way longer on the evidence than I could recoup from legal aid. One of them, Helen McAllister, even had her funding revoked because of an undisclosed ISA, and I worked the rest of the case for free! And the things they were saying, like how I locked the door at client meetings and asked them to strip, or tried to touch their breasts. Such *utter* lies. Most of the time, I barely had the impetus to make love to my own wife, let alone have anything left over to demand sexual favours from women who'd been hurt and humiliated by their husbands.

After everything I did for them, how could they do that to me?

Of course, I knew how. And who. The men outside my house, the ones involved with Carmichael's website. The ones bullying

54

me into pulling the injunction. It was a smear campaign, a step up from the leaflets but from the same playbook.

I jumped out of the taxi at Baker Street and into my car. What had they done to those women? Paid them? Threatened them? How could I prove they were lying? What if I got arrested for this? Or struck off? *What if Gabrielle didn't believe me?* I imagined her stuffing clothes into a suitcase, phone jammed between her shoulder and ear, while her mum reminded her she should have married the Cohen boy.

Gabrielle's Renault was on the driveway when I got back. I burst into the house, calling her name, hurrying through to the kitchen and finding her by the back door. She glanced at me guiltily and covered the outline of the cigarette packet in her jeans, though it was pretty obvious from the smell what she'd been doing.

'Sorry, sorry,' I said, weaving round the buffet bar, although I wasn't sure exactly what I was apologising for. I took her hands and kissed the backs of them. 'How are you always so cold?'

'The police were here,' she said.

The police! Any good standing I had left in the community would surely be gone once everyone saw my head being pushed into the back of a squad car. 'What did they—'

'They didn't come to arrest you – they just wanted to have a chat.' She pointed to a business card on the counter.

'I'd *never* sexually harass anyone. I wouldn't even know how! You believe me, don't you?'

'I'm not stupid. I know what's happening.'

We held each other tight. 'Thank you,' I said, burying my face in her neck. When we came apart, I gazed into those beautiful grey eyes. We kissed, gently at first, but then with more passion, until we were making out like we used to, before the endless days of being an adult buried us alive.

'We should do that more often,' I said, panting slightly.

'Quick! Find some clients to harass!'

'Very funny.'

We hugged again, Gabrielle laying her head on my chest.

'We'll get through this,' she said.

'I know,' I replied, stroking her shoulder.

'I mean, now you've cancelled the injunction, they'll leave us alone – right?' She must have felt my fingers freeze, only for a moment, but long enough for her to pull back and give me one of *those* looks. 'Tell me you cancelled it, Ed. After everything that happened last night, after the police have shown up *at our door*. Tell me it was the first thing you did today.'

I stepped back. 'I've not had time!'

'What did you have to do to cancel it? Send their lawyer an email?'

'There's a form to—'

'You. Are. *Unbelievable.*'

She pushed past me, fighting tears, muttering, 'You selfish, selfish bastard.'

'One, the Tube to work was down,' I said, ticking it off on my little finger dramatically as I went after her. 'Two, I was late for court—'

'Rubbish!'

I stopped her at the bottom of the stairs. 'Listen to me. I was going to ... I *am* going to. I just had to get my head together. Ally made me promise—'

'Oh! Not this again. You and that *stupid* promise.'

'I didn't want to let her down! She's so independent, she's always off these days, and I look back at her growing up and I ... I think maybe she needed me, sometimes, and I didn't always...' I shook my head. 'It doesn't matter. I'll cancel it. I'll do it right now.'

Gabrielle snorted as if I was finally catching up on something that had been common knowledge for years. 'You put your own daughter in danger because you felt guilty.'

'That's not how it is.'

She put her hand to her eyes and let out a heart-breaking sob. When I went to comfort her, she pulled away. 'I'm going to my mother's.'

'Don't leave it like this. Please, I can't do this right now.'

She didn't look round. When she spoke there was no anger, just a weariness that made my insides curl with dread. 'I don't think I can do this at all,' she said. 'Not any more.'

I stared at her back as she trudged up the stairs, trying to process what she meant. Thinking about our friends who had separated, divorced. The purgatory of shared parenthood and the horrors of the dating game, getting my balls waxed so I could meet a psychopath on Tinder. No thank you. Besides, I loved my wife. I didn't want to be with anyone else.

Those men weren't going to drive us apart. I wouldn't let that happen. I rushed up the stairs, getting to her as she pushed open the bedroom door, ready to plead my case one more time.

'*Mitchell!*' Gabrielle hissed. 'Why are you creeping around in here?'

Our son was by our en suite, hands stuffed in the pockets of his hoodie, the tense set of his face screaming guilt. We knew he sneaked around in our room – razors went missing, or drawers weren't shut, or there was just the faint murky scent of teenage boy – but come on kid, pick your time! Don't go rifling through your parents' things while they're downstairs having a row!

Gabrielle marched him out. 'Pack some things. We're spending the night at Grandma's.'

'You know what everyone will think,' I pleaded. 'If the wife leaves, he's guilty for sure!'

She flipped open a suitcase on the bed and tossed in her hair-dryer and her make-up bag. 'This has been going on for *months* now, Ed. And instead of fixing it, you just keep on making it *worse*! I'm this close to cracking. *This close.*'

'Please don't leave.'

She shoved past me to get to the wardrobe. I watched helplessly as she pulled out and packed enough clothes to last a week.

I touched her shoulder. '*Please.*'

She jerked away, zipped her case, then leaned on it and sighed. 'I just ... I can't be near you right now.'

I followed her onto the landing, desperate to find the words to get her to stay, but knowing that she was right. I should have cancelled the injunction that morning. I should have done it last night, when those men were outside our house. What did I think they were going to do? Meekly surrender their website?

Mitchell came out of his room, rucksack slung on one of his shoulders. He made to go past me as though I wasn't there, but I'd wanted to speak to him alone after what he heard me say about him last night, so blocked his path. I tried to catch his eye, but he looked past me like I was a stranger and he was trying to get to his mates.

'Listen,' I said, 'about last night. I really am sorry. I didn't mean to upset you. It's hard to explain. You're my son, I want you to be happy. You don't ... If you could just *know* ...' I stared at him helplessly, wishing he could see into my mind, so that he'd understand that I did love him and did care about him and I wasn't just the perpetually disapproving arsehole sharing a bedroom with his mum. Then perhaps he'd take back saying that he hated me without me having to force it out of him. But the words were elusive. I knew them, but couldn't put them together, at least not in the microsecond of attention my outburst allowed.

'Whatever, *Dad*,' he said, shambling round me, saying my name as though it was the punchline to a lame joke.

I followed them out to the driveway. The old busybody from across the street was peeping out of her curtains; I resisted the temptation to give her the finger. As Gabrielle opened the car door, I made one more attempt to get her to stay, but my heart wasn't in it. I knew my wife. She wasn't going to change her mind. Although she did agree to answer her phone when I called later.

Before Mitchell could climb in, I took his arm. I thought about my own father, what I did to him at the end, the guilt that had been tearing me apart since, and would continue to do so until I followed him to the grave. It crushed me to think my own son might one day do the same thing to me.

I wanted to tell him to stay, let's get pizza, watch some TV. I'd make him see I wasn't all bad. We'd just drifted apart. We could be close again. But I could tell from the way he was standing, his free arm across his chest, an expression close to horror on his face, that he'd rather be mauled by a lion than spend a night alone with his dad.

I chickened out and let him go. Watching them drive off, I knew it was a decision I'd come to regret. I just didn't realise then how much.

13

Jackie was deep in thought as DS Keyes drove them north on the Finchley Road. Superintendent Drum wanted them to go in heavy, dogs, drones, armed police, but Jackie was holding off – they'd bring Ed Truman in for questioning her way. Yes, the DNA evidence was damning – finding Truman's hair gripped in the victim's hand would be enough to take to the Crown Prosecution Service – but even so, he was a family man, with standing in the community. He had a business on the high street, and the kids went to local schools. If they got this wrong they walked away, but the memory of him being dragged into a van by armed uniforms would stay with his friends and neighbours for ever.

She wanted him to walk to the car a free man. Even if it was for the last time.

Keyes dragged the wheel left, swerving into the bus lane, accelerating past the traffic, cutting back in once it was clear. Impressive stuff. Jackie still didn't think Drum was right to be expanding the Rapid and Serious unit, and she still wished she was here with an experienced detective like Haggerty instead of taking a rookie through her paces, but to give Keyes credit, she could bloody well drive.

The success of RAS had meant a boost in their budget, and the unit now had four BMW M235is at their disposal, each tricked out like something from NASA mission control. Jackie adjusted the touchscreen, which came from under the glove compartment on an extendable arm, and scrolled down Truman's page on the Police National Computer database.

He didn't have more than a speeding ticket on his record – the DNA match had come because Truman had been part of a large cohort of men who volunteered elimination samples following a serious assault in his neighbourhood – but this last week had changed that. Three women, all clients of his legal practice, had reported claims of sexual harassment. And now this: the murder of a young woman.

Already they were piecing together his movements from yesterday. ANPR cameras had tracked him driving to Baker Street in the morning, and back home around midday. Around midnight, he took a taxi to London, getting out near Piccadilly. The pathology report put the girl's time of death at anywhere between midnight and three. That gave Truman plenty of time.

Jackie glanced at Keyes. *Let's see if she has what it takes.*

'Go on, Charlotte,' Jackie said. 'How about a theory.'

Keyes kept her eyes on the road. 'Family man, right? Married twenty years, two kids. Successful business. But he's always had these dark thoughts. Fantasies. As he gets older and the kids are growing up, he gets bored and starts trying a few things. He harasses those women at work, and gets a taste for it. He goes into town Saturday night to meet this girl—'

'He knows her already?'

'Probably met her online.'

That had been Jackie's thought as well. A warrant had already been submitted to the internet service provider for the Trumans' search history.

'He meets her in Piccadilly?' asked Jackie.

'She's out with friends.'

'Not dressed for it.'

'She lives nearby.'

'And he goes to her house? She's young to live alone.'

'Her friends are out.' Keyes rubbed her mouth. 'But if all this happens at her place, then why take the body to the Heath? He's a lawyer. He knows about evidence.'

'We're back here again. The Heath makes sense for dumping the body: it's a huge space, open at night, close to where he lives. But why leave it where it'd be found?'

'He got disturbed and panicked.'

'Maybe.'

'Guilt. He wants to be caught, to stop anyone else from getting hurt.'

'Unlikely.'

'It's a clue in some sinister serial killer's game.'

Despite herself, Jackie snorted a laugh. 'We don't do Hollywood here, Detective.'

Thankfully Keyes was also smiling. The last thing they needed on RAS was someone out to catch the next Hannibal Lecter.

Jackie changed tabs on the touchscreen, bringing up Truman's Facebook page. DS Travis and his team had already tracked down all his social media accounts. She paused at a recent picture, a holiday snap. Truman, his wife, and their two kids on a polished wooden balcony, a beautiful turquoise sea behind them. The daughter was tall and pretty, with alert eyes, while the boy was younger, shyer, half hiding behind his mum. What would it do to them if they found out their father was a murderer?

Everything they believed about themselves and their lives, gone in a moment.

*

The Truman house was large and detached, with a well-kept hedgerow running along the front, and a driveway wide enough for three cars. It was still early afternoon, but the day already had a grey tinge, washing the colour from everything. As they headed up the driveway, Jackie nodded at the garden gate. Keyes glanced around to make sure no one was watching and hurried to it. She worked the latch, darted through.

Jackie rang the bell. Silence inside. She rang it again, pressing her ear to the door, but still heard nothing. She stood back to scan the windows.

Keyes returned to the front. 'Lights all off. Place looks empty.'

'I think I've spotted the snitch,' Jackie said, tipping her head back. 'Neighbour at number 102. Nasty case of the curtain twitches.'

'You want me to have a word?'

'If you wouldn't mind, Sergeant.'

While Keyes went to charm the local busybody, Jackie lifted the letterbox flap and peered inside, trying to sense if anyone was inside and hiding. It amazed her how often she saw this: a supposedly respectable member of society, living without the financial stresses that blighted so many people's lives, getting so bored with being comfortable that they did something crazy, like kill someone. Just to see what it felt like.

Worse, Truman himself had a daughter about the same age as the victim. Didn't he put himself in her parents' position? That awful moment when they realised they would never see their child alive again?

Standing on the doorstep.

Lester opening the car door, helping Verity climb inside.

Her daughter taking one last look around. One last wave to Mum.

Seven years and still the memories sliced her open, the blades hot. How was she supposed to get through tomorrow? Maybe

Drum was right, and it was a mistake taking this case – when you went after killers, you couldn't afford to be emotional.

Jackie straightened her clothes and took a breath. She'd get through tomorrow the same way she got through every day: by doing her job. By finding the person who murdered that girl and bringing them to justice. And the next one. And the one after that.

She owed it to Verity never to stop.

'So that's interesting,' Keyes said, approaching from behind.

Jackie turned to face her. 'Go on.'

'There was a big row yesterday, about one in the afternoon. Wife and son left with their bags packed.'

'Get ANPR for the wife's car. The neighbour see Truman leave as well?'

'Said he went back inside. But there was a bit of a fracas here, a couple of nights ago.'

'Friday night?'

Keyes handed a leaflet to Jackie. 'Some men outside his house, giving people these.'

The leaflet was glossy, well produced. IMPORTANT NOTICE: THIS MAN IS A MENACE TO OUR COMMUNITY AND OUR CHILDREN. Below that was a mugshot of Truman, which she recognised from his Facebook page, except it had been Photoshopped, his eyes made sharper, his lips pulled into a sneer.

> Edgar Truman is a very dangerous person. He is not who he says he is. He is a pervert and a criminal who will stop at nothing to hide his true identity from the world. Do not be alone with this man. Do not let your children ESPECIALLY be alone with this man. BE CAREFUL! DO NOT TRUST HIM!

Maybe this had been bubbling for a while. Was that why Truman killed last night? Because the net was closing in?

A call came in from Haggerty at the office.

Jackie took it. 'What you got, Nick?'

'Ed Truman's wife, picked up from her parents'. In interview room two.'

14

Gabrielle Truman was still in interview room two – the nice one with the carpet, the view of the Thames and the chairs that didn't feel like some kind of medieval torture device when you sat on them too long – when Jackie arrived back at HQ. A smartly dressed man in his forties was beside her, his relaxed posture implying he was comfortable being in a police interview, unlike the woman, who was leaning forward, clutching one hand with the other.

'Sorry for the delay,' Jackie said, dropping a slender folder onto the table as she sat down. She nodded to the empty plastic cup in front of Gabrielle Truman. 'Can we get you another?'

'Is this about my husband?' she asked.

'Let's do this properly,' Jackie replied, switching on the machine. 'For the tape, present are Detective Chief Inspector Jackie Rose, Detective Sergeant Charlotte Keyes, Mrs Gabrielle Truman, and …'

'Steve Smith,' said the man. 'Family friend.'

'And business partner to Ed Truman,' said Keyes.

'That's right,' Smith replied, very casual.

Gabrielle Truman was more stylish than Jackie had imagined, in a navy wool skirt and grey roll-neck jumper, her nails neat and polished pale brown. A bit of surgery too, cheek fillers by the looks of it, which was odd as judging by his pictures Ed Truman was about as glamorous as a cagoule. Not the type to have a trophy wife. Was she having an affair?

Jackie pushed the folder across the table, until it was in front of the wife.

'What's this?' she asked, staring at the folder like a dead rat had been nudged towards her.

'It's about your husband.'

'Don't touch that,' Smith said. He was interesting: his style said affluent city boy, but he was a suburban solicitor. Why dress for a different part? There was a disconnect in his manner too. Charm on the surface, but something in the tilt of his head, the set of his shoulders, said different. Not arrogant, that was the wrong word. *Superior*. The kind whose first thought on meeting someone was, *I'm better than you.* He said: 'First can you tell us what this is about?'

Jackie kept her eyes on Gabrielle Truman. 'When was the last time you spoke to Ed?'

'Yesterday, around lunchtime. We were supposed to speak later but he didn't answer his phone. I got a missed call from him about eleven.'

'Nothing today?'

'I tried him this morning, but he didn't reply.' She half-turned her head and said more to herself than the room, 'No surprise there.'

'What's that supposed to mean?' asked Jackie.

'Nothing. Forget it.'

Jackie slammed her hand on the table. Both of them fell back in their chairs, shocked. Even Keyes looked startled. Enough of this messing about. '*Open the folder.*'

Gabrielle Truman's chin trembled as she turned over the front cover. Her hand went to her mouth. 'Oh my God. Is she ... ?'

Inside were stills from that morning, the girl in the park. 'Killed last night. By your husband.'

'*What?*' She shook her head. 'That's not possible.'

'We have solid evidence.'

'I know my husband.'

Jackie sat back. 'Where's Ed? Where's he hiding? Are you protecting him?'

Gabrielle Truman looked up from the stills. She blinked and a tear slid down her cheek. 'I ... I don't ...'

'No favourite fishing spot? No remote cabin in the woods?'

'No. Nothing like that. He's not the outdoor type.'

As far as Jackie could tell, Gabrielle Truman hadn't lied so far: she neither believed her husband capable of murder nor knew where he'd disappeared to. But that meant nothing. Plenty of people had secret lives.

Smith leaned forward over the table. Laced fingers, careful expression. He had that way you got with some briefs, like they'd written the law themselves. 'If you're so sure Ed did this, then why aren't you out there looking for him instead of sitting here traumatising his wife?'

Jackie ignored Smith again – she'd get to him soon enough. Instead, she placed the leaflet Keyes had got from the neighbour in front of the wife. 'Let's start from the beginning. Tell me what happened on Friday night.'

Gabrielle Truman dug around in her bag for a packet of tissues, wiped her eyes, and began. It was all to do with the daughter, Alison, how she became involved with a group of activists. They had targeted William Carmichael, figurehead for the men's rights movement – Jackie had seen him a few times on the news – and threw a milkshake at him. In retaliation Carmichael had published private details about Alison Truman on his Men's Learning Centre website. This escalated, ending with Ed Truman taking

68

legal action against Carmichael's website. The leaflets were part of a smear campaign to try to get Ed to drop the case. Same with the women claiming sexual harassment.

'You think all three women lied?' asked Jackie.

'Absolutely.'

'Why did you leave him if he'd done nothing wrong?'

Gabrielle Truman blanched. She glanced at Smith, who turned out his hands, unsure.

'I didn't leave him,' she said.

'Not what we heard,' Jackie said, nodding at Keyes.

The sergeant had out her notebook. 'At approximately 1 p.m. you and your son Mitchell were seen leaving the house with a suitcase.'

'We went to stay at my parents. For the night!'

'You always pack a suitcase for a single night?'

'I was annoyed with him! He'd said he'd cancel the injunction and he didn't.'

'So you did leave him.'

'I was going to come back today.'

Jackie folded her arms. 'Easy to say now.'

'I'm *not* a liar.'

'I can see you want to protect your husband.'

'*Ed didn't hurt that girl.*'

'How can you be so sure?'

'I've been with my husband for twenty years. I think I know him by now.'

Jackie sighed. Didn't they all. 'If you know your husband so well, why don't you tell us why he took a taxi to Piccadilly Circus at midnight last night.'

'Midnight? I don't ... I mean ...'

'Maybe you don't quite know *everything* about your husband.'

'I suppose not,' she replied, deflated. She pressed the tissue to her eyes again.

Keyes spoke up. 'What about yesterday morning? He was seen in the same area at midday.'

Gabrielle Truman shot Smith a sharp look. 'Wasn't he with you in court?'

'No,' Smith replied, flustered. 'I mean yes. He was but he left.'

'After I rang him, right?'

'I don't know.' Smith looked around like he wanted to make a fast exit. 'I was working. I had a lot of bloody explaining to do to the client!'

'You should have told me he went somewhere else first!'

Smith tightened his mouth, like he wanted to say something but was holding back. Was there some animosity between them? Sexual tension, perhaps?

'Look,' he said. 'The most important thing is that we find Ed and make sure he's okay.'

Jackie turned her attention to him. 'Are *you* covering for him?'

'Don't play bad cop with me,' he replied, as though he'd seen all this before.

'Do you think he sexually harassed your clients?'

'Ed takes his job *very* seriously.'

'That's not a no,' said Keyes.

'Okay then, *no*, I do not think Ed Truman harassed anyone,' said Smith. 'Happy now?'

'Do you also represent domestic abuse victims?' asked Jackie.

'I don't think it's appropriate to discuss my clients.'

Keyes flipped through her notebook. 'You offer free legal advice to men who have no access rights to see their children. Right?'

'That must be a point of contention,' Jackie said, a smile playing on her lips. 'He's representing the abused and you the abusers.'

'My clients are good, honest men,' Smith snapped, 'who've more often than not done nothing wrong—'

'Ninety-five per cent of defendants in domestic abuse cases are male—'

'How dare you jump to assumptions! It's that kind of attitude which prevents any kind of legitimate discussion about male equality in the family courts.'

'Male equality,' Jackie said, rasping her lips. 'Give me a break.'

Smith was gripping the arms of his chair, face flushed. 'The system is so heavily tilted towards the mother that a woman would have to walk up to the judge *brandishing* a copy of *Child Abuse Weekly* for custody to be given to the father. Tell me how that's fair?'

Jackie let the silence following his outburst settle in the room. So Mr Cool could be riled. Good to know.

'Thank you for coming in,' she said. '*Both* of you. We'll be in touch.'

Smith was still breathing hard. 'That's *it*?'

'Everything for now. DS Keyes will show you out.'

Once they'd gone, Jackie slumped onto the desk and exhaled. This case was becoming more complicated by the minute. Could someone be fitting Truman up for murder? And where did Smith fit into all this? He knew something he wasn't saying. The wife too.

Jackie picked up the photo of the dead girl.

And the biggest mystery of all. *Who are you?*

15

When Phoenix got back to the squat after meeting Ally's dad, she flung the portfolio case onto the mattress. Brighton. *Brighton*. What was Ally doing in Brighton? Even if she had got away – and that was a big *if* – why there? And with who? It made no sense!

What if Ally had planned this? What if she'd given her phone to someone, with instructions to send a text saying she'd gone away if she didn't come back? Maybe to buy a few days in case they had to disappear. It had always been a possibility that she wouldn't be able to go home. But if that was the case, why hadn't Ally told her? There was no reason to keep secrets from each other. Was there?

Phoenix paced. What if this was a trap, to draw her out? They send that text, knowing Ally's parents wouldn't believe it was from her. Her dad investigates, finds the burner phone number, maybe on an itemised bill – hadn't Ally made a test call before they went in? Phoenix tried to think back, but so much had happened, and she was too tired to remember the details. Either way, if someone like Ed Truman could track her down, how easy it would be for *them*.

She wasn't safe here. The sooner she headed to the hideout, the better.

It was just after eleven. If she got a bus out of London, she could maybe hitch the rest of the way, or at the very worst walk.

She checked her laptop – the upload for the videos was at sixty per cent. At this rate they'd be done by midnight. Perfect. It was better for her to travel at night anyway. Less chance of being seen.

Phoenix took her meds, then settled on the mattress and pulled the laptop onto her knees. She opened her software repository and began tinkering with a programme she'd been working on to analyse encrypted data packets, keen to lose herself in lines of code. This was her happy place, where she could retreat when she felt so anxious it was as though her veins were worms slithering around her body. Where she could focus on something other than the voice in her head, repeating, *You're broken, you don't work right, you're beyond repair.* Where she could quieten her thoughts, and just be her.

She was good at coding, too. Good enough to be known in the community. Aged ten she wrote an app called Angry Headline Attack Bot, which stitched together soundbites to make statements like 'Shocking Moment when Islamist Terrorist Claims Benefits for Ten Children'. The app then spoofed a URL to make the headline look like a link from a real news site, and tweeted it along with an outraged message about fake news to the news site's Twitter account. The app sold loads. By the time she was fourteen she held twenty thousand pounds in bitcoin, although the cryptocurrency crash last year trashed most of that. She didn't care. There was always money to be earned by someone with her skills.

Soon Phoenix found her eyelids drooping, exhaustion finally overpowering her always busy brain. The squat was noisy – people shouting to each other, feet thudding down the corridors, some erratic drum and bass clattering away in the background – but even so she fell into a deep and thankfully dreamless sleep.

*

73

When she opened her eyes, it was dark outside.

She checked her watch. After midnight. She'd slept for over twelve hours. Crazy. She wouldn't go so far as to say she was refreshed, but at least it no longer felt like her head was full of static. She must have needed that.

When she checked her laptop, the good feeling faded. The connection to the Wi-Fi had cut out even before the first video finished uploading. *Oh, just great.* She couldn't risk staying here another day to try again. Besides, the satellite connection at the hideout might be slow, but at least it was stable.

She packed her rucksack, and sneaked through the semi-gloom of the second floor to the fire escape. Down the stairs and into the lobby. Three guys were by the reception desk, chatting over tinny rock music coming from a mobile phone, the camping lantern on the floor casting their faces in shadow. A floral cloud of skunk drifted over to her.

This squat wasn't anywhere as seedy as some she'd crashed in, but still she kept to herself when she was here. These places were full of sketchy characters. Druggies, especially at night.

She kept her head down and walked fast, but even before she got near the men she sensed their eyes on her. They stopped talking. One stepped away from the counter to block her path.

'Hey, hey you,' he said. 'You like to party?'

She could tell from a glance he was an A-grade loser. The kind of long-haired, pot-bellied, far-gone dropout who'd seen one too many bongs to ever be normal again. He smelled funky too, like cold sausages. Yuk.

'No thanks,' Phoenix muttered, trying to sidestep him.

He moved to cover her. 'I'm talking to you.'

She tried the other side but he went that way too.

'*Please*,' she said. 'I've got to go.'

'Bit young to be here,' he said. 'You by yourself?'

74

'No.'

'That's not how it looks.' The other two were behind her now. She wanted to fling her arms out, shove them back, but she was tiny compared to them. 'How'd you like to earn some money?'

Up close he was older and grottier than she'd originally thought, his teeth bad, his breath stinking, his gut slouching over the top of his jeans. Meth head, probably. She'd heard there were quite a few junkies in the basement, although she'd never been down.

'My friends and I make films,' he said. 'We've got a whole set-up downstairs, cameras, lights, everything. How does fifty quid sound?'

'No thanks.'

He reached for her cheek, tenderly, like he wanted to kiss her at the end of a date. 'Let's call it a hundred.'

'*Just fuck off*,' she hissed, slapping his hand away.

'You're quite a rude little girl, aren't you?' He grabbed her arm. 'Perhaps it's time someone taught you some manners.'

16

Many hours after Gabrielle left to stay with her parents, I sat up on the sofa, heart hammering, a thudding pain in my head like someone had been trying to extract my brain through my ear with a plunger, wondering what the hell had just happened.

The lounge was a tip. Groaning, I took in the carnage. Cushions strewn all over the place, Gabrielle's favourite lampshade knocked over. Broken glass from the bulb fanned out the top.

I rubbed my eyes, picturing them like something from a cartoon, the capillaries red and throbbing against the whites, and caught sight of the bottle of twenty-five-year-old Laphroaig I kept for super special guests – now, of course, empty – on the floor beside a packet of my wife's Marlboro Golds, torn open as though I thought the secret to happiness might be hidden inside. Next to that was a messy cheese and coleslaw sandwich that I guess I made at some point, and then decided to use as an ashtray, although judging by the lengths of the butts sticking out, I wasn't doing much more than lighting them up and stubbing them out. It looked like some delinquent kid's art project. The stale-smoke and dairy smell hit my nose, making me retch.

What was I thinking!

Self-sabotage was one thing but drinking myself into a coma during the day was something else. I looked at the bottle and the

76

bottle looked back. Before my dad died, I'd never have done that, but something had changed. The off button had vanished. *Like father, like son.* I shuddered and wrapped my arms around my knees. The house felt so empty. A cold sensation passed through me, and I saw it suddenly like a foreshadowing, an Ebenezer Scrooge moment by the grave. *This could be your life. Your family gone.* I retched again and covered my mouth and just about made it to the kitchen sink before throwing up liquid that burned so hard it left my throat raw.

It was close to midnight. Gabrielle had rung a couple of times around seven, so I must have been passed out by then. It was good she wanted to talk. I had a hazy memory of looking up boats to Antarctica, sure our marriage was over, thinking, no doubt, *Well, if she doesn't want me, I'll go as far away as possible!* What an idiot.

I tried to call her back as I staggered to the bathroom to run my head under the shower. She didn't pick up, and the water didn't restore any clarity, although I now had a cold, wet head to add to my general misery.

Coffee. Now. As I waited for the machine to finish sputtering into my cup, I checked my messages. It was mostly friends and family wanting to know if I was okay, and assuring me they knew the sexual harassment allegations were bogus. *We're on your side*, that was what everyone said, ignoring the fact that by 'taking a side' they were already legitimising the accusations. Like there were even sides to be taken!

I hadn't done anything. Anyone who knew me would realise those claims were beyond ridiculous. And yet, some would have their doubts. People I'd grown up with, whose children I'd held, would be secretly thinking I sleazed over clients. Not just any clients – victims of domestic abuse who came to me for legal advice. No wonder drinking seemed like the only way out.

Among the messages, I found a reply from Duncan, Gordon

& Silverman Solicitors, the city sharks representing Carmichael, saying they'd received my confirmation that I'd contacted the courts to discontinue the injunction. Now *that* I did remember doing. I'd sent it off, then gone to have a drink or ten to celebrate.

But if this was over, then where was Ally? Had I really been wrong the whole time, and she'd simply slunk away for the weekend with her secret boyfriend? I checked her phone bill again. No activity all today. Texts were one thing – she only really sent them to us, thinking her parents too ancient to understand messaging apps – but no calls? It was a good job she got unlimited free minutes otherwise we'd have to re-mortgage the house to pay her phone bill. *It didn't make sense.*

I knew I should go to bed. Wake fresh in the morning to deal with the client accusations, and the fall-out from today's row with Gabrielle, and who knew what other fresh hell would also fall into my lap? But I kept thinking, *What if Ally's in trouble?* I couldn't sit there and do nothing.

The girl. The one who bumped into me today. She knew something. What if my daughter never came home? What if that girl was the only one who knew what had happened to her?

I had to find out.

17

Entering the computer room at the Men's Learning Centre, William Carmichael looked around with the same pride as always. The rows of men, cleanly shaved, dressed smartly but without ostentation, all of them working together, made his heart swell and the doubts evaporate. If only the public could see this dedication, this collaboration, this industry – all the wonderful things that men could do with such competence – they would not be so quick to dismiss the movement as hateful. In fact, they would see the opposite was true. All this was to *save* civilised society.

Carmichael passed a cluster of younger lads, late teens perhaps, tight around a workstation, discussing something serious and crucial. Who knew what states those boys would be in now if it weren't for this place? On drugs, perhaps, or living on the street, desperate for work but unable to find a decent job. The way the world rejected young men these days, allowing them to rot while minority agendas that had no relevance to the wider population were given top billing in Parliament. Why were *they* not entitled to a voice?

He paused on their shoulders to catch what they were discussing, but couldn't make much sense of it. Considering he had been speaking about these exact same issues for decades now, it seemed as though a whole language had sprung up about it in the space of a single year. 'Incels' and 'cucks' and 'taking the red pill'; humans had always sought out symbols and rituals, he supposed. Throw in a dash of ceremony and a neurotic need to categorise and it all made perfect sense – even if, all too often, what they were actually saying was indecipherable.

That didn't mean he was blind to some of the things happening under his watch. That tragic knife attack in Halifax, and the explosion in Milton Keynes only the other week. The innocent lives lost. Including one angelic four-year-old girl whose picture in the newspapers had haunted him every night since it happened. Benedict hadn't confirmed their involvement, but Carmichael wouldn't put it past the man to whip up violence.

It wasn't as though Carmichael could plead complete innocence. He'd heard too many stories too many times, from too many sources, not all of them damning, he might add, of Benedict's cruelty, his … *sadism*. There was no other word for it. Was he wrong to put so much trust in the man? Or was that the price to be paid for what they had built? None of this would be here if it wasn't for him. Indeed, wasn't Saul of Tarsus himself known as 'the widowmaker' long before he became *Saint* Paul.

When you are trying to win the most important war that has ever been fought, one at the very heart of what it is to be a man or a woman, you must use every resource at your disposal. They were battling a ruthless and relentless enemy, one that did not think twice about ripping the heart from every family on the planet by demonising the natural order of things as 'patriarchal'. As though twenty thousand years of settled living, since we first crawled from the caves, were so irrelevant that they could simply be discounted. Nonsense!

Take the shocking increase in sexual assaults in recent years. Look at what young women wore these days – less than you'd find on display at the local swimming baths! Some men were sexual predators, that was a fact. That was why at no point in the past had women dressed or acted the way they did now. The difference, of course, were the fashion companies and the cosmetic companies and the social media giants forever whispering in their ears that their female biological imperative was not enough, that they could find contentment in a sparkly new top, or at the bottom of one of those brightly coloured alcoholic drinks, or by waking up with a terrible hangover in some stranger's bed, when in truth all they were bound to discover was confusion and regret.

This wasn't bland ideology. Real people were suffering from this *liberal fever* – passed to them by psychopathic corporations as innocently as smallpox-infused blankets from British colonialists – himself as much as anyone. Almost certainly he'd lost his son Gregory to this *war*; he'd been reticent to use that term, one of Benedict's favourites, but now they were dealing with spies and espionage it seemed wholly appropriate. And if he could prevent another parent from sacrificing their child in the same way, then he would.

The world was heading down a dangerous path. If normal people didn't act soon then everything they loved and held dear would disappear for ever.

Benedict leaned out from one of the smaller offices at the back and waved him over. Inside was a grid of nine computer monitors attached to the wall. They had several AI experts at the Men's Learning Centre, mostly working on big data applications to pinpoint recruitment targets, but they'd also developed a piece of facial recognition software that could scan thousands of hours of CCTV footage in seconds to identify someone. It was this Carmichael was being called to look at.

Each screen contained a frozen image, a snatch of a young girl's face highlighted in the crowd. She was trying to stay hidden, so most showed only the curve of a cheek, or the tip of a nose sticking out from behind someone's shoulder. Then he saw a flash of silver hair.

'Why don't you leave this to me,' Benedict said, his smile chilling.

Carmichael shot him a sharp glance, once again wondering with what kind of person he was yoked to. As always, he came to the same conclusion: *Just be thankful he's on your side.*

18

Phoenix tried to stay calm as the guy tightened his grip on her arm. She wanted to scream, her lungs were tensed in preparation, but she didn't want to make the situation any worse. Besides, there was no guarantee that anyone would come to help. People generally kept to themselves in this squat. It was one of the main reasons she chose to come here. And down in the reception, with three blokes and the stink of drugs, she doubted there'd be many knights keen on charging in to save her. Same as for most of her life so far; she was on her own.

'It's not what you think,' she said, forcing out a smile, a little fake laugh. 'I'm just not really into guys. But I've got some mates upstairs who'd *love* to earn a bit of extra cash. Why don't I go up and get them?'

He let go of her, and slowly pushed his hands through his greasy rocker hair, tying it back with a ratty band from his wrist. 'You think they'd be into it?'

Phoenix tried not to let the relief show on her face. 'Oh yeah, Zara would *totally* be into it. Scarlett would probably do it for nothing!' She laughed again, freer this time, then went to turn. 'Let me get them.'

His hand on her shoulder again. *Shit.*

'Call them,' he said.

83

'Sorry. Don't have a phone.'

'Bullshit.'

'I swear I don't.'

Right then, a buzz from inside her bag. *The burner!*

'You fucking liar,' he said, shaking his head like he was genuinely disappointed by her deception. He pushed her towards the basement door. 'I reckon you owe us a freebie for that.'

Phoenix tried to pull away. His grip was too strong. She bit his arm, digging her teeth deep into the soft flesh. He slammed a fist into her stomach. A supernova of agony, radiating out. She tried to double over, but he grabbed her hair, dragged her head back. She managed a gulp of air. 'Please. Don't ... don't ...'

'No more fuss, eh?' he said, closing his hand around her neck, a dark smile on his lips. He started to drag her across the floor, his mates following. She flung her elbows back, trying to connect with his face, her heels slipping on the tiles. *This couldn't be happening!*

Behind them, someone went, 'Excuse me. *Excuse me.*'

The guy holding her neck turned, dragging her with him. '*What?*'

Phoenix saw a man holding up a phone, the screen glowing in the darkness.

'I ... errr ... I think you'd better put her down.'

*

Holding up my phone, 999 on the screen, I said again, this time with hopefully more force: 'Put her down.'

While my mouth worked away, several voices in my head were competing with one another to tell me that confronting these men was perhaps the stupidest thing I'd ever done. But this girl was someone's daughter. This could be Ally. If these men were dragging *her* away, wouldn't I want someone to stop them?

'And who the fuck are you?' enquired the portly young gentleman in the process of throttling the girl. There were three of them, more than enough to beat me senseless. I hoped to God this worked, otherwise I was facing a fun visit to the nearest hospital. Maybe staying there a while.

In a millisecond, I parsed and rejected numerous possible replies – a friend? (*Sure, her forty-year-old friend.*) Her uncle? (*What is this,* The Godfather?) – before stumbling out the only possible answer that had traction.

'I'm her father,' I said.

He let go of her throat. I exhaled, shaky with relief.

'Well, *Dad*,' he said. I heard a quick metal click. The yellow light from the lantern on the floor now glinted off the slim blade by her neck. 'We need to talk compensation.'

'Jesus, Len,' went one of his mates, 'put it away.'

'Don't tell him my name,' hissed Len.

'Screw this shit, man,' said the other.

They both skulked away, Len calling them pussies as they left. He returned his attention to me. 'Your cunt of a daughter bit me,' he said, nodding at his arm, where a set of teeth imprints were visible just below the sleeve of his Metallica T-shirt. 'Come on, *Dad*. Pass your phone over or I start cutting.'

Would he do it? Especially now I knew his name.

It wasn't a risk I was prepared to take.

I placed my phone on the floor and slid it to him, cursing myself and my stupid plan. *Great going, Detective Inspector Dumbass.* 'Now will you let her go?'

'Wallet,' he said.

'I don't have any money. Just cards.'

'Hurry the fuck up.'

As much as I wanted this girl to be safe, the thought of being trapped in the centre of London, late at night, no phone and no

85

wallet, wasn't one I was willing to entertain without discussion.

'Let her go,' I said. 'I'll walk with you to the nearest cash point.'

'Do I look stupid to you?'

There was no good way to answer that. 'Listen, I—'

Len flung his hand up in exasperation, the knife moving from the girl's neck, and started to say something. The girl didn't wait to hear his undoubted words of wisdom, driving her heel down on his toes, and in the same motion crunching her elbow into his confused mouth.

He grabbed his jaw. Blood spilled between his fingers. '*Ough* my fugging tooth you fugging—'

I rushed him, getting an arm round his ample middle, crashing us both to the floor. The knife clattered out of his hand. He tried to force me off, but there wasn't much strength to him, not as much as I'd thought, and soon I was whaling on him like a six-year-old in a schoolyard brawl, all the stress of the last few months coming out as I swore and howled and rained my fists onto his face. He appeared more shocked than hurt by my efforts, but it bought me enough time to roll off and snatch the knife.

Twitchy from the adrenaline, I feinted towards him. 'Don't make me hurt you!'

He lumbered to his feet. 'I'm going to fugging kill you, man! You're dead.'

'So are you!' I shrieked after him as he staggered out of the reception. 'So are all of us eventually!'

Once he'd gone, I put my hands on my knees, but it did nothing to stop my shaking.

The girl.

I needed to find her.

*

Phoenix ran up the fire stairs to the second floor, into the maze of corridors. She dropped to her haunches in a printer alcove, telling herself to breathe, to calm down, calm the hell down. Work out what to do next.

She needed to get out now more than ever. As great as it was that Ally's dad had saved her from those idiots, it still left the question of how he'd managed to find her. And if *he* could do it, what about the others? Unless he was already working with them. Either way she couldn't go back through reception. How was she going to—

The first floor!

The windows at the back of the building opened onto a narrow alleyway. The offices next door kept some large lidded bins there. If she could get out and onto the ledge, she should be able to creep along and drop onto the bins.

She went to take a different set of stairs. Most people who crashed on this floor had jobs to go to in the morning – even without rent and bills, living in London was expensive – so this time of night the corridors were quiet, the lights in the little rooms off.

When she came to the section of open-plan office, she stopped and pressed her back to the wall. Voices from the kitchenette. People always hung around there, even at this time, making tea and toast. But this didn't sound like chatting. More someone being questioned. Forcibly questioned, with the threat of violence.

Staying low, she darted for the first desk, and peered round the legs.

Fucksticks.

She'd recognise that ugly giant anywhere. Murph. And where there was Murph, there was *him*.

Murph was holding a girl in a pink sports top and blue tracksuit bottoms against the fridge. She looked young, terrified. Phoenix strained to hear what they were saying.

He towered over her, easily twice her size. 'Don't lie to me. You've seen her.'

The girl whimpered something in reply. A slap echoed round the office.

Phoenix saw a discarded stapler on a desk and thought about throwing it, creating a distraction. She wanted to, she hated that someone innocent was getting slapped around because of her, but she couldn't bring herself to do it, to draw that heat her way. What if they caught her? What if they *took her back*?

She crept to the stairwell and opened the door. There was nothing she could do. Nothing. She'd never spoken to that girl. Murph would realise that and leave her alone.

The stairwell was dark and empty. *Thank God.* Cold air brushed over her skin. She started for the stairs when a voice came from the shadows.

'There you are.'

The prickles on her neck felt needle sharp. *Please. Not him.*

'We've been worried about you,' he said. 'Very worried indeed.'

19

I hadn't been in many squats – that's a lie, I hadn't been in any – but this one was better than I'd imagined. Although seeing as I'd imagined a murky hellscape filled with crackheads shambling around like movie zombies, that wasn't saying much.

Street art was everywhere: a black unicorn galloping along a purple rainbow in the reception, a giraffe in conversation with C-3PO from *Star Wars* on the first-floor lift doors. Everyone seemed young and healthy and not in the least bit intent on mugging me for drug money, unlike the scrotes down in reception. I saw TVs, PlayStations, clothesrails with suits hanging from them. Most of the mattresses looked made up with clean bed linen. One ripped dude in loose fisherman pants, his torso like something from a boy band poster, nodded at me while passing in the corridor, as though we were staying in a backpacker hostel in Thailand.

I returned to the stairwell, already sure I was wasting my time. There were probably plenty of ways out of the building. The girl was long gone.

Voices from the floor above. I stopped, breath held.

It sounded like her.

The light was dim in the stairwell. I crept round the landing, staying in the shadows. A man was speaking now, but I couldn't quite hear the words. I eased up the first couple of steps.

It was him! The handsome bastard from outside my house, his back to me, talking to the girl. His big mate towered behind her.

So they *did* have something to do with Ally going missing. Them and this girl.

'Look, it's really up to you,' he was saying, his voice light, friendly, like a travel agent advising someone on the best holiday destinations for winter sun. 'We can either go now, and keep things nice. Or Murph can hold you down and I'll shoot you with so much ketamine that you'll shit yourself on the spot. Then we'll go.'

While he was speaking, I moved up the stairs, hunched to stay out of sight. I held Len's flick knife, thumb poised on the button.

The girl looked scared but resolute. 'He'd better not touch me.'

I was only a few steps behind him now. Any higher and Murph would see me. I tightened my grip on the knife and tried to picture rushing him from behind, pressing the blade into the small of his back. *What have you done with my daughter?*

Handsome rocked his head and shrugged. '*Meh*, like I care,' he said, nodding to his mate, who clamped his hand over the girl's mouth before she'd even opened it, let alone sucked in enough air to scream.

Now or never.

I darted up the stairs, flicking out the knife, and grabbed the shoulder of Handsome's jacket. 'Move and I'll sever your spine.'

He allowed himself to be pushed forward but didn't lift his hands. I swore I heard his smirk. Did he sense I wouldn't be able to go through with it? Could he tell from the pressure that I was no more capable of stabbing him than I was of taking out the man mountain afterwards with a flying scissor kick?

I pressed the knife harder. 'Where's my daughter? Tell me!'

'Hey, Murph,' he said. 'Wasn't that the girl from the other night? The one you fucked inside out?'

I barely had time to open my mouth to tell him to shut it before

I realised, too late to react, that his silky brown hair was travelling with tremendous speed towards the spot right between my eyes. Next came a crack and an explosion that detonated on the bridge of my nose, the aftershocks carrying on down my face, my neck, and on to the rest of my body, which was maybe a good thing as it meant my legs gave way before I could tumble back down the stairs.

'This guy,' said Handsome. Through my tear-blurred eyes I saw him throwing a thumb at me and grinning as if I was their joker mate. *Typical Ed!*

Well, fuck him.

I lunged, getting him round the legs. We crashed to the floor with me on top. No doubt buoyed by my own abilities, I swatted my fists in the direction of his face. Meanwhile, he grinned up at me in amiable disbelief, like he couldn't quite believe what I was doing.

A second later, I understood why.

I never knew before what it felt like to be a sack of potatoes, but I did now – so long as it was one that had been hoisted off the ground and flung into the back of a truck. I smacked the wall skull-first, and crumpled into a heap, my head a singular, ringing point of agony.

Murph lifted me off the ground and regarded me like I was a stray cat he'd just caught squatting in his flowerbed. I squirmed, flailed, kicked, you name it, but I might as well have been doing the Macarena for all the good it did me.

I glanced at the girl. She was crouched like a sprinter, ready to run. Handsome was blocking the route to the stairs.

As the big bloke slowly tipped back his wrecking ball of a forehead, I thought, *This is it. Next stop, brain damage.* I pictured myself in a wheelchair, head lolling to the side, a string of saliva hanging from my slack lips. I didn't feel heroic going out like this, just sad that I might never see Gabrielle and the kids again. In the split second before he connected, I tried to conjure a final image of them, something to take with me, but I was way too scared for anything like that, so settled for spending my last moment as a fully sentient human by whimpering and pissing my pants.

But instead of caving in my face, Murph froze. He clenched his teeth, wincing, his expression turning to horror when he looked down. The strength went from his hand, and I shook myself free.

That was when I saw all the blood soaking through his trouser leg.

The girl was backing off, holding Len's knife, her face shocked. Her hand was streaked with red.

I scrambled out of the way as Murph took an unsteady step sideways, his face pale and twisted in pain. The wound was midway up the back of his thigh. I remembered a case I helped research, an eighteen-year-old stabbed in the femoral artery in a stairwell in East London, how he bled out in less than two minutes.

'Thanks a bunch,' Handsome said to the girl. 'Did you have to do that?'

She gestured him away with the blade. 'Move.'

Murph was slumped against the wall, his low groan making him sound like he was actually deflating, the pool of blood coming out of him almost reaching the stairs. He tried to rise from the floor a couple of times but couldn't manage it.

'You need to make a tourniquet,' I said, kneeling beside him, staring helplessly at the blood. It was starting to pulse more slowly from the wound. 'He's going to die.'

Handsome shrugged. 'I'm good.'

I wanted to insist that he help his friend, that it was inconceivable for him to just do nothing, but before I could speak the girl grabbed my hand and pulled me down the stairs.

'Come on,' she said. '*Let's go.*'

Benedict crouched beside Murph and watched him die in the same way he watched anything die – with fascination, and an undercurrent of disappointment. Human, animal or insect, there was a moment when the light went from their eyes, when the thing they were ceased to be. It felt like it should be important, monumental, the culmination of a life, but it was always more of a whisper than a scream.

Shame, though. It was hard to get men that big.

Thankfully, he had a plan B. All he had to do was find a victim.

He called someone to come and clean up the mess, then went back onto the floor from the stairwell. Moving quietly, he stopped at every door until he heard someone softly crying on the other side. He entered the room and there she was, curled on a mattress on the floor. The girl Murph had been questioning before.

'Don't be scared,' Benedict said, smiling as he approached.

When he finished, he stood and straightened his clothes and got out his phone. Those two wouldn't go far. Not tonight.

Besides, he enjoyed the hunt.

20

Jackie was in the kitchen making yet another a coffee, maybe her seventh or eighth of the day – she always did herself a favour and stopped counting after lunch – even though the last one had done nothing but made her jittery. DS Keyes came in, having just shown Gabrielle Truman and Steve Smith out.

'You want one?' asked Jackie, dumping a teaspoon heaped with brown granules into her cup.

'Not for me,' Keyes replied. Then, shyer: 'I don't actually drink it.'

'You'll be the first detective in history not to down gallons of the stuff.'

Keyes shrugged. 'I stick to water.'

Jackie remembered the sleek silver reusable bottle on Keyes' desk, like some futuristic capsule. Even in the fluorescent light of the kitchen, the sergeant looked fresh, her skin unblemished, her eyes not drowning in heavy grey seas.

Give it time, Jackie thought, a little too bitterly for her liking.

'So?' she asked Keyes.

'We need to find Ed Truman.'

Jackie stirred her coffee. 'Sure he's our man?'

'I'd say so. He's unreliable, secretive. Now there's a dead girl

94

with his DNA in her hand and he's disappeared. At the very least, he's heavily involved.'

'What about the men outside his house on Friday?'

'Blackmail?'

'So you think he sexually harassed those women? The wife's wrong?'

'She doesn't want to believe it.'

Jackie nodded, and took a sip. She'd thought the same – the wife was in denial. But something about the interview wasn't sitting right. Was Gabrielle Truman holding something back? Either way, this was rapidly becoming a lot more complex than a park attack gone wrong.

Keyes cleared her throat and fingered her crucifix. 'About that …'

'About what?'

'The interview with Mrs Truman.'

'Go on,' Jackie replied, careful. She didn't like the way the sergeant's manner had shifted.

'Well, it's just that at MCU we were also told to be a bit more … considerate to the person being interviewed. Especially if we were giving them distressing news.'

Jackie felt a flicker of irritation. Considerate! A young girl was lying on a steel bed – where was the consideration for *her*? She tamped it down – the anniversary tomorrow was bound to affect her mood. *Standing on the doorstep. Lester opening the car door, helping Verity climb inside. Her daughter taking one last look around. One last wave to Mum.* She didn't want to take it out on the rookie for asking a reasonable question.

'We get results here, Charlotte,' she said. 'That's what it's about.'

'I just thought with the folder … It's a hard way to tell someone their spouse might be a murderer.'

'I had to catch her off guard, before her defences went up.'

'But—'

'But nothing.' It was bad enough she didn't have an experienced officer backing her up on this case; she wasn't going to justify her every bloody move. 'If you can't—'

Thankfully she was cut off by DS Nick Haggerty appearing in the kitchen doorway. 'Boss. We've got news.'

*

The AV system was working now in the incident room, the right screen split into four CCTV cameras, the left showing a still of the victim, lying prone on the grass.

Haggerty was at the front, leading the briefing. 'We have an ID. Ivana Kostimarov, seventeen, from Melnik in Bulgaria. She arrived in England a month ago, and was living at a squat in the old Institute of Directors building on Pall Mall.'

'Any tie to Truman?' asked Jackie.

'None yet,' Haggerty replied. 'In fact we don't know much about her. We've tried to get in touch with her family, but no progress so far.'

Jackie turned in her seat to look at DS Weston Travis, languidly sitting with his arm across the next chair along. 'You on top of her social media, Trav?'

'Team are cracking it as we speak.'

She turned back to Haggerty. 'You take statements from the squat?'

'Tried to, but the place cleared out when we turned up.'

'Funny that,' growled DS Milou Ramya.

'Okay, Charlotte,' said Jackie. 'You want to say what happened with Mrs Truman?'

Keyes swapped out with Haggerty, changed the right screen to a video of the interview, and walked them through it. Thankfully, she kept any reservations about the methods used to herself. None of the other detectives blinked at the folder of pictures, the slap on the table, the 'direct' manner of questioning. They knew how things were done at RAS. Jackie liked to think they would have gone about it in a similar fashion.

Jackie told Keyes to pause the video after Gabrielle Truman's explanation of recent events.

'What do we know about the Men's Learning Centre? Who's in charge? Who runs the website? The YouTube channel? How involved is Carmichael? He's a high-profile individual, so tread carefully. Let's not make ourselves a target for his followers.'

'I'm on it,' said Ramya.

'Okay, Trav,' Jackie said. 'You're up.'

Detective Sergeant Travis sauntered to the screens. Six foot two, broad-shouldered, with smooth skin and a dimple in his right cheek when he smiled, he had the easy charm of a chat show host. Jackie told herself he was a good fit for Rapid and Serious because of his technical knowledge, but even she had to admit that maybe, like most of the other women in the unit, she might have a tiny crush on him. Not enough to think about pursuing it – she didn't have the time or inclination for a relationship, let alone with someone at work. Although there had been that one night, out celebrating a major success, when he'd cocked a drunken eyebrow at her. She'd patted his cheek, told him to go home, she'd see him in the morning, then tossed and turned all night thinking what it might have been like.

Trav pointed to the top-left section of the CCTV screen, which showed the back of a car driving through traffic. 'Here's our guy,' he said, 'heading into town, Saturday morning.' Next the top-right screen, a man hurrying down the street. 'He parks up at Baker Street, then double-times it to Westminster Magistrates' Court, arriving at approximately 9.35. But...' Trav indicated the bottom left screen, a bus camera, and there, looking directly at them: Ed Truman. 'Twenty minutes later, he's on the bus, getting off at the West End.'

'His business partner corroborated that,' Keyes said. 'Steve Smith. They were supposed to be joint counsel in court, but Truman disappeared and didn't come back.'

Jackie sat forward. 'He gets off very close to Pall Mall.'

'Less than five minutes' walk to the squat,' Trav replied.

'He's meeting her,' said Ramya. 'He's setting it up, for that night.'

'The taxi Truman takes into town at midnight,' said Jackie. 'Where does it drop him?'

Trav pointed to the last screen, a London street in darkness, Ed Truman in a hurry. 'Literally round the corner.'

Not only did they have his hairs, they had him close to Ivana Kostimarov's digs around the time she was killed. That was a whole heap of circumstantial evidence to add to the forensics. Surely she should be feeling the case starting to close? Why, then, did it feel more open than ever?

'Milou,' said Jackie, 'you get the warrant yet for Truman's office?'

'Just come through.'

'I want their computers. All of them.'

Ramya made a face. 'The seize description only says to take his.'

'I couldn't give a shit what the description says. Laptops, tablets, even a bloody palm pilot. If it's got a hard drive, I want it here.'

'But—'

Jackie cut him off. 'We've got a dead teenage girl and a DNA-matched murder suspect on the loose. So if you're not capable of going above and beyond to bring him in before he kills again perhaps you need to step aside for someone who can.'

Ramya made to say something but chose to keep it inside. Good for him.

'I'll get them, boss,' he said.

'Nick,' Jackie said to Haggerty. 'Bank statements, medical records, internet search history. Social media to the max. If Ed Truman liked a picture of someone's dog on Facebook at three in the morning last Thursday, I want to know about it.'

Haggerty shook a thick folder. 'Way ahead of you.'

'Let's get to it, people,' Jackie said, clapping. 'Nick, leave me that.'

Keyes hung back while the others left. Jackie knew already she wasn't going to like what the sergeant had to say. 'What now, Charlotte?'

'What you said to DS Ramya? About the seizure warrant?'

'What about it?'

'Well . . . won't that open us up to being sued?'

'It's a local solicitor, right?'

'Right.'

'Well, it's not a good look, is it? Suing the police while they investigate a murder where your business partner is the prime suspect.'

'But still—'

'But nothing. Same goes for you as Ramya. If you can't handle it in this unit, step aside for someone who can.' She moved close enough to Keyes to smell the floral scent of her body spray. 'I didn't ask you to join RAS, and I won't shed a tear if you leave. Understood?'

Keyes stood her ground. 'You know we've met before.'

'Is that so?'

'I did your close combat class at Hendon.'

Jackie searched her memory but couldn't place the sergeant. Then again, she'd been giving the same class for years now, teaching countless cadets how to disarm an opponent, or to turn a weapon back on the attacker. It made her proud to think that the knowledge she'd shared might have saved a fellow officer's life.

'Well, I hope you found it useful,' she said.

'I thought you were amazing.' Keyes' stare was unwavering. 'I guess it's only when you meet your heroes that you realise they're just human too.'

'That everything?'

'Yes, ma'am.'

Jackie nodded to the door. 'You'd better get busy, then.'

*

She was still bristling when she got back to her office. This was why she liked to control who joined her team, so she didn't have to explain herself to some cookie-cutter trainee who probably didn't go for a shit without checking the proper protocol. What if Truman went on a spree? What if he thought, *Screw it, I'm going down anyway*, and the clue to catching him was in a hidden directory on the Smith Truman Solicitors server?

She flicked through the casefile. Less than a day and already it was huge. What started out as a slender document folder, containing the crime log and SOCO stills, was now so full the sides bulged. She stopped at an article about Ed Truman's charity work from the *Barnet Gazette*. The photo had him in a community centre, dressed in beige chinos and a light blue shirt, beaming at the camera, his arm around a robust young woman with a lanyard around her neck – but in a fatherly way, looking proud of a job well done. The very model of respectable. Someone who'd make you feel safe.

Something wasn't adding up. She could feel the knot in her mind. You had this family man, local hero, picture in the papers, and all of a sudden he switches. Fine, she could buy that. She'd seen that before, too many times. But at the same time as his family is caught up in a running battle with this website?

Was Gabrielle Truman right? Could someone have forced those women accusing him of harassment to go to the police to build a smear campaign? But what about Ivana Kostimarov? Was she involved with Ed Truman? Or the men outside his house? Where did Carmichael fit into this? Was the trouble between them really over the Trumans' daughter, or was there something more?

The mental knot started to throb, and no amount of kneading her temples helped.

A knock on the door. Jackie called, 'Come in.'

'Got the warrant for the Truman house,' Keyes said, stepping into the office.

'Head down to the car. I'll be there in a minute.'

'I just want to apologise for before, ma'am. I didn't mean to step out of line.'

Jackie remembered what the super said to her first thing that morning – *be nice!*

'You're still getting used to how we do things in the unit,' she replied. 'Don't worry about it.'

'Thank you, ma'am.'

When she'd gone, Jackie picked up the newspaper article again and sighed.

Where are you hiding, Ed Truman?

21

EARLIER THAT DAY
6.45 A.M., SUNDAY

Maybe if I were still a teenager, I would have found a comfortable way to sleep rough, perhaps by fashioning a bed from litter and fallen leaves. As it was, I spent the hours until dawn sitting rigid on the glacial plastic slab that passed for a seat in the bus shelter, and juddering like someone who'd tried to fix the electrics with a fork. I guess I might have been warmer if I hadn't given Phoenix my jacket, but I couldn't let her freeze.

After fleeing the squat we'd scuttled through the dark back streets of the city. At first I'd argued that we had to go to the police, tell them what happened, but once Phoenix pointed out the murder weapon in her back pocket and big bloke's blood soaked into one of the knees of my jeans, I backed down. She said she had a hideout. We could work out what to do there. It seemed like a better idea than anything I could come up with, which was nothing, so I followed her.

At King's Cross we'd sneaked on the back of a night bus packed with drunk students, taking it all the way to the end of the route, and then walked, walked, walked until we found the bus shelter, giving me plenty of time to go over the events of the last few days, and try to work out how I had messed everything up so badly. Gabrielle was right. I should never have got involved with that website. At a minimum I should have backed down once those blokes started harassing me after the hearing. Thank God Gabrielle and Mitchell were staying at her mother's last night – if that handsome bastard turned up at ours looking for me, he'd find an empty house.

The jacket shape in the corner stirred, and Phoenix groggily appeared. 'Ugh, Jesus,' she muttered. In morning light, with that silvery-grey hair, she looked like a ghost emerging from my Berghaus windbreaker.

'Can't believe you slept,' I said, so cold even the words came out shivering.

'You can't call that sleep.'

I rubbed my hands and breathed into them, but failed to make them feel like anything other than lumps of cold iron welded onto my wrists. 'So now we're safe, are you going to tell me how you know my daughter?'

'We're not safe.'

'We're safe enough for you to tell me what's going on.' I caught her eye and held it. 'Yesterday, outside the courts. You didn't just bump into me.'

'Honestly,' she said, picking at a thread coming loose from the collar of my jacket, 'I really don't—'

'People only say *honestly* when they're lying. How do you know her?'

She was about to say something – I could tell it was going to be another lie by the arch of her eyebrow – but then she seemed to change her mind and sighed instead.

'Okay,' she said. 'Yes, I know Ally. But I didn't mean to trick you. I ... I've been worried about her as well. I was supposed to meet her a few days ago and she didn't show up and I thought that—'

'What? What did you think?'

'I thought they might have got to her.'

'"They" meaning those blokes in the stairwell.'

Phoenix nodded. She was smaller than Ally, barely five feet, and slight too, her features so delicate they put me in mind of filigree lace. Running across the base of her throat was a pale, puckered line, about an inch across. Most likely she had her thyroid gland removed. That happened to an aunt of mine, and she had the same scar. Still, it couldn't be nice for such a young girl to have that, so I made sure I didn't glance at it when I spoke.

'Let me guess,' I said. 'You're involved in the group that milk-shaked Carmichael.'

'Something like that.'

'Could they have hurt Ally?'

'You don't know what they're like.'

'I've got some idea,' I replied, and explained the harassment on Friday, outside my office, and later my house.

'That's nothing. That's them messing with you.'

'So you don't know where Ally is? Or if she's okay?'

Phoenix shook her head.

I tried to rub some heat into my legs. 'You mentioned going to a hideout, but shouldn't we try to get you home?'

'I don't have a home.'

'Where do your parents live?'

'They're ... they're dead.'

Now I felt rotten. 'I'm so sorry. I didn't—'

'My life is nothing new to me,' she said, giving me a wan smile. She pushed her fringe back from her eyes. She looked so young, so innocent. What had these girls got themselves involved in?

Down the street a door slammed, and something I hoped was a cat screeched. A faint smell of frying bacon wafted from the house behind us. The world was starting to wake, and we had to decide how to face the day ahead.

'Let's go back to mine,' I said. 'We can get changed, get warm. Work out what to do next.'

'You can't go back to yours.'

'You think they'll be waiting?'

'Probably.'

'I'll buy some new jeans, then we'll go to the police.'

'They've got people in the police.'

'Isn't that a bit paranoid?'

'I'm *serious*. You can't go home, you can't call anyone—'

'I need to ring Gabrielle,' I said, my hand going to my pocket, checking my phone was still there. After that, a taxi. I was out of it last night, dazed from the booze and the events at the squat, so didn't put up much of a fight as Phoenix led me to the back end of nowhere, but one thing a few hours freezing at a bus shelter will do is focus the mind.

Her gaze was intense. 'If you use your phone, they'll find us. If you use your bank cards, they'll find us.'

'You're being ridiculous.'

Her lip quivered, her chin crinkling, she looked away.

'I'm sorry,' I said. 'I've just ... I've got to get back.'

'Please,' she said. 'You've got to trust me on this. You can't use anything that can be traced.'

She had to be exaggerating. More than likely she thought I wanted to leave her, and was terrified of being alone.

'Listen,' I said. 'I'm going to go to the police and tell them *every-thing*. They can escort me home and check no one's hiding in the cupboards. You're welcome to join me, or you can stay here. If you don't want to come, we can go to a cashpoint and I'll give you enough to get a hotel, new clothes, whatever you need. And when that runs out, you call me. Okay? Whatever you need, I'll help you. Not just money. If you want to come and stay with us, you can. And if anything happens about last night, with that man

Murph, and you get arrested for it, then I can help with that as well. I'm a pretty good lawyer. At least when I'm not sleeping in bus shelters.'

'*You can't go.*'

'Please, Phoenix—'

'If they find you, they'll torture you. They won't stop until you tell them where I've gone.'

I remembered how that handsome bloke stood there watching his friend die, when he could have made a tourniquet, maybe saved him. My next thought saw me strapped to a table, him standing over me, eyes impassive, as he asked for the last time, *Where is she?* before hammering a nail into my kneecap. Somehow, against all possible laws of nature, my freezing body broke into a sweat. I'd always assumed that I'd get through life avoiding torture of any kind. A little too casually, so it appeared. Torture was what happened to people in horror films, or to detainees in Guantanamo Bay, not to middle-aged lawyers living in Finchley.

It sounded crazy, I didn't believe it, but I saw the conviction in her face. *She* believed it.

At least for the moment, going home was on hold.

I checked my wallet, but I had no cash. 'Tell me again why I can't take out any money?'

'What have you got? Visa? Mastercard? They can put a trace on those like that.' She clicked her fingers, in case I didn't understand how fast it would be. 'Soon as you use your card, *ping!* Your exact location.' She pulled herself upright and handed me my jacket.

I put it on gratefully, almost moaning as the warmth of her body transferred to mine. 'And my phone? Why can't I—'

'They'll have a trace set up on your number. You call anyone, they'll know where we are in seconds.'

My head was throbbing, my mouth as musty as an old cupboard.

This was too much to take in. 'What do they want with you? What have you *done*?'

She scuffed an old chocolate wrapper with her trainer. Her voice was broken when she spoke. 'I've got something they want, but if I give it to them, I won't be *me* any more.'

'I have a right to know what it is.'

'It's ... it's personal.'

If she wasn't going to tell me, what could I do? Take a lead from the blokes after us and torture the truth out of her?

'*Fine*,' I said, in a way that I'm sure told her it was anything but. 'So what do we do now?'

Phoenix examined the map on the bus shelter. 'How about some breakfast? Look, we're not far from Potters Bar Station. Let's get something there.'

'But we haven't got any cash.'

'Maybe not, but I have a plan.'

22

We were inside Potters Bar Station, spying on the coffee counter near the ticket barrier, when Phoenix told me her plan.

My reply: 'You have got to be kidding.'

There were packaged muffins next to the till, and she wanted us to steal them. Me. A lawyer of over twenty years. If I got caught, I would be struck off the roll of solicitors in seconds.

'It's so easy,' she said.

'You do realise stealing is a crime.'

'I'll remind you of that when you're watching me eat.'

Even in the comparative warmth of the station I was freezing; the cold gnawed through to my bones, with nothing of substance in my gut to make enough heat to drive it away.

She pointed to the far corner. 'That's the only camera, and it's facing the ticket office. We'll be away before anyone even realises what happened. I've done this a hundred times.'

'And I've done it zero times.'

'Great. So it evens out.'

'That's not how it works.'

'If we get caught, I'll be the one in trouble.'

'That's better how?'

Phoenix rolled her eyes in a *duh, dummy* way I recognised from my own kids. 'Because *I* can talk my way out of it.'

I thought about what it would be like to bite into the soft sponge of a muffin, and my stomach rumbled encouragement at her terrible plan. I sighed. 'What do you need me to do?'

She pointed to the ticket barriers. 'Create a diversion. Something that's going to get people's attention.'

'What? Like fake a heart attack?'

'Just make it interesting. Think big. The bigger the better.'

Oh, balls. This wasn't my thing at all. Call me British and repressed, but I didn't enjoy public displays of humiliation. 'I don't think I can do this.'

'Let's swap. I'll do the diversion.'

I tried to imagine pilfering muffins from the counter while the server was looking away, but that sounded even worse.

'Okay,' I said. 'Wish me luck.'

I approached the ticket barrier, wallet out, footsteps echoing in the quiet concourse, trying to keep my breath steady while my heart jitterbugged around my chest. A bored station attendant with wispy blond hair and a shark tooth necklace was secretly checking his phone down by his waist. I got to the gate and pretended to slide a ticket into the slot. I gave it a second, then banged the machine, glaring angrily at it.

'Excuse me,' I called to the attendant.

He glanced up and smiled genially. 'Yes, sir.'

'I put my ticket into the machine, and now it's gone. The doors didn't open.'

'Let's check that for you.' He pulled a set of keys from his back pocket, came through the barrier, and flicked through them for the right one.

What little plan I had collapsed. I was hoping to get in a row with the attendant, possibly with some swearing and pushing as I demanded to be let through, but instead he was going to open the machine and I wouldn't have a clue about the last card, where the train was going or what time. I glanced at Phoenix, loitering by the cafe's display case. She gave me some *hurry up* eyes.

'These old machines are always playing up,' the attendant said, showing me the key.

Shit. Shit, shit, *shit*.

Time for plan B.

I dug my fingers into my ribs, mouth twisted to the side. An agonised groan slipped out. The attendant took my arm, asked if I was okay, did I need to sit down? Behind him Phoenix gestured for me to ramp it up. I groaned again, louder now, slipping to my knees. The attendant grabbed his walkie-talkie. '*Emergency. Emergency.* I need an ambulance!' Phoenix shook her head and sliced her hand under her chin. I sprang up, rubbing my chest, backing away from the now *very* confused attendant.

He gestured to the machine. 'But . . . your ticket.'

I started to say something, but my mind wasn't working near the speed needed to come up with a cogent explanation for the last sixty seconds. Instead I grimaced profusely, then turned and ran.

Outside, Phoenix shook her head in disbelief. 'That was *so lame.*'

I leaned against a metal strut, sucking lungfuls of frigid morning air and cursing my love of late-night snacks. 'I don't . . . I don't usually . . .'

'Rule one. *Be* the person. If you're a guy in a hurry, don't stroll to the barrier. And don't choose something that can be checked, like tickets. Remember, the more irrational the better. You should've just steamed in, demanded to be let through, said you had to say goodbye to someone. Get emotional. Grab everyone's attention. I only needed a second.'

'Okay, okay,' I said. 'Give me a minute and I'll—'

'I don't think so. I need to eat.' She nodded to a long kiosk selling newspapers and chocolate bars by the side entrance to the station. A bus was pulling up to the stop beside it, the back door busy with people readying to get off. 'I'll go in loud and fast, so grab what you can.' I started to object, but she set off, gesturing for me to follow. '*Come on.* Crowds are good.'

She walked chin up, shoulders back. I stayed close, scouring for passing police and telling myself this was no different to the 'stealing bread to feed your family' philosophical dilemma that all young lawyers ask themselves. Thankfully, the unshaven man slumped inside the kiosk was in even worse shape than me.

Phoenix got there as the bus was emptying. She grabbed a young man wearing a leather jacket he clearly didn't feel comfortable in, and yelled, '*Hey! What do you think you're doing?*' He gawped at her, bewildered, and not a little scared. She truly looked horrified, violated, furious.

People stopped to watch, the man in the kiosk rubbernecking with the rest of them. I snatched chocolate bars from the counter and ran. He clocked me from the corner of his eye, but was slow to react, and I was already round the corner before he could get out of the kiosk.

I ducked behind a car, legs trembling, ready to set off again. A few minutes passed, then Phoenix appeared at the corner. I waved her over.

I'd managed to grab two triple Mars Bars, two Cadburys Boosts, and three bags of peanut M&Ms. 'Good haul,' she said. 'Later I'll teach you joys of dumpster diving.'

'That sounds suspiciously like scavenging for food in a rubbish bin.'

'It's not as icky as you'd think. Some chains throw their morning sandwiches out at three – don't you think that's *so* wasteful? I saw one on the high street.'

'Can't wait,' I muttered, picturing my gleamingly clean, always full fridge back home.

How could this be happening to me?

*

We sat on crates behind Starbucks, close enough for Phoenix to hop onto the free Wi-Fi.

'You shouldn't use sexual harassment that way,' I said, opening a Mars Bar. 'When it happens for real, it's nothing to joke about.'

'It worked, didn't it?' Phoenix tipped a bag of M&M's to her mouth, crunching through them as she logged into her surprisingly smart laptop.

'How you do something is as important as the outcome.'

'It'll be a funny story to tell his mates. *Some psycho bitch accused me of touching her up. Huh, huh, huh.*'

'You don't know what kind of person he was.'

Windows flashed open on the screen as she typed. 'Think of it as collateral damage.'

'You're hardly advancing the good name of the sisterhood.'

'You can't bring a knife to a gunfight.'

'That's a bit much, isn't it?'

'Feminism isn't just a PR stunt,' she said, fixing me with the weary stare of a journalist who's seen too many machine-gun totting child soldiers in the Sudan. 'It's war.'

'Things are changing – the world's changing.'

'*We're* changing the world.' She turned the laptop screen to me, and pointed to a red dot next to a village called Saddleton . 'Here's where we need to get to.'

'What's there?'

'It's a hideout. It's not far – you can message people safely from there.'

'How far is not far?'

'I mean it. Especially if we can get a ride.'

'You mean hitch?'

'Sure, why not.'

I saw us in the cabin of an articulated lorry, pleading with the driver to let us out, as he chuckled menacingly and pulled a bowie knife from the shadows. 'I don't think that's a good idea.'

She joshed my shoulder. 'No one's going to murder us. Well . . . not on the road, anyway.'

'Ha bloody ha.'

*

Unfortunately – or fortunately, depending on whether you believed that hitching was a surefire way to having your remains found in a ditch – no one stopped for us. The rest of the day was spent trudging along the country road in the direction of Saddleton, and praying that the dark clouds massing above us didn't decide to empty their rain.

As we passed through a three-road village, I realised how I could get in touch with Gabrielle without being traced. I was desperate to tell her about the psycho who might be looking for me, and to suggest she should go back to her mother's, just to be on the safe side.

Phoenix said I couldn't call home with my phone. She didn't say anything about using someone else's.

We came to a pub called The King's Head, a tatty place with peeling paintwork and a St George's flag sagging in the cob-webbed window. I told Phoenix I was nipping in to use the loo. She said she'd wait outside.

The light in the pub was dull, the air stale and smelling of gloom. I passed a line of dead fruit machines and a smattering of mis-matched tables on the way to the bar, where a couple of old lags were on stools, nursing pints of swampy brown ale. Behind it, an old lady with bare arms like badly stuffed sausages scowled when I approached, like she was daring me to order a drink. Nothing would have made me happier than to get a pint, and maybe a couple of dozen whisky chasers to go with it.

'Excuse me,' I said to her. 'I need to call home, and I've lost my phone. Do you have one I can use?'

'No phone here,' she snapped.

'Please, I—'

'Knock yourself out,' mumbled one of the blokes at the bar, sliding his mobile to me. It was small and battered, with real keys. I thanked him profusely and called Gabrielle, but her phone was off. Next I tried home. After three rings, she picked up.

'Gabrielle, it's me,' I said. 'Listen, I—'

'Hi Ed,' said a woman on the other end. 'Hold on. I'll get her for you.'

Who did I just speak to? I tried to match the voice to one of Gabrielle's friends, but couldn't place it. Above the bar the TV was tuned to a rolling news channel. The sound was down, but the weather was on – navy-blue pixels sweeping over the map made it clear rain was coming, and in great amounts. Maybe getting a lift wouldn't be a bad idea after all.

A minute passed, and Gabrielle still hadn't come to the phone. What could be taking so long? The four o'clock news bulletin started, and in the silence of the pub my mind filled in the thunderous theme music to go along with the clip montage of celebrities, disasters and political leaders shaking hands.

Then the presenter came on and I froze.

This couldn't be real. No way was this real. It was my face on the screen. *My face.* And below that, the headline:

Man wanted in connection with murder of teenage girl.

23

A squad car was already at the Truman house when Rose and Keyes arrived with the search warrant.

'One of you here,' Jackie told the constables waiting outside. She pulled on some latex gloves. 'The other bagging and tagging. Keep an eye out for electronics. Phones, tablets, computers – the usual. Let's head upstairs.'

They started in the daughter's room. Neat and prim, everything in its place, a sweet scent in the air, like someone had been chewing bubblegum. A single bed in the corner with a duvet cover saying 'Be Your Own Kind of Beautiful' in gold script. Miniature gift bottles of shampoo and face cream arranged in clusters beside a vanity mirror. Lots of posters, Lorde, Lana Del Rey, 'There Is No Planet B' above a picture of the world, 'Feminism: The Radical Notion That Women Are People'. Jackie felt a crawling in her throat, something dark and desperate inside her still searching for a way out. Was this what her own daughter's room would have looked like?

Jackie forced herself to focus. If she got sidetracked, she might miss something. They searched under the bed, the mattress, in the cupboards and drawers. No diary. Shame.

The son's bedroom, in comparison, was disgusting. They sifted through the layers of soiled clothes, crusted tissues and eviscerated crisp packets covering the floor. Typical for a teenage boy, sure, but somehow it felt more so, like buried beneath the petrified socks they'd find something rotting.

'Glad we're wearing gloves,' Keyes said, shoving a pile of grotty underpants out of the way to peer under the bed.

In the corner was a gaming set-up. Desktop PC, monitor, head-phones. 'Grab that,' Jackie said to the constable, nodding to the computer.

'Here we go,' Keyes said, pulling a shoebox of tech from deep beneath the bed. Hard drives, old phones, ancient SIM cards.

Jackie crouched beside her and sifted through it. 'Trav's going to hate us for bringing all this back.'

'I was lucky to have a walkie-talkie.'

'I was lucky to have a couple of tin cans and some string,' Jackie replied. 'Bag it up.'

Next they checked the master bedroom, taking the iPad on the dresser and a loose-leafed organiser with a leather cover from the bedside drawer. The en suite was immaculate, with vitamin bottles on the window shelf, expensive lotions beside the sink, a dark grey body scrub brush hanging in the shower stall. No liner in the bin, though. She paused. The bin was clean, and there were clips for a liner, so why wasn't one there?

She indicated the toothbrush. 'Bag that, then let's go down.'

The curtains in the living room were closed. A couple of flies twisted in the sour air. 'Looks like a party for one,' Keyes said, nudging the empty bottle of whisky. Cushions were everywhere, and a tall lamp had been knocked over, the bulb smashed.

Jackie saw a congealed coleslaw sandwich spiked with cigarette butts on the floor. 'Didn't think much of the catering.'

'Left in a hurry.'

'Got very drunk, *then* left in a hurry.'

That worked, right? Big argument with the wife. She storms

out, says she's leaving him – he's furious, drinks to oblivion, and thinks he has nothing to lose. Time to give in to his darkest desires.

So why did the knot in her mind get tighter?

Truman, the dead girl, the men outside his house on Friday, the allegations of sexual harassment by his clients, and looming over all of this, William Carmichael, an incendiary public figure with a huge following. When Jackie tried to put the pieces together, the edges clashed and rebounded away. Nothing fitted any single rationale.

They went through to a bright, modern kitchen. Skylights, dove-grey cabinets, a wide granite-topped island in the middle, wooden stools lining one side. Jackie looked at the framed photos on the wall. The perfect family, the perfect life. What if Ed Truman was a psychopath? Cold and deadly behind the mask. Except that didn't tally with the uncontrolled mess in the lounge, or the panicky way the body was dumped in a public park . . .

A phone started ringing: a land line attached to the wall by the fridge.

'You get a trace put on that?' asked Jackie.

Keyes nodded. 'Approved before we left.'

Jackie went to the phone. She shook out her shoulders, picked it off the cradle, and listened.

'Hi Ed,' she replied. 'Hold on. I'll get her for you.'

24

I stared at the television screen in the pub. The picture of me on the news stared back.

In that moment, I saw the truth about life: we are all on borrowed time. Something will happen, a diagnosis, a death, a car crash you could have avoided if only you weren't messing with the radio, spinning you into a different and altogether worse direction, and everything to that point will be as much use to you as someone else's memories.

Man wanted in connection with murder of teenage girl.

The picture changed to the girl in question. She had a slender face, curly blond hair, a cheeky smile. She looked like a good laugh, someone who probably had lots of friends.

And now she was dead.

That handsome man must be behind it, the one trying to find Phoenix. He and his thugs killed this girl and planted enough evidence to suggest I'd done it. I wasn't a criminal lawyer, but I knew enough to surmise that the police didn't start a national manhunt unless they had the reason to do so.

Phoenix was right. I had no idea what these people were capable of.

Well, I did now.

The only positive, and it wasn't much, was that the crone behind the bar and the two old duffers drinking at it hadn't noticed my face peering down at them. As casually as possible for someone who's just realised his entire existence had been flung into a wood chipper, I hung up the phone, slid it back along the bar, and muttered a croaky, 'Thanks.'

Outside, the clouds had gathered together in the sky. Everything seemed darker. In shadow. Phoenix was leaning against a postbox, rubbing her thumb over the tips of her nails.

Looking up, she said, 'Oh no, what now?'

'Don't panic,' I replied, only realising as I said it that nothing would be *more* likely to cause panic. Keeping my tone calm, I explained what I'd seen on the news.

'I *told* you. They're ruthless.'

'I need to call Steve, my business partner. He's got a better grasp of criminal—'

Phoenix waved her hands like I was about to back over her in a car. 'No, no, no. You can't call anyone. *Especially* now. The police will have traces set up on ... what? What is it?'

'About that,' I said, shifting my weight to the other foot. 'I ... *ummm*. I might have gone inside to call Gabrielle.'

'*You turned on your phone?*'

'No! Of course not. I used someone else's.'

'Did you get through?'

I nodded.

She covered her eyes. 'That's it. We're done.'

As reactions went, it wasn't the most reassuring. 'But it wasn't my phone!'

'They can trace all incoming calls! How long were you on for?'

'I don't know, a minute. I didn't speak to Gabrielle, just ...'

Just who? Who did I speak to? I'd assumed it was her sister, or one of her friends, Natalie, Reyna, but thinking about it the voice matched none of those people. In fact, it matched no one I knew.

'We've got to get out of here,' Phoenix said.

The village wasn't more than this pub, a newsagent's, a cafe, and a few streets of cottages. In any direction the countryside was less than five minutes away. We hurried to the nearest corner, and froze.

A police car was coming our way.

25

Keyes swerved between the motorway lanes, passing the slow
Sunday traffic, the stately home day trippers and the dads driving
with deliberation after a boozy Sunday lunch. Jackie could spot
them every time, the way they were hunched to the wheel, going
sixty in the middle lane, like that made up for the fact they were
putting their lives at risk. Just two drinks *doubled* the chance of a
fatal crash. If you told someone their family were a hundred per
cent more likely to die if they ate cornflakes, they wouldn't eat
cornflakes. Say that about a couple of lunchtime pints and they
thought that was an acceptable risk.

Jackie's phone rang on her lap. DS Travis from the office.

'What you got, Trav?'

'The phone Truman used belongs to a Mr Bernard Nutt. Sixty-
eight, retired labourer. Lives local with his sister and her son. Bit
of previous in his younger days, fighting at the football, but nothing for a *long* time.'

'You called our Mr Nutt back?'

'He's still at the scene, waiting for the local uniforms.'

'They're not there yet!' *For fuck's sake.* She resisted the urge to
beat her phone against the glove compartment.

'Don't think they've got much of a force up there. Probably just
two blokes and their nan.'

Jackie checked the time. Seven minutes since the call from Ed Truman, with at least another twenty-five until they arrived. They wouldn't get there much before the armed response, dispatched from Warren Street. Those local coppers bloody well better have him penned in when they arrived.

'How you doing with his phone?' she asked.

'I've managed to get into some of his online accounts. Same password for most of them, the stupid sod. I'm sure if I switch some of the letters to digits I'll get into his cloud. Depending on what OS version he's running on his handset, I might know a way of enabling the GPS when he turns his phone on.'

'Whatever would we do without you, Trav?'

'Hunt for crims with an Ordnance Survey map and a magnifying glass.'

Jackie laughed and hung up. Out the window, green fields stretched into the distance. People thought Britain was a small country, but try searching it for someone who wanted to stay hidden. Then you realised how enormous it really was. Nearly a hundred thousand square miles of towns, forests and marshland, with every remote shed, abandoned farm and secluded cave in between. Civvies always gasped when you told them how often murderers were never found, even when their identity was known.

Would Ed Truman be one more to add to the list?

26

We dived behind the front wall of a cottage, getting scratched up by the rose bushes on the other side, and crawled across the lawn to a narrow passageway leading to the back garden.

'If the police are here,' Phoenix said, '*he* won't be far behind.'

'It's me they want. I'll create a diversion and you run for it.'

'But you know where I'm going.'

'So go somewhere else.'

'There *is* nowhere else.'

I crept to the front bushes and peered through the thorns. It was a pretty idyllic English country scene – over the road was an old dear in her front garden, pruning her wisteria, while further along a young lad in a bright yellow baseball cap was loading fruit and veg into a cart from the back of a local grocer's van, the afternoon so quiet I could hear his off-key whistling. Even the police car next to the pub seemed kind of quaint, the officers leaning on the bonnet and chatting amiably to the blokes from the bar.

It wouldn't last long. In ten minutes this place was going to be swarming.

What choice did I have?

'Look at me,' Phoenix said when I got back to the passageway, clearly about to read my thoughts. 'Best case scenario, you go to prison.'

'I'm a lawyer. I'll fight my case.'

'What if you lose? Don't you want to go home?'

An image of a typical Friday night flashed in my mind, all of us sitting at dinner, everyone happy, even Mitchell. Gabrielle and I always lingered at the table long after the kids were gone upstairs. After tidying up, we'd hang around the kitchen, chatting and hugging. I felt Gabrielle's arms around me, the place on my shoulder where she always rested her head, the reassuring smell of her hair. I'd close my eyes, inhale the scent of her, and know everything was okay with the world, at least in that moment, no matter what dramas were going on outside of her embrace.

If I went to prison, I might never get any of that back.

'And don't think you'll be safe from him inside,' Phoenix went on. 'He can get to you anywhere. He'll do whatever it takes to make you tell him where I am.'

'Okay, okay. You've made your point.'

We hurried to the back garden. It was large with well-tended beds of colourful flowers, and a little stone pond in the corner. At the back stood a fence made from chicken wire laced with spiky metal nuggets. On the other side lay a field of knee-high yellow grass. Trees rose in the distance, maybe half a kilometre away.

Could we make it to them without being seen?

I pressed my ear to the damp brick wall of the house. No TV on, no one talking. There was no car in the driveway either, so maybe they were out. I wasn't as fit as I used to be when I played squash three times a week, but I figured I could make that distance. Would I get over the fence without ripping off my trousers? Of all the ways this could work out, some super-fit constable wrestling me to the ground in just my boxers was down there with the worst of them. Talk about final indignities.

'We doing this?' asked Phoenix. She tried for a determined smile, but I could tell by her eyes she was terrified. She barely touched five foot. The chicken-wire fence came almost up to her neck.

I tried to reply with words, but couldn't stop swallowing long enough to speak, so settled for curt nod.

'All right,' she said. 'On the count of three.'

We readied ourselves like running club teammates at the start line, waiting for the gun.

'One, two—'

A buzzing noise cut her off. Very quickly it got louder, until it sounded like a flying lawnmower about to dive bomb us. Phoenix pushed me back against the side of the house and gestured for me to get down. Then I saw it, floating above the back garden. A drone.

I like to think I'm pretty open to new technology. I Uber this and Amazon Prime that – once, when a new iPhone came out, I queued outside the Apple store on Oxford Street for two hours so I could get it on the first day. But I've never been keen on drones. There's something insidious about their spidery shape, not to mention all the future surveillance implications. And I certainly wasn't thrilled to see one now.

I nodded at the field and shrugged. Phoenix shook her head in reply, eyes wide, in case I didn't catch that was a hard *no*.

She waited for the sound of the drone to fade a little before whispering. 'That's an R60,' she said. '360-degree camera. They don't usually have thermal imaging as standard, but in the open they'll definitely see us.'

So that was it. Prison. The bullying and the beatings, the sadistic guards and the sound of the bars clanking shut. The bare metal toilet where everyone got to watch you taking a shit. Fucking fantastic.

Phoenix crawled on her elbows to the front of the house. The buzz was fainter now, down to an industrial fan instead of a lawnmower. She pointed in the direction of the pub and made a *maybe* gesture. She went further out to the rosebushes, then scurried back fast.

'Okay,' she said.

'Okay, what?'

'I've got an idea.' She indicated the road. 'There's someone delivering groceries a few doors down.'

My chest shrivelled in disappointment. 'What are you saying? We make a stir fry?'

She explained her plan. It was only marginally better.

'We're going to get caught,' I said.

'We're going to get caught if we stay.' She took my hands and looked me in the eye. 'You can do this. You're a badass.'

I'm a badass, I thought, trying it on for size.

It didn't fit.

This was a terrible idea – but it was the only one we had.

*

As the grocer was passing the top of the driveway of the cottage, I called and waved to him from the front door.

He looked late twenties, stocky in a way that suggested he liked a pie and a pint at lunch, and dressed in shorts despite the weather. At first, I didn't think he'd notice me – earphone cords came out from under his yellow baseball cap, plugging into the phone pulling down the chest pocket of his Golborne Groceries vest – but my flailing arms must have caught his eye. He came up the driveway, nodding along to the beat, wheeling a cart behind him.

I'd rubbed my hands in the dirt, and Phoenix had put a smear of mud on my cheek, like I'd been doing a spot of gardening, but I was sure he'd know I wasn't really the owner. Even if he didn't notice my agitation, the beads of sweat collecting between my eyebrows, he probably knew the real owners by name. *Or what if he'd seen me on the news?*

Too late now. He smiled at me without recognition, and I had to stop myself collapsing with relief right there.

'Afternoon,' he said, and went to check his cart. He scanned a clipboard attached to the front, and turned back frowning.

I glanced to the side. Phoenix was watching from the end of the passage, mouthing, *Come on, come on.*

Go hard and fast. Don't fuck this up like the train station!

'You've got some nerve showing up here,' I said, fishing desperately for something to hold his attention. 'After ... the *mess* last time!'

He took one of his headphones out quizzically. A brash rap beat drifted from the discarded earbud. 'What's this about, mate?'

'My fruit! My *pineapples!*'

He was about to turn to his cart when I realised my mistake – *nothing that can be checked!*

'Last delivery,' I blurted out. 'They were broken. Destroyed! And I'm holding *you* responsible.'

'Sorry, mate,' he replied. 'I'm new on deliveries, so it wasn't—'

'This isn't the end of this matter. What's your name? I'm taking this to the top!'

I clenched with embarrassment. To the top of what? The local grocery store?

'I'm not giving you my name, mate,' he said. He went to turn around but I grabbed his arm just in time. He faced me again, his expression grown dark. I didn't know what to do next. I kept hold of his arm, my heart pounding in my throat, my mind filled with white noise. I felt immobile, like time had stopped.

'I'm lonely,' I said. 'My wife left me, and I have no friends.'

He looked at my hand, still clamped to his wrist, but didn't pull away. If anything, he seemed more confused than annoyed. 'I'm sorry to hear that, pal, but what's that got to do with me?'

'Well, you seem like such a nice young chap, and wondered if you wanted to get a drink?'

Now he removed my hand. 'You're all right.'

'Sorry.'

'If you've got a problem with your delivery, then give the shop a call. I'm sure they'll help you out.'

'Sorry. I'm sorry.'

'That's all right, mate,' he said, pushing his cart away. At the top of the drive, he gave me one final, perplexed shake of the head before continuing down the street, leaving me to slump against the front door, panting and sweating and wondering, *Was that enough?*

27

Jackie got the message from Trav as they were approaching the turn-off for the pub where the alarm had been raised. She tapped the link on the touchscreen and a map opened. A grey dot was flashing on the outskirts of the village.

'Got you,' she muttered. They were five minutes away.

'Intel from Sergeant Travis?' asked Keyes, flashing her a grin.

'Eyes on the road, please. We're not there yet.'

'Yes, boss,' Keyes replied, swerving onto the hard shoulder and accelerating past the queue for the turn-off.

As they sped through the village, they heard the buzz of drones and saw them rise over the houses up ahead. If one thing had made their jobs easier, it was drones. Before, you had to drag twenty uniforms to an area to lock it down, now you could stream the visual to the station and have as many eyes on it as you needed.

They swung onto a long and wide tree-lined road. At the same time armed response tore up the other way. The ARV jack-knifed to a stop next to a small white van with 'Golborne Groceries' on the side. Keyes screeched to a halt beside it.

The armed officers took up strategic positions, submachine guns raised and ready to fire. Jackie jumped out and advanced on the van, warrant card out, saying loud enough for the man in the driver's seat to hear, 'Step out of the vehicle, right *now*.'

He was young and scared and started scrabbling in his lap. Jackie ran to the door and yanked it open. She grabbed him by the arm. *'Down! Down!'*

A cigarette paper fell from his hand, scattering fragments of tobacco into the road. On his lap was a bag of cannabis.

He stared at the black-clad officers aiming at him. *'It's only a bit of weed!'*

'Not him!' Jackie called over her shoulder. She nodded to Keyes. 'Check the back.'

Keyes slid the van's side door open. Except for a cart and some crates, it was empty. 'Nothing, boss.'

Jackie jumped in, confused. She flipped over the crates, opened the top of the cart. *Oh, for fuck's sake!* She fished inside, coming out with a phone. Truman's phone. He'd tricked them. Their suspect was smarter than she'd given him credit for.

She got out. Countryside in every direction. He'd be long gone. They'd had him, they'd *fucking* had him. But they'd lost him.

And there was only one person to blame.

28

Benedict appraised himself in the mirror. He was pleased with the retro style he'd achieved: late seventies, early eighties. Blow-dry and a leather jacket. Classic. Truman's wife had only seen him from her window at a distance, and the light had been fading, but he liked to be meticulous. That was why he always won and others always lost. Most people were sloppy, covering their deficiencies by handing their lives to nonsense concepts like fate and destiny, when in reality all that existed was the world and your will. Everyone could take whatever they wanted, if only they chose to do so.

Even before meeting William Carmichael, Benedict had been ambitious. As a teenager he joined a white nationalist group to prove himself, quickly rising through the ranks, but the whole skin colour thing was so last century. Restless, he sold his services as a contract killer on the dark web, to crooked cops and gang-land bosses and Russian oligarchs looking to remove a rival. Those should have been the best years of his life. He had wealth and prestige – ruthless and efficient, he was always in demand – but something was missing. He had too much vision to be *just* a killer.

Everything came together the night he saw William Carmichael speak at his 'The End of Intellectual Discourse' tour. Finally, it all made sense. Race, religion, they were just sideshows to the main event, to the war that had been raging for as long as humans had drawn breath. Men against women. The battle of the sexes.

Men had always been dominant, but in recent times women had fought back. More than that, they'd turned the tide, joining together under the banner of feminism to take control. What had men done in reply? Nothing. They'd remained disparate, ineffective, easy to subjugate, while women cemented their position.

The night Benedict saw Carmichael speak, he knew what he had to do.

He saw his path to *real* power.

It wasn't hard to organise a chance meeting, to charm his way into the old man's life and make himself indispensable. Carmichael had the ideas, but ideas die without someone to broadcast them to the world. How many people would still be quoting Jesus if it wasn't for his apostles spreading the good word?

A few years later, and here they were. Poised to turn the tide. To put men back in their rightful position, now and for ever.

This was a new politics for a new world: people connected not by country or culture, but by ideology; brothers tied to a single belief system. The men they'd recruited weren't just supporters. Many were victims of the institutional and systemic misandry pervasive in the Western world: men cast out by the feminist demagogues who were the lawmakers, judges and juries of hyper-liberalism. These empty shells were gathered, filled back up with masculine pride, taught how to fight, how to feel pride in their strength, not shame, as they had been brainwashed to do. What would the police do if they took to the streets in their hundreds of thousands? What would the government do if they all rose up together and asserted their rights? Even the army would be massively outnumbered.

Change is coming, and we are the change.

Smiling at his own largesse – if you don't celebrate your achievements, why should anyone else? – Benedict brought himself back to the present, turning his face from side to side in the mirror. How would Gabrielle Truman like him to look?

She'd had work done. Cheek enhancements, nose to mouth lines, eight hundred and sixty pounds at Cosmetics Skin Club on Harley Street. This was a woman who craved a new life. She wanted to look young, so he too would opt for a youthful style, his hair faded around the sides and back, swept over the top. Black-rimmed glasses, large and square to suit his jaw. Stubble, but neat, groomed. A slim-fitting blazer to go with his Santoni brown leather loafers. Modern and precise, perfect for her.

Given her situation – husband on the run for murder – most would think she'd have no interest in being seduced. But that would show a lack of understanding of the human condition. He'd had sex with more than a few women whose husbands were still cooling in the casket. The high tension, the feeling of life on the edge, only made it easier, as long as you were well prepared – and he had a very reliable source on every detail of her life.

He'd go as far as to say he was quite the expert on Gabrielle Truman.

*

One of his tech boys had tricked her into installing spyware on her phone – an email about her upcoming exhibition, containing an attachment that wouldn't open no matter how many times she tapped on it – so he could track her GPS movements. He pulled up in his Jaguar F-Type coupé as she swung her drab little car onto the driveway. They even opened their doors at the same time.

'Excuse me, hi,' he said.

Gabrielle did a double-take and fumbled her handbag, spilling lipstick, tissues and a blister packet of pills onto the gravel. He hurried to help gather her things.

'Sorry, sorry,' she said.

'No, I'm sorry. I shouldn't have surprised you like that.'

They looked up at the same time. He recognised the slight alarm on her face at being close to someone so sexually attractive. He allowed his smile to grow, his lips slightly parted, the hint of a crease in his brow, as though he were a breath away from a super-model, not some suburban hausfrau.

'Are you . . .?' she mumbled. 'Can I help . . .?'

He made a show of snapping out of the spell. 'Oh, I'm sorry. I just . . .' He coughed into his fist, bashful. 'It doesn't matter. Anyway, hi – hello. My name's Benedict Silver and I'm after Ed Truman. I thought he lived here.'

'He . . . he does.' Some tension returned to her face. 'Who are you?'

'I'm a business contact. Well, actually, that's not right. He's my lawyer. I run a venture capital firm, and he's been helping out with some of our contracts.'

'Oh! Okay, right. I'm Gabrielle. I'm his wife.'

Benedict offered his hand, and she took it. He carried on holding it as he said, 'It's funny, because he never mentioned a wife. I don't even remember him wearing a ring.'

She cocked her head, confused. 'Really?'

'Yeah, it's strange.' He let go of her hand, noticing with satisfaction that it stayed in place for a fraction of a second before she realised he was no longer holding it. 'I always got the impression he was single.'

'Oh,' she said. 'Okay.'

He pretended not to notice her disappointment. 'I've been trying to get hold of him for days. We've got a deadline this afternoon.'

'Haven't you seen the news?'

'Sorry. I don't really watch TV, and I've been so busy trying to finalise this deal.' Benedict leaned towards her conspiratorially. 'It's worth a tidy sum you know. Do you know when Ed's going to be back?'

She looked behind him to the street. 'I don't really want to talk about it here. Why ... why don't you come in? I was just about to make a cup of tea.'

He checked his watch, rocked his head, like he shouldn't really ...

'Go on, then,' he said. 'I've got a few minutes.'

She was wearing a fitted navy skirt. As she walked to the front door, he watched the way it clung to her arse. Not bad.

He was going to enjoy this.

29

When we stopped running, I slumped against a mossy rock wall and grabbed a protruding root, my legs quivering like twanged elastic bands, sucking in air as though the world was one big inhaler.

The wet leaves squelched as Phoenix approached. 'You okay?'

Tiny squiggles wormed across my vision. When I tried to speak all that came out was a strangled retch, followed by a long string of saliva that stretched, incredibly, all the way to my waist. The back of my throat had a rusty metal taste, and I wondered if I'd managed to rupture a lung in our escape. I hadn't sprinted like that since, well, for ever.

'We can't take too long,' she said.

'Do you ... do you ... do you think they'll ... they'll find—'

'I'm more worried about us finding a road or something before it gets dark. Otherwise we're going to get *really* lost.'

The string of saliva snapped. I wiped the back of my mouth and muttered, 'We wouldn't want that, would we?'

She got the accusation in my voice. 'What have *I* done? I got us out of there!'

I couldn't bring myself to look at her. 'What have you *done*? You've ... you've dragged me into this whole mess! Not just me, but my daughter—'

'I didn't drag Ally into anything.'

'From the moment we met all you've done is lie and steal and get me into just … just *insane* amounts of trouble.'

'I'm sorry, I'm sorry—'

'I mean, who are you? *Who the hell are you?* And what could they possibly want that is so important that they'd kill someone to find you?'

'I told you—'

'Bullshit! You told me nothing! You side-stepped and prevaricated and said it was too personal. Well, I'll tell you what's personal to me – *my life*. My *family*. I'm wanted for murder – murder! I could go to prison for the next thirty years because of you.'

Hands bunched by her chest, Phoenix was so young and frail and scared that the anger drained right out of me. It wasn't right for me to take my fear out on her. Did she ask for any of this? Okay, I couldn't answer that. But at the very least she too was terrified. She too was exhausted, and starving, and staring down the barrel of more of the same and possibly worse if those men found us.

I exhaled, long and slow. 'Okay, I've calmed down now. I'm sorry. It was wrong to shout at you like that.' Offering her an apologetic smile, I said, 'I guess this is another fine mess you've gotten us into.'

Her confused frown told me she didn't get the reference.

'Laurel and Hardy?' I said. 'You must have heard of them.'

'Larry and who? Are they your friends?'

'No, they're…' I shook my head. 'Whatever. It doesn't matter. I might as well be making pop culture references about the dinosaurs.'

'I think you already were.'

It was nearly dusk, and the air was getting cold. Tree shadows lay over everything. 'Do you think we'll get to your hideout tonight?'

'We're still miles away – that's if I can even work out the right way. We don't want to start walking in the wrong direction.'

That was a no, then. 'It's going to be dark soon. We need to find somewhere warm to spend the night.'

All she had on was a thin black hoodie, and beneath that a T-shirt. She wrapped her arms around her chest and shivered. 'I'm so cold.'

Same as last night in the bus shelter, I sighed and slipped off my jacket. It was the least I could do after my freak-out. She hesitated, but only for a moment, then took it and put it on. 'Thanks.'

'But when we find somewhere,' I said as we set off, 'you're going to tell me *everything*. The truth this time. Okay?'

'Okay.'

'You promise?'

'I promise,' she replied.

More fool me for believing her. Promises are like dreams: great while you're making them, but worth fuck all to anyone in the morning.

*

We carried on through the forest, ears straining, hoping to hear the distant growl of a passing car. Evening was coming on fast, our bodies dissolving into the darkness, and we increasingly caught our feet on roots, or found ourselves wading into waist-high shrubs that scratched through our clothes. The last thing I wanted was to get lost for days. For one, we had no food. For two, I had the survival skills of an evicted agoraphobic. Judging from the way Phoenix grumbled at the mud on her trainers or clawed at her face when she walked through a spider's web, I figured she was equally uncomfortable in the wild.

All too soon, it was night. Thankfully there were gaps in the clouds, so we had enough moonlight to keep going, albeit at a slower pace. My body ached as though I'd done back-to-back marathons. I needed to soak in a hot bath for most of the next decade.

'Ssssh,' went Phoenix. 'Stop.'

I heard it as well, a sheep *baaing*, the sound long and plaintive in the silence.

'Let's find it,' she said.

'You want to ask it for directions?'

I cringed at how petulant I sounded, but in my defence I was freezing, miserable, and regretting my generosity in giving her my jacket, again.

'Where there are farm animals, there's usually a farm,' she replied, more patiently than I deserved. 'There might be a barn or something we can sleep in.'

The sound wasn't continuous, but we heard it often enough to find the field it was coming from. We followed the line of barbed-wire fence to a gate, and despite a couple of hazardous moments that wouldn't have been out of place in a silent slapstick comedy, managed to make it over the slippery metal bars.

'There,' Phoenix said, pointing to a dome of hazy yellow light in the dark. 'Got to be a farmhouse. If they've got Wi-Fi, I can connect my laptop and find where we are.'

If someone saw us, the police would be swarming round here before we knew it, and there wasn't much chance of us pulling off another great escape. Not in the dark. Not if they had dogs. But what choice did we have? The sooner we got to this hideout, the sooner I could work out how to find my daughter and get us both back home.

'Lead on, Macduff,' I said.

'You really do say the weirdest things,' Phoenix replied, her voice full of wonder.

The farmhouse was large and sprawling, ramshackle even in the dark. We crept around the perimeter, staying in the undergrowth, Phoenix with her laptop open, trying to get a Wi-Fi signal. The kitchen window was open, and the sound of people chatting wafted out, along with a smell of roast lamb that sent my stomach into back-flips of hunger.

'Okay,' she whispered. 'I've got something.'

We found a place to hide in the shadow of a shed. She got to work, spinning up little black windows and typing fast into them. 'Who still uses WEP keys?' she murmured. 'They deserve to be hacked.'

I crouched next to her. 'What are you doing?'

'Something I'll be able to do much faster without interruption,' she replied, her face tinted blue from the screen. 'You know what we need? Water. I've got a couple of empty bottles in the bag.'

As soon as she said it, I realised how parched my mouth was. We'd not had anything to drink since taking a few tentative sips from a shallow stream that we quickly decided tasted too murky to be clean. When I reached for her rucksack, she did a double-take and snatched it first.

'Here,' she said, finding the bottles. She put the bag down beside her, her arm lying across the top of it as though she thought I might grab it and run.

'Oh-kay,' I said, taking the bottles. I made a mental note to see what she had stashed in there at the earliest opportunity.

We'd passed an overgrown area with a sizable greenhouse near the front of the house. I'm not much of a gardener – the only time I'd get green thumbs would be if gangrene spread to my hands – but even I knew that anything growing in there needed water.

I crept toward it on high alert, waiting for the moment when a door crashed open and someone hollered, 'Oy! You!' in my direction. In fact, didn't farms have dogs? Especially ones with sheep. Hence the name, *sheepdog*. What if they had more than one? Or a pack? Charging at me, knocking me down, their bare teeth snapping at my throat. I picked up the pace. Thankfully the front of the house was quieter, the windows black, the night silent.

The greenhouse was accessed by a gate that gave a tortured screech as I eased it open. On the other side, a winding path flanked with weeds and rusting wheelbarrows led to the greenhouse. The door opened more quietly, thank God, and I slipped inside, moaning as warm air smothered my face.

For the first time in hours, my shivering subsided. Perhaps we could stay in here for the night? We'd be up at dawn. The ceiling, after all, was made of glass. We could be out before they realised we were here. I felt the plants, and found small, shiny-skinned vegetables hanging from the stems. I pulled one close and took a sniff. Tomatoes! Well, that settled it. We were having a tomato party! I twisted one off and took a bite, certain in that moment I'd never tasted something so sweet and delicious as—

Torchlight slapped me in the face. I staggered back and threw an arm up in defence.

'And the other one,' snarled the voice behind the torch. 'Both hands where I can see them.'

I looked around for a weapon, another way out, but abruptly stopped when I heard the distinctive clunk of a shotgun being cocked. His next words dispelled any doubts.

'And put my tomato down,' he said. 'Or I'll blow your fucking balls off.'

30

I lowered the tomato to the workbench like it was a loaded pistol, then raised my hands again. Could I rush the farmer? Catch him off guard? Barge him out of the way and head into the darkness, praying he was a bad shot? What about Phoenix? I couldn't leave her here. Maybe I could clobber him over the back of the head with one of the wheelbarrows outside. But I'd probably miss completely and land on my back with a load of rusty metal heading for my face. Talking my way out of it seemed like a better bet.

'I'm sorry,' I said, wincing in the torchlight. 'I've … I've not eaten all day, and—'

'And you thought you'd break into my greenhouse and steal my veggies?'

I knew a rhetorical question when I heard one. I searched for where his face might be behind the light, and fixed on my most pleading expression.

'I was out camping with my family,' I said. 'I went for a walk in the forest. I got lost, and … and…'

'So that's why there were helicopters out? They looking for you?'

'Maybe,' I said, cautiously. That was a little too close to the truth. 'I got lost this morning. My family must be frantic.'

142

'I'm sure they would be.' The shadow by the door moved in such a way as to imply the shotgun was being lowered. 'I guess we'd better get you back to them.'

I wanted to pump my fists in celebration that I was getting to keep my balls, but settled for lowering my hands very, very slowly.

'I've got my phone,' he said, putting the torch to one side. 'Let me call the police.'

That was it, I had to run. 'Shouldn't we go to the house?'

'The missus won't like that. She hates trespassers. She'll want to know why I didn't shoot you! Ha ha ha.' I laughed along with him, even as my insides crumbled. 'You're warm here, aren't you? Go on, help yourself to some toms. There's peppers, too, if you like.'

The light from his phone came on when he unlocked it. He was older than I had thought, with sagging jowls, capillary cheeks and a nose that suggested many years of being thrust into a glass of red wine. Now would be the time to go for him, while he was distracted. But it wouldn't take much to swing up his shotgun and fire. Was it worth the risk?

A crash of breaking glass, coming from the main house.

The farmer reared up from his phone. 'Thought you were on your own.'

I flapped my mouth, hoping I looked as bemused by the sound as him.

'You wait here,' he said. He slammed the greenhouse door and slid a latch across. I ran to it, shook it. Nothing. I thought about kicking it open but remembered that bloke in the stairwell with the slashed artery in the leg and thought better of it. I'd spotted a trowel by the door, so grabbed it and slammed it on the glass. It bounced back. I rapped the pane with my knuckle. Plastic! I thought greenhouses were made from glass! I tried the door again, shaking it in the frame, wondering if it sounded loose enough to break off the hinge. I placed my foot on the metal beside it and prayed for a burst of superhuman strength. One, two, *thr*—

The latch clicked and the door flew open.

I staggered back, dropping onto my arse and throwing my hands up in the same graceless motion. 'I wasn't … I didn't …'

'What you doing on the floor?' Phoenix shook her head. 'Doesn't matter. Just come on – and hurry!'

We careened round the house, rushed to the top of the drive, the farmer bellowing for us to stop, and sprinted up the narrow country road, our feet slapping the wet tarmac. I spotted a gate and pulled Phoenix towards it. We scrambled over and into a field and carried on running, slipping in mud, getting tangled in long grass, until we got to some trees and headed deep into the forest.

*

Of course, being lost in a forest at night couldn't *quite* be bad enough. Huge raindrops fell between the canopy of bare branches, slapping us like water balloons. Pretty soon we were drenched.

We found a rocky overhang that just about covered us. The temperature had dropped and we huddled together, shivering beneath my jacket. My feet were freezing, my trainers waterlogged, and I thought wistfully about my slippers back home. I'd watched a documentary about survivalists, and remembered leaves could be used as insulation, so we stuffed handfuls of them under our clothes, an idea which took an already terrible situation and made it ten times worse. Not only did it have zero impact on my body temperature, but it now felt like a million bugs – many imaginary, but some no doubt real – were crawling over my skin.

It wasn't all bad, I guess. At least being thrust into this misery was stopping me from drinking, something which I found impossible with a fully stocked wine cabinet at home, and about eighty thousand off licences within a two-mile radius. The truth was, I drank every day, and increasingly *during* the day. You couldn't get away from the facts. I always woke up with the best of intentions, but determined morning me and worn-down afternoon me were two very different people. Either way I usually went through between a quarter and a half a bottle of scotch a day, depending on how shit I was feeling, plus sometimes/ often a beer after work, or a glass or two of wine over dinner, or the occasional celebratory can of gin and tonic. Or maybe all three. You get the idea. A high-functioning alcoholic, I called myself in moments of elevated self-esteem. A wino in waiting, the rest of the time.

Back home I had a handle on it. The handle being, I drank. But without it I could sense the restlessness in my head. It felt like my mind was filled with Escher-like stairs, all winding round one other and leading nowhere, and I was trudging along them looking for the exit. A couple of drinks down, that feeling faded away. Now there was no escape.

I focused on the patter of the falling rain, hoping the sound would calm me down, but it did nothing. How was I going to make it through to morning? It seemed impossible.

'You don't talk about your son much, do you?' Phoenix's voice startled me from my mental plummeting. She sounded annoyed, although I guess that wasn't surprising, considering how the day had panned out.

'What do you mean?'

'He barely gets a mention from you. I don't think it's fair.'

'That's not true,' I replied, although right then I didn't have a clue what I'd told her about my family. Quite a lot had happened.

'I asked you about him, and you just shrugged and said that he'd changed. He was *difficult* now. Difficult for you, maybe.'

Where was this coming from? Why was she being so pissy with

me? What right did she have to take so personally the fact that my son and I were barely on speaking terms?

'Phoenix, while I appreciate you sticking your nose into my relationship with Mitchell, I don't think—'

'He's not who you want him to be, so you don't love him. Men are *such* sociopaths.'

'You don't know anything about him – or me.'

'I know you don't tell him you love him.'

'Of course I love him.'

'That's such a lawyer answer. When was you last time you told him?'

I didn't need to think too hard. For a long, long time now, nothing close to the word 'love' had appeared in the standard exchange between my son and me.

'People are who they are,' I said. 'Not everyone has to shout their love from the rooftops to feel it inside.'

'You're a shit dad. You're all shit dads.' Her voice cracked. 'None of you know anything.'

She hadn't gone into detail about her relationship with her father before he'd died, but from the bits she'd revealed I got the impression they hadn't shared the same opinion on many things. I knew what it was like to keep hold of those unresolved feelings. To go through that so young must be awful.

'I bet your dad loved you,' I said, swallowing. Tears pushed at my eyelids. 'I bet you were everything to him.'

She sniffed hard. Her voice was broken when she replied, bitterly, '*What do you know?*'

We were both quiet. Just the rain and the rustling of leaves as we scratched at the bugs. I tried a few times to say something more, but everything I could think of sounded either stupid or crass. After a while, her breaths became longer, heavier, and then I was alone in the endless night, alone with my thoughts, with no way to make them stop.

31

Jackie threw down the printout and rubbed her eyes. She hated wading through people's internet search history. It always made her feel a little deflated and slightly sick, as if she'd eaten too much of a cake that she didn't even like. *What will future civilisations think of us if all they ever find are Google's archives? That we were a bunch of sordid, celebrity-obsessed, body fascists?* The most disappointing thing was they probably wouldn't be too far from the truth.

But that, of course, was only part of it. Today was the day. *The* day. A whole year had vanished and here she was again. Perhaps the super was right. She was stupid to take this case – she hadn't slept last night, couldn't force down any food so far this morning. How was that fair to Ivana Kostimarov or her family? A killer was out there, and the case's senior investigating officer was too busy wallowing to focus.

If Lester could see her now he'd say, *Cut yourself some slack.* He'd rest a hand on her shoulder and say, *You need to give yourself a break or you're going to burn out.*

Whose fault was it that he wasn't here to say those things?

Seven years, and in that time a scab had grown over the grief, but it had not healed. The wound beneath was still raw. She'd learnt not to pick at it, but right now all she could think of was Lester

147

and Verity by the car, her daughter lifting her hand to say goodbye. Ten seconds later Lester started the engine, and her whole world exploded.

It should have been her. She'd recently been drafted into the National Counter Terrorism Security Office, and was working hard to bring down an ethno-terrorist group called Pure Resistance; they were suspected of planning multiple synchronised knife attacks around the country. Usually she dropped Verity at school on the way to the office, but that morning she'd been exhausted. Lester told her to take an extra half-hour, he'd do the school run.

Her daughter taking one last look around. One last wave to Mum.

Not a day went by when she didn't wish she'd died with them.

A knock on her door – that'd be Trav. She called him in.

'You wanted to see me, boss?' he said, heading to sit down.

'Don't bother,' Jackie said. 'This isn't a social visit.'

His easy smile faded. He paused with his hand on the back of the chair, like he was waiting for her to crack a grin and say she was joking.

That wasn't going to happen.

'You made me look like a fucking idiot yesterday,' she said.

'What? I—'

'You made me think you'd got into Truman's phone and activated his GPS, but he turned it on himself, didn't he? It was nothing to do with you.'

'I didn't mean—'

'Don't bother, okay? That was vital information, *Sergeant*. We might have gone in differently if I thought he was trying to pull something. Instead you held out on me to make yourself look better.'

He swallowed hard. 'I'm … I'm sorry, boss. It won't happen again.'

'Next time, park your ego. Understood?'

'Understood.'

Jackie caught the tight expression on Trav's face as he closed the door on the way out. He didn't appreciate being spoken to like that. Well, tough. Because of him they'd diverted all their attention to following the phone, instead of splitting to contain the wider area. It had given Truman more than enough of a head start to get away.

She got up from her desk and prowled around her office. What about the girl Ed Truman was with? Was she involved in the murder? That had been the biggest surprise – he wasn't travelling solo.

Once they knew where to start, finding CCTV images of Truman leaving London hadn't been too difficult. He was in the city at midnight, and twenty miles north the next day, so he had to get there somehow. Driving seemed doubtful. Truman's car was still at home, and he hadn't used his cards to take money out, or his phone to book a taxi. They scoured the night buses heading in that direction, and sure enough there he was, sneaking onto the back of the N91 at King's Cross at 2.48 a.m.

He rode it to the end of the line, getting off at Cockfosters at 3.22. That was when they saw her. A young girl with pale hair, in black leggings and a hoodie, a slip of a thing. Yet on the CCTV, she was the one leading the way, turning and hurrying him, while he shambled behind, looking around as though he'd just woken up after falling asleep and missing his stop.

That feeling again, the knot in her mind, the sense that they were getting this wrong. Truman just didn't *seem* like a man on the run.

She printed some stills of the footage. Time to take this to the super.

*

Superintendent Drum was hunched at his desk when she came in, holding a pen over a report like he wanted to stab it to death.

'Oh, hi Jack,' he said sombrely. 'How you doing today?'

'Fine, fine.'

'You don't look fine.'

'I don't want to talk about it.'

He sat back in his chair, and said like a suggestion, 'Maybe you should.'

'Back off, Andy.' She put the stills of Truman and the girl on his desk. 'It's about the case.'

She could tell he didn't want to leave it, but he knew her well enough to understand that if he pushed she'd only push back.

He picked up a still. 'What's going on?'

'We need to find out who this girl is.'

'A hostage? Have you checked the mispers list?'

That was the first thing she had done, but nothing matching the girl's description came up.

'I'm having doubts,' she said.

'Go see a priest.'

'I'm serious.'

'We've got DNA on the victim's body and a suspect on the run. What part of that are you not sure about?'

'None of this makes sense. He's so smart one minute – that phone in the grocer's cart – but before that he's so stupid he actually calls his home.'

'Misdirection. Guilt. A bloody cry for help. Bring him in and we'll find out.'

Jackie pushed the CCTV pictures towards Drum. '*She's* leading *him*. Was she there when the other girl was killed? Or did he meet her after?'

'You've got questions? *Bring him in.* We'll get the answers.'

'I don't like it, boss. This is all wrong.'

Drum slumped back in his chair. 'You know why I like you, Jack?' He saw she was about to speak and waved her down. 'Just shut up a minute. I mean you're a good detective, probably the best I've worked with. You don't get a suspect then force the evidence to fit. You know if you mess it up the CPS will throw it out, and that means more rapists on the street. More murderers and child abusers. I get where you're coming from. But you've been given a gift from the gods here, an open-and-shut case. Stop second-guessing yourself. Okay?'

Bullshit. She didn't need his stupid pep talks. She needed him to *listen*.

'All we've got is circumstance and a few hairs,' she said. '*This is all wrong.*'

'You've got a DNA match, a history of sexual harassment – he's our man. Everything's pointing to him. So *stop*—'

A knock at the door. Drum sighed aggressively, and shouted for them to come in.

Charlotte Keyes pushed the door open, apologetic. 'Sorry to interrupt, sir, ma'am, but I thought you might like to see this.'

She handed a printout to Jackie. It was the internet search history from Truman's work computer; Keyes had highlighted the important lines. For months he'd been accessing extreme websites with names like www.strangulation-porn.xxx and www.deathrape.com. More recently he'd been researching where to buy chloroform, and whether duct tape or cable ties made a better restraint.

Jackie blew out her cheeks. *Some timing.* 'This was found on Ed Truman's work computer?' It looked like Drum was right after all. Everything was pointing to Truman.

So why did the knot just get as tight as a noose?

This is all wrong.

'Well,' Drum said. 'Satisfied?'

Jackie nodded at Keyes. 'Come on, Sergeant. We're heading out.'

First on the list, Helen McAllister. One of the women who had accused Truman of sexual harassment. Her husband, Dennis, was currently in Pentonville prison, sentenced to a six-year stretch for grievous bodily harm. Would she really sell out the person who had saved her? Time to find out.

McAllister lived in a housing estate comprising three tall concrete blocks, standing against the gloomy London sky like a line of middle fingers flipping off the city. Keyes parked between a rotting Ford Fiesta and a shopping trolley left on its side. They got out of the car to the stink of clogged drains.

Keyes grimaced at the huge silver bins in the rubbish area, all of them overflowing with bags. 'No wonder some people feel forgotten.'

Jackie headed for the entrance. 'You can call the council when we get back.'

'What are we doing here anyway? She's already spoken to uniform. Twice.'

'I'm thinking that maybe they didn't ask the right questions.'

The front door to the block was wide and metal, with a square of reinforced glass in the middle that had somehow still been cracked, although judging by the orange-stained tiles and the sharp stink of piss, people used the entrance mainly as a toilet. The panel of buttons looked equally unsavoury, the metal covered in grey finger smears. Jackie found a tissue in her pocket to press the numbers for McAllister's flat.

'Let me do the talking,' she said to Keyes.

A woman's voice echoed through the intercom. 'Who's there? What do you want?'

'Just the post. Got a delivery for a ... Mrs McAllister,' Jackie said. In the pause that followed, she offered a tight smile to the sergeant's glance of bemusement. When the door buzzed she pushed inside.

The lift was out of order, so they jogged up the steps, their footsteps echoing off the walls. McAllister lived on the fifth floor. They paused to get their breath when they reached it.

Jackie glanced down the corridor, making sure it was clear. She didn't want any witnesses to what she was going to do. 'Follow my lead. Okay?'

At McAllister's door, Jackie steadied herself, then knocked. A dull shuffle of footsteps on the other side, coming closer. The woman's voice was muffled. 'Just leave it there.'

'Sorry, need a signature,' Jackie replied.

The click of the latch being turned, the door opening an inch, a fraction of an eye peering out.

Jackie shouldered the door open, warrant card out. 'Helen McAllister, I am arresting you for perverting the course of justice.'

The flat opened straight into the living room. Sagging sofa, threadbare beige carpet, a smell like meat left out of the fridge for too long. The TV was on low and tuned to some glamorous soap where everyone was toned and tanned and rich – a world away from McAllister's tired face, her sallow neck, her skin the colour of cigarette ash.

'What's going on?' she whimpered. 'What's happening?'

Jackie pulled a set of cuffs from her jacket pocket. 'Don't mess us about, all right?' She turned McAllister, the woman offering little resistance, and snapped the first cuff on her wrist. 'You do not have to say anything, but it may harm your defence if you do not mention when questioned something which you rely on later in court.' She closed the other cuff in place, turned her back round, and looked her in the eye. 'Anything you do say may be given in evidence.'

McAllister was wincing at the restraints, tears filling her eyes. 'I don't … I don't understand.'

'Ed Truman,' Jackie said. 'You lied about the sexual harassment, didn't you?'

Recognition, then horror. '*I didn't do anything!*'

'We know you lied. You and the others. They've both confessed – and dumped you right in it.'

'That's not true!'

McAllister tried to pull away, but Jackie tweaked the cuffs and she yelped in pain. She leaned in close to the woman's ear. 'Take one last look around. This will be the last time you see your home for *years*.'

'My children! They're at school!'

'They'll be taken into care.'

'Please! It wasn't me!'

'Save it for the station,' Jackie said, pushing her towards the door.

McAllister's eyes were wide and terrified. 'He told me to say it!'

'He?'

'He said if I didn't go to the police he'd hurt my kids.'

'That's more like it.' Jackie steered McAllister to the sofa. 'Now, let's sit down, and you can tell us what exactly he told you to say about Ed Truman.'

32

If I thought the few hours freezing at the bus stop was bad, that was like luxuriating in a five-star hotel compared to spending the night soaked and crawling with insects. Trying to get comfortable on ground that seemed to be solely comprised of knobbly tree roots, beneath a rocky overhang that frankly offered fuck-all protection once the wind shifted and the rain blew into us, all the while failing to squish a ball of leaves and muck into a pillow. No thank you. Never again.

And yet, remarkably, as the day wore on, it got worse. I would have thought that the worst part of sleeping rough was the cold. But it wasn't. The worst was getting wet. With no change of clothes and typical miserable British weather you stay wet for days. Within an hour of walking, sores bloomed on my inner thighs, my elbows, around my collar. Anywhere the material rubbed. Before long, every step was a test of endurance. The chafing couldn't have been more painful if someone were going at my skin with sandpaper.

All day we trudged through that forest, tripping over branches torn down in the storm the previous night, sinking up to our ankles in mud. Phoenix was leading the way, but that was overstating her contribution. We couldn't have been more lost if we'd woken up in a maze on the moon.

We scrambled up endless sludgy escarpments, trying to get to higher ground in the hope of seeing cars, but at the top were greeted with just another rise, this one steeper and slippier than the last. Phoenix covered her eyes and held back a sob. We hadn't eaten all day, and were both starving and scratchy and wishing we were anywhere but here, deep in some spooky woodland that wouldn't look out of place in a horror film, with little hope of finding our way out before the sunlight once again pissed off somewhere else.

We took five minutes before facing the next climb. She booted up her laptop, thankfully kept dry in a waterproof sleeve. Although she'd managed to download directions to the hideout from the farmer's Wi-Fi, they hadn't proved to be too much use to us, seeing as we'd run off in some random direction.

'No, no, *no*,' she moaned, slapping the trackpad. The little battery icon in the corner of the screen both had a line through it *and* was flashing red, which you didn't need a degree in computer science to know were bad signs. That was the problem with technology. For all the wonderful things it had brought to the world, a pencil never ran out of battery, and a piece of paper didn't shut down.

I tried my best to join Phoenix in memorising all the villages near the hideout, but I was so tired and hungry that the words wouldn't stick in my brain. She might as well have been trying to teach me Japanese. Still she kept at it, reciting names and road numbers, forehead creased in concentration.

The screen faded to black. After a moment she closed the laptop lid.

'Come on,' she sighed. 'We'd better go.'

We started on the next escarpment. As I dragged my aching body up the slope, slipping in the mud and flailing for roots to stop myself plummeting back down, I thought about Gabrielle, what she'd say if she could see me now. How she'd hold me and make me warm. How, when I finally made it back home, I'd tell her things were going to change, *I* was going to change – and right then I wondered if she was thinking about me the way I was thinking about her.

33

6 P.M., MONDAY

Gabrielle Truman reached for her previous outfit, the burgundy maxi dress, and struggled back into it. She'd spent over an hour trying on clothes, all the while drinking too much wine and trying not to think about what she mustn't do tonight, what would be disgraceful and insane and so utterly wrong to do tonight, but what the excited twist in her stomach told her she might do – she could imagine it happening, had imagined it on repeat since meeting Benedict yesterday – going over and over it until she wanted to scream. Although that was hardly surprising. Not a moment went by these last few days when she didn't feel like screaming.

She straightened the straps of her dress in the mirror, pleased at how the pleated fabric hid the worst of her stress eating, then staggered into a pair of beachy sandals with ivory shells studding the strap. Was this too much? Shouldn't she be in sackcloth and sweatpants?

She felt the indignation unfurl inside her, and grabbed onto it before it could disappear again. Why should *she* be the victim? She'd thought continuously about the half-hour spent with Benedict yesterday, her stomach jumping each time, but what else was she supposed to think about? Her daughter? As if Alison Miriam Truman ever gave two thoughts to anyone else! Sneaking around with her double life and expecting her mum to come up with lies to cover for her – and she was sick of doing it! This wasn't the first time their daughter had disappeared. It was just the first time Ed had found out about it.

Thank God she was safe though, that was the main thing. Gabrielle had been sick with worry that their daughter was in danger, but then another text came from her at lunchtime today, as brief as the last one, saying she was going to stay away a bit longer. You'd think, what with her Ed being accused of *murder*, she'd race back to be with her family, but maybe she hadn't seen the news? Gabrielle said in her reply that she needed to come home, as in right *now*, but Alison didn't respond. Why couldn't she just sit her father down, and say, *Dad, I'm gay*. How hard would that be? Ed had watched *Ellen*. The world was full of lesbians! What did she think he'd do if he found out? Disown her? Demand she stopped seeing her girlfriend? Although maybe it wasn't surprising Alison was so self-absorbed, with Ed as a father. *What had he dragged his family into?*

Gabrielle felt tears surge towards her eyes and just about managed to cut them off with her fingers before they ruined her mascara. The last couple of years had been *so hard* for her, trying to get her career back, and now she was teaching and getting commissions and putting on an exhibition and instead of supporting her like she'd supported him for *all these years* he'd sunk deeper into his self-indulgent rut. And heaven forbid she try to talk to him about his drinking! Now all *this*. On the run with some *girl*? She'd seen the CCTV pictures of them on the news, on the night bus like they were coming home from a drunken bar crawl. Was he sleeping with her? Was he going to meet her when he took that taxi to town on Saturday night? How long had he—

The shriek of the doorbell ripped through her thoughts. *That's him.* Her heart went wild in her chest, hurling itself against her ribs, wine surging back up her throat and filling her mouth with an acid taste. *Stay calm. Don't think this into something more than it actually is.* Benedict was just coming over to keep her company. Nothing more sinister than that. He was a good listener, that was all. Who else was she supposed to talk to? Mitchell? The garden shed would be more responsive than her son. Even without his computer, he barely set foot outside his room. As for her friends, they were kind and supportive and always on hand, but she knew everything they were going to say before they said it, and talking to them just reflected her own worry back on herself, intensifying her anxiety.

She could speak her truth to Benedict – that she was furious with Alison, beyond furious with Ed – without him looking at her in horror. Not like that mean cow who interviewed her at the police station, who'd *repeatedly* asked her why she'd left her husband if she didn't think he sexually harassed those women, despite her saying that she *didn't* leave, she just went to stay with her parents for the night to get some *space* from him after he'd lied. The detective didn't look married. How could she possibly hope to understand what it was like? Sometimes you needed a night or two apart.

Gabrielle opened the front door. She caught her breath and tried to pass if off in a smile. He was even more attractive than she remembered. She couldn't move her eyes from him. He was dressed more casually than last time, in a grey polo neck and a black jacket with a slight military cut. If she was honest, she'd always wanted Ed to dress like this, but he'd never been in stylishness, preferring jeans with just about everything.

As he handed her a bottle of red wine, her mind flooded with images of them as a couple – walking arm-in-arm through Soho Square, sipping Prosecco at the opening of the latest hot young artist at White Cube, relaxing beside the pool of some white-washed Aegean villa – and she had to give herself a stern telling off to get her shit together, because what she was thinking was crazy. Crazy! She was married. Okay, not always *happily* married, but who was? She and Ed had their issues, but day-to-day they got by just fine. In twenty years, she'd never even been tempted by anyone else, yet here she was daydreaming a whole life with a stranger. *Pull yourself together, woman!*

Yet, even in this telling-off, another voice was saying, *Isn't it how these things happen? That you meet someone new when you least expect it?*

Could there be any more unexpected time than now?

On the way to the lounge, Benedict paused by a set of three framed prints on the wall. They were from her new collection, experiments in form and material, the bodies of the life models who'd posed for them twisted into whirlwind shapes, above shadows made from crushed glass.

'These are incredible,' he said. 'Who's the artist? I'd love to get some for our city office.'

Her hand went to her throat. She felt the heat creeping around her neck. 'I . . . I did those.'

He looked at her closely, then shook his head, like he was snapping himself out of a trance. 'Well, you are one talented lady, let me tell you that. I'm impressed! A real artist! I dabble a bit myself. Just watercolours, fields and clouds, horizons, that kind of thing. Nothing like . . . this.' He nodded to the bottle of wine in her hand. 'Now let's get that open, and you can tell me all about where you get your inspiration.'

Benedict settled on the sofa, as out of place on their family-worn furniture as a Monet in a pub toilet, while she went to the kitchen to find the corkscrew. Her hand shook as she dug through the drawers. She should tell him to leave. She saw the way he was looking at her; she knew what he'd come here for. *Just because you find each other attractive, it doesn't mean anything has to happen.*

She couldn't ask him to leave straight away, not after he'd made the effort to come round. One drink, they'd have one drink, then she'd say she had a headache. That was okay, right?

'Here's the thing,' he said, after they'd toasted their wine and taken a sip. 'If you want to talk about your husband, that's fine. If you want to talk about something else, that's fine too. I'm just here to keep you company. I know what it's like when life becomes … traumatic. I…' He frowned, cleared his throat. 'When I lost my wife, I remember thinking how much I just wanted to have a normal conversation with someone. You know? Just a … a *chat*. Without them tilting their head and nodding like it was okay if I wanted to cry. Exactly like you're doing now.'

'Oh God,' Gabrielle said. 'I'm so sorry. I just – you know – your wife…'

'That's okay. It's many moons ago now. I'll always love her, but…' He gave a sad smile and waved his hand. 'You can't live in the past. I'm ready to love again.' He broke into a sudden laugh. 'That sounds cheesy! But it's true. I spent so many years fighting feeling that way, and I don't want to fight any more. I want to live.'

She heard a sound behind her and noticed Benedict looking over her shoulder. She turned her head and saw Mitchell in the doorway – *Mitchell*! How could she forget he was here? Of course he was. Where else would he be?

'Hi sweetie,' Gabrielle said, pulling up the top of her dress, even though it hadn't slipped down. 'Would you like something to eat? This is my … friend, Benedict.'

But Benedict was already up, already striding towards Mitchell, his hand out to shake. She expected her son to shrink into himself, like he always did around new people, but instead his face did something she hadn't seen for a long time – it opened into a smile.

'A fine-looking young man,' Benedict said, as they shook.

Mitchell straightened his back and mumbled something about

getting a snack. He returned a moment later with a giant bag of Doritos clutched to his chest, and even gave them another grin as he headed out of the lounge.

'Wow,' Gabrielle said. 'You got more smiles from him in the last two minutes than I've got in the last two *years*.'

Benedict shrugged like it was no big deal. 'The secret with boys like that is you've got to treat them like men.'

'I should write that down.'

'I can't imagine how hard this must be for you – and for him.'

'*Hard?* I … I don't even know where to begin…'

He put down his glass and gazed kindly into her eyes. 'Begin wherever you want. I'm here to listen.'

She started slow at first, talking factually about her family, the kids, where she met Ed and how long they'd been married, but whether it was the wine or exhaustion or just the freedom to speak without fear of him running off to gossip to everyone she knew, she found herself opening up like she was lying on a therapist's couch, telling him things that she'd been too ashamed to admit, even to herself. How in her marriage to Ed she always felt in competition with his work, how it made him stressed and distracted to the detriment of their relationship, but there was never any question of putting her first – maybe he'd pay her more attention if she was one of the battered women he was so fond of defending. And wasn't she an awful person for even thinking that! (No, no, he murmured. You're not.) Why couldn't *he* have stayed home to raise the kids? Put *his* career on hold? Yes, he earned enough, but who knows how much she could have earned? She loved her family, she'd given the last sixteen years to the kids, but she was finally getting *herself* back, producing the best work of her life, and now this was happening, and what? She was supposed to just sit here and pick up all the pieces while her husband and daughter swanned off and her son ignored her and here she was with so much to offer the world—

She'd held back the first sob for as long as possible, but once that broke from her mouth the dam came crashing down, and soon she was crying hard. Benedict held her, telling her it was okay to feel her feelings, they were her feelings and she shouldn't be guilty about having them, because there was no right and there was no wrong. There was just here and now.

'I'm a horrible, horrible human being,' she said.

'No you're not.'

'I deserve everything that's happening to me for even thinking these things.'

'You're a beautiful, wonderful person.'

When he placed his hand on her cheek, an electric spark ran thrillingly down her neck. This was wrong. She needed to stop this *now*.

'I can't,' she whispered. 'My husband.'

'Your husband's not here,' he replied, touching his lips to hers. 'But I am.'

34

As they sped towards the Truman house, the sun dropped behind the trees, the sky the purple of a faded bruise. Jackie extended the touchscreen from under the glove compartment and brought up the internet search history from Ed Truman's work computer. All that extreme pornography, the searches for cable ties and chloroform. She tried to imagine him sneaking up behind someone with a soaked cloth in his hand. She just couldn't see it.

Drum's voice: *Stop second-guessing yourself.*

When pressed with the details – the dropped bank note, the threat to their children – the two women who had filed charges against Truman had cracked as quickly as McAllister. Now she wanted to chat to Gabrielle Truman again, to see if she'd been approached by the same men who'd coerced those women.

Jackie glanced over at Keyes. The detective sergeant was still glaring through the windscreen, saying nothing. She'd been that way since they left Helen McAllister's. At first Jackie had let her get away with it, this petulant child act, but she couldn't have her like this when they were questioning the wife.

'Go on, then,' Jackie said. 'Out with it.'

'Out with what, boss?' Keyes replied, deadpan.

'This attitude.'

'No attitude.'

'*Charlotte*.'

'Concentrating on the road, boss.'

'Stop with the "boss" shit, okay? Just pull over.'

'We're on the motorway!'

'I don't care. Pull over – pull over, now. That's an order.'

Keyes dragged the wheel left, swerving them onto the hard shoulder and screeched to a stop. Her lips were pressed so tight they'd all but disappeared into her mouth.

'Detective Sergeant,' Jackie said, and waited for Keyes to look at her. 'I'm going to give you one chance to say whatever it is you have to say, or we'll go back to the office and I'll find myself a real copper to work the case with me.'

Keyes squeezed the top of the wheel, breathing heavily through her nose. The car rocked as an articulated lorry went past in the slow lane. Red taillights sped into the distance.

'You do realise we're after *murderers* here?' Jackie said. 'While you're sitting there with the fucking hump.'

'I didn't like you roughing up Helen McAllister. It's not right.'

'She was in cuffs for less than a minute.'

'The whole good cop, bad cop thing. It's like something from the eighties.'

'Oh, grow up.'

'But—'

'What happened to being *desperate* to work for me?'

'It's not right to lie to the public.'

'She lied, so why not us?'

Keyes gripped the wheel harder. 'We're the police. We're supposed to be above that.'

Jackie snorted. *Saint fucking Charlotte Keyes.* 'Listen to you. Where'd you transfer from? The Girl Guides?'

'I know what's right and what's not.'

'Tell me, Sergeant. Has anyone you love ever been murdered?'

'What? No, but—'

'I used to be the same as you,' Jackie said. She couldn't deal with this. Not today. 'No doubt you'll learn the hard way that you're wrong.'

Keyes looked at her pleadingly. 'If we don't stay on the right side of law, then what's the point?'

'The *only* point is to catch the scum that murdered an innocent girl.'

'I just feel—'

'Okay, Sergeant, your opinion has been noted.' Jackie waved towards the road. 'Let's get on, eh?'

'But—'

'I said *drive*.'

35

Gabrielle jerked her head away from Benedict. The shrill ring of the doorbell had cut through the haze of his kisses like a fire alarm. Their initial tenderness had rapidly given way to more passionate fumbling, and her lipstick was smeared, her maxi dress up round her thighs. What if that was Ed? They stayed frozen, facing each other, Benedict panting slightly, a bead of saliva still on his lips.

The truth of what she'd done – *cheated on her husband* – slammed into her. She pulled out of Benedict's arms and dragged a tea towel over her mouth like she was wiping away fingerprints. Wine burned back up her throat. How was she going to explain what she was wearing, the empty glasses, the *other man* in Ed's place?

The bell went again, followed by the metallic clank of the letterbox being flipped open. A woman's voice called through. 'Mrs Truman? Are you there? It's DCI Jackie Rose and DS Charlotte Keyes.'

Oh God, what if Ed was hurt? What if he was *dead*?

Gabrielle rushed to open the front door. 'Is it Ed? Is he okay?'

On the step were the detectives from the station, the short one with the bitch face, and the taller, younger one.

'Mind if we come in?' Detective Rose said, stepping into the house before Gabrielle could reply.

Gabrielle checked her dress straps, feeling like one had slipped off her shoulder. 'I just … I've got—'

'A friend come to keep her company.'

All eyes went to Benedict, standing in the entrance to the lounge. Detective Rose flashed her warrant card at him. 'And you are?'

'Just a friend,' he replied.

'Well Mrs Truman, and *friend*' – the detective said the word as though she'd been watching them through the window – 'can you spare us a few minutes of your evening? We can either do it here, or if you'd prefer at a local station.'

'I can't leave,' Gabrielle replied. 'My son's upstairs…'

Detective Rose made an *after you* gesture to the lounge. 'I guess we'll do it here. That is, unless you're not interested in helping us find your husband?'

'No, no, of course. Please come through.' Gabrielle led the way, her heart still pounding in the hollow of her throat. 'Can I … do you want a drink?'

'That'd be lovely,' Rose said. 'I'll have a tea, please. White, one sugar. Charlotte, you'll have one, won't you?'

The other officer cleared her throat. 'Sure, okay.'

In the lounge, Gabrielle's cheeks flushed at the empty wine glasses, the smushed sofa cushion, the tea towel smeared with lipstick as bright and red as arterial blood, the whole scene reeking of guilt. She felt like a kid caught by her parents bunking off school. It was clear from that bitch detective's sneer that she knew what had been going on. And what she thought of it.

Detective Rose gave Gabrielle a forced smile. 'How about that cuppa, eh?'

*

Jackie stared at the man hovering by the sofa after Gabrielle Truman went to make the drinks. The man stared back.

He didn't fit the description exactly – the hair was different, and he wore glasses – but straight away Jackie knew two things. One, this was the man who'd threatened the women into filing the sexual harassment reports against Ed Truman. Two, he was serious trouble. A proper bad guy.

How did she know? Easy. Most normal people, when faced with the police, especially those investigating a murder, got flustered, over-polite, glancing round like they'd just fled a crime scene. What they did not do was make hard eye contact, unblinking, like a gunslinger waiting for someone to shout, *Draw!*

'I'm sorry,' Jackie said. 'I didn't catch your name.'

'Benedict Silver,' he replied. 'I'm a business associate of Gabrielle's husband.'

'Bit late in the evening to be discussing business, isn't it?' Jackie said. 'And difficult without Mr Truman here.'

'I'm also *her* friend.'

Jackie made a point of taking in the wine glasses, the messy sofa. 'I can see that.'

'I didn't realise you were the friend police.'

'Good job, isn't it? Otherwise you'd be under arrest.'

His eyes still hadn't moved from hers. 'What for?'

'I'm sure we could find something.'

Keyes cleared her throat. The wife was back with the teas. Jackie took one off her, then sat in the armchair.

Gabrielle Truman perched on the end of the sofa, her hands clasped and face set like she was expecting the worst. Benedict Silver, if that was his name, stayed standing.

'Please, sir,' Jackie said, nodding for him to sit, 'make yourself comfortable.' He lowered himself down. *Good boy.*

She opened the case folder and stalled for time by flipping

through it – no point in asking Gabrielle if she knew the man who'd forced Helen McAllister and her husband's other accusers to go to the police when he was sitting right here. She grabbed the CCTV stills of Ed Truman and the girl.

'These are images taken on Sunday morning,' Jackie said, passing them to Gabrielle. 'You probably saw them in the papers. Your husband and this young woman took the 2.38 a.m. bus from King's Cross, arriving at Cockfosters at 3.22. Do you know where your husband might be going at that time? Any friends? Relatives?' She glanced at Silver. '*Business associates?*'

'No...' she replied. 'No one I can think of.'

'And the girl? Do you recognise her?'

Truman shook her head, her mouth sour. 'I've never seen her before.'

'Could she be one of your daughter's friends?'

'Not one that I know.'

The wife handed the pictures back. Instead of putting them away, Jackie paused, then held them out to Silver. 'How about you, sir? Would you care to take a look?'

He cocked his head at her, a bit cautious, a bit amused, a whole lot of something she couldn't read. 'Why would *I* need to look?'

'You never know.'

'Sure,' he said. 'Okay.'

He took the pictures. The muscles around his eyes tightened. 'Sorry,' he said, leaning forward to hand them back. 'I don't know her.'

When Jackie took hold of them, he kept his grip for an extra second. A shiver ran across her shoulders. *Trouble with a capital T.*

His smile crept higher. 'Looks like you're not far from blowing this case wide open, Detective.'

Jackie froze as she put the stills back in the folder. Her heart seemed to stop for a very long time. 'What was that?'

'I said,' Silver replied, a glimmer of mischief in his cold eyes, 'that it looks like you're not far from *blowing this case wide open*.'

He knew about Lester and Verity. He knew how they were killed.

Jackie closed the folder and stood up. 'Well, we'd better get back,' she said, and looked wistfully at her tea. 'Such a shame, I never get to finish my cuppa. One of the downsides of the job.'

Gabrielle Truman's hand went to her throat. 'That's it?'

'That's all for now,' Jackie replied. 'Sorry to disturb your evening. Don't get up, we'll show ourselves out.'

'No update, or—'

'Sorry, ma'am. We'll be in touch.'

As they left the room, Jackie didn't need to look round to know Silver's eyes were following her the whole way.

Outside, the road was lit by streetlights. Keyes rubbed her arms against the chill and said, 'It's him. That bloke in there? Blue eyes, well built, handsome. We've heard that description three times today. Let's bring him in.'

'On what charge?'

'Coercion, assault. Perverting the course of justice.'

'If he's working for Carmichael he's probably got a room of lawyers ready to get him off on a technicality. Besides, I want him for what we *can't* prove yet.'

Keyes looked confused. 'What's that?'

'Murder.'

'There's no evidence.'

'Call it a hunch,' Jackie replied.

For the first time in days, the knot in her mind had loosened. She knew a killer when she saw one, and there were never two of them in a case like this – if 'Mr Benedict Silver' didn't have a direct connection to the death of Ivana Kostimarov then she might as well hand in her card and take up fishing.

'And what about Truman's DNA at the scene?' asked Keyes. 'The fact he's on the run?'

'All good questions, Sergeant.' Jackie pulled out her phone. 'Give me a second. I need to make a call.'

She waited for Keyes to walk away. A sporty blue Jaguar F-Type convertible was squatting outside the house, incongruous among the saloons and station wagons parked along the street. No doubt it had an in-built GPS connecting to Jaguar's cloud service. All you needed to access those records was a warrant.

Well, usually.

'Evening, Trav,' Jackie said, when the call connected. 'Remember how you owe me a favour? I need to cash it in. Off the books...'

36

Gabrielle pitched forward on the sofa. What was she *doing*? How had she let herself get into this situation? She wanted to drag her nails down her face, to tear out clumps of her hair, to scream herself hoarse. Her family was falling apart and here she was getting off with some bloke like a cheap slapper after last orders.

'It's okay,' Benedict said, rubbing small circles on her back. 'You've done nothing wrong.'

'I'm sorry. I'm so sorry.'

'So this? Us?'

'I can't…' She caught his sorrowful expression. 'It's not you. You're great. You're … perfect. You're handsome, and funny, and kind.'

'And rich!' he chimed in.

She smiled, wiping her eyes. 'There's that too. But—'

'I hate it when there's a but!'

'I'm married.'

He took her hands, looked deep into her eyes. 'Are you sure you don't want to be with me? The other option might not be as good.'

Gabrielle flinched. Did he mean Ed? Her husband of twenty years reduced to 'the other option'?

'I can't, Benedict,' she said. 'Really—'

'Please, say no more. I understand.' He nodded towards the

kitchen. 'Before I go, do you mind if I make a cup of tea? I just need something to help sober up before I hit the road.'

'Of course, of course,' she said, starting to stand, but he gestured for her to sit.

'I run a global venture capital company. I'm pretty sure I can make a round of tea.'

If she was honest, she'd rather be on her own. She had a lot of thinking to do, some deep soul-searching, and she wasn't sure she was going to like what she found.

'Come on,' he said, flashing her that smile, his hands up, unarmed. 'Let's not end the night with the police and tears. Let me get you one too. Just milk, right?'

He was being so good about it. Plenty of men would be fuming at her for leading them on. And she was going to make herself one anyway when he'd gone …

'Go on, then,' she said.

He came back a few minutes later with two steaming mugs. She felt terrible about this, he was such a sweet man. 'Have you tried internet dating?' she asked. 'I've got so many friends who married people they met online.'

Benedict twisted his beautiful lips like this was a stance he regularly had to justify. 'Call me old-fashioned, but I like to *meet* someone in person before I ask them on a date. Anyway.' He lifted his mug, and when he spoke his voice was soft with nostalgia. 'Meeting you will be a sweet memory.'

What if this was a mistake? What if he was the best thing to happen to her, and she was letting him go?

No, this was the right thing to do.

'To sweet memories,' she said. Their mugs made a gentle *tung* when they touched.

They drank their tea and chatted for a while about her new class on tonal value in colour. He told her about a funny incident that happened during a pitch in Geneva last month, where he didn't know the investor was Swiss-German. He thought the man was asking for nine per cent of the company, whereas in fact he was just saying *nein*...

As Benedict spoke, Gabrielle suddenly felt her body slipping sideways, until she was leaning against the back cushion. At first she thought she must be drunk, but she knew that wasn't right, she hadn't had nearly enough wine. Was it a delayed reaction from the police visit? Her body going into shock and shutting down? She tried to open her mouth, to tell Benedict. Only then did she realise the truth.

'Ah,' he said, his smile warm. 'I think it's working.'

In her head she was screaming for her body to work. All the voluntary movements she'd taken for granted were gone. How to open her mouth, or kick her legs, or curl her fingers into a fist. She watched as he lifted her arm – feeling his fingers grasping her wrist – and let it drop. The impact reverberated up to her shoulder. She ordered her muscles to *Move! Move!* Nothing happened.

'Shhh, don't panic,' he said, giving her the charming smile that only an hour ago had her dreaming of a new life with him. She cringed inside at her stupidity. 'It's only an ammonium compound. It works to block neuromuscular activity. You'll still be able to breathe, and it'll wear off in a few hours. You'll be fine. I promise. Okay?' He stroked her cheek with the back of his fingertips. 'It's a shame, though. I think you would have enjoyed it. Now, not so much.'

He left the room, and came back a few minutes later. She watched him root through a rucksack and bring out a red, silky eye mask with little white hearts embroidered on the front, the kind of thing you might wear if you were being kinky with your husband.

'A smile can be touched up,' Benedict said, slipping the mask over her head. 'But you can't do much with the eyes.'

He kissed her tenderly on the lips, then he began.

37

Phoenix and I carried on trudging through the mud. Eventually we saw a stretch of road in the distance that she thought went to Kimpton, which we could follow to Allenby, a village near to the hideout.

We rushed downhill, across a field, the air thick with the smell of wet cow dung, and crouched behind a thick hedgerow until we were sure no cars were coming. Staying behind the hedge, we followed the road, finding an old-fashioned wooden sign, the pointed hands engraved with town names and the distance down to a quarter-mile.

Allenby 2—.

Phoenix whooped and pumped her fist. I remained less enthused – the afternoon was fading fast. As the vast country sky darkened, we upped the pace, staying on the road now, but neither of us had much in the tank. The light was already a heavy shade of grey by the time we hit the outskirts of Allenby. I was so ravenous I could think of nothing else. It felt like my stomach was digesting itself in the hope of finding something lodged in the lining. My thoughts were getting reckless. *You're a lawyer, right? Just give yourself up and worry about it later. By the time you get out, this whole thing will have blown over. Until then you could get some warm food, some dry clothes, a bed and a blanket and—*

I forced myself to remember what Phoenix had said about torture. It wouldn't be hard to get to me in a prison cell, to extract the details of the hideout. I bet I'd recall them pretty quickly if someone was waterboarding me with a bucket of urine.

It was too densely wooded to go round the back of the village. We went through it instead, alert to any people or passing traffic. A couple of residential turn-offs, a little garden square bordered by a newsagent, a charity shop and a deli with some dusty-looking doughnuts on its display shelves, and then we were out the other side. We headed down a narrow country road to Saddleton, the village closest to the hideout. Less than a mile to go.

The world was an ominous shade of charcoal, the clouds low and looming with rain. A light drizzle started. I kept my head down, pushing one foot forward, then the next, wincing at the ache in my muscles, the million sores beneath my clothes. Every step was an effort of will. I doubted I would last much longer.

Phoenix started whimpering. Even though I could barely make out her face I saw the panic on it all too clearly. 'This isn't right,' she said.

'What do you mean it's not right?'

'The road! It's not this one! We should have seen a turning for Saddleton by now.'

She couldn't seem to catch her breath. I held onto her, telling her it was okay, we'd just retrace our steps, but she was losing it, hunger and exhaustion ripping down her defences. She was trembling and clinging onto me as I guided us back the way we had come, but we were moving slowly. Soon it was so dark it felt like we were stumbling through a void.

We shuffled forward with our hands out, trying to stay on the road. The drizzle quickly turned into a downpour as the wind kicked up. Soaked and shivering, we pushed on, the going soft, until we came to a sheer wall of vegetation. Where had the road gone? I turned us around, tried to retrace our steps, but the tarmac had vanished. Phoenix gripped my arm, her teeth chattering.

'D-don't leave me,' she said. 'Please don't leave me.'

'It's okay,' I replied. 'We're okay.'

Everything was black. We couldn't see a thing. The grass was slippery and tilting slightly down. *Where's the fucking road!* I tried to slide my feet along, but must have misjudged it, because suddenly the ground wasn't there. Reality shot out and up, hung in the air for a long horrifying second, during which I wondered if I'd flown over the side of a precipice, then slammed down with full force on my right hip. I began sliding. I thrashed around to stop myself, flinging out a hand, grabbing something jagged that cut into my fingers, but managing to hold on.

Phoenix was screaming. The sound was moving away from me, then abruptly stopped. I dragged myself back up the slope, hollering her name into the wind, straining to hear a reply.

'Stay where you are!' I shouted to her, trying to work out where her cries for help were coming from.

I skidded on my side down a shallow incline, dragging my fingers in the mud to keep control. Her voice was getting louder. I found her foot, her leg, then the rest of her. She grabbed onto me, shaking.

'I-I thought ... I thought you were going ... to leave me here.'

I helped her up. 'Let's find some shelter.'

We were in serious danger. One stop from hypothermia, the doors closing fast. We found a dryish spot in the dirt beneath some branches, and I wrapped the jacket around us.

Phoenix was shivering so hard it felt like she was having convulsions. 'I ca— I can't stop ... shiv— shiv—'

'It's a good sign. It means your body's trying to produce heat. If you're cold and you stop shivering, *that's* when you need to worry.'

She tried to speak again, but I told her to save her energy. I remembered the scar on her neck – what if she was still recovering from her illness and her immune system was shot? The only thing that could possibly make my situation even worse would be the police finding me with *another* dead girl.

I wrapped myself around her. After a while her shivers subsided, her breaths going low and shallow, each one so faint it sounded like her last. I carried on holding her, trying to rub some warmth into her back, praying for the storm to calm down so we'd make it through the night. Although once the rain had subsided, the wind fading to a chilly breeze, I kind of wished it would come back again. If only for the distraction.

That was the problem with being sober: clarity.

All day, my subconscious had been churning the conversation with Phoenix from the night before, and now, without a drink to fuzz the lines, I saw where they led so clearly that it made me want to cower. The state of my relationship with my children was all down to me. I pushed them away to protect myself, then spent years drinking the pain of this decision into submission.

My father wasn't a loving man. One of my earliest memories was of his giant hand looming down, then the sharp sting of his slap on my skin. We all lived in fear of his moods, especially when he'd been drinking – I didn't see him hit my mum many times, but I heard it all too often from the top of the stairs, where I'd crouch with my younger brother Noah and listen to them row. When I was old enough to understand that it wasn't right, I asked Mum why she stayed with him. She said Jewish families didn't get divorced. What she meant was that the shame of being a pariah in the community would hurt more than being slapped around. My dad knew that too. That was the first time I understood the power that one person can have over another, and how easily that power can be abused.

I never forgave my dad when he was alive. In fact, we never

mentioned my childhood. I thought about bringing it up, especially once Mum passed away, and I was the only one left to look after him – Noah had buggered off to Australia long before and had no interest in coming back to share the burden – but I'd learnt to push my feelings down for so long that I didn't even know where to find them any more. Instead I punished him by letting him die alone.

He'd been ill for a while, so I was expecting the call from the care home, the one saying I had to come and say goodbye. When they rang, I let it go to voicemail. On the message they said he was asking for me. I needed to come *right now*. I didn't go. I sat in my office, drinking and working. I worked all through the night. When I called back in the morning, he was gone.

Not even Gabrielle knew about that. I should have told her, but I was too ashamed, and was happy for her to mistake my self-loathing for grief.

I don't think I ever understood how to love my children. I was at my best with them when they were toddlers. We had so much fun, and I thought that I had this, being a dad. I could do it. Then Ally started growing up and, perfectly naturally, wanted her own space, her own life. I still remember how much that hurt, and how stupid I felt for being that hurt, because she wasn't rejecting me, not like my father rejected me and my brother, but I couldn't seem to stop feeling that way, and maybe when Mitchell turned that age I was a bit more ready for it. Maybe I'd always kept a distance from him, so as to not get hurt again. That was why my son told me to my face how much he hated me.

I said I'd never be drunk and abusive like my father, but instead I'd been drunk and elusive, which might even be worse. I barely knew my children, and they barely knew me.

If I got another chance I wouldn't mess it up. I'd cut back my hours at the practice, maybe even take on another partner, be there to consult rather than represent clients. I'd let Gabrielle take me clothes shopping – and next time perhaps we could *both* get our faces injected with chemicals. I'd not only drop Ally off at demonstrations, but march alongside her, and really listen to what she was telling me instead of smiling and nodding and saying, *That's so awful/great/interesting, sweetie*, while thinking about when I could have a drink. I'd sit with Mitchell and tell him he could talk to me about what was going on in his head, his life, no judgements, just so he knew I was there if he needed. It tore my heart to think of him as being as unhappy as me.

I knew that if I could make it home, I would be a better father, a better husband, a better man.

The first step to doing that was getting my daughter back.

I'll find you, Ally. I promise.

38

THE BOX

Her name. What was her name? She'd been clinging to it like a life raft, but now it was gone. She couldn't hold onto any of her thoughts. As soon as one appeared it drifted away from her, fast as a soap bubble on a breeze, leaving her mind blank. Emptied out.

Okay, forget her name. Focus on the box. There had to be a weakness, an emergency exit, a way to get out. Inside was dark, lit by a single inset LED near her neck, so weak that anything past her waist was in black. Screens made from some kind of toughened plastic covered the front and sides – you could scratch your fingers down to the bone and not leave so much as a mark. Steel cords ran from the plastic manacles around her wrists, ankles and neck into the back. She could turn on her side, lift her knee to her chest, stretch enough to keep her muscles from seizing, but not enough to ever be comfortable. When a session started, the cords retracted and locked her in place on her back, so she couldn't curl up and cower from what he was making her endure.

Once more she ran her fingers in methodical lines along the walls, feeling for an imperfection, a hidden button, something that might open the box from the inside. The movement was also keeping her calm. She felt it churning, a burning stew of anguish and panic and dread in her stomach, and if she stopped her focus even for a second it would bubble out and slosh through her body, spreading its poison to every part of her until she was shrieking and clawing at the walls, begging to be let out. In other words, how she reacted when she was first imprisoned. It did no good then, and she was sure it would do no good now.

Nothing. No hidden compartments or secret levers. Only the screens, the manacles, and the drinking tube running in from the left side. At first she'd refused the tube – a green light beside it flashed when it was starting – but he sent such a powerful electric shock through the metal pads embedded in her shapeless grey clothes that next time the green light came on she couldn't suck the tube fast enough. A thick, fishy slush that put her in mind of frogspawn had flowed into her mouth. For days, that was all she'd eaten.

Had it been days already? It must have been, although she really had no idea. There was nothing to judge it against. Either she was here, alone and in silence, or she was being forced to watch the videos. Once they started, they went on for hours. Sometimes they were snippets of sitcoms, or sunny home movies from some family she'd never seen before, and during these the electrodes would warm pleasantly. There must be drugs in the slush because despite everything, this hell she was trapped in, she felt euphoric watching them. When the other films came on, that was when things got *bad*. Women kissing other women, or little boys dressing as girls, along with enough volts going through her body to arch her back, teeth gritted, straining against the manacle around her neck. By the end it always felt as though a wrecking ball had smashed through her brain, reducing it to rubble. She feared that was the point.

She started on the right wall with her finger, sweeping it in long, careful lines, top to bottom. There had to be *something*.

The screens came to life.

Oh God, it's starting!

The manacles retracted, pulling her into place. All around her was a red, pulsing landscape, a rolling, sliding, convulsing nightmare of shadows and indistinct shapes that loomed close to her and shifted quickly away. *What's happening?*

A weird soundtrack started, rending metal and insect clicks and a faint noise like someone screaming far away. She tried to focus on a single point because she was losing it, really losing it. She couldn't get her breath. This was too much. It felt like she was being sucked deep into the throat of a demon. She had to get out of there. She tried to move, but the manacles held her tight. Something pricked in her arm and when she looked she saw a needle retracting from the side of the box. What had he given her? The images came faster. Something dark and awful seemed to pass into her eyes, burrowing into her soul, where it ripped and shrieked and writhed as she strained against the manacles and screamed for it to get out, get out, *get out—*

39

Jackie got home close to ten. The lights were off, the air was cold. The house, as always, was empty.

She went through to the kitchen and fell heavily onto a chair. The first five minutes back were always the worst, even on a normal day. Right on cue, the masochist in her mind served her vivid memories – Verity at the table, her curly black hair spilling over her face as she bent close to her colouring book, always so meticulous about keeping inside the lines; Lester at the cooker, stirring spices into a sizzling pan. Jackie closed her eyes and inhaled, conjuring the smell of his chicken fajitas, her favourite. It was a good job he was such an amazing cook. Left to her, they would've subsisted on overcooked scrambled eggs and tomato soup straight from the can. As she did now.

She knew she should eat something then go to bed, get some rest, she'd been going full tilt for days, but once the box was open it was impossible to stuff the pain back inside and close it up. How could it be otherwise, with only the hum of the fridge and the tick of the wall clock and the endless thoughts of what had been stolen from her for company? How different she'd been all those years ago, back in training. How naive and idealistic – not so different from Keyes. *Everyone deserves a second chance* – that used to be her standard reply when asked about criminal justice. Try saying that

186

once you've watched your husband and daughter being blown up by a car bomb meant for you.

Seven years since they were murdered. Seven years since her life was stolen.

It was late, but fuck it. She needed to work this off.

In the basement, Jackie stripped off her blouse and trousers, and faced up to her battered wing chun dummy. She'd been a UK junior martial arts champion at fifteen, and in another life might have turned professional, if she hadn't been so set on joining the force. Her father had been a DI in the Met, and from before she could remember it had been her dream to be a detective like him.

She started on the top half of the dummy, building up speed as she moved through combinations, centre line punches, turning punches, working the different hand shapes, glad for the solid slap of the wood on her skin. *Standing on the doorstep. Lester opening the car door, helping Verity climb inside. Her daughter taking one last look around. One last wave to Mum.* Jackie slammed the posts harder, tears streaming down her cheeks. What would their life be like now if they were still here? Verity would be eleven, off to secondary school, thinking about what she wanted to do with her life. She was so smart, even at that age. She could have done anything. Such a sweet soul, too, with just enough mischief to make her an interesting person to be around, even when she was a baby.

Jackie switched to leg drills, calf, thigh, knee to the middle. The lactic acid in her muscles was building up, but she gritted through it, welcoming the chance to transfer the pain in her mind into her body. *Oh, Lester.* No one had ever understood her like him. He knew that she was intense, focused, and never took her frustration with a case as irritation with him. He was too well-grounded for that, too sure of his own beliefs, his own place in the world – and right then she saw his smile, heard his laugh, the low *uh-huh-huh* chuckle he saved for something *really* funny, their wedding day, his eyes when she said *I do*, the feel of his lips, the tender way they would press their faces together after a kiss, the smell of him on the bedsheets, the contented sound he made when he had his first sip of coffee in the morning, and she slammed her elbow into the top of the dummy, making it spin around.

Panting hard, she draped herself over the top of the varnished wood. Time to shut the box again. She needed to stop thinking about murders past when there were murderers on the loose right now.

*

A hot shower, then Jackie set up at the kitchen table. Laptop, case file, jar of peanut butter and a spoon.

That man, Benedict Silver, the one with Gabrielle Truman. He was the key. But who was he? One of Ed Truman's 'business associates', as he claimed? And what was he doing with Mrs Truman? Were they having an affair? Was this whole thing a way to get the husband out of the picture? No, it was too intricate, too *involved*. It would be just as easy to kill Ed Truman himself as some innocent girl.

Looks like you're not far from blowing this case wide open.

Jackie ate a spoon of peanut butter. One thing was for certain, Benedict Silver knew who *she* was. Sure, it wouldn't be hard to find out about her past – even now a search of her name online threw up news links about what happened – but it was the way he used that information to taunt her, like he wanted to draw her attention to him.

Why was Ed Truman being fitted up for murder? Because that was the truth of it. Jackie felt it from the way her shoulders were loose; she knew it from the clarity in her mind. Silver was their man.

He had killed Ivana Kostimarov and planted DNA evidence on her so the police would find Truman for him.

Jackie put down her spoon, mouth absently working as she processed this theory, probing it for weaknesses. What about the searches on Truman's work computer? How to explain why Truman had been looking for chloroform? *Hmmm...* She'd have to come back to that.

Next question: was Silver taking orders from William Carmichael? How involved was Carmichael in all this anyway? Was this campaign against Ed Truman really all because Alison Truman threw a milkshake at Carmichael? Jackie had tried to bring the daughter in for questioning, but apparently she was away with friends – although hearing about how Carmichael's followers went for her, all the stalking and bullying online, she could be forgiven for going to ground. Even so, now her father was involved you'd think she'd make an appearance.

If this *was* all about Alison Truman, then why go after Ed Truman at all? Yes, he'd filed the injunction against the Men's Learning Centre website, but that had been withdrawn.

Jackie rolled up her dressing-gown sleeves and opened a web browser. Time to do some honest plod work – well, the modern version of it anyway, hunched over a laptop instead of pounding the streets. Carmichael *had* to be involved. She remembered seeing him on some news programme, spouting off against diversity, full of the usual conspiracy crap. He was a professor of clinical sciences at some university or other, with a background in psychology – his academic credentials gave him the veneer of credibility, but scratch the surface and you found the same old hatred. Why couldn't these people let others live how they wanted?

The background image on Carmichael's website showed a man at a workbench, gazing lovingly down at his tools. He had a checked shirt, a neat beard and a muscular build, like a cross between a carpenter and a lumberjack; an ideal of man, honest and reliable, someone who made his own furniture and always smelled faintly of cigars. She clicked into the About page, and the image changed to a man in his mid-fifties, serious, academic, face stern as he leaned forward on his lectern.

William Carmichael.

She clicked on the banner ad for the Men's Learning Centre. That was where he'd been milkshaked, at the grand opening. What did they actually do there? On the Courses page – after some pseudo-intellectual spiel about rejecting the post-feminist interpretation of man – she found there'd be classes in computing, construction and survival skills, as well as a daily exercise regime and, interestingly, *worryingly*, combat training. No mention of cost, but on the r/MLC Reddit thread they reckoned prices started at a thousand pounds a week. You could apply for something called a 'permanent scholarship', which was free, perfect for ex-military, especially those who'd not been able to integrate back into society. Could Carmichael be building a personal army?

What if that was only a fraction of his power? His most popular YouTube video, called 'The Gender Game: How Women Play to Win', had been watched over thirty million times. Thirty *million*! That was almost half the population of the UK. If he could mobilise a fraction of those people … think how much damage he could do before someone stopped him. *If* anyone stopped him.

She watched video after video. Carmichael's intelligence was compelling, and the way he manipulated facts made them sound convincing. She could see how someone who'd been mistreated by a woman – someone who already blamed his bad luck or bad choices on that relationship – might watch this rhetoric and buy into the argument that *all* women were at fault.

Jackie stabbed the space bar, stopping the video. There he was, Benedict Silver, walking across the stage behind Carmichael.

Longer hair and no glasses, but she was sure. Most of the time he had his head down, but for a split-second he glanced up, directly at the camera, giving her a clean shot of his face. *Got you, you fucker.*

She screenshotted it and sent the image to the office with instructions to put it through the facial recognition software. DC Samantha Sen was running the night shift for the tech team. She replied straight away that she was on it.

It was past two in the morning. Part of Jackie wanted to stay downstairs, keep on researching, rather than risk struggling to sleep for the next few hours, but her eyelids felt as though they'd been weighted down. She stumbled up the stairs and fell onto the bed.

Images of Ivana Kostimarov, her glazed eyes staring up at the grey sky, drifted through her thoughts along with outtakes from the day: Helen McAllister's tearful confession, Silver taunting her at Truman's house, Carmichael at his pulpit. *Looks like you're not far from blowing this case wide open.*

Silver's eyes as he saw the CCTV stills…

Jackie shot up in bed, prickles spreading from her spine. Silver didn't want Ed Truman at all.

He was after the silver-haired girl.

40

Gabrielle felt the drugs wear off slowly, like she was thawing out. When she was able, she tore off the eye mask. She was still on the sofa, naked. He'd touched her, pressing his hands to her breasts; at one point he'd put his face so close to her crotch that she'd felt his breath on her inner thigh. All of it, no doubt, part of some sick game. Who was he? *What had she invited into their house?*

She was still too weak to stand. She crawled off the sofa, reaching for her maxi dress, gulping down a sob as her chest loosened. Shock moved into the space left by the drugs. She pressed the dress to her face and screamed. She deserved this, as penance for what she'd been preparing to do. *Thou shalt not commit adultery.* She'd been brought up in a religious home; although she didn't practise now, the beliefs were deeply ingrained, and they were finding their voice now. *Slut. You brought this on yourself.*

She crept out the lounge, seeing shapes in every shadow, still feeling Benedict on her skin, the smell of his aftershave in her nose. Climbing the stairs, she pressed her side to the wall, nerves poised with expectation that any second he was going to leer out of the darkness, grab her throat and start the whole ordeal again. Somehow she made it to the top.

Mitchell's door was shut. She edged towards it, hand out, breath quivering. *Please let him be okay.* She pressed the handle

192

soundlessly and went in. He was in bed, sleeping. Benedict had said he wouldn't hurt him, and he hadn't. That brought her more relief than she deserved.

She crept out and closed the door. In her own bedroom she fought the urge to dive to the floor, see if he was hiding under the bed – or maybe in the wardrobe. Or— *Stop. Stop!* She dropped to her knees and began to cry. She pulled the duvet tight to her face, howling into it. How could she have been so stupid?

She wanted to crawl into the shower and turn the water scalding hot so she could burn every trace of him off her, but her body was evidence now. She needed to go to the police. A predator like that, who knew how many other women he'd drugged? He could be out there now, hunting his next victim. She couldn't let him get away with it!

But if she went to the police everyone would find out. *Ed would find out.* She'd have to tell the truth, about Benedict, what she might have done with him. *No, don't lie.* What she was *definitely* on her way to doing before those detectives showed up. *The detectives!* They'd seen the glasses of wine, the state of her sofa, the state of *her*, and known exactly what was going on. Her only hope would be if a toxicology report showed up the drug he'd given her, but it had already been hours since she drank the tea, and no doubt there would be plenty more before she was tested; Ed had told her many times that spiking victims often had nothing left in their system by the time they gave a sample. That settled it. She wouldn't go to the police. She didn't want to go to the police. She didn't want to think about last night ever again.

Gabrielle dragged herself upright, taking strength from that resolution. She wasn't going to tell anyone. She didn't have to, and she *wasn't going to*. Even thinking that sparked something inside. This was her decision. She still had some autonomy, some power. Benedict hadn't stolen everything from her. Not yet.

In the shower, she scrubbed her body as though trying to remove a stubborn stain. She could get it back, her marriage, her family. Things had been strained with Ed for a while now, and if she was honest that was as much her fault as his. It was easy to blame him, his drinking, to say the death of his father had messed him up – and hadn't she put up with Ed's weird relationship with his parents enough when they were alive? Now she had to put up with that *and more* when they were dead – but Ed was a good man. He was kind and intelligent – and attractive. She still fancied him. That had never changed. Sure, the spark might have gone out recently, but when was the last time she'd blown on the embers? No, she'd been too busy insisting this was *her time*, as she must have reminded Ed every other day.

So what? The kids didn't need her any more. Was she not supposed to a build a life for herself?

A life? Ha! She'd been building a life *raft*, that was the truth – for when their marriage finally capsized.

Gabrielle slipped down in the shower and grabbed her hair. *You brought this all on yourself.* She wanted to beat the back of her head against the tiles until she blacked out. Instead she rolled on her side and curled up, the water burning as it splashed onto her, and quietly sobbed.

It was already three in the morning. There was no chance of sleeping tonight, so she went downstairs, made a coffee, and sat in the kitchen. Where was her family? Why hadn't she kept a tighter hold on the people that mattered most? They were everything to her, *everything*, but somehow she'd fallen into the trap of believing they would always be there, and now her family had been snatched from her, and she might never get it back.

She rested her head on the table. Once she'd shut her eyes, she couldn't open them again. Her body needed to recover. She fought the first twitches of sleep but soon slipped into an anxious dream where she was running through a corridor, looking for the right door, but every time she grabbed at a handle it wasn't there. An alarm started to ring, telling her she had to get out, it was time to go, get out, *get out, GET OUT!*

Gabrielle's eyes shot open. She was in the kitchen. What was she doing there? What time was it? A dark morass of memory rolled back over her. *Oh God.*

The doorbell rang. She grasped at the end of the dream. That must have been the alarm, the doorbell. Who could be there? Not him again? It was light outside. The morning was bright through the window.

A man's voice came through the door. 'Mrs Truman? Are you home?'

Gabrielle came into the hallway, heart pounding hard enough to shake her whole body.

'It's Barry Flynn from *The Sun*, Mrs Truman. We're just here to get your side of the story.'

Her side of the story?

What story?

She edged to the door and peered through the spy hole. She gasped at what she saw on the other side. Journalists were clustered on the lawn, camera crews alongside them. News vans crowded the top of the drive.

This couldn't be real. This must be a joke. A prank. Or maybe a hallucination. Yes, that was it. That had to be it. The whole thing was a bizarre drugged-up fantasy, and all she had to do to get rid of them was demand they leave her alone.

'Go away!' she said. 'I don't want you here.'

'How long have you had a lover, Mrs Truman? Was it before your husband murdered Ivana Kostimarov?'

Gabrielle yanked open the door. 'I don't have a lover. I don't know where—'

The reporter flashed his phone at her. On it was a photo of a woman, naked, her cheeks flushed and mouth caught in a loose moan of pleasure. The back of a man's head – Benedict's head – hovered by her breast.

A silky red mask covered her eyes.

41

5.02 A.M., TUESDAY

I lay with my thoughts through the impossibly long hours, until the sky began to grow light.

We were on a dirt track running beside a cattle fence made from metal bars. A line of narrow, denuded trees leaned over the top, which was what must have been keeping us dry. Well, dryish.

I shook Phoenix awake. We needed to take advantage of the early hour to find the hideout. She opened her eyes and stared past me, face slack, saying nothing. For a moment I thought maybe she'd suffered some sort of breakdown – I wasn't far from one myself. Then she took a long breath through her nose like she was inflating something inside her body, and sat up.

'You okay?' I asked.

She nodded but didn't reply.

The slope we had come down was close by, and not anywhere near as steep as it had seemed last night. 'Come on,' I said, helping her up.

We quickly made it back to the road. 'This way,' Phoenix said, leading us towards the sleeping village. It couldn't have been much past five.

This time we took the right road.

Twenty minutes later, Phoenix excitedly tugged on my sleeve. We ducked down a muddy bridle path, going deep into the forest, taking a left onto a different path, then a right, staying on that until we got to a wide tree stump at the top of a shallow hill.

'Mind if we take a break?' I asked, going to sit on the stump.

'Wait,' she said, shooing me off it. She crouched and felt around the base, fingers digging into the dirt. A click echoed round the trees and the top of the stump lifted open. Inside, unbelievably, was a ladder. She swung her legs over and headed down. I watched her disappear from view.

'Hurry up,' she hissed from the bottom.

I clambered into the stump, feet scrambling, feeling as though any second I'd lose my grip and plummet to the ground, hilariously breaking both ankles. As it happened, it wasn't far down, and easy enough once on the rungs. I even dropped the last metre, landing in a crouch like the little bloke from *Mission: Impossible*.

We were in a wide tunnel with an arched corrugated iron ceiling, lit by a single bulb on a wire, the dull yellow light not quite making it all the way to the corners. The air was damp and stale, like it had been trapped down here for a long time. I brushed my fingers along the lichen-stained brick wall. 'What is this place?'

'It's a secret bunker from the Second World War. There's an old military base nearby. They used to keep some of their computers here, the same ones that cracked the Enigma code, so they could keep going if the base got bombed.'

She was by a rickety desk, like something from a 1950s classroom, connecting her laptop to what appeared to be a power socket, although it was hard to tell from all the moss growing on it.

'Don't tell me there's electricity here,' I said.

Phoenix glanced at the bulb dangling from the ceiling.

'Ah,' I replied.

'The cables were already here,' she said, opening the laptop and starting it. 'I just hacked onto the grid and switched the power on.'

'*You hacked into the National Grid?*'

She shrugged like it was no big deal.

'How do you even know about this place?'

'I grew up near here.'

I didn't want to ask anything about her upbringing that might upset her, like I did the other night. Not given how fragile she seemed this morning. So I just said, 'Oh, okay,' expecting to leave it at that. But then I saw she was leaning on the desk, her shoulders moving like she was about to cry.

'Are you okay?' I asked.

'I thought you were going to leave me last night.'

'Why would I do that?'

She stayed facing away, head tilted down. When she spoke her tone was heart-breaking. 'I … I'm not normal.'

'There's nothing wrong with you. You're just a kid.'

Phoenix wasn't saying anything, so I put my hand on her shoulder. She turned and buried her head in my chest, sobbing hard, her body shaking, grabbing onto my jacket like she was hanging off the edge of a cliff. I was never particularly good at comforting Ally and Mitchell, at least not once they were old enough to have real-world problems, but patting Phoenix on the shoulder and saying, 'It's going to be okay,' in a soothing voice seemed to help, so I did that for a while.

'Sorry,' she said, wiping her eyes and nose with her hand. With nowhere else to clean it, she rubbed it down the back of her leg, shuddering and pulling a disgusted face. 'I'm really sorry.'

'Have you seen the state of me? I think smearing snot on my trousers would actually *improve* my look.'

She snorted out a laugh. 'Save a fortune in tissues.'

'Are you going to tell me what's going on?'

Phoenix looked at me for a long hard moment, then she pushed her hair behind her ear and sighed and nodded. 'First, tea.'

She'd clearly been stocking the bunker for a while, and had a whole corner shop of snacks and canned goods, including, best of all, biscuits. If I have a weakness for any food, it's chocolate digestives. As soon as I saw that distinctive blue packet among the treasure trove I grabbed it, opened it, and stuffed the first one in my mouth before she had time to speak.

'Want some biscuits with your biscuits?' she asked, lifting out a packet of bourbons.

I folded another digestive in two and shoved it in. 'No, I'm good.'

As she heated a pan of water over a camping stove, she told me about her upbringing. Her mother died of a postpartum haemorrhage only minutes after Phoenix was born, so she was raised by her father. A cold, distant man, all he ever did was work. He couldn't wait to hand her over to boarding school as soon as she turned six.

'He didn't want to know me,' she said, chin hard.

She poured the boiling water into tin mugs, stirred in powdered milk, then handed me one. The tea was weak and insipid, the colour of used dishwater, but right then it was the finest cuppa I'd ever tasted.

I blew on the top to cool it down. 'I'm so sorry, Phoenix.'

'You're not like him. It was wrong for me to say that. Ally, and your son...'

'Mitchell.'

'They're lucky to have you.'

I dunked a biscuit. 'Let's not get carried away.'

'Look what you've done to try to find her.'

I glanced around the bunker. 'I'd hardly call being here a raging success.'

Phoenix turned and rooted around a plastic storage box under the desk, coming back with what looked like a compact, incredibly hi-tech radio.

'Not so far,' she said. 'But that's all about to change.'

42

I watched Phoenix wire the radio device to her laptop. 'What's that?'

'Satellite phone. To connect to the internet.'

'I'm not sure how checking your email is going to help us right now.'

'Give me a minute, I'll explain.'

I waited while she switched on the device and typed furiously on her laptop, switching between different windows. She double-checked something on the satellite phone, twisting a dial on the top. A line of green lights appeared in the display.

'Yes!' She pumped her fist like she'd just served a tennis ace.

'What? What's happening?'

She turned from the desk and blew out her cheeks. 'They're uploading.'

'What's uploading? What's going on?'

'Okay,' she said, and seemed to steady herself, suddenly nervous. 'I ... I shouldn't be here with you.'

'Trust me, this wasn't where I expected to end up either.'

She frowned like I wasn't getting it. 'I mean I should be here with someone else.'

As much as I appreciated the tea and biscuits and shelter from rain, I was still exhausted and not really in the mood to interpret hidden meanings. 'Just spit it out, Phoenix.'

'Ally. I should be here with her. That was the plan.'

'*What plan?*'

'Please don't be angry!'

I forced my expression to soften; I didn't want her to shut down and not tell me. Or worse, make up more lies, which by now I'd realised accounted for a high percentage of the words out of her mouth. 'I'm not annoyed. I just want to know the truth. Please, Phoenix, if there's something you're not telling me about my daughter, now is the time. *Please.*'

She nodded, and then nodded again, and just when I thought she was going for three in a row, she began to talk. 'People see William Carmichael as this far-right talking head who gets wheeled out every so often because he's a professor, and they can't usually find someone with his views able to speak in more than a series of grunts. They think the people that watch his videos are sad blokes looking for something to fill five minutes before they get back to watching porn. But it's not true. He's dangerous.'

'Exactly, he's dangerous. So why did you pick a fight with him?'

Phoenix closed her eyes, trying to gather herself. I wanted to grab her and shake out the truth.

'He does these … procedures,' she said. 'On people.'

'What kind of procedures?'

'He claims that anything not a biological imperative is a conditioned state that can be reversed. So, like, he says being trans or gay isn't "natural" – and he thinks you can change people back.'

'What? You mean like conversion therapy?'

'Kind of, but times a million. Carmichael does all these horrible brainwashing things with drugs and electric shocks, until their whole fucking mind blows a fuse. His big thing is transgender children. You get the super-rich, like Saudi royals or Russian oligarchs, who don't want a trans kid, so they pay Carmichael to make them "normal" again.'

Although I'd not had much involvement with transgender issues, I was supportive of someone's right to lead their life the way they wished, free from inequality and hatred. Clearly, if Phoenix was telling the truth, it was beyond abhorrent. Carmichael should be going down on charges of torture.

That, however, was a big *if*.

'You don't believe me,' she said.

'That's not true.'

She beckoned me to the desk. 'Look at this.'

I hauled myself to my feet, my back stiff as a cinder block, and hobbled across the dirt floor to join her. She started a split-screen video. On the right was a pleasant family scene, a picnic on a sunny day, the mother and father lounging on a tartan blanket beside a fine deli spread, the children, a boy and a girl, chasing each other beneath a perfect blue sky; on the left was webcam footage of a young boy, maybe ten years old. The boy was wearing shapeless grey clothes. He was lying down, narrow walls surrounding him. Eyes slack, a loose smile on his lips, he was staring up at something, presumably at the video playing on the other side of the split.

I glanced at Phoenix. 'What is this?'

'Watch,' she replied, dragging the cursor along the bottom of the video player, fast-forwarding the image. When she stopped, the right screen now showed two men kissing passionately – on the left side, the boy was squirming, teeth clenched. He popped forward, like he'd been shocked, and when his chin lifted I saw a restraint around his neck.

'Oh my God,' I murmured. 'This is disgusting. How … how can someone … ?'

'You see now,' she said, shutting the video down.

'Where did you get that?'

'We broke into the lab at Carmichael's Men's Learning Centre last week and stole it. I've got lots more.'

'What do you mean, *we*?'

Phoenix didn't say anything. She didn't have to – I already knew. 'Where's my daughter?'

'A door shut behind me as we were getting out of the lab. I couldn't open it. Ally was on the other side.'

'Maybe she found another way out?'

Phoenix's look told me she didn't think so. 'I wanted to go back for her,' she said, her eyes glistening. She rubbed them with the back of her hand. 'But I had to make a decision. I had to get the videos out. Ally would have done the same.'

I steadied myself, knowing what I had to ask next, but terrified of what I was about to hear. 'Is she still alive?'

'I ... I don't know.'

My ears were ringing, my mouth suddenly so dry I couldn't swallow. I told myself not to be annoyed with Phoenix, that if Ally had been the one to get away I would've been happy for her to keep running, but I could see my daughter trapped and scared and calling desperately for someone to help, and the anger surged through me. '*So you dragged*—'

'I didn't *drag* anyone. Ally's just as involved as me.'

'And now she's gone – because of you.'

'*That's not true.*'

'Isn't it?'

'Ally knew what she was doing.'

'Oh, *right*. I get it now. I'm here, she's not, and that's just bloody fine with you?'

'It's *not* fine with me.'

'You knew if you told me before now I'd try to find her; then it'd be *you* in danger because I might lead them back here!'

Phoenix fixed me with a hard stare. 'You don't know your daughter as well as you think you do.'

'I might not have been the best dad in the world, but I do know my own child!'

'Do you know she set up the whole thing?'

That pulled me out of my rage. Set what up? What was she talking about?

'It was all her idea,' Phoenix said. 'The milkshake. To give them a *reason* to dox her.'

Until recently, I had no idea the word 'dox' even existed, but after seeing what the bastards on that website did to Ally, I understood it intimately. They ransacked her life, digging through it and posting it on their forum. Not just her address and phone number, which would've been bad enough, but her social media login details, her debit card numbers, pictures of her as a child. How they got half of it, I'll never know. Every time I sent them a letter ordering them to take something down, or risk legal action, ten more things appeared.

'It wasn't them,' said Phoenix.

'Will you stop talking in riddles!'

'They weren't the ones posting that stuff about Ally.'

'But if they didn't, who did?'

'We did.'

'What do you mean, "we"?'

'Me and Ally.'

'Ally posted all that private information on the Men's Learning Centre forum?'

Phoenix nodded. 'We'd phished admin user account details, then posted stuff and locked the account so it couldn't be taken down.'

I couldn't believe what I was hearing. All the abuse Ally received, all the dick pics and death threats. She'd brought that on herself? It didn't seem possible. 'But why?'

'So *you* would go after them for harassment. So you'd do some legal shit to shut down the website.'

I shook my head, about to tell her, *No, no way, that's crazy, my daughter would never do that.* Then I saw Ally pleading with me to promise that I wouldn't withdraw the injunction, no matter what happened.

You don't know your daughter as well as you think you do.

Everyone said it, and everyone was right.

'We'll get her out,' Phoenix said. 'I'm uploading the videos to a secure site, then I'll send them a link so they know I have them – if they don't let Ally go, I release them to the media.'

'But surely wasn't that your plan anyway? Otherwise why steal them?'

'I don't—'

'What I mean is, why should they believe you? You could easily release the videos after they let Ally go.'

Phoenix looked crestfallen. 'I…'

'Is there even anything on the videos themselves to tie them to Carmichael?'

'There's some metadata on the files that show—'

'Unless the camera pans round to show Carmichael at the control panel, pressing the shock button himself, no respected media outlet is going to run with it. They'd get sued so fast the same paper would be able to run the story in the afternoon edition.'

I turned away from the laptop feeling unsteady, the biscuits from before threatening to come back up. If that was all Phoenix had, it was hopeless. The world was awash in fake news. These videos would be brushed off as one more pointless piece of internet litter.

'I won't stop until we get Ally back,' Phoenix said. 'I promise.'

I'd heard her promises before, and as fond as I was of her as a person, I didn't believe a word she said. At least I knew where Ally had been the night she didn't come home: Carmichael's Men's Learning Centre.

*

The connection over the satellite phone was as slow as a 56k modem, and it'd take a long time to upload all the videos. I wanted to stay awake, to assimilate what Phoenix had told me, try to work out what to do next, but once she pulled out the sleeping mats and bags she and Ally had stashed in the hideout, I took a set gratefully. The first step in getting my daughter home had to be rest. I was wiped out and needed to get back some strength.

At first, I thought I'd fall asleep – my eyelids were so heavy I couldn't force them open – but as soon as I lay down my mind spun out of control. Soon I was sitting back up again, feeling more spaced out and groggy than before, which was quite saying something. How was I not asleep?

Phoenix, as usual, was having no such problem. Her soft, puttering snores echoed off the corrugated ceiling.

I crept over to the laptop and opened a web browser, wanting to find out the latest on the case. It felt weird to be doing something so normal as checking the news. I probably did it twenty times any given day, never thinking about it, but now I was doing it from an underground bunker, on the run from the police. I couldn't get my head round it. It seemed impossible. What evidence could they possibly have to pin the murder on me?

As the page painstakingly opened, one line at a time, I spotted Phoenix's rucksack. The zip was open. Remembering the farm when she handed me the water bottles, I shuffled over to it and peered inside. Inside I could see T-shirts, old tissues and wrappers from the chocolate bars we had stolen. I glanced around at her. Still asleep.

Fuck it. I thrust my hand in her bag and rooted around, hoping her secret wasn't a collection of antique razor blades. At the bottom were some large plastic bottles that rattled when I shook them. I lifted one out. It was pale brown and unlabelled – and full of pills. I put the bottle back in and tried a different one. Same again. What was going on here? Was she sick? Should we be at a hospital, instead of holed up here?

I shoved the bottle away, feeling ashamed now for going through her stuff, for violating her trust. What had I expected to find in there? A map leading to Ally? *X marks the missing daughter?* Pathetic.

I turned my attention back to the laptop screen. The news had loaded.

Time froze. I couldn't believe what I was seeing.

On the homepage was a picture of my wife. Her cheeks were flushed, and over her eyes was a sexy red mask.

MURDER SUSPECT'S WIFE SNAPPED
WITH SECRET LOVER.

43

Jackie woke early, as always. No matter how exhausted she felt at the end of a night, or how late she came to bed, it was the same. Maybe it was just part of getting older. Or maybe even in sleep she saw the need to punish herself, like she didn't deserve to feel well rested.

Watery light filled the bedroom. *Another year gone, another anniversary passed.* She didn't know whether to cry or feel relieved, so settled for trying not to think about anything at all, instead trudging downstairs to brew the first of the day's many coffees.

Her laptop was still open at the kitchen table. A reply from Samantha Sen from the tech team had arrived an hour ago. Did she already have results for the facial recognition scan of Benedict Silver? Jackie opened the email, tense at the screen, *come on, come on. . .* Direct hit! They even had a file on him.

Multiple names, as to be expected. Not wanted in connection with anything, but a person of interest for *many* years, although disappeared as of late. Rumoured to be heavily involved in the rise of nationalist gang culture in the noughties – White Tigers, Truth & Valour, Pure Resistance.

Jackie sat back. Pure Resistance was the organisation she had been investigating when Lester and Verity were murdered. Although she was never able to prove it at the time, she was certain they were behind it. She knew it in her gut. For six months she had hunted for the killers, paying any snitch and twisting any arm she could find. A couple of times she had sensed she was close, but at the last second her lead would vanish, and she'd be nowhere, again.

That explained how Silver knew about what happened. No doubt her story had been laughed about in gangster pubs all over London. If he was involved with Pure Resistance, he'd have heard it a hundred times. *Looks like you're not far from blowing this case wide open.* Ha, bloody ha.

You'll slip up, Silver. Cocky bastards like you always do.

Her phone buzzed – Detective Sergeant Travis was calling.

Jackie picked up. 'What's new, Trav?'

'Got a trace on that Jag you told me to check out. It's on the move. Heading down the Westway.'

Silver's car. Why would he be on the Westway? Who could he be— *Oh, no!*

*

Benedict pulled up in the car park of the decaying housing estate. The two men he'd bought for the job got out with him. One of them opened the boot and took out a brown holdall that sagged down his back when he slung it over his shoulder, like there was something metal and weighty inside.

As they approached the block, all three pulled down balaclavas.

The safety glass in the centre of the wide metal door was already cracked. One swing of a sledgehammer later, and it was gone completely. A gloved hand swept the glass away, then reached in to turn the latch. The lift was out so they took the stairs to her floor, where one of the men silently picked her lock. As soon as it clicked, Benedict pushed open the door.

'Hello?' he called, lifting off his balaclava. 'Anyone home?'

They found Helen McAllister in the kitchen, draping socks over a plastic drying rack. She paused, staring at them like they were apparitions.

Benedict gave her his most charming smile. '*Helen*. It's so lovely to see you again.'

McAllister shook her head, backing into the corner. 'I ... I—'

'Sorry to scare you. I just want us to have a little chat.'

She glanced at the two men beside him, still with their balaclavas pulled down, one of them resting a sledgehammer on his shoulder.

'Don't worry about these guys,' Benedict said. 'They're just for show. Now, should we go sit down?'

He waited for her to nod, then took her hand, cold and damp from hanging up the clothes, and led her through to the living room. He sat on the sofa and patted the cushion beside him. She lowered herself down.

'I'm going to ask you something really important,' he said. 'I want you to think before you answer. Has anyone come here to ask you about me? A couple of police detectives perhaps?'

He watched her already pale face go white.

'I spoke to the police,' she said. 'Like you told me to.'

'If there's one thing I really hate, it's a *liar*.'

McAllister's tongue darted out to wet her lips. 'Please,' she murmured. 'I haven't done anything...'

'I'm going to ask you one last time. Did two detectives come and speak to you about me?'

She started to shake her head again, then paused and looked down. Tears dripped onto her lap. She nodded instead.

'That wasn't so hard, was it?' Benedict gave her a friendly shake on the shoulder. 'Now, what did they ask you? And more importantly, what did you tell them?'

Between sobs, McAllister explained how the detectives tricked her, bursting in, pretending they were going to arrest her for lying. She didn't want to tell them anything, she really didn't, but she was scared and they caught her off guard and they seemed to know everything anyway. But she hadn't mentioned him, she'd said nothing about him. She told the police that she didn't get a good look at the men who'd threatened her, which he could see was a lie, but it was amusing to watch her try to get out of it.

'Thank you so much for being honest,' he said.

'I promise I won't say anything to anyone else.'

'I know you won't. And you're also going to take back the statement you gave those detectives, aren't you?'

She nodded with relief. 'I promise. I promise.'

Benedict stood and made to leave, but stopped, his finger in the air. 'There's just one thing.'

He gestured to the men, who moved towards her. One of them clamped his hand over her mouth, his arm around her neck, and hoisted her off the sofa. The other grabbed her thumb and held it out, the bottom joint exposed.

Benedict unzipped the holdall. 'Remember when we first met? I told you that if you betrayed me, I would chop up your children and force you to eat them? Unfortunately, they're not here. But *you* are.'

McAllister's eyes grew wide and she bucked against the men as Benedict took out a set of gleaming metal bolt cutters.

'I guess the only question now,' he said, testing the cutters for tension, 'is how would you like your thumb? Boiled, or fried?'

*

Jackie screeched to a stop in the car park. She jumped out and ducked down as the door to Helen McAllister's block opened.

Silver, flanked by a couple of thugs, the three of them laughing and joking. *Damn. Too late.* She hoped they'd only given McAllister a telling off.

Careful to keep her movements to a minimum, Jackie retrieved the pepper spray from her back pocket, and palmed it. She watched them approach their car in the wing mirror.

Silver stopped and turned around, nose in the air, mouth turned down, like he was smelling something bad. 'Get a load of that,' he said to his goons, sniffing again, facing where she was hiding. 'I'd say that was either ten kilos of spoilt tuna, or Detective Rose's mouldy old cunt.'

How did he know she was here? Had he watched her drive in from Helen's window?

Jackie stood from behind the car. 'Benedict Silver, right? Also known as Sam Cornelius, Michael Ripley and Carter Lambert.'

'The one and the many,' he replied, big grin. 'Fancy seeing you here.'

Jackie moved round her car, a swagger in her step. Confidence was everything with this kind of scum. Silver's smile didn't falter. She stopped five metres away, readying to get into a fighting stance if they attacked. The two men beside him looked prepared to pounce at his word.

'You visiting someone?' she asked.

'An old friend.'

Jackie glanced at his gleaming Jaguar. 'You have old friends here?'

'Sure.'

'What's her name?'

'I don't like to kiss and tell.'

'So it's a woman?'

If Silver was concerned about being caught here, his face didn't show it. He clicked his key fob and the car beeped. 'Well, as lovely as it is to see you again, we really must be going.'

Jackie took another step. She had to try to bring him in – if McAllister was hurt, she was more likely to tell them what really happened if Silver was already under arrest.

'How about you come down the station,' she said. 'Just for a chat.'

'Are you charging me with something?'

'I don't know, am I?'

'This is harassment.'

'Let's head upstairs and speak to Helen McAllister about harassment.'

'Ask who you want. I doubt you'll hear much.'

'Shame we couldn't find Truman for you, though.'

Silver's mouth went tight.

'It's the girl, isn't it?' Jackie said. 'That's who you want. I've seen it before, with men like you. You're getting old, a bit saggy, losing your touch, so you start liking them younger and younger. It's called over-compensation.'

'You think I'm scared of you? It's the police! I'm *soooo* scared. You have nothing. You know nothing. Because if you did, it wouldn't be you here, on your own, in a quiet car park on a quiet morning. Where you could get hurt, maybe even killed.' Silver cocked his finger – the men moved towards her. 'And no one would ever know how or why.'

Jackie hunched her shoulders, hands up by her face, in her favoured Brazilian jiu-jitsu stance. It was perfect for big idiots like these two, who thought size gave you the ultimate advantage over any opponent. They didn't realise speed and technique beat dumb muscle every time.

She feinted one way, then the other, waiting for one of them to lunge, knowing they didn't have the patience to try to find her weaknesses. The one on the right went for her. She caught his arm at the inner elbow, placed her foot on his instep, and rolled him over her back, flicking her shoulder up at the last moment, so there was further for his head to fall. His skull hit the tarmac with a sickening crack.

She was the wrong way round, but anticipated which side the other one was coming at her. She spun under his flailing arm, firing the pepper spray into his eyes as she completed the turn, blinding him. A kick in the chest sent him staggering backwards.

Silver was already in his car and speeding out of the estate. Jackie jumped into hers, started the engine, swung backwards and swerved around the two men staggering to their feet. She tore after Silver, but by the time she got out of the car park, the road was empty.

44

8.03 A.M., TUESDAY

I stared at the picture of my wife on the news, her flushed cheeks, the silky eye mask, my heart pounding so hard it was a surprise Phoenix didn't wake up and ask where that drumming was coming from.

MURDER SUSPECT'S WIFE SNAPPED WITH SECRET LOVER.

After Gabrielle got her face done, I wondered briefly if she was having an affair. I even snooped around, checking her email, her phone – we knew each other's passwords for everything – but without any great intent. I guess, in my heart, I always trusted her. We were just too, I don't know, *affectionate*. I'm not saying we spent every moment draped over each other, and Lord knows we rowed enough, especially of late, but not a day went past without a few kisses and at least one 'love you'. For her to go from that to ending up in bed with another man? I could never see it.

Well, I could now. Me and just about everyone else.

I stared at the photo, trying to work out from the back of the head covering my wife's right breast if it was someone I knew. The style was different, but the colour ... what if it was that guy? The

217

handsome one after Phoenix? What if he had seduced Gabrielle to get information about where I was hiding?

I scanned the article, but it was filled with supposition. *It has been reported. We have learnt.* No names, no details. Ninety per cent was a rehash of the murder investigation.

The truth of what had happened began to sink below the surface of my brain, deep into my gut. I'd wanted so much to get home that I hadn't considered there might not be a home to go back to.

If I lost Gabrielle, I lost my family.

I lost everything.

That was it. Enough. I couldn't sit here any longer, waiting for something to happen. Phoenix had no plan. Those videos could easily be refuted, or ignored, and then what? It was time to take matters into my own hands – go straight to the police, insist on protective custody for Gabrielle, Mitchell and myself. I'd tell them everything, about Carmichael, Ally's disappearance, how I'd been framed to find Phoenix, the videos of the 'procedures' she stole from the Men's Learning Centre. If that meant I ended up with someone trying to wring Phoenix's whereabouts from me with a pair of rusty pliers, so be it. I would deal with that when it happened.

I crept to the ladder and stepped on the bottom rung, wincing at the metallic creak, holding my breath as I took the next step. Thankfully, it was quieter. I eased myself up, only realising near the top that I didn't know whether it would even open. What if something at the bottom needed to be pulled or prodded or pressed to release the lid? I felt around in the dark, found a metal lever, pushed up. After a little resistance, it gave, and the top of the stump lifted. I climbed out and eased it back down.

I jogged along the bridle path until I came to a T-junction. Which way? I couldn't remember. I strained to hear the sound of traffic over the tweeting birds and my own laboured breaths. Nothing. The one to the left had fresh footprints in the mud, so I took that one, figuring that if other people had been that way it must lead somewhere. Nearly an hour and another couple of turns later, I was about to give up on ever finding my way out of the glorious bloody English countryside when the path came out onto a road. I froze. A car was coming.

What was my story? Quickly, I rubbed mud on my cheek, tore the collar of my T-shirt, and grabbed my side. A red VW Beetle came round the corner, a couple of old dears in the front seats. I lifted my arm.

The car stopped, and the lady in the passenger side lowered her window. 'You okay, love?'

'I came off my bike,' I said, face clenched. 'Can you give me a lift to the nearest village?'

She looked worried. 'Do you need to go to the hospital?'

'No, no, that's okay.' I dialled down the pain. 'It's just a knock.'

I got in the back, thanking them profusely, and asked if they had a phone I could use. I wasn't going to throw myself at the mercy of the police. That would be crazy. No, I was going to go to them with one of the finest criminal lawyers I've ever known, who just happened to be my business partner.

I called the office, one of the few numbers I knew by heart, and paused as it rang, clutching the phone to my ear, pulse throbbing in my hand. Finally he answered: 'Smith Truman Solicitors.'

'Steve.'

'*Christ*, Ed.'

Relief flooded over me at the sound of his voice. Finally, I was going home. I just prayed there was something there for me when I got back.

'Listen,' I said, 'I need your help.'

45

Steve Smith waved off his nine o'clock client and slumped back in his chair rubbing his face. How was it only nine-thirty? He'd stayed up until the early hours catching up with Ed's cases, made all the more difficult by the fact the police *still* had the practice's main office computer, but it was either that or letting down clients, and he wasn't prepared to do that. It wasn't their fault their lawyer had gone AWOL.

His next client was already waiting in reception, but he needed another brew, *stat!* He went through to the kitchen and steeped his second cup of matcha green tea. It hadn't been easy to get over his addiction to double espressos, which he used to throw down like tequila shots between clients, but it was all part of his drive to be a better person. To be a better man. Ten years ago, if someone had said to him, *This'll be your life*, up before the birds, in the office while most people were still shuffling into the kitchen in their slippers, he'd have thought they were having a laugh. But times change and people change and now it was two cups of green tea in the morning, then water the rest of the day. Booze only on the weekend. Fags, never.

Steve carried his tea to his desk while checking the news on his phone. Gaby, Gaby, *Gaby. Who's been a naughty girl, eh?* Karma, that's what it was – or irony for the spiritual, as he liked to say.

When he and Faith separated, old Gabs was so sanctimonious, making a point of taking Faith's side, even though they'd known each other for five minutes compared to how long he and Ed had been mates.

Back at his desk, he tapped the trackpad to activate his laptop, and loaded the article again to carry on reading it. He'd warned Ed about her when she got those fillers. You don't do something like that without telling your husband. Unless you're doing it for someone else.

'Hello, Steve.'

Steve swore and shoved back his chair. It was the detective, the woman who had interviewed Gabrielle and him on Sunday. She was leaning against the back wall, shorter than he remembered, in a shapeless navy pantsuit, her face sinewy in the way some middle-aged women got when they worked out too much.

'Are you trying to intimidate me, Detective?'

She pushed off the wall, but didn't approach the desk. 'Benedict Silver?'

'I don't know who that is.'

'How about Sam Cornelius, Michael Ripley or Carter Lambert?'

'I don't know any of those people.' He'd met detectives like this before, hard nuts who thought their very presence sent you into spasms of fear. Well, not him. 'You know I can still sue the police for going beyond the bounds of the seizure warrant. It said Ed's work computer *only*.'

'What's stopping you?'

'Because I, too, would like to find him. I want to know what the bloody hell is going on. I'm running this place on my own, and can barely manage—'

She walked up to his desk and placed her hands on the edge. Close up, Steve could see her clothes were scuffed, and her cold blue eyes had a sharpness to them that made him pull his neck back.

'One of the women who accused Truman of sexual harassment has just had her thumb cut off. Her *fucking* thumb. She's in the hospital right now being sewn up. Now I'm going to ask you again. Benedict Silver. Sam Cornelius. Michael Ripley. Carter Lambert. Do any of those names sound familiar?'

'I'm sorry, *Detective*. I've never heard of those men. Now if you excuse me, you are keeping my next client waiting.'

She put her hands up in surrender. 'Only trying to do my job.'

'I'm sorry too,' he said, realising as the words came out that she hadn't actually apologised. 'The past few days have *not* been easy.' He cleared his throat and leaned towards his laptop. 'Now if you'll excuse me.'

'You've got two boys, right?'

'That's right.'

'Are they close to Mitchell Truman?'

'Of course. They grew up together.'

'How about you? Are you close to him?'

'To *Mitchell*? He's fourteen! Why would I be close to him?'

The detective nodded, like she hadn't thought of that – but she wasn't stupid. He felt queasy. What was going on here?

'I have no idea what you're implying,' Steve said, standing. 'But unless we are going to conduct this as a formal interview, which will include asking your superior if it is common practice for you to break into someone's office and try to *bully them*—'

She took a step back, hands up again. 'I didn't mean to rile you. I'll leave you in peace.' At the door, she turned back round. 'Last question, I promise.'

'What now?'

'Ed's work calendar. How accurate would you say that was?'

'*What?* How should I know?'

'If it said he was in court on a certain day, would he definitely be there?'

'Why don't you check with the courts? They keep records.'

The detective smiled. 'I'll do that. Thanks for your time, Mr Smith.'

Steve fell back in his chair, shaking his head long after she'd left. *Unbelievable.* If this was how the police acted, what hope was there for society? He sipped his tea, but it was cold. Did he have time to heat it up? He was already over ten minutes late for his next client, and if he wasn't careful the rest of the day was going to turn into a pile-up.

The phone rang. He didn't really have time to answer it, but was expecting a call. 'Smith Truman Solicitors.'

'Steve.'

'*Christ*, Ed.'

'Listen, I need your help.'

46

The old dears dropped me in a village called Brayford Downs, at a grassy square so Ye Olde England it even had a red phone box. They offered to stay until someone came to get me, but I assured them I was okay, and thanked them until they left. It was a chilly morning, the grey clouds sitting heavy. I thought about heading down the cobblestoned high street to the cafe I could see in the distance, but the last thing I needed was someone recognising me and calling the police.

Instead I sat on a bench, watching for Steve's silver Merc, and trying to work out how this might play with the police. What could I do to stack the cards in my favour? They must have good evidence – CCTV or DNA – so it all came down to my alibi. I had one – Phoenix. To use that I'd have to lead the police to the hideout. She'd have to give them a statement. Could I really betray her that way? She was a smart girl. That was her thing, being smart. She'd work out that me going would mean she'd have to leave as well. But if she left, so did my alibi.

'Ed! Ed!'

'Steve!' I leapt from the bench, overjoyed at seeing a familiar face, and grabbed him into a hug.

'You fucking stink,' he laughed, patting me on the back.

'No doubt!'

He held me out by the shoulders. 'It really is good to see you.'

Something was wrong. His eyes were helpless, his manner hesitant, like he'd come a long way to deliver bad news.

I shrugged off his hands. 'What's happened?'

'I'm so sorry.'

'You're sorry? Why are you sorry?'

He gestured with his eyes over my shoulder. I spun around. *Oh, no. Please God, no.*

Standing behind me, grinning innocently, was the handsome bastard bent on destroying my life.

'How about we start again?' He held out his hand. 'I'm Benedict.'

*

As we followed Benedict up the high street, I ignored Steve's urgent whispers in my ear about how he'd warned me not to get involved with these people, and how he had to protect his own kids, but his words washed over me. A numbness had spread from my face, down to my chest, and out to my limbs. It was like someone was dragging me forward with a rope. The office phone was bugged, he was saying, they knew I'd called. He had no choice but to lead them to me. No choice.

Benedict opened the cafe door for us. Inside, it was loud and steamy. Steve weaved between tables to take one in the corner. I stayed close behind him, ducked into my jacket, the smell of my dirty clothes ripe in my nostrils.

I sat opposite Benedict, Steve beside me, hunched and sheepishly fiddling with his hands. Benedict looked around expansively and cocked his finger at the waitress to come over. She was short and young and pretty, with gold hoop earrings and a small Indian symbol tattooed on her wrist.

'What can I get you?' she asked.

'Full English for me,' Benedict said, flashing her a smile that made her visibly swallow. 'You got a decent coffee machine?'

She nodded, colour rising in her cheeks, clearly smitten.

'I'll have a macchiato, then. Chaps?'

I had to admire the gall of the man. Everything he'd done to my family, to get half the police force in the country hunting me, and not only did he seem as calm as if we were old friends meeting for a catch-up, but happy to finish his breakfast before breaking my fingers to find out where Phoenix was hiding. Well, *fuck him*. I was going to call his bluff. Let him call the police. Let them come and arrest me. I'd tell them everything.

'Come on, Ed,' he said, genially. 'You look like you could do with a feed.'

'I'm *fine*.'

'Suit yourself.' He ordered for himself, then sat back, stretched. 'Grim weather, isn't it? You know that in October—'

I made fists on the Formica top. 'You haven't destroyed my whole life to sit here and talk about the *weather*.'

Benedict glanced at Steve, eyebrows lifted, sucking a sharp breath through his teeth, like I was embarrassing them. My former best friend at least had the good grace to keep his eyes down.

I tried to calm my tone. 'I'm done playing your stupid games.'

His 'who me?' expression almost had me lurching over the table to throttle him.

'I want you to stay away from me, my wife—'

'Have you ever heard of an alpha widow?' Benedict smiled, like he expected to enjoy this. 'An alpha widow is a woman with an average sexual market value. Say, for example, your wife. She falls under the lure of an alpha male, in this case me, sacrificing the long-term relationship with the lower market value man in her life – that's you, by the way – to be with him. The alpha male discards her once she has fulfilled her purpose, making her his widow.'

'Did you rape her?'

He gave me an *as-if* eye roll. 'You should be thanking me for showing you the truth.' He sighed and leaned forward. 'She invited me to your house. She wanted to have sex with me.'

'You're an animal.'

'No. *You're the animal.* I'm something far superior.'

I put my hand to my eyes, feeling tears trying to push their way out, but no way was I going to cry in front of that psychopath. 'Why are you *doing* this to me?'

'You know why, Ed. Tell me where she is.'

'It's near here,' I said, suddenly drained, the fight in me gone. *Sorry, Phoenix, this is your mess you dragged me into.* 'It's a bomb shelter, I think. When I left, it took me ages to find the way back to the road. Nearly an hour. Then I got a lift. It was only about twenty minutes' drive, so it's not far.'

Benedict took a few seconds to process this. 'I'm going to need something a bit better than that.'

'That's all I know.'

'Not good enough.'

'I don't know what to tell you.'

'How about we get that old memory of yours jogging?' He got out his phone, made a call. When they answered he passed it to me. 'I think there's someone who wants to have a word with you.'

I took the phone, carefully, feeling like I was heading into a trap. 'H-hello?'

'*Dad?*'

Mitchell. They had my son.

'Are you okay? Have they hurt—'

Benedict snatched it from me. 'That's enough.'

'Please,' I said. 'Whatever you want, I'll give you. What I have is yours.'

'Where is she?'

'I've told you everything.'

'One dead child is bad luck. Two? That's just negligent.'

My face went numb. 'What do you mean *one dead child*? Have you done something to Ally?'

'*Focus*, please Ed. Your son doesn't have long.'

'Don't hurt him. Please don't hurt him.'

'That's down to you.'

I grabbed Steve's arm, but he bit his lip and shook his head, a tear slipping out the corner of his eye. Just as long as it wasn't one of *his* sons.

'It's hidden – underground. You get in through a secret entrance, a tree stump. It's down a ladder.'

'And where is this stump?'

'In the woods, off a bridle path.'

'But you couldn't lead us there.'

I rooted through my memory, trying to locate the roads we took to get there, but I couldn't remember them then and I didn't now. '*Please*. I've told you everything.'

Benedict made a shrinking sign with his finger and thumb, telling me to keep it down, like I was making a scene. 'One more chance, otherwise that's the last time you speak to your son.'

'Don't do this.'

'Such a shame. Seemed like a good kid.'

'*Please!*'

This wasn't happening. It couldn't be possible. I frantically tried to recall anything that could lead them to the bunker – a landmark, a road sign, a giant fucking tree – but my mind was blank. There was nothing. I knew nothing. 'I'm sorry. *I'm sorry.*'

'Go ahead,' Benedict said into the phone. He gave me a look that could almost be called compassionate, then added, 'Make it quick, eh? Don't let him suffer.'

Tears ran freely over my face. 'Please, stop. You've got to stop.'

He shrugged as though there was nothing he could do. The decision had been made.

Something Phoenix said when we first arrived at the bunker – the Second World War, an old military base nearby, how they had computers set up there in case the base got bombed.

'Wait!' I said. 'I've got it.'

'I'm listening.'

I relayed what I remembered.

'Get *everyone* on it,' Benedict said into the phone. 'Call me back when you've found something.'

I forced myself to stare him in the eye. 'If you hurt my son, I'll kill you. I swear to God, I'll kill you.'

'No, you won't,' he replied. His voice became low, confessional. 'I realise you've been through a lot, but I just want you to know that there'll always be a place with us when you get out of prison. I don't know when that'll be, maybe not for many years – long after your family has given up on you.' He rested his hand over my still quivering fist and gave it a caring shake. 'Our doors will always be open for all men.'

I pulled my hand away and stood up. I couldn't bear to be near him a second longer. The sooner we got this done, the sooner I could get back to my family.

'Hold on a second there,' he said, motioning for me to sit.

'Can't we—'

'Right here,' he said. The waitress was coming up behind me with his breakfast. She slid the plate in front of him, grinning like a groupie.

I stared at him in disbelief. 'You're seriously going to eat that.'

'Never rush a good breakfast,' he said, picking up a corner of toast and smashing it into his fried egg. 'It's the most important meal of the day. Didn't your mother teach you anything?'

47

Phoenix sat up, panting, sweat sticking her clothes to her skin, and looked around the bunker, confused for a moment as to how she'd ended up there. She flopped back in her sleeping bag. Some nightmare. At the end it had been dark and hands had been clawing at her, and she'd been screaming, screaming, screaming for them to stop.

'Ed,' she said, her voice croaky. She finished the dregs of her cold tea and called his name again. His sleeping bag didn't move. Was he still asleep? As her eyes adjusted to the dark she realised his sleeping bag looked too flat. She scrabbled over to it, panic rising, patting it from top to bottom. *Where was he?*

What if he'd gone to try to get Ally out? No, that would be insane. What was he going to do? Burst into the Men's Learning Centre and demand they hand his daughter over? *But what if he had?* He'd lead them right back here! She'd been stupid to trust him. Stupid, stupid, *stupid*. Why did she tell him *anything*? Because she'd fallen for it, that was why. Because she'd allowed herself to believe that someone actually gave a shit about her. She remembered the stupid thoughts that had crowded her head, like how maybe Ed would invite her to live with them after they got Ally back. Maybe she'd go to school and take her A levels. She'd have a normal life, a family life, instead of having to crash on couches or live in squats. She wouldn't call him 'dad', that would be too weird, but he'd be there to turn to when she needed help. He'd be someone she could look up to, or ask for advice, or just hang with if she was sick of being on her own *all the time*. She beat the side of her head. So. Stupid!

Ow. She rubbed her head regretfully. Maybe he'd gone to get some air, or to the toilet? Why didn't she think of that instead of sprinting to the worst possibility? She got up, filled a pan with bottled water, and put it on the camping stove. While it boiled, she checked the uploads. The first video was nearly complete – only half an hour to go. Then she could think about how to use them to get Ally out.

But what if Ed was right about those? She hadn't considered that the videos would be ignored or dismissed as fake. Planning the raid on the lab, they'd imagined it being front-page news, the scandal to bring down Carmichael. But now she was beginning to see the videos for what they really were. Just files, easily deleted.

No. She couldn't think that way. She'd make this work. First she'd get Ally back, then go after Carmichael.

Where was Ed?

Phoenix paced the bunker. If he'd gone to try to get Ally, then she needed to evacuate, and fast. But to go where? This was the hideout! The place she came to as a last resort. There *was* nowhere else.

A clunk overhead, followed by the creak of the stump being lifted. A circle of sunlight hit the dirt floor.

She ran to the bottom of the ladder and squinted up, starting to say, 'Where have you…?' but something was wrong. Too many bodies coming down.

She stumbled back as Benedict Silver dropped the last few rungs. He swung a gun level with her face.

'There you are!' he said, giving her that pleased-with-himself psycho grin she knew so well. 'We've been looking for you *everywhere.*'

More men were coming down the ladder, Ed too, cowering, apologetic. Fat lot of good that was going to do her. *That's what you get for trusting someone.*

Benedict nodded at the ladder. 'You want to walk up or be carried?'

This was it, her worst nightmare. She knew it was pointless to beg, but she did it anyway, saying, 'Please, please, don't take me back there' – catching Ed's eye and imploring him to do *something*, even though she knew he wouldn't, except apologise over and over, because what could he do against three of them? *He'd do something if it was Ally.* And all the while Benedict moved towards her, still with that superior smile, like the world was supposed to bow down because he had cheekbones, and pressed the cold metal of the gun between her eyes. She was shaking so hard she couldn't catch her breath.

'What have we got here,' he said, reaching between her legs and shaking her crotch, like he was checking to see if it was on properly.

'Fuck you,' Phoenix said, and went to spit in his face.

'Don't push your luck, *freak,*' he said, grabbing her mouth. He spun her around and pushed her towards the other men. 'Grab the hood and cable ties. Looks like we're carrying it out.'

Then the hood was over her head, and the world went black.

48

As soon as Jackie stepped into the office, DS Keyes ran up to her. 'What's this about Helen McAllister? Is she hurt? I heard you called her an ambulance.'

'Charlotte, just the sergeant I need. Can you get down the hospital? Make sure she gives a statement.'

'What statement? What's going on?'

Jackie motioned for her to come for a quiet chat by the printer. 'I had a run-in with our man Silver, this morning. At McAllister's place.'

'On your *own*.'

'Last minute tip-off. No time to call it in.'

'You should have asked for back-up,' said Keyes, looking personally offended. 'You could've been killed.'

'I can take care of myself.'

'That's not the point.'

'I'm sick of arguing with you, *Sergeant*. He cut her fucking thumb off, okay? Now either you get down there and take a statement before she works out a story, or fill in a transfer request. Your choice.'

'You know, I used to really look up to you. That's before I worked for you.'

Jackie sighed and walked away. 'Go to the hospital,' she called over her shoulder. 'Get a statement. Do the job you're paid to do.'

Back in her office, she checked her messages. The other two women who'd reported Truman for harassment were unhurt. Trav had carried on tracing Silver's car, but it was dumped soon after he got away. He could be anywhere by now. Especially as he knew she was onto him.

She opened the recycle bin on her computer, and moved the cursor over the solitary folder there, called 'Investigation'. The one she'd never been quite able to delete. She hadn't read through the folder in at least five years, not since they set up Rapid and Serious. What if Silver was high up in Pure Resistance, the group that killed her family? What if he knew the person that planted the bomb?

What if this was finally her chance to take revenge?

She right clicked the folder and moved the cursor over Restore. *Don't do it. Don't—*

A knock on her door. She closed the window and called for them to come in.

Sergeant Haggerty entered. 'Got a minute, boss?'

'What's up, Nick?'

'News on the daughter, Alison Truman.'

'Away with friends, right?'

'Maybe, maybe not.'

Jackie motioned for Haggerty to sit. 'Go on.'

'Remember she sent her mum some texts saying she'd gone to ground in Brighton.' He cleared his throat, uncomfortable. 'It seems Alison Truman was leading something of a double life.'

'Don't be coy, Nick.'

'She was in a homosexual relationship,' Haggerty replied, the tops of his cheeks flushing. 'According to her best friend, Jasmine Anaisha.'

'So Alison Truman has disappeared with a mystery girlfriend. Did this Jasmine have any info?'

'Here's the thing – no. None at all.'

That was strange. Girls that age usually told each other everything.

'There's more,' Haggarty went on. 'I've been through Alison Truman's phone records, her social media, everything, and from what I can see she's got no friends or contacts in Brighton.'

Was she really there? Or did someone have her phone? Was that person trying to buy time – making out that Alison Truman was safe when she was not?

'Good work, Nick,' Jackie said. 'Can you get her on the mispers—'

'Already done, boss.'

'You're wasted as inside sergeant.'

'You were the same when I started,' he said, getting up. 'I mean, how you're being with Charlotte. That first month was the worst of my life.'

'And look at you now.'

They traded smiles, and he shrugged. 'Sink or swim, isn't it?'

The phone rang as Haggerty was leaving. Jackie saw it was the super, so picked up. He wanted a quick five minutes, but she could tell by his tone it was something more. *What now?*

*

Superintendent Drum welcomed Jackie at the door to his office and led her to the chair.

'What's going on, Andy?' She took a seat. 'Am I being put down?'

He laughed without humour, then became serious. 'What happened today?'

'Just another day on the job.'

Drum leaned forward, his black jacket straining against his shoulders. 'Then why is Helen McAllister in hospital, raving about police brutality in general – and you in particular?'

'There may be someone else involved in the case, a real criminal.'

'McAllister's saying you threatened to arrest her unless she lied.'

'He's making her say that.'

'Who is?'

She couldn't tell Drum about Silver, not yet. If he found out about the gangs Silver used to be involved with, he might say she was compromised and pull her off the case – and she couldn't let that happen. This was much bigger than one murder.

'A person of interest,' she said. 'Nothing concrete yet.'

Drum rubbed his eyes. 'Jackie. You've been here since the start. You know how hard we've grafted to build RAS.'

'I know.'

'There's additional scrutiny on us now.'

'Trust me. You don't need to worry. I've—'

'You're not *listening* to me!' Drum was leaning forward, gripping the armrest of his chair like he wanted to rip it off and beat someone to death with it. He took stock of himself and sat back. 'I'm worried about you, Jack. That's all. How many years have we worked together? Ten? Twelve? This is the wrong case for you. It can go to Aleksy. You take—'

'No way.'

'It's not your decision.'

'Please, Andy.' She sat forward. 'This is *my* case.'

He held her gaze but looked away first. 'Okay, fine, Jack. But I'm watching you now. So, please, don't fuck it up – because if you do, you might bring us all down.'

49

For a long time I sat in the bunker, reliving what had just happened. Phoenix struggling against the restraints, the way she threw her head around and snapped her teeth as the hood went on, her muffled whimpers as they hauled her up the ladder. Benedict's last words to me. *Don't forget, there'll always be a place for you with us.*

Not for the first time in my life I wished I were a stronger, braver and maybe altogether different man from the spineless creature I seemed to be. I didn't have a choice in betraying her, not when my own son was in danger, but it was still my fault they'd found us. She'd told me not to call anyone. She'd told me not to trust anyone. I hadn't listened.

Sitting there in the dark, I wanted more than anything to get drunk. To feel whisky scald my throat. Scrub the world, fade into oblivion, and repeat. But that wasn't an option.

Not only was Ally's fate in my hands, but Phoenix's too. I'd do whatever it took to get them back.

I searched the bunker. They'd taken her laptop but left everything else. Inside her rucksack I found the flick knife that killed Murph, and an old-school Nokia phone. From the food supply I nabbed a stack of brown square sachets each stamped Pure Whey Protein in bold black letters. In a lockbox hidden under blankets in the far corner was a money clip containing about five hundred pounds in twenties, and a photo of Ally and Phoenix together. They were on a picnic blanket, arms around each other's shoulders, grinning into the sun.

One dead child is bad luck. Two? That's just negligent.

What if Benedict was telling the truth, and my daughter was already dead? I pressed the photo to my eyes and quietly sobbed. I couldn't allow myself to think that way. He was taunting me, trying to get a rise. When the tears stopped, I kissed the picture of Ally and held the photo to my heart. *I'll find you. Both of you.*

I headed up the ladder and opened the stump, ready to pull the knife if someone was there, but the forest was quiet. I followed the bridle path, maintaining a steady jog, wanting to push on faster, to outrun the thoughts forcing their way to the front of my mind – Gabrielle's flushed cheeks, Phoenix trussed and squirming, Mitchell's voice on the phone – but I had a long way to go, and I didn't want to burn out before I got there.

My whole life, I'd been scared by the thought of death, of that instant when you went from being to nothing. But something had switched. If being alive meant doing nothing while a young girl was kidnapped in front of me, then I wasn't sure if I deserved life. I would rather be dead than that person. I'm not saying I was suddenly fearless. I didn't want to die in great pain, and spiders could still keep their distance, thank you; but on that long jog back to the road, when I thought about the many ways trying to find the girls might lead to my end, I no longer felt afraid.

*

Barely days on the run, I'd lost weight. That, and the stubble, and the plain black jacket/baseball cap combo I bought at a petrol station meant I was unrecognisable from the picture of me on the news. I pulled the cap low and walked the A road to Luton, then bought a ticket for the train to St Pancras, getting in late afternoon. The Men's Learning Centre was out west, but I had somewhere to go first.

It was evening by the time I got to Finchley. When I saw my house, something inside me cracked, and I wished more than anything to wind back a week, to cancel that bloody injunction and ground Ally for the next five years.

Whatever happened next, my life how I'd lived it before was over. Whether or not I managed to clear my name, my career as a serious solicitor was in ruins, and my legs were too old and slow to start chasing ambulances. As for my family, even if I found Ally and brought her home, we were all going to be scarred beyond recognition by what had happened. There'd be no more Friday nights, not like before.

Gabrielle's silver Renault was in the driveway. Staying in the shadows, I crept round the side of the house. I peered into the kitchen window and saw her at the buffet bar, sitting on a stool, her chin resting on one hand, listlessly scrolling through her phone. An almost empty bottle of red wine stood beside her glass. When I rapped on the window, she sprang off the stool like someone had thrown a grenade into the garden.

I gave her a little wave. She seemed unsure at first, no doubt confused by the baseball cap, something I'd never worn in my life before. Then she ran to the window and pressed her hand to the glass. My heart broke at how tired she looked. Something had gone from her, a confidence in how she carried herself; it was like she was a ghost, and wasn't sure if I could see her. I put my hand to hers on the glass. We stayed that way for a long second, looking at each other, and I realised that I probably seemed just as alien to her. Our warm nest was gone. We were different creatures now.

Gabrielle opened the back door and I stole into the house, moving quickly to the hallway, away from all windows. We paused, like there was still a barrier between us. Then we collapsed into each other's arms.

50

Benedict sat before the grid of monitors, trying to lose himself in the petty dramas playing out on them. Whenever he dipped into someone's life, he liked to leave a camera or two around their home, so he could see how the ripples of his actions continued to spread. Nothing excited him more than watching a family tear itself apart after he'd intervened in their lives. He loved to send the tops spinning, then sit back and watch, letting them spin whichever direction they pleased. That was the reason humans had free will: so the gods remained interested.

It was just after seven and most people were herded round the dinner table, their faces in the trough. Prime time for conflict. Teenagers especially loved to flip out at meals, which always struck him as bizarre, seeing as the people they were screaming at had just given them food. That was what made watching people so interesting. The irrationality, the absurdity, the capacity to destroy themselves and those around them simply because they were feeling upset. It made up for having to see them eat, which he always found mildly disgusting.

Some interesting scenes were playing out – that McAllister woman in particular was having a bad time, cradling her bandaged hand while her brat of a boy, goading her with his eyes, slowly tipped his eggs and beans onto the carpet – but still he couldn't engage. Truman, that was the problem. Had it been a mistake to let him live?

At the time Benedict had dismissed him as a nothing, a nobody, no more capable of coming back to bite him than an old dog dumped in the wild. He'd been looking forward to the pathos of watching Truman's homecoming on the cameras left in his house, and his no doubt wretched attempts to hold onto his family while they waited for the return of the daughter who would never come home.

Now Benedict wasn't so sure. No amount of rationalisation could ease the tension in his shoulders, the restlessness in his legs, the sensation of clamouring in his brain. At the very least, he should have taken Truman to the police. Tie the threads of that murder case into a neat bow.

Benedict switched one of the screens to the live feed of the operant conditioning chamber – or, as he called it, the Box – and watched her squirm as the shocks ran up and down her spine. On a different screen, he checked her hormone levels, and added an 80 mg dose of Tamoxifen. How long had she been on this sequence? Just over an hour. Another ten minutes, then he'd switch her to the family scene, and pump her with MDMA. Really capitalise on how broken her defences must be.

He had a real knack for working the Box, so much so that Carmichael now left that side of the operation to him. They had a very exclusive client list, and at up to a hundred thousand for a week's therapy, it was that more than anything which had funded their phenomenal growth.

Only this week, the Men's Learning Centre itself had passed a million sign-ups, many of them *paying* subscribers, and was now in a position to take over some of the smaller players. Both the militant Alpha Activists group and the milder Justice Now Alliance had accepted offers to come under the Learning Centre banner, selling the group their websites and mailing lists for a fraction of their true worth. A shadowy group called Coalition for Celibacy – who owned KillStacey.com and the Men's Rights Movement Facebook page, with over two hundred and fifty thousand followers on its own – were days away from accepting a merger. By the end of the year, they were projecting a mailing list of well over two million, worldwide.

The numbers were increasing faster than ever, and it was all down to him. How many men did he have on the computers now? Some were on the social media frontline, trolling SJW losers on the MeToo hashtag. Others were undercover on women's forums, arguing that they preferred it when men were strong instead of sissies, promoting #WeNeedStrength and #BringBackTheRealMan. Plenty were recruiting too. Scouring 4chan and Reddit for lonely alienated teenage boys to bring into the fold. His men would have three or four chat sessions on the go, each saying the same thing: *You are being taught to feel anxious. You are being made to believe your masculinity is toxic. But these are lies. Women are liars. Look at the way they paint their faces then tell you not to look. You don't need them or their lies. You are powerful. You are a* man.

His position was all but untouchable, so why was he ill at ease? Why couldn't he stop thinking about Ed Truman? That loser hadn't done anything particularly surprising or ingenious, but he was unpredictable, especially with his home life in ruins. The detective wasn't a problem – someone was already on her – but Truman was out there in the world. Who knew what mischief he might cause?

On a whim, Benedict clicked onto the Truman house cameras and turned up the sound. There she was, *Gabrielle*. On her own, sinking yet another bottle of wine, looking glum. He wouldn't have thought she'd be interesting ... and yet there was something so *watchable* about her. Drama loves drama, he supposed. On more than one occasion he'd imagined what the expression in her eyes might be when she died. Perhaps he could pay her another visit, maybe even—

Gabrielle jumped to her feet, hurried to the window. A moment later she opened the back door.

Benedict allowed himself a smile, a wry shake of the head. Then he called the police hotline.

All that stress, and for what?

He should have had faith the gods always find a way.

51

THE BOX

On the screen were the mother, the father, the boy and the girl. They were sitting on the floor in a large lounge, close together on the cream carpet, celebrating something – maybe an exam result, or was it Christmas? It was hard to focus. Their voices faded in and out along with her concentration. It didn't matter. She was warm and her body was warm and her brain hummed with warm thoughts, and she only wished that she could stay in this moment for ever, watching this family. She *loved* this family. There was just so much tenderness flowing between them. Sometimes when she zoned out she was there, with them, part of it, she was the girl, that cute little girl with her long hair in a very pretty plait that went all the way down the back of her cute mermaid pyjamas.

Something rippled in her heart. *Her hair.* It was all gone, wasn't it? She tried to reach up to feel but realised she couldn't lift her arms more than a few inches and saw the manacles, the water tube, and straight away it all came back, she was trapped, she was trapped, she was—

Take a deep breath. Nothing has changed.

She shifted position, flexing the muscles in her legs, wincing against the pain. What snapped her out of the spell? The girl's hair. *That bastard!* It took *so many* years to grow her hair. Some girls, they only had to wake up in the morning and their hair was an inch longer. She was lucky if she got that in *three months*. Now it was gone – he'd shaved her head. And she knew it wasn't important, not compared to the bigger picture, the one where she was locked in a nightmare having her brain pulped. *But her hair!*

On the screen, the girl was getting a present. It was her birthday and everyone was crowding excitedly to see what she would unwrap.

'I hate you,' she said to the girl, and spat at the screen. 'You don't fool me, you *bitch*.'

Even when she was expecting it, the electric shock caught her by surprise. Her back arched, pushing her against the limits of the manacles around her wrists and neck.

She dropped back down. 'Fuck your myth of the happy fucking family—'

The next shock lasted so long that it seemed to rip her right up the middle. When it finally stopped, she slumped, jaw slack, the sweat on her skin freezing, and continued to spasm for a few seconds. She heard a click, and hazily watched as a needle extended out from the side of the box and jabbed her in the leg. Then the *whirrr* as the manacles retracted, moving her back into place.

She couldn't remember closing her eyes but when she opened them again the family were on the beach. Everything was so vivid, so fresh, she could feel the warm breeze on her face, hear the soft crash of the waves, the dad asking, *Who's coming into the water?*

I am, she called after them. *Wait for me!*

52

I clung onto Gabrielle in the hallway, both of us crying, neither of us wanting to let go, because breaking the moment would mean we'd have to face up to the real world again, and I didn't think either of us were ready to do that.

'You look rugged,' she mumbled into my neck.

'I probably smell pretty rugged too.'

She pulled her head back, and when she spoke her bottom lip trembled. 'I can't believe you're here.'

'Where's Mitchell? Is he okay? Is he here?'

'Where else would he be?'

'He's not been anywhere else?'

'You think I'm going to send him to school with all this going on?'

Had Benedict tricked me? Had he got a recording of my son's voice, and used that to fool me into telling him where Phoenix was hiding? And I'd fallen for it!

'I heard from Alison,' Gabrielle said. 'She's still in Brighton. She's staying—'

'She's not there.'

'But I got another text—'

'Someone must have her phone.'

'So where is she? Do you know?'

247

'I think so.'

'We have to tell the police.'

'How about I give them a quick call?' I could see from the hurt in Gabrielle's eyes that the joke had come out mean. 'She sneaked into William Carmichael's Men's Learning Centre with another girl, Phoenix. They were stealing evidence of some messed-up psychological experiments they're doing on kids. Ally got caught.'

'What do you mean *caught*? Is she still there?'

'I don't know. But I'm going to find out.'

'*How?*'

'I ... I'm not sure.'

'You're not sure!'

'I swear, if I have to search that whole place—'

'What if they *kill* you?'

The words hung between us. There was nothing I could say to that.

I started up the stairs. 'I want to speak to Mitchell before I go.'

'Wait, Ed.'

Now the initial euphoria at seeing her had subsided, all I could think about was the picture of her on the news, her head thrown back, another man's head at her breast.

'You saw it,' she said.

'Benedict Silver?'

She had her hand to her throat, like she was about to throw up and was desperate to hold it down. My wife, my beautiful wife, who I'd loved almost from the minute I saw her. I felt light-headed, not able to catch my breath, my pulse pounding so fast I thought my heart was going to rupture. I'd been dreading this moment, had pushed the thoughts away as soon as they came to me – there was too much other stuff going on – but now I was here I realised I'd been in denial the whole time. This was what mattered. As much as anything else, it was this.

'He told me you invited him round.'

Gabrielle opened her mouth to speak, but instead looked away.

'So it's true?'

'I wasn't ... I didn't ... I didn't know what I was doing.'

'Okay. Right.'

'Please, Ed. I'm sorry. I was scared, I wasn't thinking straight. You weren't here and ... I'm sorry. There's no excuse. I'm so, so sorry.' Gabrielle squeezed my hand and I went to squeeze it back, but all my strength was gone. I was empty, emptied out, nothing left.

We sat on the stairs, and she explained what had happened. How it was supposed to be just a drink, but things got out of hand, and then the police came round, and once they left she asked him to go, but instead of leaving he drugged her and took those pictures and now she just wanted to die from the shame of it all. I held her and stroked her hair as she wept onto my shoulder. I wanted to forgive her. I knew she was devastated and truly sorry. She'd been manipulated by a cruel, charming psychopath, who'd probably tricked a hundred women in the same way before her. Even so, we'd been together twenty years, and all it took to forget about me was a handsome face.

'I've got to go,' I said.

'There's a detective – Chief Inspector Rose. She was here last night. She met *him* too. Maybe you could call her.'

That had been an option before, but now without Phoenix as an alibi, or the videos to at least entice the police into investigating Carmichael, I couldn't think of anything worse than being arrested.

'I have to find Ally.'

She grabbed my arm as I started up the stairs. 'You're not going.'

'I have to.'

Tears ran down her cheeks. 'Please Ed, don't.'

We stood in silence for a long while, our fingers laced.

'I'm sorry,' she said. 'I'm so sorry.'

'I'd better speak to Mitchell,' I replied, pulling gently out of her hands.

Gabrielle nodded. 'I love you,' she whispered.

'I love—'

A fist banging on the front door cut me off.

'Mrs Truman? Are you in there? It's the police.'

53

Gabrielle and I froze. That wasn't a coincidence or a courtesy knock. A neighbour must have seen me and called the police. I bristled at the thought that someone I'd lived next to for fifteen years, whom I'd smiled at, chatted to, maybe even had over for a barbecue, could turn me in like I was a burglar trying to jimmy open the bedroom window.

I thought about bolting for the back door, but figured they already had someone waiting there. Instead we crept upstairs.

'You have to go with them,' Gabrielle whispered. 'What else can you do?'

'Even if they can't get the charges to stick, I could still be away for days, and I need to find Ally *now*. What if she's still alive, and something happens to her when I'm locked away?'

'Call Steve.'

'That snake? He's already sold me out once.'

'*What?* When did you—'

'I'll tell you later. I've got to go.'

'Go where? They're outside!'

I glanced at the loft hatch.

Gabrielle figured out what I was thinking. 'Are you crazy? You'll *die*!'

'If I don't look for Ally, then who will?'

She opened her mouth to speak, but closed it again, knowing I was right.

Mitchell was watching from his doorway, dressed in his pyjamas and dressing gown. He shrank away as I went to him, about to go back in his room and slam the door, but I got there first and dragged him into a hug. 'I just want you to know', I said, 'that none of this is your fault. We've not always got on lately, and I'm sorry for my part in that. I … I could have been better, and I'll try harder. I promise. You're my son, Mitchell. You're my son and I love you with all my heart.'

I don't know what I expected his response to be. Maybe I'd watched too many soap operas, and was primed for the big reaction, for him to fling his arms around me and say I was forgiven, that he loved me too, or to shove me away and declare that he wished I was dead. Instead, his chin trembled, he nodded like he understood, then made a squirming motion with his shoulders that signified I was to let go. He closed the door without a word.

When I turned back to Gabrielle my escape plan seemed even more difficult than before, and it already felt the wrong side of impossible. She gave me a *been there, bought the T-shirt* look. 'He never comes out any more. I just leave plates of food for him by his door, and during the night he puts the empty ones back outside. God knows where he's peeing.'

'I'd better go,' I said, pulling the loft hatch down.

'Ed?'

'What?'

She grabbed me by the lapels and kissed me with a fierceness I'd not felt since we first started dating. 'Come back to me. It's *you* I want. No one else.'

I held her close, wanting to cry, but the only thing that would make what I was planning to do even harder would be to do it half-blinded by tears.

'You've not seen the last of me,' I said into her mass of curly hair. Then I started up the ladder.

*

Jackie turned onto Truman's street, the uniform waiting at the corner waving her through, and pulled up outside the house. DS Keyes was at the bottom of the drive, briefing two more officers.

Keyes greeted her with a sparse nod. 'Got cars covering the south exits. Other end is the high street – you want it cordoned?'

Finchley had a busy high street filled with wine bars and Italian chain restaurants named after famous chefs who probably had as much to do with running them as the pot washer. Jackie didn't want to cause panic by clearing the area and throwing up tape.

'Just get some extra patrol,' she said. 'Chopper here soon?'

'In twenty.'

She waited for the uniform to go, then eyed Keyes carefully. 'Have you got a problem with me, Charlotte?'

'No problem, ma'am,' she replied, although the flat set of her mouth said different.

'So this is how it is now?'

'How what is?'

Jackie sighed. Whatever. Keyes thought she knew it all, but she was wrong.

'Fine,' Jackie said. 'If that's how it's going to be, then maybe when you get back to the office you should look at filling in a transfer request.'

'I went to the hospital, as you asked.'

'You've made your feelings clear, Sergeant. Let's move on. Who's round the back?'

'Sanghvi and Clark.'

'Other exits? Flat roof? Dormer?'

253

Keyes glanced sheepishly at the house. 'Surely you don't think he'd—'

'I've seen people climb onto ledges ten storeys above moving traffic to avoid getting arrested.'

'Okay, sorry.' Keyes got out her radio. 'I'll—'

Jackie motioned for her to put it away. 'I'll go round.'

She hurried in the shadows to the side of the house, moving low and fast. She found DC Clark, mid-fifties, not front line but dependable. Through whispers and signs, he communicated that the lights were on, but they'd not seen anyone yet.

At the back, DC Sanghvi was crouched behind a hedge within lunging distance of the back door. He gave her a quick nod, then returned his focus. She scanned the back of the house. A skylight in the roof, big enough to climb out of. Not far to the end, then a short jump to the next house, maybe a metre. Easy enough. All he'd have to do was clear a couple of houses, drop into a garden, get lucky with the fences, and he'd be gone again.

She crept to the wall on that side. Bricks went up to shoulder height, with three-foot panels on top. She gave them a push. Rickety, but they probably wouldn't collapse under her weight.

A click from above. Jackie looked up just in time to see the skylight opening.

*

I'd always said I wasn't especially scared of heights – falling to my death seemed no better or worse than all the other ways to die – but as I looked out of the window, I realised that I'd never been scared of heights before because I'd never been in a genuine position of falling from one. Halfway out of that skylight, the ground looking much further down than I thought, I wasn't so much scared as downright shit-your-pants terrified. *What the fuck am I doing!*

I grabbed the casing at the top of the skylight, and lifted my foot from the crate I was standing on, trying not to pitch forward and slide headfirst down the tiles. How steep was this roof? It didn't look this steep from below. I pictured myself losing my grip, spinning off the side, slamming onto the flagstones. If I thought thirty years in prison was bad, how about serving it in a wheelchair? No picnic, I was sure, not unless that picnic involved getting shanked with a screwdriver. That's if I didn't die on impact. *Just climb out first, then worry about staying alive.*

Movement below, in the bushes. The police were in the back garden. I swung my other leg out and in the same motion managed to pirouette my body, falling onto my front, getting a handhold on the tiles. I couldn't believe it. I was out!

A woman's voice called up to me from the ground. 'Come on, Ed. Is that such a good idea?'

I craned my neck over the eaves and saw her in the garden. Bad idea, looking down. The world tilted sickeningly, and I gripped the frame harder. Eyes front from now on, and go, just go. *Go now!*

I started along the roof, pressed to the tiles, hoping that friction was enough to keep me from plummeting to the ground. The surface was as slippery as wet grass. I didn't know where to put my feet. *Shit, shit!* I inched sideways, gripping what I could with my fingertips.

'Long way down, Ed,' called the woman. 'Just stay there, and don't panic. Chopper will be here in a couple of minutes with a ladder.'

A chopper! Oh, for piss sake. I had to push on faster. Roofers walked on these things all the time. How hard could it be? It was all a matter of confidence. The ridge running along the top was only a few feet above. If I got up there I could straddle it and make it to the end faster. I pressed my forehead to the tile, trying to steady my breath. *You can do it! You're a badass!* I readied myself on my toes, then scrabbled up, hands searching for the ridge, just about throwing my fingers over the top before my foot slipped. I dangled like that for a few seconds, then flung my other hand over and hauled myself up.

'We've got the whole area locked down, Ed. There's nowhere for you to go.'

I managed to stand on the ridge, one foot either side, arms out like I was crossing a tightrope, and headed for the end of the house. We'd lived next door to the Cunninghams for the last six years. Although they were just starting out in married life, their twin girls too young to play with my pair, we got along well with them. They were quiet and uncomplaining. In short, great neighbours.

And now my life depended on leaping across the metre or so gap between our houses.

It didn't seem far, but maybe the distance was deceptive. Maybe I'd sail halfway then run out of steam, dropping, cartoon-style, onto the paving below. I tottered to the edge of the ridge and went to glance down but managed to stop myself. What good would that do? None. None at all. *Oh Lord. Oh balls.* I forced myself to think about Ally. *You're doing this for her.*

Now or never. I primed my legs to jump, but something short-circuited. I began to topple forward instead. *Oh great. Just fucking great.* I was literally going to fall face down. At the last second, something kicked in and I thrust outwards, not so much leaping as bridging the gap, my forearms clattering onto the neighbouring roof. An adrenaline-burst of strength allowed me to swing a leg and get first my knee up, then the rest.

I lay on my front, chest heaving, head spinning, thinking I was going to be sick. I made it! *Unbelievable.* Below was movement, the fence between our garden and the Cunninghams' shaking. Someone was climbing over it. That bloody detective!

I half-stumbled, half-crawled forward, getting to my feet

more easily now. At the other end I got right to the edge and leapt, this time getting a knee onto Mrs Mishra's roof. She was a nice old lady whose cat I helped to feed when she went to visit her son in Scotland, although I didn't think she'd welcome this new phase of our relationship, me as a fugitive, jumping onto her tiles.

A memory – her cat in the garden, disappearing through the fence at the back. Mrs Mishra saying, *I keep meaning to get that hole fixed, but it's not doing any harm.* If I could somehow get down, through the gap, out onto McClure Street ... Damian and Anushka lived at thirty-eight, and I knew they had a gate at the back of their garden. Leading where? What did it matter? *Get there first, then worry about it.*

I skidded down the roof tiles, aiming for the flat roof over the kitchen extension, but I was moving too fast. My foot hit the gutter and tore it from the wall. Way too close. I turned on my front and slid carefully over the edge, until only a foot remained to fall. I dropped down into the garden.

I picked my way through the long grass to the back, and looked among the bushes for a cat-sized gap in the fence. A whole panel was missing. I hopped a concrete lip into the next garden, where a new house was being built, the bottom floor still only a shell of steel and foundations.

I tore past it, stopping behind the skip on the front drive, fully expecting to see a police car waiting to see if I'd come this way. There wasn't. Maybe they hadn't seen me drop down. I wasn't going to wait to find out. I sprinted for Damian and Anushka's house, almost vaulting their front wall, sending thanks to anything and everything in the universe that might have had a hand in helping me escape. I ran round the side, picturing their pretty little garden, with its blossoming beds and art deco fountain. The gate was in the far-right corner. *I was going to make it!*

Just as I thought that, something slammed into me, very hard and very fast, knocking me to the ground.

*

Jackie grabbed one of Truman's hands on the way down and twisted it behind his back. He tried to buck her off, but she shoved his hand higher, until he yelped and stopped struggling.

'Give it up,' she said. 'It's done. You're done.'

She stayed tense, expecting him to push up, make another break for it. Most blokes she nicked tried that, thinking she was too small to keep them down. They were wrong.

'Edgar Truman, I am arresting you on suspicion of the murder of Ivana Kostimarov. You do not have to say anything, but it may harm your defence if you do not mention when questioned something which you later rely on in court.' He dropped his forehead to the ground and moaned. 'Anything you do say may be given in evidence. Do you understand?'

'I didn't kill anyone,' he mumbled. 'I'm being set up.'

'Now I don't have any cuffs on me,' she said, lifting slowly off his back, 'so I'm going to have to trust you not to try anything. If it helps make your mind up, I'm a seventh-degree red belt in Brazilian jiu-jitsu, and a close combat trainer for the police force. I'll let you stand if you want, and walk with me back to the car, but I am not the most patient of people. If you—'

He jerked up, pushing her back, getting onto his toes and almost breaking for it, but she managed to hook his ankle with her foot. An elbow came flying towards her as he spun around, trying to stay on his feet. Jackie pulled her neck back, avoiding it at the last second, stepping into the gap, and getting Truman by the throat. She shoved him against the side of the house.

'Let's have no more of that, eh?' she said.

'*They have my daughter.*'

'Tell me all about it at the station.'

Truman looked gaunt and scruffy, a different person to the one stuck to the whiteboards at the office, the tanned dad on holiday, the respectable lawyer getting recognition in the local papers for his work in the community.

'If you take me in,' he said, 'they'll kill her. I know they will. If they haven't already.' Moonlight caught the tear tracks on his face. 'She's at this place called the Men's Learning Centre, in Marlow. It's run by William—'

'Carmichael.'

'You've heard of him.'

Jackie nodded. 'You could say that.'

'She broke in with a friend—'

'The girl you were with?'

'Her name's Phoenix. I don't know her last name. They were after her too. That's why they killed that girl in the park, so you would track us down for them.'

'You had no dealings with Ivana Kostimarov?'

'On my life – on my children's lives. I'd never heard of her before I read about her death in the news.'

'What about this other girl? This Phoenix?'

'They've got her as well now.'

Blue lights from a passing squad car swept through the passage and were gone.

'What do you know about Benedict Silver?' Jackie said. 'White, tall, athletic build. Brown hair, side-parting. Good-looking.'

'That fucking psycho. He was the one after us. *He* killed that girl, not me.' Truman's eyes became animated. 'You know about him, don't you? You're the detective Gabrielle mentioned. Please, you've got to let me go. As soon as I've found them, I'll hand myself in. I promise.'

'You and everyone else,' Jackie snorted.

'I know how this works. Even if you believe me, you'll never get a warrant to search Carmichael's place. If my daughter's in there, I've got to try to get her out.'

Helicopter blades throbbed in the night sky, getting closer.

Truman wasn't the murderer. She knew it in her gut. And he was right that they'd never get a warrant for the Men's Learning Centre. On what basis could they?

Even so, she had to take him in. See what he knew.

Jackie grabbed his arm. 'Come on, let's go.'

'I don't know you,' he said. 'I don't know if you've got kids. But if you do, just imagine what it'd be like if one of them was taken.'

One last look around. One last wave to Mum.

She paused, suddenly unsure. *Don't do it. Whatever you're thinking, don't do it.*

Truman noticed. 'I have to find her. *Please.*'

The mistake was looking him in the eye. She saw the same desperation that had stared back from her reflection every day for the last seven years. What she would have given for someone to offer her the chance to save Verity.

Jackie's hand opened. Truman freed his arm cautiously, then bolted.

Had she just made the biggest fucking mistake of her career? If anyone found out she just let the prime suspect in a murder investigation go, it might not just be the end for her, but for the whole of RAS.

She turned to head back, stopping when she saw who was watching her from the top of the passageway. Detective Sergeant Keyes.

'How much of that did you see?' asked Jackie.

'All of it.'

54

'So,' Jackie said. 'What now?'

Keyes' eyes were hard in the moonlight. 'Speak to the super. Remove yourself as senior investigating officer from the case.'

'Why would I do that?'

'You had him. You had him, and you let him go.'

'He didn't do it.'

'You don't know that.'

'I know.'

'He gave you some sob story about his missing daughter – who he's probably buried under his back patio – and you believed him.'

'He didn't kill that girl.'

'You know what I think?'

'Go on,' Jackie said, stepping towards her. 'What do you think?'

Keyes stood her ground. 'I think you bottled it, guv. I think he served you a plate of horseshit and you ate it.'

They were close enough for Jackie to feel the sergeant's body heat. 'I was catching killers while you were still wetting the bed.'

'You're not fit to run the case.'

'He slipped out of my hands.'

'Bullshit.'

'Your word against mine.'

'You're a disgrace.'

'And you couldn't catch a fucking cold in flu season, let alone the people behind all this.'

'You're not going to speak to the super.'

'Not until I've got something to tell him.'

'Then maybe I will.'

'Go home,' Jackie said, moving past Keyes. 'I'll see you in the morning.'

Keyes, Truman, that smug bastard at the Men's Learning Centre pulling the strings, they could all fucking jump. She was done with this for the night.

*

When Jackie pulled up outside her house, a chill spread through her chest. Why was the upstairs light on?

She slipped through the front gate and crept to the door. It was ajar. She eased it open with her shoulder, pepper spray in her hand, tensed to strike in case someone loomed at her from the shadows. The streetlight showed dirty bootprints on the hallway carpet. A lingering stink of cigarette smoke in the hallway. She stayed still, listening. Nothing.

This was a warning. Someone was telling her, *I know where you live, and I can get in whenever I want*. Otherwise why make it so obvious? Either way, she wasn't going to risk staying.

Back in the car, she made a call. 'Peter, I need your help.'

He told her to come straight over.

*

Jackie had known ex-DCI Peter Brennen for over twenty years. He'd been her first boss at the Met, when she was an ambitious constable keen to prove herself as a detective in a world still dominated by surly men in trench coats, who somehow managed to stumble over criminals between pints down at the pub. Peter had never been like that. A teetotal vicar's son, he'd been the one to instil in her the importance of keeping a clear head, trusting her instinct, and understanding that the right thing to do wasn't always the *right* thing to do. Now in his early seventies, Peter was a long way past active service, but when he got a call from an old colleague asking for a favour, he never said no.

'It'll just be for a few days,' Jackie said.

'Stay as long as you need,' Peter replied. 'Coffee?'

Jackie followed him through to the kitchen. At the table, she eased her shoes off.

'I think I might have messed up,' she said, when he put her cup down. She took a sip, wincing at the bitterness, pleased that her caffeine tolerance was such that even a cup as strong as this would have little effect on her exhaustion.

'Go on,' he replied. Tall and lean, with a dimple in his chin and a sweep of hair, Peter had always put her in mind of a matinee star, the kind who beat the baddie and got the girl, all without causing a single crease in his tailored suit. The years were catching up to him, though. A cloudiness had come to his pale blue eyes, a slight tremor to the fingers of his right hand, and Jackie was once again reminded that nothing stays strong for ever.

'I let my emotions get the better of me.'

'So what's the problem?'

'You following the Ed Truman case?'

'Of course.'

'I had him, and I let him go. He told me he didn't do it, and … I believed him.'

Peter nodded, considering this. 'You know what I think?'

Jackie looked up from her coffee. 'What?'

'You're never going to know if you made the right decision or not, because you'll never know what would've happened if you brought him in. You went with your gut. That's never a bad thing.'

'What if my gut threw away the one chance we had to catch the killer?'

'You're not going to work anything out sitting here and going over it again.' He patted her hand. 'Sleep on it. Let your subconscious do the work. The mind is much more powerful than people imagine.'

'But—'

'Get some rest.' Peter finished his coffee and stretched, grimacing at a pain in his shoulder. 'That's an order.'

He showed her to the spare room and said goodnight. Jackie sat on the bed, then slumped back, so drained that she couldn't even move her limbs to get undressed. And yet her mind continued to churn. What if Truman had played her? What if this was the one chance to bring him in and she had blown it? She remembered the super yesterday: *I'm watching you now. So, please, don't fuck it up.*

What if she'd made the biggest mistake of her career?

55

I burst through Damian and Anushka's garden gate, turned left, and sprinted. In another reality I would have run straight into a waiting officer, but in this one I came out on Layton Road and darted for the sprawling housing estate at the end. I used to cut through there walking the kids to school, so knew my way around the maze of walkways and gated bin areas.

I came out at the entrance to Evershot Park. It was quiet at this time of night, the moon hidden behind clouds. I hurried past the tennis courts, deserted save for some teenagers smoking by the nets, and ducked into the trees. A helicopter passed overhead. I crouched low in the bushes.

Why did she let me go? Did the police already suspect I'd been framed? Or just her? It had to be just her, otherwise they wouldn't have swooped down on the house to catch me. Still, one was better than none. At the very least it meant that bastard had made mistakes. Although perhaps not enough to prove my innocence.

The sound of the helicopter faded away. I stayed kneeling in the dirt for hours, until my thighs ached, and my feet were numb from the cold. By the time I left the park, it must have been midnight.

Hood up, I trotted towards the minicab office near the shopping centre. Even though it would be easier and cheaper to wait until morning and get the train to Marlow, I didn't want to risk being seen on CCTV. That detective knew where I was going, and might change her mind about bringing me in. The sooner I got there, the better.

I had my spiel ready for the taxi – drunk after a work do, missed the last train – but the tired Chinese bloke in the dispatch booth, the bags under his eyes the purple of ripe aubergines, cut me off. Sixty pounds. Car will be here in five minutes. I had plenty of cash from the hideout, so said that was fine. He nodded for me to wait on the rutted wooden bench by the door, then turned back to his screen and joylessly carried on his game of Minesweeper.

The car arrived. As we sped through the dark puddled streets of North London, I tried to work out what I was going to do once I actually got there. Knock on the front door in the morning and ask them what they were teaching? Where I could apply? If the stuff going on there was as dodgy as Phoenix claimed, they weren't likely to be having open days.

How did those girls even get in? Don suits and wigs and stroll through the gates pretending to be dudes? I wished I'd asked Phoenix at the hideout. I pictured myself struggling over a security gate, slipping and impaling my bum on an iron spike. Scratch that.

*

Forty-five minutes later, we passed the *Welcome to Marlow* sign. I told the driver to drop me at the station. I'd been to Marlow a few times, so knew my way around a little. It was a picturesque enough place on the bank of the Thames, the high street lined with estate agents, boutique galleries and charity shops stocking designer clothes. As affluent an English town as you could imagine. Not the kind of place you'd picture Carmichael setting up his base.

I walked around the quiet streets, shivering as the wind picked up, but couldn't find any signs for the Men's Learning Centre. It didn't help that I hadn't a clue what I was looking for – and seeing as it was nearly two in the morning there was no one to ask, either. Marlow was the kind of place that went to bed at ten o'clock and didn't have anything in particular to get up for in the morning.

Eventually, my legs were too tired to keep going. I found a small grassy square with a bench and a bronze statue of a man crouching beside an old-fashioned wheel, which, judging from the stains on it, looked to be the communal toilet for all the local pigeons. As with so many of my nights of late, I was freezing, the wooden slats of the bench cold and hard as iron. If this was what it was like to be homeless, shivering and aching and filled with dismay, no wonder they were all taking drugs and getting pissed at midday.

*

In the morning it felt as though someone had spent the night using my body for origami. If it weren't for the bench's arm rests to push against, I'd probably still be there, trying to stand. I trudged back to the town centre, feeling vulnerable now it was daytime. If someone recognised me and called the police, I wasn't likely to get another officer who believed me and let me go. I needed to fix my appearance.

Near the station was a GO Outdoors shop. It didn't open for a couple of hours, so I passed the time shivering behind a skip in a nearby alleyway, then went in and bought a black beanie hat, a black ski jacket and, remembering how cold I had been the previous night, treated myself to a six-pack of hand warmers and a merino wool thermal vest. I kept everything on when I paid, and got a bag for my old baseball cap and jacket, which I planned to dump.

I asked the cashier if he'd heard of the Men's Learning Centre. He told me it was on the campus of the now defunct West

Buckingham University, a quick bus ride or a twenty-minute walk out of town. Fearing cameras, I chose the walk, following the main road south, taking the third left and the second right, noting sourly to myself how proud Phoenix would be with me for remembering the directions – but then I saw her squirming and bucking as they carried her up the ladder, and I had to lean on a garden wall, feeling physically sick. *I'm so sorry, Phoenix.*

By the time I saw the main entrance, my heart was beating so hard it seemed to be shaking my whole body. Behind the high front gates was a modern glass-fronted reception, and further back some taller buildings, maybe five or six storeys. Signs warned of dogs and security men. Prosecution for trespassers.

I carried on round. Where I could get close to it, the perimeter wall loomed a couple of feet above me, and on top of that were railings coated in anti-climbing paint. Plenty of stretches were new, as if they'd been fortifying the place in case of attack. They clearly didn't want anyone sneaking in.

At the back of the ex-university campus was another entrance, probably for deliveries. Two men in an orange Portakabin manned the barrier. I found a hiding place in the trees where I could watch.

A steady stream of men filtered in and out, both on foot and by car, most of them looking like cast members of a particularly brutal gangster movie, all scars and tats and foreheads designed to crumple your nose. As they passed the Portakabin they showed ID cards to the men inside, although the speed at which they produced them and put them away suggested the examination was far from forensic.

Could I somehow make a fake one? But I had no idea what a real one looked like, and the last thing I wanted was to draw attention to myself. For all I knew, all these hard bastards could be friends from nursery school, and that was why they were being waved through.

About eleven, the guards changed over, although the new pair of hard bastards didn't look any friendlier than the last. What would Phoenix do? How would she get in? Could I dress as a plumber or something and say I'd been called out for an emergency? What if they took me to a leaky pipe and told me to fix it? Maybe I should stay closer to home. *Hey, fellas! Any of you call for a lawyer?*

Oh boy. This was hopeless.

How the hell was I going to get in?

56

Jackie woke at half six. Had she even slept? Time had passed quickly, but she didn't feel rested. The tiredness from last night was still deep in her eyes. One thing, though – the knot in her mind had gone. And right then she realised she had it, she had all of it, the case laid bare.

Ed Truman's daughter sneaked into Carmichael's Men's Learning Centre with this other girl, Phoenix. They got caught; Alison Truman was grabbed, but the other girl got away. She must have taken something, though, as Carmichael sent his attack dog, aka Benedict Silver, to go find her. Silver knew that Ed Truman and Phoenix were together, so he killed an innocent girl and planted Truman's DNA on her – the police find Truman, he finds the girl. When that didn't work, Silver assaulted Truman's wife and planted the pictures in the media. Just as Silver had planned, Ed Truman saw it and came home – though he'd missed Ed's arrival at the house, for some reason.

Where were Alison Truman and her friend now? Had they really been taken back to the Men's Learning Centre? Why did they even break in there to begin with? What had they been looking for?

Peter was up already when Jackie came downstairs. They had tea and toast together at the kitchen table, and he regaled her with tales from his service days. In his twenties he'd been a Class 1 driver, the ones they called in for the fastest, most dangerous pursuits. She'd heard the stories before, how he chased jewellery robbers round the narrow back streets of Hatton Garden, or the time he clipped a barrier and tilted onto the side of his wheels while going ninety down the M6, but it was good to see his eyes come alive as he told them again.

On the way to the office, she thought about how to handle the Keyes situation. What could she tell Drum? How they tricked McAllister into telling them the truth? Or about confronting Silver on her own? He'd laugh Keyes out the office for stuff like that. What about last night, letting Truman go? It was the sergeant's word against hers.

Andy wouldn't be happy if any complaints were lodged against her, but she'd worked with him for a long time. He'd know that if she *had* let Truman go, there would have been a bloody good reason for it.

*

When she walked into the office, Drum was loitering in his doorway. He looked harried, pissed off, sweating through his shirt, like he'd spent an hour searching for his wallet and still couldn't find it.

'A word, please,' he said to her. She spied Keyes behind him, sitting at his desk. Opposite her was Tanya Goodman, the union rep, tall and narrow, with a short shock of black hair. What was she doing here? Was this a disciplinary?

Jackie nodded to the kitchen. She needed to buy some time to think this through. 'Mind if I get a coffee first?'

'A word, *now.*'

She followed the super into his office. Tanya greeted her with a curt nod, Keyes with eyes that suggested their first-name terms had been cuffed and thrown in a cell. A chair was set out next to Tanya. Jackie guessed that was for her.

Drum gave her a tense smile. 'If you're wondering why your rep's here, it's because I don't want you to feel ambushed by this.'

'Which is exactly what her being here makes it feel like.'

Tanya's smile got even curter. The unions weren't keen on intervening in specialist units, preferring to speak for the honest plod walking the beat. 'Shall we start?' she said.

'What exactly are we starting, Andy?' asked Jackie.

Drum and Keyes exchanged a glance. 'Detective Sergeant Keyes has brought certain ... *incidents* to my attention, and' – he sighed hard – 'I am duty-bound to investigate them.'

'What kind of incidents?' Jackie replied.

Keyes leaned forward, lips tight to her teeth. '*You let him go.*'

'Let who go?'

'You *know* who. Ed Truman. Last night.'

Jackie looked around the room in surprise. 'Are you trying to stitch me up?'

'You arrested him, then you let him go.'

'You're mistaken, Detective Sergeant. I had a scuffle with him. He got away.'

Drum didn't hide his scepticism. 'He got away from you?'

'Lucky punch, boss.' Jackie shrugged. 'What can I say?'

'What about Helen McAllister? She's saying you attacked her.'

'Is she saying I cut off her thumb?'

'Well, no—'

'So when did I attack her?'

'When you were there with Sergeant Keyes.'

Jackie looked at Keyes. 'Did I attack Mrs McAllister?'

'You intimidated her,' Keyes replied.

'Perverting the course of justice is breaking the law, Sergeant.

I had every right to place her under arrest – should I have said "please" first?'

Drum leaned forward on his desk, his shoulders straining against the seams of his shirt. 'What about this *other person*?'

'Which person?' Jackie replied.

'The person of interest.'

She felt her stomach fall. He knew. 'You speak to Sergeant Sen?'

'She gave me a copy of the file she sent you, for Benedict Silver.'

'I'm perfectly capable of separating my personal life from—'

The union rep cut in. 'What's this about?'

'One of the *suspects*', Drum said sharply, 'in a current murder investigation has links to a terrorist group, Pure Resistance.'

'How's that relevant?' asked the rep.

'They killed my family,' Jackie replied.

'Oh God,' said Keyes, her hand to her mouth. 'I'm sorry.'

Drum rubbed his face, dragging his cheeks down like they were stuck to his palms. 'For God's sake, Jackie. Why didn't you tell me?'

'Because you'd have pulled me from the case.'

'I've got no choice.'

'But I'm there, Andy. I'm *there*.'

'I'm officially removing you as SIO, and recommending you go on gardening leave until a review can—'

'I'm working a *murder* investigation here, or have you forgotten what that's like?'

'I'm just trying to follow the proper procedures to ensure—'

'Fuck your procedures.'

'That's enough.'

'Look at you, in your uniform. Proper respectable, aren't you?'

'RAS needs to be seen—'

'Yeah, yeah, yeah.'

'Do you want to go on suspension?'

'What else do you call *voluntary gardening leave*?'

At least Drum had the grace to appear genuinely unhappy. 'I'm sorry, Jackie. My hands are tied.'

'This is big. We're talking major organised crime. Domestic terrorism.'

Drum shook his head. 'I'm sorry—'

Jackie shoved back her chair. 'You know something, Andy? You used to be a real detective, but you've gone soft. And you, *Charlotte*. You wouldn't know a killer if they served you a severed head for breakfast. Next time, why don't you stay behind your desk? Let some real detectives get the job done.'

As she left the office, she heard Keyes calling after her – 'Wait! Ma'am!' – but Jackie didn't look back. She didn't care what that excuse for a detective had to say.

*

Driving back to Peter's house, Jackie replayed the meeting, cringing at how petulant she'd sounded. She was out of order talking to Drum like that. He was her superior, and that mattered to her. Plus he was right. She should have told him about Silver's links to Pure Resistance. And to tell him to go fuck his procedures when he was just trying to do the right thing – if someone had spoken to her like that, they'd be out the door before they'd finished the sentence. She'd have some apologising to do once she'd calmed down. Maybe some grovelling too. No way was she being taken off this case.

She pulled up outside Peter's house ... and felt suddenly cold. Something gave in the back of her throat.

Why is the front door open?

Jackie fumbled the handle, her hands suddenly useless, shoving the car door open with her shoulder. Every step seemed like wading deeper and deeper into a swamp. At the porch she palmed her pepper spray, composed herself, then crept into the house.

She sneaked through the hallway, peered into the front room. Empty. TV off. Perhaps he'd gone out and forgotten to close the door. That was possible, right? Except it didn't feel that way. Not at all. She'd been to enough crime scenes to know how one felt. Too quiet, a bad taste in the air. A sense that something was very wrong.

When she got to the kitchen, she saw them: droplets of blood, dark red against the white tile floor.

She ran through the house, checking every room, calling his name. Peter wasn't there. He was gone. And it was all her fault.

57

I needed to put myself in Phoenix's mindset. If she were me, how would she get into the Centre? She'd do something daring, be dressed for the part, like when she tricked me into thinking she was an art student. She'd swoop past the guards before they could even wonder if they'd been had.

First, I needed to look like them.

The men at the centre had a certain appearance. Not a uniform, as such, but a way of dressing. Jeans were in, which was fine by me as I lived in them anyway, as were plain white T-shirts, black work boots – polished so hard you could do your hair in them – and hoodies in dark hues. I had a feeling there was a hierarchy attached to the colour of your hoodie. Most of the younger, seemingly less sure blokes wore black, whereas the ones in burgundy looked older and more in charge. Everything was clean, spotless, even, and neatly pressed, like they were all expecting a visit from judgy in-laws.

I rushed back to Marlow, bought yet another set of clothes, then went to Boots and picked up some scissors, shaving foam and a razor. Standard hair in the centre was either short back and sides or a buzzcut. In the disabled toilets at the train station I went one further and shaved my head down to the skin. When I passed a hand over my smooth scalp, I shivered. I'd always been protective of my hair, was constantly pushing it back to check whether it was receding, silently mourning every strand I found swirling in the plughole after a shower, so it was strange now to see it gone. I did miss it – having no hair didn't suit my face – but I felt more alert after doing it. Sharper. A little bit deadly.

I felt the flick knife in my back pocket, and tried to imagine pulling it in a fight, thrusting it into someone's gut. The give of the blade as it slid through their flesh. Watching the life vanish from their eyes.

Could I really do that?

*

I got back to my hiding spot by the back door. It was lunch time, and groups of men were coming out. I waited for a sizable one that looked in high spirits, then stepped from the undergrowth, hurrying after them.

They turned off about a quarter of a mile down the road, went past a long-abandoned business park, and piled into a clapped-out boozer called The Lord Nelson beside what looked like an abandoned freight railway line, the weeds growing over the tracks. Inside were men in shadowy corners, hunched over their tables, staring menacingly at their drinks. It stank of sour beer and deep-fried scampi, with a back-note of piss spilling out of urinals.

The group I'd followed were sitting at a long table near the back. I took a stool at the bar, ordered a pint from the bored bloke messing with his phone on the other side, then pretended to watch the football on the caged screen above the lifeless jukebox. My plan, as much as I had one, was to try to speak to some of them, see how they got a place in the centre, and somehow use that information to blag my way in. At the very least, I wanted to see their ID badges. Maybe I could create a fake one.

One of the men came to the bar. He had that cocky, stand-on-the-street-drinking-pints vibe. In the past, I might have been nervous speaking to someone like that, at least socially – I had about as much in common with him as the stool I was sitting on – but not now. I tipped my beer at him in greeting, and he nodded back.

'You with those lads over there?' I asked.

'That's right.'

'Let me get you a round.'

He cocked his head, suspicious. 'How come?'

Phoenix's voice in my head – *Go for it! Go big!*

'Cos I just got out, innit,' I replied, taking on this cockney Del Boy twang I'd neither planned nor knew was part of my repertoire. 'I've got some dosh and it's no fun drinking on your tod.'

He began to smile. 'You do a stretch?'

Fortunately, Gabrielle and I were partial to the occasional gritty prison drama, and I'd practised my story. 'Got a two for GBH,' I replied. 'Cunt 'ad it coming. Been messin' around with my missus.'

'That right?'

'Shanked the fucker in the arse,' I said, affecting a croaky, cigarette-ruined laugh. He joined in and, like a couple of six-year-olds, we laughed together at the thought of me stabbing someone in the bum.

'Good on you, man,' he said, holding out his hand. 'I'm Mikey. Go on, get us a round. I'll bring you over to the boys.'

Minutes later we were both carrying trays of slopping lagers to the table. Mikey did the introductions, then I slipped into the chair beside him, proposed a toast to being free, and joined in the joyous clanking of glasses. A couple of leading questions later and they were telling me about life in the centre, how it was a bit like being in the army, which many of them had served in – except with more boozing and fewer 'ragheads' hiding in ruined buildings, waiting to blow you to bits. Mornings were devoted to fitness and combat training, the afternoons to education, mainly IT or construction skills. Everyone pitched in with the cooking, maintenance and, especially, the cleaning.

'S'all about keeping your life in order,' Mikey said. Sage nods round the table. 'Shows you got self-respect.'

This was just the London base. Apparently, there were over twenty centres around the country. None as big as here – they confirmed there were over a thousand men on campus – but some were quickly establishing themselves.

'I'm up to the Middlesbrough chapter in the mornin',' said a tall old lag with chunky plastic glasses. 'Gonna be huge in the North East. You know up there they've got the highest male suicide rates in Europe. In bloody Europe!'

Grumbles of agreement. A toast 'to the fallen comrades'.

I didn't want to drink, even the thought of it made something rear up inside me, but I knew I had to fit in, so nursed my first pint and barely touched my second. When they went to get another round, I said I was driving. All the while I asked questions about life on the campus, how you went about joining up, what was the vetting process. I noticed one of them, a stumpy, stubble-headed bloke, his forearms thick as thighs, had his ID card on the table, so went round to talk to him. While I made up some rubbish about being sure he'd dated a girl I knew – *Kirsty, you know a Kirsty, right? Or was it Cindy?* – I studied the details on his card. Along with a picture, it had his name, number and block, which I assumed was where he slept.

Around two, they headed back. I shook hands with them all then waved them off, saying I hoped to see them in there soon. By the time I returned to the Portakabin, the entrance was quiet. I hurried to it, a panicked vein throbbing in my temple, sweat sluicing off my neck, hoping my genuine terror would convince them that I'd really gone out for lunch and forgotten my ID card.

The man at the window was mid-fifties, on his elbows reading the paper, his thinning hair slicked back over his scalp.

'Sorry, I'm really sorry,' I said, bustling up to him. 'I've only been here a week, and I went to the pub, and I left my card on my bunk.'

He looked up at me, scowling. 'You what?' Then he called over his shoulder to the bloke behind him monitoring a CCTV screen, 'You hear that, Ray? This twat forgot his card.'

'Tell him to fuck off, then,' Ray replied, without turning round.

The bloke at the window shrugged. 'You heard him. Fuck off.'

A fresh load of sweat squirted from my pores. 'Please, you've got to let me in. I'm already late and—'

'Go round the front. Take it up with reception.'

I dredged Mikey's afternoon schedule from my memory. 'That'll take ages! My woodwork class has started, and it's computing after—'

'How's any of this my problem?'

'*Please*, I don't want to be late. I promise I'll never forget it again. I remember all my details. I'm in Block 2B, and my ID number's XD44215—'

'All right, all right, for fuck's sake, I don't need your life story.' He nodded past the barrier. 'Go on, just this once. Don't forget it again.'

I thanked him profusely, sent an extra thanks to Phoenix, then ran past the barrier.

Finally, I was in.

58

Jackie sat in her car, eyes on the sliding glass doors at the front of RAS HQ, waiting for him to come out. Did he know Peter had been taken? He must by now. The snake. The lowest of the low. He didn't deserve to live.

The doors slid open. Sergeant Travis rushed out, glancing at his watch, gym bag slung over one shoulder. Jackie watched him walk through the gates, then got out of the car.

She stayed behind him as he turned onto the main road. It was quiet, the commuter rush dying down. Jackie saw her chance, a side alley behind the Woodman, a pub they'd been to countless times. She remembered that night there, after cracking the Mildew twins case, when Trav made a move on her. Was he dirty back then?

She rushed him from behind, a razor blade between her fingers. He turned as she got close, his usual smile in place. It dropped when he saw her.

'Afternoon, Sergeant,' she said, grabbing his belt. She pushed the razor into the small of his back. 'Have you seen spinal nerves before? They spill out like worms.'

'What the fuck, boss?'

She dragged him by the belt into the alley behind the pub, and pushed him against the bins. 'Don't play stupid with me.'

He had his hands up, his look of innocence almost convincing. 'I don't know what you've been told, but—'

She pressed the razor to his sternum. 'Shut up, or I swear I will slit you up the middle.'

'Up the middle? In the spine?' He went for that smile again. 'Who said women were indecisive?'

'You fucking shit, Trav. You fucking, fucking shit.' Her hand wavered, her voice was cracking. She tried to control it. 'A good man might be *dead* because of you.'

'I swear, boss. On my life. I don't know what you're talking about.'

'How did Silver know I was at Helen McAllister's?'

'When were you at hers?'

'Yesterday morning. You rang me to say the jag was on the move.'

'I said it was on Westway. How could I have known where it was going?'

She looked into those brown eyes, that handsome face. The trust built up over years of working together bubbled to the surface. Was her head so messed up by the case and the anniversary and now Peter's disappearance that she'd imagined the connection? McAllister's flat was on the fifth floor; wasn't it possible Silver saw her pull into the car park from a window in the tower block?

She lowered the razor. It made her head jam up thinking she could be wrong about this. But it was possible, right?

Trav puffed out his cheeks, his shoulders slumping. 'Holy moly, boss. You had me going there. *Fuck.* You looked crazy!' He let out a strangled laugh. 'I thought you were going to gut me for a minute. Let's go back to the office and talk—'

Jackie didn't move. 'I keep asking myself, who could have known I was staying at his place?'

'Who you're talking about now?'

'Peter Brennen.'

'I'm sorry, boss. I don't know—'

'You don't know that name?'

'On my life, boss.'

'You really don't remember? We were out for a drink and talking about old bosses. I told you about Peter, I know I did. I said I stayed with him if I needed somewhere to hide out. And the reason I remember is because you made this big deal about some old CID mate whose house you crashed at when you were undercover.'

Trav was shaking his head, his expression apologetic, like he wished he knew what she was talking about, but no, he still hadn't a clue.

'What was that friend's name again, Trav? The one you used to crash with. Because I remember.'

'I … I—'

'*What was his name?*'

'I'm sorry, I—'

'You fucking scum.'

'Listen, boss,' Trav sighed – then jerked his head to the side. 'What was that?'

His punch couldn't have been more obvious if he'd pulled out a whiteboard and explained his plan. Jackie slipped his flailing fist and closed the distance between them, wrapping her arms around his body and pushing him back, getting in two jabs to his solar plexus before he could react. Trav folded forward, mouth open, not breathing, his throat making a strange clicking noise. She hooked her foot around his ankle and yanked his body from under him. He landed flat, the back of his head bouncing off the cobblestones.

One knee on his chest, Jackie pressed the gleaming silver tip of the razor to the hollow below his Adam's apple. 'How about we do it a third way? I puncture your windpipe then watch you squirm as your breath leaks out before it gets to your lungs?'

Trav was panting, face red, still not recovered from the slam. 'You psycho … fucking … bitch.'

She pressed the razor hard enough to pierce the skin. A thin red trail ran down to his collarbone. 'Do you want to see how psycho?'

'*I don't know what you're talking about!*'

'Get out your phone and call Silver. Tell him you need to see him.'

'Listen to yourself, boss! You've gone mental!'

'I'm not getting through to you, am I?' Jackie lifted the razor and pressed it to Trav's cheek. 'You may not give a shit about dying, but I bet you wouldn't want go around with your pretty face all cut up.'

For the first time there was real fear in his eyes. He went pale and she felt a cold sweat against the back of her fingers.

'Peter's one of our own,' she said. 'You don't deserve the badge.'

She pressed in the blade, dragging it down Trav's cheek, his scream echoing around the alley until she chopped him in the throat with one hand. The sound abruptly stopped.

Jackie leaned down, until there wasn't an inch between their eyes. 'Call. Him. *Now.*'

Trav scrabbled in his pocket, found his phone. His hand shook as he unlocked it.

'Make it convincing,' she said. 'Or by the time I've finished, your face will be hanging in ribbons.'

59

I wandered around the Men's Learning Centre at random, feeling unreal, strangely disconnected, remote-controlled. I was in a maze of small buildings, connected by paved pathways, the grass between them yellow and overgrown. It was clearly designed to hold many thousands of students, a lot more than the number of men here, so away from the main path there was a strange silence, as if it was deserted.

The buildings were old, the brickwork water-stained. Through the windows of some I saw men at their lessons, heads bent to their desks as they took notes. Other structures looked like they hadn't been used in many years. I darted into an empty one and padded down a magnolia corridor lined with musty seminar rooms. In a recreation room at the end I found some sofas, vending machines and a campus map pinned to the wall.

I searched the map. Along the right-hand side were clusters of small blocks with names like Higgins and Kogan, most likely famous people connected to the university. I figured I was in one of those. In the centre of the campus was a courtyard, surrounded by a refectory, a sports centre and various administrative offices. Three towers of lecture theatres stood behind the reception at the front entrance, which must have been the ones I saw from the gates.

Where could Ally be? A feeling of hopelessness crept up the back of my throat, heading for my brain. I swallowed it back down. I hadn't come this far to lose faith. If she wasn't here, then I'd find someone who knew where she'd been taken.

Or buried.

No. I couldn't allow myself to think that.

I needed to speak to some of the men, ask questions. Someone had to know something. I needed to be careful though – if I said the wrong thing, I'd be found out for sure. Then again, why should anyone suspect me? Middle-aged and grim-mouthed, scarred with the knowledge that the woman I loved had betrayed me; maybe I wasn't so different from them. Maybe, in another life, I could have been one of them.

*

As evening came on, I hung around the central courtyard. A bar called the Good Monk opened onto it, and despite the chilly air people were standing by the doors, drinking pints, joking around. I bought a beer, took it outside and found a group large enough that I could linger beside it without anyone noticing.

Some greaser was boasting about how he'd infiltrated a Facebook group for romance novel fans, convinced them over time to make him an administrator, then deleted the group. The men around him laughed. I joined in. When they stopped, I turned to the bloke next to me – a youngish lad with a brown fringe and gold ear stud – and said, 'Name's Mikey. Just got here a few days ago.'

'Wade,' he replied, shaking my hand. 'How you getting on?'

There was this weird noise in my head, high-pitched, almost a squeal. 'Like we're all fucking brothers here.'

He chinked his glass to mine. 'Amen, brother.'

I told him I was recently out of prison, here on the invite of

286

a friend, fleshing out my story with some of Mikey's anecdotes from his time inside – the cell mate who got so messed up on spice he thought the toilet was a drinking fountain; the guard who got done for assault and ended up in the same block as them.

'No way!' Wade cried, slapping me on the back. He related the story to the bruiser beside him, who guffawed just as loud.

During a raucous cheer, I tipped out half of my pint, then only pretended to take sips. When a shooter came my way I flung the contents over my shoulder before lifting the glass in victory and howling. I started asking around about the break-in, keeping it casual, joking around. *I heard some dumb bitches tried to get in here last week.* But I got either shrugs or slight looks of suspicion, so quickly changed tack.

'Where can I get some pussy,' I slurred at Wade, holding onto his arm as though without it I'd pass out face first on the paving stones.

One of his eyelids was drooping lower than the other. Not surprising considering how many shooters he'd dispatched. 'No worries on that part!'

Then he told me about the Club.

'S'all free, mate,' he said, and downed the rest of his pint. 'Whatever you want.'

My heart kicked up. 'They keep girls here?' I realised how that sounded, so quickly added, 'We can have 'em whenever we like, eh?'

'No old slappers, neither. Some of 'em are total babes.'

I pictured him forcing himself on Ally, and felt such a rush of anger that it took all of my control to keep the reaction off my face. Was that where they were keeping my daughter? Was she being assaulted by these animals?

'Sounds like heaven, mate,' I said. 'I gotta get to this place! Is it open now?'

Wade managed to shift his eyelids into what I thought was a wink. 'The Club is *always* open.'

*

He directed me to the maze of blocks on the south of the campus, close to where I had come in. I soon found a long squat building with pornstar pink windows and Ayia Napa dance crap pulsing out of the back room. A young man was out the front, face down on the grassy verge, empty vodka bottle still in his hand. I guessed this was the place.

I headed inside and followed the music down the corridor. The party was going on in what had been a university common room. It was busy, maybe twenty men and almost as many women, with most of the women done up as if they were going to an aerobics class in a fetish club. The air was warm, viscous, and the sheen of moisture on my skin felt less like my own sweat and more the condensation of other people's bodily fluids. All the armchairs had been pushed to the sides, and lots of the action was happening there, kissing, fumbling, one couple either having sex or trying to beat each other to death with their pelvises.

A couple of women by the drinks table were eyeing me. One wore a black one-piece bathing suit, like she was going to a public swimming pool, the other was in a bra with big scallop shells covering her breasts. The one with the scallops swayed over and grabbed my arm. Her bra was too big for her skeletal frame, and her lipstick was smeared up her cheek, like she'd recently wiped her mouth.

She took me in with bleary eyes. 'Let's have a dance.'

I glimpsed the rotting remains of her teeth when she spoke. Not even her perfume, slathered on like sun cream, could mask the stink coming from her mouth. It took all I had not to recoil.

She draped her arms around my neck, and we slow-danced. The hi-NRG beats broke into a vocoder solo, some guy warbling about his *chiquita's* sexy smile. Somehow I doubted he was singing about this *chiquita*.

I took the chance to whisper in her ear, 'I'm looking for a girl.'

'Right here, sugar.'

'She's called Ally.'

She pressed her bony crotch to mine. 'I can be anyone.'

The music dropped in a hail of trumpets, the drum machine going at least five hundred beats per minute. I tried not to think about the ten different types of herpes she was no doubt breathing onto me. Scallops slid her hand in mine. It was cold and hard, a bit slimy, like a dead fish.

'You got something for me?' she mumbled. I noticed the track marks on her arm. She saw me looking and did nothing to cover them. 'I'll do whatever you want.'

'It's not like that. I'm searching for someone.' The interest faded from her eyes, and she started to turn away. 'I mean yes. Whatever you need, I can get.'

She led me out the way I had come. We took a corridor off to the right, past a woman in a dilapidated Playboy Bunny outfit, the black bowtie skewed and one of the ears torn off, sitting against the wall with her head in her hands. Scallops opened a door into what might once have been some professor's office, but which now contained a camp bed, a dressing table and a lot of empty bookshelves, which, for some reason, depressed me almost as much as anything else I'd seen tonight.

She sat on the bed and nodded for me to join her. Instead I loitered by the dressing table, on which stood a grimy tub of E45 cream and an even grimier teaspoon, the bottom crusted black.

She reached for the cigarettes on her nightstand. 'You got any ice? I need a bump.'

'I'm looking for my daughter. I think she might be here.'

'She on the game?'

'It's not like that.'

She lit her cigarette and regarded me. She was younger than I thought, maybe mid-twenties, but tired and used beyond her years. 'So you're one of *them*, are you?'

'One of what?'

She spread her legs. 'Like to fuck daddy's little girl?'

'Christ, no! I'm talking about my daughter, my *real* daughter. She's … disappeared. I thought she might be here.'

'Why would she be *here*?'

'I just heard she was.'

Scallops took a long drag of her cigarette, regarding me over the glowing tip. 'How long's she been missing, your girl?'

'Since Friday.'

'What's she look like?'

'She's sixteen, tall, long brown hair. Wavy.'

Her hand froze as she was stubbing her butt on the sad foil ashtray by her bed. When she sat back, her eyes were feral. 'What's it worth?'

I took the rest of the hideout money from my pocket, still over two hundred pounds, and held it out.

'This do?'

She took the money and flashed me a grey-toothed smile. 'Wait outside a minute, eh?'

As I went out the door, I flushed with regret. Had I just been played?

60

THE BOX

She turned her head once more in the unbearable darkness and strained her neck to search for the drinking tube. Her tongue caught the end and she guided it to her teeth, clamping on and sucking, begging for something to come out. Her throat was so dry she couldn't even swallow.

Still nothing.

When had the last video ended? The one with the family on the beach. She'd been caught up in it, imagining herself frolicking with them in the sea, feeling the sun warming her skin, the water splashing against her chest, then it ended and . . . nothing. She'd expected the cords attached to the restraints to loosen, so she could lift her arms and legs and neck, but they'd remained locked in place.

How long ago was that now? Many hours, at least. A day? Each minute probably felt like a thousand, in the silence, unable to move. Her muscles were painfully seized up. Any shift of position caused blades of pain to dig into her body.

What had happened? What had changed? Was she just going to be left in this box to die? She wouldn't last long without any water. Was that their plan all along? Why even begin the treatment? Everything she'd fought for, all the struggles she'd overcome to try to be the person she was meant to be, it couldn't end this way. *It wasn't fair!*

She felt the pressure building again in her eyes, and fought against it. You will not cry. *You will not cry!* But it was hopeless. Huge sobs shuddered through her as she pulled against the restraints, the scream building in her throat, until she could no longer stop it from bursting out.

61

Jackie took Trav's car to the abandoned warehouse complex where he'd agreed to meet Silver. She got out, took up a position behind a low wall, and waited.

Half an hour passed, an hour. The sky grew darker, the backdrop of broken buildings and sagging chain link fences becoming more desolate as the light faded. Had Trav double-crossed her? Somehow given away on the phone it was a trap? He'd said nothing suspicious, just to meet at the usual place – Silver said to be there for six – but maybe there'd been something crucial unsaid, something that let Silver know it was a set-up.

Five more minutes, then she was opening that boot, getting Trav by the throat, and asking in a not nice manner what was going on. What she had on him, he'd better not be lying to her. It wouldn't be just his job, his reputation, and more than likely his freedom; bent coppers were one thing, but bent coppers who caused harm to another officer were an altogether different league of scum. If word got out he'd been involved in Peter's kidnapping, it wouldn't just be a few cuts on his cheek. It'd be the end. And not a quick or happy one.

A black BMW swung round the side of the warehouse, pulling up close to Trav's car. Silver climbed out and leaned against the bonnet, calm and unhurried, a wistful smile tugging at his lips, like he'd just arrived at a holiday rental on the beach and wanted to soak it all in.

'I'm not stupid, Detective,' he called out. 'I left you a trail right to me. If it's *not* you here, then I seriously overestimated your capabilities. And I'm not in the habit—'

'Okay, Silver,' Jackie said, standing up from behind the wall and shaking out the cramp in her thighs. 'I don't need to hear another speech about how great you are.'

Silver grinned charmingly. 'Come on. Let me.'

'If you knew it was me,' she said, walking back to Trav's car, 'I take it you've come to hand yourself in.'

'I always suspected there'd be a time when knowing where you liked to scurry off to hide would come in handy.'

Jackie froze. How long had Trav been with the unit? Five years? And when did she tell him that about Peter? At least two, maybe two and a half—

'I can see you're crunching the numbers,' Silver said, his grin growing wider. 'Wondering how long I've been monitoring you for. How about if I say, *seven years.*'

'I get it. You know about my family. You and every other piece of London pondlife. But I know about you too, Silver. I know the gangs you used to run with. Pure Resistance, right?' She shrugged. 'If that's all you've got, if that's your big reveal—'

'*Bye, sweetheart,*' Silver said, affecting a woman's voice. '*Be a good girl today, and I'll see you after school.*'

The last words she ever said to her daughter. Jackie was back there, crouching by the door, holding Verity and kissing her smooth cheek, feeling guilty for taking an extra half-hour to herself, but grateful to Lester for doing the school run. Looking forward to a long, hot shower. On a whim, after shutting the front door, she went to the window to see them go.

Her daughter taking one last look around. One last wave to Mum.

Then the explosion that tore her life apart.

Pinpricks of light flashed in her eyes, like she'd been socked bare-knuckled in the teeth. Something broke deep inside her. What spilled out was cold and black.

'You ... you were there?'

'I was more than just *there*.'

'You killed my family?'

'I figured you might work it out at some point.'

She made for him. 'You piece of shit. I'm going—'

Silver tapped his phone and held it up, screen out. He was still a car length away, but even so it was clear enough what she was seeing – Peter in a dingy room, gagged and tied to a chair. Beside him stood one of Silver's goons. Something sharp glinted in his hand.

'Don't you dare hurt him,' she said.

'Or what?'

'I swear on my life...'

Silver gave a thumbs-up to the man on the screen. He grabbed Peter's hair, pulling his head back, exposing his neck. His tendons were taut and he tried to thrash his head. The knife moved to his throat.

'Stop!' Jackie lowered her hands. '*Please*, stop. Okay? I'm here. You've got my attention. Whatever you want me to do, I'll do. Just don't hurt him.'

'You understand the situation now?'

'Yes. I understand. Okay? I *understand*.'

'You're a liability to me, Detective. You know too much. Now I could just kill you, but that's not how I like to do things. I'd much rather watch you squirm.'

'So what—'

Silver pressed his finger to his lips. 'Hush now, girlie. The man's talking.'

Now she got it. That same old story. Power. Dominance. For all his calculations and flourishes he was still so stupefyingly *alpha male*. She kept her mouth shut. *Play along. That's all he wants.*

He took a flick knife from his pocket and tossed it to her. She caught it and popped the blade. Weighed it in her hand, judging.

'Don't even think about it,' Silver said. 'Try *anything* and you'll watch your friend's neck turn into a fountain.'

'What do you want me to do with this?'

'I want you to cut out your tongue. If you do that, I'll let him go.'

'You're crazy!'

He licked his top lip and seemed to be panting. 'For the rest of your life, it'll be a reminder for you not to open your mouth about me.'

'This turn you on, Silver?'

'You don't want to know what turns me on.'

Jackie shuddered. No, she did not. She weighed the knife again. 'I—'

'Shame,' he said, and nodded to the screen. Peter bucked in the chair as the man pressed the knife, drawing blood.

Jackie lurched forward, hand out. 'Wait! Wait! Look!'

She stuck out her tongue, held the knife to the base.

'You've got until I count down,' Silver said. 'What's it going to be? Your tongue, or your friend?'

Was she really going to do this?

'Three…'

She pressed the sharp metal, feeling it cut into her flesh, tasting blood.

'Two…'

Fuck! Fuck! *Fuck!*

'One.'

Sergeant Keyes stepped from the shadows, warrant card out,

Taser in her other hand. 'Benedict Silver, I am placing you under arrest.'

Silver stared at her, head cocked, a *how could you be so stupid* look forming on his face.

Jackie flicked the knife underhand. It thumped into Silver's stomach. He dropped the phone and staggered back, hands in a wide circle around the hilt sticking out of his shirt. A bloodstain grew around the wound. He took a quick step to the side, then dropped to his knees, jaw clenched in pain.

Jackie moved fast to him and took the knife's handle. 'Where is he?'

Silver smirked, bubbles of blood on his lips. 'He'll be dead by now.'

She grabbed the phone off the ground. The video call was still live, the man at the other end staring into the camera and going, 'Boss? *Boss?*'

'Tell him to stand down,' Jackie hissed, tweaking the knife.

Silver gritted his teeth harder. 'Fuck you, cunt.'

She pressed down. Silver jerked forward, face in agony, sucking in a breath like he was coming back to life. 'Stand down!' he ordered them, defeated. From the distance came the sound of an ambulance siren.

'Why don't you rest,' she said. 'Got a lot of questioning to do after they've patched you up.' Leaning close, she gave the knife one last twist. 'I've not *finished* with you. Understood?'

She took his agonised grimace as a kind of agreement and stood, wiping her hands on her trouser leg.

Keyes was by the car, Taser still trained on Silver. 'You never cease to amaze me, ma'am.'

'I told you to wait until I gave my signal.'

'Cutting off your tongue wasn't signal enough?'

'I might have missed.'

'Lucky for you that you didn't.'

Jackie smiled. 'You know something? We may make a real detective out of you yet.'

'And you asked for back-up this time, so maybe we're both learning something.'

'Maybe we are, Charlotte. Maybe we are.'

62

I waited in the corridor, the seconds slowly ticking by, imagining the woman inside opening the window and climbing out, or texting some of the campus thugs to have me removed, or just lying on the bed, counting the cash I'd given her and laughing at my naivety for handing it over. I should have given her half now, half if she managed to find my daughter. She didn't even say if she'd seen Ally. It was just instinct, seeing her hand freeze as she stubbed out her cigarette, that made me think she had. *How could I be so stupid!* Now I was out of money, which made looking for—

Scallops stepped out of the room, glanced up and down the corridor, then closed the door.

'Don't fuck me over,' she said, which I took to mean, *Don't steal the money back once we're done.*

'I could say the same to you.'

'Come on,' she said, heading back the way we came.

'Where are we going?'

'To the basement.'

We skirted past the main room, round a corner and through some double doors into a stairwell. We headed down, our feet echoing off the concrete steps, my heart hammering. *Please let her be here.* At the bottom was a fire door, and beside that a short plank of wood. She pushed the metal bar in the middle of the door to open it. Murky air wafted out.

Scallops looked at me expectantly. When I didn't move, she nodded to the wood. 'Use that to keep the door open, otherwise you'll get locked in.'

I peered into the gloom. The only light came from some security LEDs on the walls, dulled from years of dust. 'My daughter's here?'

'If she's anywhere.'

'How do you know?'

'She's not upstairs.'

I heard a groan from inside, coughing. 'Who's in there?'

'Here's where you go if you're … difficult.'

'*Difficult?*'

She gave me a humourless smile. 'If you say no.'

'Oh, okay. Thanks.'

I placed the plank at the bottom of the door, and stepped into the basement, expecting to hear the sound of her yanking it away, the door slamming shut, her evil cackles receding into the distance – but when I turned my head the door was still propped open, and Scallops was gone.

I moved deeper into the basement. There was a strong smell of bleach, but it didn't quite cover the swampy underlay of sweat and excrement. I made out some mattresses, heard the low moans of the women on them, against the faint *buddha-bud, buddha-bud* of the dance music coming from above. I still had the crappy old phone I'd found in Phoenix's belongings at the hideout, so turned it on, hoping the handset was advanced enough to have a torch. It wasn't and didn't, but the green screen gave me some illumination if I got in close enough.

In the gloom I could see a line of mattresses, a woman on each one, curled up under filthy blankets. I crept among them, hoping none of them freaked out at a green light in their face, but most were coma-tose. Every mattress I'd get a surge of hope, but then it wouldn't be Ally. I was beginning to think it was hopeless, I'd looked at every bed and she wasn't there, when I saw a mattress next to a pile of black bags I hadn't yet checked. She had her face covered, but I knew from the shape of her body, the way she was lying. I just knew.

'Ally,' I whispered, crouching beside her. I eased the blanket down, and there she was, my baby. Starved and filthy and beaten, but alive. I gathered her into my arms, knowing I needed to get her out of there, but unable to do anything more than cry and hold her and kiss her forehead.

She was out of it. Her eyeballs were rolled back when I lifted her lids. She was in just her underwear, so I wrapped her in my hoodie then hoisted her over my shoulder, and navigated through the dark back to the stairwell. I left the plank in the door.

I rushed up the stairs, through the corridor, desperate to get out of there before anyone saw me. A couple of blokes were by the entrance. Was there another way out? I tried to picture the block from outside. Fuck it. I swapped speed for swagger.

'Evening lads,' I said. 'Just taking this one somewhere more pri-vate. Ha ha ha.' They were too drunk and cared too little to look closely. Instead they joined in my laugh, one of them wished me luck, and then I was outside.

I set off at a trot, staying close to the building, aware of the cold, how Ally must be freezing, but wanting to put some dis-tance between us and that awful place. Eventually I saw a small, seemingly deserted building and found a way in. It soon became clear from the dusty instruments and sheet stands this was a music block. I remembered Ally learning the guitar, how she huffed with frustration as she slowly picked through old Neil Diamond songs, 'Sweet Caroline' and 'Forever in Blue Jeans'. And Mitchell's abortive attempt at playing the clarinet – the way Gabrielle and

I would stand at the top of the landing, listening to the reedy screeches coming from his room and trading proud but pained smiles. We never were a musical family.

Upstairs I found a large study with wood-panel walls, a writing desk and a soft leather sofa, so well used the cushions were cracked up the middle. There was even a tweed blazer hanging on the back of the door, complete with brown suede elbow patches.

I laid Ally on the sofa. It wasn't much warmer in here than outside, so I wrapped the blazer around her legs, then got behind her, hoping my body might warm her up. Her skin felt so cold, her breath so shallow. For hours I lay there, rubbing her arm and back, singing her the same nursery rhymes as when she was a baby.

Just as I was nodding off – it must have been one or two in the morning – I felt her shoulder shift beneath my hand. She sat up suddenly, taking a huge breath, like she was surfacing from deep water. She scrabbled away from me, voice panicked. 'Where am I? Where am I?'

'It's okay, Ally. It's me.'

'*Dad?*'

She started to cry, harsh sobs that seem to be wrenched from deep inside her. I gathered her in, soaking up each anguished shudder, stroking her hair and pressing my head to hers and telling her it was okay, she was safe now, even though we both knew I was lying. Busting her out of the basement was just the first step. How was I going to get her off the campus?

Ally wiped her eyes with the sleeve of my hoodie. 'How did you even know I was here?'

'Through your friend, Phoenix.'

'*What?* How did you find her?'

'She found me.'

'Is she okay?' Ally's excitement disappeared when she saw my expression. 'What happened? Where is she?'

'I don't know. They took her somewhere.'

'Who took her?'

'Some bloke, working for Carmichael, I think. His name was Benedict Silver.'

She went still. 'Oh God.'

'What is it? What have they done to her?'

'How long ago?'

'A couple of days, almost.'

'No – *no!*'

'What have they done to her, Ally?'

63

Jackie waited in the hospital canteen until the doctors had patched Silver up enough for her to see him. Her fingers kept twitching into fists. The pulse in her neck shook her jaw. *Don't do anything stupid. Nothing you do to him will bring Lester and Verity back.* At least Peter was okay. True to expectations, Silver's goons had shown as much nous as a tin of beans. They'd continued using their phone despite the police having their number. Ten minutes after Silver was arrested, a disused fire station in Kennington was surrounded, and Peter brought out unharmed.

Silver was already sitting up in bed, his gown hanging loose on his muscular frame. If he was at all worried about being under arrest, or in a room alone with the person whose family he'd murdered, then his relaxed smile and the steady *bip-bip-bip* of the heart monitor machine gave nothing away.

'Detective!' he cried. 'Great to see you again.'

Jackie stood at the end of the bed. 'Don't you find it tiring, being you?'

'I'm sorry I don't have your self-esteem issues, Detective.'

'You can't get to me, Silver.'

'Those clothes, so shapeless. And really, come on, run a brush through your hair. You do realise people have to look at you all day.'

304

She pictured herself pulling the IV tube from the cannula on the back of his hand and throttling him with it.

Think about the case.

'You know what I think,' Silver said, his smile growing. 'You don't *want* people to find you attractive, because if they did you'd have face up to how small and sorrowful your life—'

'That's *enough*.'

'Getting too close, am I?'

Before Jackie could stop herself she was round the bed, grabbing him by the throat, pushing his head onto the bed frame. Could she get away with it? Say he attacked her?

Think of the fucking case!

She let go. Forced herself to take a breath.

'All I'm saying,' he said, rubbing his neck, still with that same shit-eating grin as before, 'is that you could be quite pretty if you bothered to make a bit of effort.'

Enough of this bullshit. She knew already he would talk. He wasn't the type to spend the next thirty years in prison, not when some other patsy could take his place.

'What's it going to take, Silver?'

'Please, call me Benedict.'

'What do you *want*?'

'Why, the same thing as you, of course. Justice for Ivana Kostimarov. That poor young girl, so cruelly struck down—'

'By you.'

'Where's your evidence?'

'I'll find it.'

Silver stretched, then put his hand to his stomach, wincing at the pain. 'You got me good there, I'll give you that.' He mimed throwing a knife, making a *pee-ow* noise. 'I might learn how to—'

'If you want to cut a deal I'll listen, otherwise stop wasting my time.'

'It's hardly as if you have anywhere else to go.'

Jackie ignored the taunt. She was rapidly learning to tune them out. 'We've got you already for assault, blackmail. *Kidnapping.*'

He waved her away. 'I'll be free before you've had your first sip of coffee in the morning.'

'Don't worry, Silver,' she said, leaning in again. 'The evidence will turn up.'

The threat hung between them, chilling the air.

'All I want', he said, 'is to tell my side of the story.'

'Let me guess. You're a poor underling, a nobody, the wrong person in the wrong place. We can talk about knocking that murder charge down to manslaughter.'

His eyes went sharp. 'How about accessory? And forget the other charges.'

With good behaviour, he could be out in five. On appeal probably even less. She swallowed the bitter taste at the back of her throat. But what was one loose cannon, when she could bring down the whole castle?

'I need enough for a warrant to the Men's Learning Centre,' she said.

'That', he replied, casual again, 'shall not be a problem.' He began to talk.

Jackie didn't know how much of Silver's version of events surrounding Ivana Kostimarov's murder she believed – he knew about it, but none of the details, and was certainly nowhere near when it happened – but the information about the terrorist acts being planned was dynamite.

'Okay,' said Jackie, when he'd finished, 'I'll see what I can do.'

'You want all that on tape, you'll make it happen.'

'You'll still do time.'

'You think I'm scared of prison?' Silver gave her a good-natured shake of the head. 'Please. I'll *thrive* inside.'

'And if they come after you for being a grass?'

'Who says I won't go after them first?'

Jackie sighed, sick of Silver and his spiel, wanting to be any-where but near him. 'I'll send someone in to take a statement,' she said, heading for the door.

'Oh, and Detective?'

When she turned again, his face was strangely blank. *Inhuman.*

'I didn't enjoy killing your family,' he said. 'I gave you that impression to get a rise out of you. Really, I didn't have feelings about it either way. It was pure business.'

Was he taunting her again? It didn't seem that way – so what did he want?

'Is that supposed to make me feel better?' she said.

'In fact, I really dislike killing children. I didn't expect your daughter to be in the car.'

'But you did it anyway.'

Silver rocked his head, button-eyed. 'What should I have done? Run out and said, "Don't start the car?" I'm not the one who changed my schedule, Detective. Besides, I don't know why you're being so coy. You've killed before, haven't you?'

Jackie paused, sensing a trap. He waved the question away. *Whatever. Some you win, some you lose.* Like she was unlucky to be born with a conscience.

A shiver ran through her. *Jesus.* If that was him unmasked, then put the fucking mask back on.

'Okay,' Jackie said. 'I'll send someone in.'

'I look forward to it,' he replied, smiling again, the Silver from before firmly back in place. Jackie hurried out of the room, hoping never to see the real him again.

In the corridor, she rang the super. 'Andy, it's me. I'm going to Carmichael's. Send back-up. The works.'

'What did Silver say?'

'More than enough for a warrant.'
'At this time of night?'
'Better get busy, boss.'

64

My first reaction to what Ally told me was that it couldn't be true. It was too horrific. As a parent, I found it inconceivable. But even when she was a young girl, my daughter always told the truth. From little things like sneaking a snack before dinner, to the time, only last year, when she took my car round the block with her friends and pranged the bumper, she fronted up to what she'd done, accepting the consequences as though doing so were a point of principle.

'I hope it's not too late,' she said, her chin trembling again.

'And you know where she is?'

Ally nodded. 'Our plan was to get whoever was in there out, show the world first-hand what they were doing to people. We both memorised the codes to the building and the security system.'

She started to tell me, but it was complicated stuff. I was too exhausted to remember everything, at least to the point where I'd be *sure* not to make a mistake, so I tore around the study looking for a pen. Then I remembered I still had that old phone. I typed everything into a text message and saved it as a draft.

I didn't want to leave her there, hated the idea of her still being in this awful place, scared and alone, but the thought of what they were doing to Phoenix was even worse. She wasn't my daughter, but I'd been more of a dad to her in the last week than her scumbag father had ever managed. It was my fault she was here. And if

I left her here, after everything I now knew, I would never be able to live with the guilt.

Ally promised me she'd stay quiet, just in case anyone came into the building, but the layer of dust covering every surface told us she wasn't likely to be disturbed. Then I headed back out.

It was still deep in the night, the campus quiet. Staying off the paths, I left the maze of blocks and skirted the silent courtyard. Considering how much drinking was going on here last night, it was remarkably clean, not a pint glass or empty packet of cigarettes in sight. On the other side of the refectory, I crossed the car park, and hid behind a thicket of scrubby bushes in sight of the buildings where Ally had said the lab was.

It all fell into place now: the scar on her throat, the pills in her bag, the fact that she had to keep the truth about herself hidden from her father. But even considering who he was and what he stood for, he was a monster to do that to his own child. Someone had to stop him.

The lab was in a line of two-storey concrete buildings. I watched from the bushes for a few minutes, to see if I could spot movement in any of the windows. The place seemed empty. Ally had said it was the second one from the end. I crept towards it, flick knife palmed, ears pricked for sounds. I prayed I wasn't too late.

As I approached, I noticed the extra security here – bars on the bottom floor windows, motion sensor cameras attached to the wall by the entrance. None of the other blocks I'd been to had been locked, but this one had a heavy steel door. The keypad was illuminated beside it. I needed to move fast in case there was someone watching on a monitor.

I committed the code in the draft text to memory, then strode to the keypad like I was supposed to be there. When I typed it in and there was a double beep I stifled my excitement, instead pulling the door open with purpose.

It led into an airy, modern reception. The fire escape sign on the other side bathed everything in a pale green light. Behind the desk was a computer. I slid into the chair and turned it on, eyeing the camera in the corner of the room as it loaded. If anyone was watching they'd know I wasn't supposed to be there. I logged in with the username and password Ally had given me, expecting at any moment a shrill alarm to cut through the silence, the reception to be flooded with security.

The screen changed to a plain blue Windows background. Following the instructions, I opened a search bar and entered *cmd*, making a small black box appear, similar to the ones Phoenix was so keen on spinning up on her laptop. I typed the commands from the phone, not even trying to make sense of them, hoping that I hadn't made a mistake inputting them back at the music block. After the last one, the black box appeared to freeze. Had I put it in wrong? Had it been intercepted? I waited, muttering, 'Come on, come on, come—'

Operant conditioning chamber unlocked.

Was that it? Was that done? I shut down the computer, took the double doors and carried on to the end of the corridor. At the stairwell, I went down and found the other locked door Ally had described. I typed the code for that one. Double beep. In.

It was pitch black. I used my phone to find the light switch, and flicked it on. Above a desk was a bank of monitors, and behind that, another room. I went through. A white box lay on a metal bed, as long as a coffin but twice as wide, with readout screens along the side. A stream of cables came out the far end.

I ran my hands over the lid. How did you get inside? On the other side, I found a lever marked *emergency release* and shoved it down. Something clicked. The top began to lift.

As the box opened, I caught my breath.

I couldn't believe what I was seeing.

65

3.30 A.M., THURSDAY

'The super isn't going to want a stand-off,' Keyes said.

'We might not have a choice,' Jackie replied.

They were at the back entrance to the Men's Learning Centre, waiting by the cars, watching the uniformed officers talking to the men in the Portakabin. Despite the late hour – it had just gone three-thirty in the morning – the warrant to let them onto the campus had been issued, but it was having little effect. The guards were resolute that the police could not come in. Armed response units were already on their way.

'They'll outnumber us ten to one.'

'And the rest.'

'Do you believe what Silver said, about what's going on in there?'

He'd told them about storerooms filled with guns and explosives, computer rooms packed with men grooming teenage boys online or cyber-bullying women. He'd gone into detail about a terrorist attack being planned by Carmichael's men, from stabbing liberal activists in public to burning down women's refuges, giving names, dates, and the location of incriminating documents.

Jackie glanced at the campus, sensing movement at the top of some of the buildings near the entrance. 'If even half of it's true...'

Keyes touched her crucifix. 'Do you get many people like *him*?'

'Not a lot,' Jackie sighed. 'But more often than you could ever want.'

Drum's car screeched to a stop nearby. He slammed out and strode towards them, jacket off, sleeves rolled past his forearms, face set to barely concealed rage. 'What the fuck's going on? Why aren't we inside yet?'

'I'll go check,' Keyes said, heading to the Portakabin.

Once she'd gone, Drum said, 'You got lucky.'

'In what way, boss?'

He gave her a look of limited patience. 'Letting Truman go.'

'He slipped out my hands.'

'He was the main suspect in a murder investigation.'

'What can I say?'

Drum made a resigned sound. He wasn't buying it, but neither did he have the inclination to carry it on.

Jackie cleared her throat. 'I'm sorry, boss. For some of the things I said.'

'About me going soft?'

'You're not going soft.'

'Bloody shortbread,' he muttered, pressing his middle.

'Does this mean I'm not on gardening leave?'

'I'll have to check. The paperwork may have been mislaid. How's Peter?'

'He's at home,' Jackie said. 'They didn't hurt him. He's just shook up.'

'I'll send a car down. Keep an eye on him, eh?'

'Thanks, Andy. I'd appreciate that.'

Drum paused like he was weighing up the best way to broach a difficult topic. She was tempted to watch him squirm, but it was nice for him to be concerned. Not many people in this world would be.

'It's okay,' she said. 'I'm fine.'

'I'm amazed he's still alive to give testimony. If he'd done that to my family… So why didn't you?'

'It wouldn't have brought them back, would it?'

Drum put his hand on her shoulder. 'No, it wouldn't.'

'It's for the greater good,' she said, nodding at the campus. 'Besides, who knows what's going to happen after the trial. Silver plays it cool, but there's going to be a lot of people after his neck, and it's hard to be charming when someone lets themselves into your cell in the middle of the night.'

'Let's hope he gets what's coming to him.'

The truth was, she didn't know how to feel about Silver's admission. It brought no closure, that was for sure, no sense of her life being different with the knowledge of who had murdered her family. There was still anger, a compulsion for revenge, but it was fading from the initial fire. *It was pure business.*

Silver didn't deserve to have his blood on her conscience.

Keyes and the uniformed officers came back, their sour expressions showing they'd failed to convince the Portakabin guards to cede to the warrant.

'Did you tell them armed police were on their way?' asked Drum.

PC Gomathi shrugged. 'Seemed keen to tell us how many assault rifles they had.'

'All licensed, I'm sure.' Jackie waved the constables away. 'How long until SCO19 arrive?'

Drum checked his watch. 'Two minutes max.'

'You know there's a thousand men in there?'

'Call's already gone to the military.'

'You really want that shoot-out? Tens, maybe hundreds dead?'

Drum kneaded his face with the heel of his hand. 'Do me a fucking favour, Jack. If you've got any smart ideas, now is the time to share them.'

A police van swung into view, siren blasting, *ARMED*

RESPONSE UNIT in capitals above the blue and neon yellow stripe. It swerved to stop near the entrance, blocking the road. A moment of silence, then the back doors burst open and black-clad officers spread out, taking positions, submachine guns trained on the Portakabin.

'Better move out of the way,' Drum said, ushering her and Keyes behind the cars.

Movement on the campus side, at the top of the buildings, what looked suspiciously like men with guns taking up positions behind the parapet walls.

'This is going to get messy,' Jackie said. 'Unless...'

Drum frowned. 'What is it? I don't like that look.'

'I think I may have an idea.'

66

I stared at the kid in the box. She was almost unrecognisable. Gone was her long platinum hair, shaved now into a severe crew cut. Her cool T-shirt and funky trainers had been replaced by stiff grey clothes. It was less Phoenix than her dull twin brother, the kind of boy who collected stamps and thought a visit to the National Maritime Museum was a fun day out.

Her lips were slack, her eyes open and staring into the distance. *Was I too late?* I checked her neck. Her pulse was slow and weak against my finger. I tried to lift her out, but she was stuck. Restraints around her neck, wrists and ankles. They seemed to be attached to the box. I pulled at them, but they were made from some kind of thick material, like woven plastic. I tried again, harder this time, twisting them, all the while pleading for Phoenix to wake up, *please wake up*, but it was hopeless, she remained trapped and catatonic. That was it. I had no more instructions. I'd come so close to getting her out, but it was all for nothing.

The energy went from my body. I dropped to my knees, suddenly and overwhelmingly exhausted, the last week and everything that had happened in it slamming into me. I banged the box with my elbow, cycling through every curse I knew, and many I invented on the spot.

'If you want people to know you're here,' came a croaky voice from inside. 'Keep on shouting.'

I jumped up and leaned in, going again for her manacles. 'How do I get you out?'

'Release. Other side.'

I went round. There were lots of different buttons and lights and panels. 'Which one?'

'Square blue button, bottom left.'

When I pressed it, something clicked. Phoenix took a long slow breath. 'Thank you. Oh my God, thank you.' Even her voice was different. Deeper. She clung onto me as I lifted her out and lowered her to the floor. She stayed holding onto me, burying her head into my shoulder. 'Look at what he's done. I'm a monster!'

'You're not a monster. Your father's the monster.'

William Carmichael – Phoenix's dad.

'I know everything,' I said. 'Ally told me.'

Phoenix pulled back. 'She's okay? Where is she?'

'She's fine. She's safe. We're going to go back to her now, then call the police.' I showed her the phone. 'I found this at the hideout.'

'That's amazing,' she said, looking at me in awe. 'How did you even get on campus?'

'Because I'm a badass.'

'You're the baddest of asses.'

We crept back up the stairs and through to the reception. The dark was grainier than before – it was starting to get light. The men got up at daybreak for their first exercise session, so we needed to move fast if we were going to return to the music block without being seen. Time to get out of there.

I pressed the release button beside the door, but before I could even grab the handle, it opened from the other side.

The man standing there smiled sadly at me. 'I'm so sorry about this, Ed.'

What was *he* doing here?

67

Jackie had spotted the Thames Water roadwork signs on the drive in. They were set up on the route from Marlow to the campus. She raced there in her car, jumped out and searched behind the barrier. *Yes!* A manhole hook. She hurried back, pulling up in a quiet spot away from the stand-off at the back entrance, and stalked the perimeter towards the front, finding a manhole cover close to the outer boundary. She slid in the hook and strained to lift the cover. The thud as it hit the tarmac echoed around the quiet country road.

A faecal cloud wafted out to envelop her. *Oh, the glamour.*

She climbed down the ladder, torch on, holding her breath at first, but quickly realising she couldn't hold it for ever. She'd get used to it – this wasn't her first time sneaking through the sewer system. She just hoped her path wasn't blocked by any fatbergs. Fortunately, she saw a ladder up less than fifty metres from where she started. Now for the hard part. Lifting that bastard cover to get out, and doing it without being seen.

She climbed the ladder, grimacing as she pressed her head to the grimy underside of the cover. It seemed quiet enough on the other side. She put her shoulder to the cold metal, braced herself, and pushed. At first nothing happened, and she worried she'd got this wrong, that she wasn't going to be able to lift it, but then it shifted just a few millimetres, and that encouraged her to push harder. With a grunt she heaved it high enough to shove to the side. Then she was out beside it, kneeling on a grassy verge, sucking in clean air.

No one around. It was starting to get light. She needed to move fast. She jogged to a long brick building nearby and pressed her back to it. A slow wail, like an air-raid siren, started to sound. Behind that she heard someone speaking over a tinny Tannoy system. '*The weapon store is now open. Collect your allocated weapon and assemble in the main courtyard.*'

Jackie shuddered. *Collect your weapon?* If this got out of hand, it could turn into a bloodbath.

Her plan, as much as she had one, had been to sneak to the front gates and open one of them, so they could get some armed officers inside, but this escalation was making her rethink. She wasn't going to be responsible for a suicide mission.

She darted between buildings, staying low, in the shadows. At the edge of a floodlit courtyard, she crouched in the dirt and watched the men hurry to line up. More than a few looked ex-army. Her uncle had served, she knew the type. She could tell by the way they carried themselves. Even from a distance they looked serious.

A flurry of activity from the other side of the courtyard. A group of men hurrying somewhere, and in among them, a face she recognised. She *knew* it. Now it all made sense.

68

My brain wouldn't process what my eyes were showing it. On the other side of the doorway was a man I'd known for over half my life, someone I saw more often than my own family, whose children called me Uncle Ed. A man whom I once rushed to at three in the morning, days after his wife kicked him out, and talked with until sunrise because he was so scared of being alone that night, of what he might do.

Steve. Standing there with this bullshit sombre sorry-for-bad-news look slapped on his face, all furrowed brow and hunched chin, like he'd done all he could for me but lost. And these were the consequences.

'I told you months ago that Ally needed to back off,' he said. 'I told you she was messing with dangerous people.'

'And you're one of them, right?'

'You should have done more to stop her.'

Was he trying to say this was *my* fault? 'They kidnapped Ally. They left her locked in a basement, filthy and starving.'

'She'd be dead already if it wasn't for me.'

I wanted to go for him, but he wasn't alone. Behind him were two men. Armed men.

How was this possible? I tracked back through years of morning chats at the coffee machine, car journeys to court, post-work

320

beers, looking for how I could have missed this. Yes, he was a passionate defender of men, and we would often get into heated but good-natured discussions about why there were so many refuges and resources for women in trouble, whereas men more often than not ended up on the streets. When did *that* spill over into *this*?

I looked him up and down. 'So how does this work? You providing counsel to Carmichael, or moonlighting as a henchman? I hope you're charging him by the hour.'

'It's not like that, Ed.'

'So what's it like?'

He motioned for me and Phoenix to move back, then stepped into the reception. The bigger of his tag-along thugs – bent nose, leather jacket, gun the size of my forearm – came with. The other one stayed outside.

'Listen,' Steve said, putting his palms together, prayer-style. I'd seen him make that gesture a hundred times before a judge, usually when he was trying to wheedle an extra inch of sympathy. 'It's nothing personal, okay? And if anything, I've tried to protect you – and Ally.'

'By keeping her locked up—'

'I put my own bloody neck on the line to save her!'

'—and fucked off her head on drugs?'

'Who do you think's been sending Gabrielle those texts from her phone! If you'd just kept your head down I could have got her out.'

'Why should I believe a word you say?'

'They were going to kill her there and then.'

Hot tears sprang to my eyes. 'You've known Ally since she was a baby!'

'Bloody hell, Ed,' Steve said, exasperated. 'Put it away, will you? At least try to act a *bit* more like a man.'

'Oh yeah, some big man,' said Phoenix.

Steve looked at her like a stepchild he'd always hated. 'Shut it, freak. If you weren't Carmichael's kid you'd be long gone.'

I stepped in front of her. 'If you touch her...'

'Then what, Ed? What are you going to do?' He shook his head, disdainful of my ability to offer any kind of protection. 'But you know what,' he said, clicking his fingers at the goon next to him and taking the offered gun, 'maybe it's best we don't take any chances.'

'The police know I'm here,' I said.

'For all they know you've fled the country.'

I couldn't believe this. It felt like one of those dreams where you realise none of it is real but you still can't figure out how to wake up. Thirty years we'd known each other. Thirty years! And here he was casually working out whether it would be best to shoot me now or later.

'Why are you doing this, Steve? Doesn't our...?' I felt the pressure behind my eyes again. This time I pushed the tears back down. 'I thought we were *friends*.'

'Don't you see? It's taken years to get the message out there, to get people to even start to see what's going on. All we want is equality – in the courts, in social settings. Why should women be allowed full rein to both make and enforce the rules? This is an uprising, Ed, and neither your daughter, nor' – he waved towards Phoenix – 'whatever that thing is, nor the entire cunt church devoted to destroying what it is to be a man, is going to stop that.'

I flashed on an image of him from our graduation party. He was slow dancing with Faith to 'Unchained Melody', supremely smashed, more slumped on her than standing on his own feet, this dopey grin spread over his face. For a second he cracked an eye, saw me watching, and swung a thumbs-up, like he couldn't imagine being any happier than he was in that moment.

Whatever had happened in the intervening years, that Steve was gone.

And this Steve wanted me dead.

'I've got the videos they stole,' I said. 'I've left instructions to release them if I don't come back.'

'Bullshit,' he said, snorting, but I knew him well enough to see the glimmer of doubt in his eyes. 'Who would you leave instructions with? Nice try. You're lying.'

'If people found out what you *really* did here. Child abuse, brainwashing—'

'I don't believe you.'

'You willing to take that risk?'

'Tell me who,' he said, levelling the gun at my face.

I was trembling almost too much to speak. 'Let us go.'

Steve kept the gun on me for another second, then lowered it, starting to smile. 'Why don't we give Gabs a call, see if she knows where those videos are?'

'Leave my wife alone.'

He got out his phone and swiped the screen to unlock it. 'In fact, I'll send a couple of men over to ask her in person. It'll be more persuasive that way.'

'Don't do this. *Please.*'

'Tell me if you're lying,' he said, thumb hovering over call.

I hadn't thought this through. I had nowhere to go. It was either me and Phoenix, or Gabrielle and Mitchell. There was nothing else I could do.

'Okay, Steve,' I said. 'I'm—'

A slow wail, like an air-raid siren, went off outside. The way it was echoing, it sounded like it was over the whole campus. Steve swore, and got a different number up on his phone. He held it to his ear as it rang.

'Where the hell is Benedict?' he muttered. 'Of all the times to disappear...' He hung up and nodded to the bloke beside him. 'Go find out—'

The reception door opened. At first I didn't recognise the man coming in. Slight, bearded, in a smart grey tracksuit. Then Phoenix said, '*Dad?*'

My mental image of William Carmichael was as this stooped academic in a brown suit, but at that moment he looked spry, like he was just on his way out for a morning jog. 'Oh, for heaven's sake, Gregory.'

Did he mean Phoenix? I felt her shrink against my shoulder.

Carmichael shook his head like he'd deal with her in a minute. 'You know the police are outside,' he said to Steve. 'With a warrant!'

Steve nodded to his thug. 'Head back to command. Siege manoeuvres.'

Siege? I had to get the girls out of there.

The flick knife in my back pocket.

Somehow I needed to incapacitate Steve, get the gun off him.

'And *you*,' Carmichael said to Phoenix. 'How can you ever expect to be *normal* if you won't finish the treatment!'

'It's not treatment,' she hissed. 'It's *torture.*'

'Nonsense. Torture is what you were doing to yourself, with that silly *fad* of yours.'

'It's not a *fad*. It's who I am!'

'You really are the most obnoxious child. Do you realise just how obnoxious you are?'

'I am what you made me!'

'You always wanted to be *different*.'

I reached behind my back. Phoenix caught my eye, saw my hand go to my back pocket, knew what I was doing. She pushed past me, making for Carmichael. '*You made me different!*'

Carmichael caught her arms as she went to slap him, and looked at Steve. 'Don't just stand there.'

I had the knife out, flicking the blade, at the same time as Steve whipped the butt of the gun into the side of Phoenix's skull. He saw me too late and tried to turn. I got him on the right side of the chest, pushing the knife in to the hilt. We fell back, the gun spilling from his hand. He was stronger than me, but weakened from the wound. His punches to my kidney were half-hearted.

'Get the gun!' I screamed to Phoenix. '*Get it!*'

I sensed a scramble behind me. I wanted to look round, but Steve was trying to buck me off. He seemed to be regaining some strength. I was having to use my body weight to keep him down. Phoenix screamed, '*Ed!* Watch out!'

I rolled off Steve and scrabbled back on my heels. Carmichael had the gun pointed at me. Phoenix dragged his arm down as he fired.

I felt the thud in my side and my whole body went cold, like I'd been flash frozen. The pain built in seconds from an ebb to a pulse to a great dark howl. I curled up, clenched, praying for it to peak but it kept getting worse, spreading in ever more awful aftershocks through my chest and groin.

Steve's right side was soaked in blood. The blade was still sticking out of his body. He staggered a couple of steps my way and booted me in the side, sending fresh waves of agony down my legs. He doubled over, then dropped to his knees, bloodied saliva hanging from his mouth, heaving in breaths. 'I think … you got … my fucking lung!'

'Oh, Christ,' said Carmichael. 'Where's Benedict?'

'Don't know,' Steve replied, on all fours now. He'd gone the same off white as the wall. Sweat was pattering from his forehead onto the linoleum floor. The alarm was still wailing in the background, and behind that, someone was issuing orders over a Tannoy.

Carmichael waved the gun at Phoenix. She had her hand to the red welt on her temple.

'Let's start with you going back downstairs,' he said.

Clenching against the pain, I sneaked a shaking hand into my pocket, got what I wanted, and set it up. If I died then at least this might be found.

'No,' she replied. 'I'm not going.'

'I won't let you embarrass me any more.'

I rolled onto my back, one arm cradling my stomach, not daring to look down in case my intestines were spilling out. It didn't feel that way, but I couldn't be sure. A worrying but merciful numbness was spreading from my chest.

'You, Carmichael,' I said, 'what kind of father are you?'

He swung his head at me. 'What do you know?'

'Torturing your own child.'

'Not you as well!'

'Locking her in a box. Trying to brainwash her into being something she's not.'

He waved the gun, exasperated. 'Who cares about the method of delivery? It's the results that count! No one complains about their ribs being cracked open for heart surgery.'

'I never asked for your *surgery*,' snarled Phoenix.

'There you go again,' Carmichael replied. 'Always trying to garner sympathy by pretending to be the victim.'

She turned to me. 'He did the same when I was young. He'd keep me locked up for days. If I did the wrong thing, he gave me electric shocks. There was a tube for water, but sometimes it wasn't water. Sometimes it *burned*.'

'Oh, now you're exaggerating,' Carmichael said. 'It was one time, and it was *just* chilli sauce. Nothing more harmful than that.'

I couldn't believe what I was hearing. 'You really are crazy.'

'Was B. F. Skinner crazy? Was John B. Watson crazy? Or were they not some of the finest minds the field of psychology has ever seen?'

'You locked your own child in a box and gave her electric shocks?'

'You're worse than he is!' Carmichael snapped. 'Gregory used to love being in there.'

'*Don't call me that!*' Phoenix screamed.

'I couldn't keep him out of it!' The muscles around Carmichael's mouth were twitching, flecks of spit caught on his beard. 'Which, in fact, was part of the process, generating the positive reinforcement protocols to allow him to enjoy being in there. Do you not see how amazing that is? People pay huge sums of money for my methods!'

Phoenix clenched her fists, staring fiercely at her father. 'I hate you.'

'You always were a contrary child,' he sighed. 'Now come along—'

The front door swung open. I expected it to be Steve's man from outside, perhaps with some update about the police, but instead it was the detective who had chased me down at my house, a gun held before her in both hands.

'William Carmichael,' she said. 'You are under arrest. You do not have to say anything, but it may harm your defence if you do not mention when questioned something which you later rely on in court. Anything you do say may be given in evidence.'

He looked at her, confused and incredulous. 'You can't arrest me. I haven't done anything!'

The detective glanced at Phoenix. 'We have received credible allegations of historic child abuse against you. If you'd like to accompany me to the station for questioning, you can discuss the matter with your solicitor.'

Carmichael shook his head. 'I'm not going anywhere with you.'

'If you don't want to come willingly,' the detective said, taking some cuffs from her back pocket, 'I'll have to make you. And trust me, you do *not* want it to come to that.'

He gestured with his gun. 'And if I don't?'

'One of us is a highly trained police officer wearing a bullet-proof vest. The other is you.'

Smiling, Carmichael lowered his weapon. 'Take me to your *station*, then, oh officer of the law. I'll be out in half an hour.'

'Maybe you will. Maybe you won't.'

'What proof do you have? Where's your evidence?'

'We'll worry about that later.'

'The word of a troubled youth with a history of mental instability? Of a man on the run for murder? Of a copper with a personal vendetta?' Carmichael smiled. 'That's right, I know all about you too, Detective Inspector Rose.'

'That's Detective *Chief* Inspector Rose to you.' Her finger tightened on the trigger.

His smile became a snarl. 'This is why women don't do well in positions of power. You lack the rational intelligence of men—'

Phoenix's voice cut him off.

'He'd keep me locked up for days. If I did the wrong thing, he gave me electric shocks. There was a tube for water, but sometimes it wasn't water. Sometimes it burned.'

A couple of nights ago, shivering on that bench in Marlow, I'd been messing with Phoenix's phone, and found it had a voice recorder. At the time, I'd captured a melancholy message for my family, to be recovered after my almost certain death. Now I'd been using it to record everything Carmichael had said.

'Oh, now you're exaggerating. It was one time, and it was just chilli sauce. Nothing more harmful than that.'

Carmichael blanched. Sweat was running from his hairline. He turned the gun on me.

'I wouldn't do that,' said Detective Rose.

'You locked your own child in a box and gave her electric shocks?'

His hand wavered. I braced, waiting for him to shoot.

'*You're worse than he is! Gregory used to love being in there.*'

Carmichael let out a defeated sigh. He lowered first his head, then the gun.

EPILOGUE

FRIDAY NIGHT

While Ally and Mitchell set the table, Gabrielle and I prepare the dinner. We move quietly in the kitchen. At one end of the counter Gabrielle stirs sauce into the pasta, and at the other I chop a rudimentary salad from the meagre stock of vegetables in the fridge. I keep meaning to go shopping, but the last week since the stand-off at the Men's Learning Centre has been insanely busy. It's probably for the best. If I take the time to think about what's happening tomorrow morning, I don't think I'll be able to hold it together.

Slicing tomatoes, I steal a glance into the dining room, where Mitchell is laying place mats. He looks so caught up in his fear that even if I was standing in front of him blaring dirty limericks through a megaphone it would not pierce his shell.

At the table, we go through the motions of eating, spinning our forks in the spaghetti and lifting them to our mouths, but I can tell no one's mind is on the food. Mitchell keeps pausing, brow creased, as some new imagined horror comes to him. I try to distract everyone with stories, like when the kids were young and Gabrielle went away for the night with all the keys – I took them to the Holiday Inn down the road, where we worked through the room service menu and mainlined cartoons until midnight. Or the time on holiday in Spain when we received an astronomical food bill at check out, over eight hundred euros for a five-night stay, and I demanded to see the manager.

'You remember?' I say, and put on the manager's confused Catalonian baritone. 'But Meezter Truman, that iz not the food bill. It iz the *room number*!'

That got the usual laughs. 'The look on your face,' Gabrielle says. 'That was funny.'

I put my hand on Mitchell's arm. His chin quivers, and his eyelids are glistening. 'You'll be *okay*,' I say.

He swallows his tears down. Doesn't want to cry in front of us. I understand.

We eat in silence until the moment has passed, then Gabrielle asks Ally how it went today. She did a segment for *This Morning* about her ordeal, and becomes animated as she tells us how supportive Holly Willoughby was after the show.

'They had a tray of amazing biscuits in the green room,' she says. 'And Michael McIntyre told me jokes! But I don't remember any of them.'

'You should be taking it easy,' I say.

Ally shrugs, as though I've got no idea what it's like to be young.

'Are you coming with tomorrow?' she asks me, then glances at Mitchell. '*Sorry.*'

But he's not heard her. He's off imagining beatings and bullying and how it will be to be alone.

She means am I going to the hospital with her, for when Phoenix is discharged. Both girls seemed to have made a quick recovery, at least physically. Phoenix especially was in a bad way. When they ran tests on her at the hospital they found she'd been pumped full of drugs – stimulants, depressives, hallucinogens, and super strong doses of testosterone. Yet within a day she was sitting up in her hospital bed, computer on her lap.

Both girls are meant to go to Birmingham on Sunday morning

to speak at an Extinction Rebellion rally, and then to Italy mid-week to take part in protests against the rise of the far right in Europe. I have my reservations. Okay, I feel sick at the thought of them being so far away. But at least they'll be together, so they can look after each other.

*

After dinner Ally goes to meet friends. The rest of us watch TV for a while, then Mitchell and finally Gabrielle head up to bed. As recently as last week I would have sat here working through a bottle, and it's not like part of me wouldn't love to do just that, to tune the world out, even for a little while, but the thought of taking even a single drink makes me seize up inside. *What if Mitchell needs me during the night? What if Carmichael's men show up at the door, seeking retribution? What if, once I start drinking, I can't stop?*

Instead, while I'm changing my dressing – thankfully the bullet passed through my love handle, leaving only flesh wounds – I think about Mitchell, the young offender's institute he'll be taken to while we await trial. The things that might happen to him there. When Jackie first spoke to me about bringing him in, she told me that I shouldn't feel betrayed by what he did, that the people who groomed him were meticulous and professional. My son didn't have a chance.

Don't hate him, she said, as though that would be the natural way to feel.

Nothing could be further from the truth.

If I'd been closer to my son, if I'd been more present in his life, then Steve wouldn't have been able to dig his claws into him. All those times he picked up Mitchell to take him back to play with his boys, he'd been turning my son against me. It started over a year ago, apparently, when Ally and her friends first began their campaign against Carmichael. Steve got Mitchell to spy on Ally and report back. But that wasn't why Jackie was coming in the morning. The police were taking my son in because he was the one who stole the hairs from the plughole in my bathroom and gave them to Steve to be planted on that poor girl from the squat they killed. That's how my DNA evidence appeared at the scene.

If I'd been a better father, the police wouldn't be arresting my son for conspiracy to commit murder.

So no, I don't hate Mitchell. I don't feel betrayed by him. I'm just mortified that I wasn't there to protect him.

Steve is also up on a charge of conspiracy, not only for collecting the hairs, but also because he planted the incriminating web searches on my work computer. Jackie deduced they were all done when I was at court, as confirmed by the court records, and no one else was in the office but him.

He had an idea of what Ally and Phoenix were doing, hacking into the Men's Learning Centre website and posting Ally's personal information on it, hoping I would get involved. Putting the searches on my work computer was part of his plan to discredit me.

Steve, however, is rigorously denying the accusation of grooming, showing a vindictive streak that makes me wonder if I don't owe Faith a few years' worth of sympathy back payments, if this was what she had to deal with. According to him, I'm a drunk who ignored his children, and his relationship to Mitchell was one of nurturing and support. It was my son who presented him with the hairs and suggested how they could be used to get back at me for years of neglect.

Grooming is hard to prove at the best of times, and right now Mitchell is facing seven to ten years. With a plea deal.

The thought of Mitchell not getting out until his twenties, his whole childhood gone, is too much. I'm still wiping away my tears when I notice him by the doorway, his own eyes red. I go to bring him to the sofa. He's almost my height, but still curls into me, his head on my lap, his knees clutched to his chest. I hold him that way while he cries.

'I'm scared, Dad,' he says.

'I know you are.'

'I don't want to go.'

I kiss his forehead. 'I know.'

After a while, his sobs fade. His breaths become slow and deep. I hold him like that throughout the night, thinking, thinking, thinking. There must be something. An angle. I can't let them take my son.

We're still there when the door goes at seven. Mitchell wakes with a start, but he seems less scared now, and I shoo him upstairs to get ready.

Jackie is here on her own, and in an unmarked car. The neighbours don't need to be gossiping about our family any more than they are already.

I ask if she wants to come in for a coffee, but she shakes her head. 'Want to get him processed before the duty sergeant starts her shift.' She gives me a conspiratorial smile. 'You know ... paperwork.' She was supposed to take him in yesterday, but wanted to give us a bit more time.

'Thank you,' I say. 'It's made a big difference.'

'How you holding up?'

'Still alive.'

'That's no small thing.'

'I hear congratulations are in order.' It was in the *Evening Standard* last night, the new counter-terrorism unit being set up in London, with her at the helm.

'One guess who we're going after,' she replies.

334

They'd taken Carmichael in, but he has some powerful backers, and was soon out again. Even so, with Silver's testimony Carmichael has taken some big hits. All the social media and video-streaming platforms have taken down his content, and his Men's Learning Centres are permanently closed.

'Give it six months,' Jackie says. 'He'll be joining his pal Silver inside.'

Footsteps on the stairs. I turn to see Mitchell coming down. Showered, his hair combed back, dressed in jeans and a white shirt, he looks older than his fourteen years. He looks like the man he will become.

Gabrielle didn't want to say goodbye at the door. I can hear her crying softly at the top of the stairs.

'Okay, then,' Jackie says, reaching for Mitchell.

I can't let this happen. I won't let them take him.

'Wait,' I say. 'He didn't do anything. Steve got the hairs from me.'

She looks at me sharply. 'Don't do this, Ed.'

'I'm being serious.'

'So am I.'

She bustles inside and shuts the door. Shakes me by the arm. 'What are you trying to pull?'

Gabrielle has come down the stairs and is watching from the banister, an arm around Mitchell's chest.

'I used Steve's comb at work,' I say.

Jackie pulls me face-to-face. 'We have your son's computer. We have the chat messages where they planned it.'

If that and Steve's testimony is all they've got then maybe I have a chance. 'That was me, pretending to be Mitchell.'

'You made a *statement* saying you had nothing to do with—'

'Which I'd like to amend.'

She throws her hands up and looks at Gabrielle. 'Are you in on this bullshit too?'

My wife shakes her head, eyes wide, a hand to her mouth. She pulls Mitchell in tighter.

'You'll go to prison,' Jackie says.

'I know.'

'You'll mess up the case.'

'Not true. My evidence will help.'

She carries on looking at me like I'm insane, clearly waiting for me to put a stop to the madness, but I just stare back at her. Finally, she sighs. Then she reads me my rights.

Ally comes down. There are many tears, but not from me. I feel elated as Jackie leads me out. The sun is shining, the morning is calm. At the car door, I turn and raise a hand to my family, safe together at home. I can't stop smiling. I'm ready.

ACKNOWLEDGEMENTS

Acknowledgements are funny things. They feel a little like writing a wedding speech, although I guess it's the opposite. The moment when the book and I say farewell.

We'd never have got this far without the fantastic people who made it happen. Thanks to my agent Jordan Lees, for seeing the potential in the manuscript, helping me buff it to a shine, and finding it the perfect home at Viper. To Miranda Jewess, Queen of the Vipers, for being generally brilliant, but also for her ninja editing skills, untangling my convoluted timeline, and pointing out where I had somehow, even after six drafts, not noticed that the narratives were a day out of sync. Similar editorial kudos must go to Sam Matthews, whose keen eye picked out errors and inconsistencies buried deep in the manuscript. To them and everyone else at Viper, you have my heartfelt gratitude.

Equal praise must go to those who suffered through the early versions of this book. Huge thanks to Jilly, Jonny, Tash, and my brother Adam, in particular, for insisting that I had to change the ending. I'm fortunate to count among my friends more than a few lawyers, so special thanks to Jonny (again), Oliver, Regine and Richard for always being on the end of a WhatsApp chat to answer my many questions. If there are any remaining legal mistakes in the manuscript, they are one hundred percent my own.

It's been a long journey to get to this point, and if I'm not careful I could be thanking people for days. So I'll just give a special shout out to those without whom I definitely would not be writing these words – Alex Keegan, Matt Thorne, Betsy and Fred at Bloodhound. I'd also like to mention all the wonderful readers I've met and become friends with online, particularly those who have supported my writing in my advance reader group, and especially Mark 'Book Mark' Fearn.

Now's the moment when I think of my family and risk sobbing over the keyboard. Much love to my mum and dad for absolutely everything and, more recently, childcare. Thanks to the constant support from my brothers Richard and Adam (your one book a year, bro) and their families. It's maybe only as you get older that you realise how lucky you are if you have loving people around you. I certainly appreciate it now.

Closer to home, my own home in fact, and my amazing daughter. You make it easy to get out of bed in the morning, and I'd open every box for you. My best friend and blind bundle of slobbering fur, Boddington, whose stinky morning licks make me wish I'd stayed in bed after all. And finally, and always, my beautiful wife Delia. It's not easy being married to a writer, so thank you for giving me the space to get on with it. I love you.